Castigation

Middle East Literature in Translation
Michael Beard and Adnan Haydar, *Series Editors*

For a full list of titles in this series,
visit https://press.syr.edu/supressbook-series
/middle-east-literature-in-translation/.

Castigation

Sultan Raev

Translated from the Kyrgyz by
Shelley Fairweather-Vega

Syracuse University Press

This book was originally published in Kyrgyz as *Janjaza* (Bishkek: Turar, 2013).

First Edition 2025

25 26 27 28 29 30   6 5 4 3 2 1

A version of the passage from page 236 to page 240 first appeared in *Turkoslavia*, issue 2, 2023.

Publication supported by the generous donors to the SU Press Gift Fund.

For a listing of books published and distributed by Syracuse University Press,
visit https://press.syr.edu.

ISBN: 9780815611936 (paperback)
      9780815657484 (e-book)

Library of Congress Cataloging in Publication Control Number: 2025013424

The authorized representative in the EU for product
safety and compliance is Mare Nostrum Group B.V.
Mauritskade 21D, 1091 GC Amsterdam, The Netherlands
gpsr@mare-nostrum.co.uk

Like a flash of lightning,
Like a vanishing drop of dew,
Like a ghost: the thought of oneself

> Prince Ikkyu

The absurd is not in man, and not in the world,
but in their coexistence.

> Albert Camus, *Le Mythe de Sisyphe*

Hundreds of times, I grew as grass
along the banks of fast-flowing rivers.
Hundreds of thousands of years, I was born and lived,
in every body there is on Earth.

> Mansur Al-Hallaj

Then shall the dust
return to the earth as it was;
and the spirit shall return unto God
who gave it

> Ecclesiastes 12:7

Contents

Castigation

The people who walked out of the psychiatric hospital at dusk one evening find themselves in the naked desert by noon the next day. There are seven of them. The Emperor is their guide. Of the other six, the oldest wears glasses, and once was an actor. Nobody knows his real name, but everyone calls him Lear. Whenever an attack suddenly comes upon him, despite his advanced age, he flings back his long, ashen hair and starts to declaim a monologue by the insane King Lear, but before he reaches the end he starts howling, writhing, digging his fingers into the earth, cursing and damning his daughters and detested sons-in-law who have stolen away all his wealth in the clear light of day. It is usually at the full moon that he recites King Lear's monologue, which has gotten stuck in one corner of his brain, but in his previous life, people say, he had been a shameless ladies' man, and there was no counting the women he'd taken and the children they'd borne him. Once, when somebody commented that his amorous adventures would pursue him to Judgment Day, he answered with a laugh: "Where is this Judgment Day of yours? Why isn't anyone judging me?" And then he tore some pages about life after death out of the Holy Book and trampled on them with his feet. This is the deranged old man who knows no God: he and the six with him set out at dusk on their long journey. The youngest of the seven, whose adolescent acne has not yet quit his face, is thin as a sapling, and he bears the name Kozuchak, given to him by nobody knew who; maybe it is his real name, but nobody knows that, either. Anytime someone says the word "Kozuchak," he immediately answers, "That's me." And there are two women among them. One of them, though she is long past fifty, and though her hair is suffused with gray, is lively in her movements, yet the hair on her head has long been greased in place and there is no record of the last time it was combed. Everyone calls her Thaïs the Athenian, and nobody knows her real name. (Here is part of the entry in this woman's medical chart. "Profession: Philosopher, knows three languages. Diagnosis: Schizophrenia. Incongruity of affect.") The other woman is younger, clean and shapely, with a straight nose, and pale face, and she is perhaps twenty-five years old. But she is the least amiable one, not prone to conversation, reticent with her words. Everyone calls her Cleopatra. People say that was what the psychiatric hospital director had called the lady. But she prefers not to speak her real name to anyone. (Recently, the young lady forgot her real name, herself.) The son of some big shot, or of a king (who knows), anyway: the son of a king fell in love with this beautiful woman, and when the king's wife found out, she began looking for a way to be rid of her, the woman who kindled her son's fiery adoration, to sweep her away so that her son would take for his wife the daughter of the king of the neighboring realm. Nobody knew this part of Cleopatra's history, and they were all astounded to learn that she, too, had joined the group of escapees. When Kozuchak confided in her that they were secretly preparing to flee, the young beauty asked to be included: "Take me with you, please." Kozuchak told nobody he had let Cleopatra into their group. Why not, though? Having a beautiful young woman with them on their journey would make it even nicer. But all that aside, she had caught Kozuchak's eye a long time ago, and he felt very attached to her. When they brought Cleopatra to the hospital, Kozuchak was the first one to see her, and as soon as he did his soul trembled inside his body, and he got a warm feeling inside his chest. He liked her. He remembered, when they pulled her out of the psychomobile (a yellow van), she had been sobbing and shouting "I won't stay here!" and stomping her feet, raising a fuss, tearing at the gowns of the hospital orderlies. Kozuchak had long wanted to flee that comfy nest (that's what they'd always called their mental hospital), but after the wind blew Cleopatra to the comfy nest, the place became easier for him to bear, so he stayed, for a while. Feeling as he did for her, Kozuchak started hinting to Cleopatra about the escape they were planning, to make her into his companion for the long journey, and then, without thinking it over too much, he told her that the time had come; but he told nothing about all that to anyone else

who was planning to flee. Now it was too late to change anything. Cleopatra has shown no fear before the long, unknown road to come. Kozuchak
knows people say Cleopatra was bitten by a poisonous snake, and after
that she contracted some incurable disease and ended up in their hospital.
That's what they say. Anyway, either a snake bit her, or they forced her to
take to the needle, then said she wasn't herself and gave her a place in the
comfy nest. In the two years Cleopatra spent there, not a soul came to see
her. Her parents are simple people, they say, with no idea whether their
daughter who the prince fell in love with is alive, whether she still walks
this earth or whether she is no more. For them, it's a mystery. A man in a
hat came, just to see her, that's true. He observed her from a distance or
might have sat in the head doctor's office without speaking, in a chair in
the far corner, and listened to her answer the questions somebody asked
her. Cleopatra didn't know who that man was or where he worked, and the
mystery of him thoroughly surprised her; at the end of the conversation,
he wanted her to recite Japanese poetry from memory. As if she'd expected
that, Cleopatra immediately began to recite:

Oh how light, light.
Oh how light, light, light.
Oh how light, light.
Oh how light, light, light, light
Is the moon!

She recited that poem in an unusually gentle way, with ineffable sadness
and humility, her face gorgeously inspired . . .

The other two members of this group are extremely intriguing. One of
them is called Genghis Khan, and the other is Alexander the Great. There
is no record of when these two came to the comfy nest. Look, though, at
the diagnoses of these last three, Cleopatra, Genghis Khan, and Alexander the Great: "following a snakebite . . . following a snakebite . . ."

The Seven

In the heat of midday, these seven walked across the naked steppe on their long pilgrimage, after fleeing the psychiatric hospital under the cover of night . . . Now a great distance separates them from the Nation of Nutters and Psychos . . . And the goal of their journey is the Holy Land.

The seven of them are the Emperor, Genghis Khan, Kozuchak, Alexander the Great, Cleopatra, King Lear, and Thaïs the Athenian.

There are seven of them. The Emperor walks in front, using a stick to support him, and he walks slowly, muttering something inaudible under his breath . . . What joined them was a desire to escape the hospital, reach the Holy Land, and pay their respects there, and ask the Creator for forgiveness and mercy, and rid themselves of all their human sins . . . The road was long, and they had already left behind them mountain passes, rivers, deserts, green valleys, hills, and plains . . . While they experienced much hardship and deprivation on their way, they all agreed they could tolerate any hardship to achieve their goal. On they walked to the Holy Land despite their hunger and thirst. The Emperor said that once they reached it, they would all be rid of their sins; they would know all the joys of life, and they would be forever rid of the Nation of Nutters and Psychos back there, far away. Those thoughts gave them new vitality and saved them from exhaustion . . . Onward they walked: the unsociable Emperor; Genghis Khan, whose sword had subdued every land; Alexander the Great, who had made Asia kneel before him; the hysterical Lear; the wanton Thaïs; the shapely Cleopatra—many years after forgetting their real names . . . On they walked to the Holy Land, having left their real names in the Nation of Nutters and Psychos, under the names the head of the mental hospital had given them, having forgotten their genuine names . . . Perhaps it was only Kozuchak, who was practically a boy, whose name was his own.

Although the Emperor, guide of the group, had never been to the Holy Land, he always led them, controlling and governing the people. Kozuchak led Cleopatra by the hand, as the long journey was difficult for her, and stayed next to her everywhere, like her shadow . . .

Before dawn on this day, they had emerged into a great desert, a realm of sand . . . The water in the Emperor's plastic bottle, which he carried hanging off his belt, became warm as soon as the sun rose over the earth. He felt it when he rinsed his mouth with the water. The most difficult part is through these sands; after the endless desert, the valleys lush and green begin . . . and then it will be just a little longer to the Holy Land . . . This is what the Emperor extravagantly assumed, but, as a matter of fact, he had no clear idea what awaited them beyond this sandy desert, or what awaited them on their way . . . But the other participants in this escape knew nothing of his secret doubts . . . It was very difficult to walk barefoot across the scorching sand under the hot, beating rays of the sun . . . When they had reached the start of the desert, they had decided to have a rest, lying in the shade of the black saxaul shrubs . . .

Thaïs the Athenian, who had dropped behind the rest as they shuffled along slowly in the heat of the sun, suddenly threw down her knapsack, which she carried on her back, and pulled her skirt up over her head, and started a crude lament:

"Oy, mother of mothers! Where have we come to?" she cried, hoisting her skirt, baring her fat ass to the sun. "Sweat is running down all my cracks! What is this place? The Taklamakan? The Gobi Desert? Mount Sinai? The Malakum or the Karakum? What is this place?!" Maybe the sun had boiled her brains.

Thaïs the Athenian's long-unwashed, oily hair shone in the sun, and a repulsive stench spread all around her. She said she was a philosopher by trade and interpreted dreams in foreign languages . . . But later she caught this terrible disease, she lost her mind, she ended up on the street . . . And there was a reason she was given the name of the real-life feather-brained coquette Thaïs of Athens . . . Once, a well-to-do landlord fell in love with this modern-day harlot. They say he fell hopelessly, thoughtlessly in love with her. And after she told him, "If you genuinely love me, burn down your house," this man, people say, did burn his house down . . . Those rumors instantly soared around town, setting hundreds of tongues clacking . . . Ptolemy, who was the right hand and close confidant of Alexander the Great, once burned down a whole city, turning it to ashes, at one word from his notorious mistress, Thaïs of Athens. That city went down in history as a place completely burned up and annihilated at the word of a hetaera. Maybe that is why they called the woman philosopher Thaïs the Athenian. Nobody knows a thing about the rest of her life or biography. About three years have passed, now, since she appeared in the psychiatric hospital. Now she is truly out of her mind; when other people do anything, she always repeats after them; so she left with the rest of them and fled the hospital . . .

Thaïs the Athenian

After the needle entered her vein, her thoughts dissolved, and a thick fog came to swim before her eyes . . . She feels she is swimming and spiraling in air that is light as a feather . . . This air, light as a feather, seems to be moving toward her, but none of her movements, no strokes, are bringing it nearer, as if she could not move from that place. She wants a better look at the events transpiring past this thick fog, and her soul strives desperately to catch a glimpse of what is there; she wants to join the silhouettes of the people who are beyond this fog, as if, if they move away, if her hands cannot reach them, she will drown undiscovered in this viscous fog, becoming fog herself . . . And these terrifying suspicions urge her on to more desperate efforts; she strives not to be left alone in his ragged, gray fog . . . She wants to join the people who seem so close to her . . . And now, in this thick fog, she has caught sight of a fragile, yet bright, ray of Light . . . The Light spoke to her, and she recognized its voice immediately . . . If Light could speak, it would speak just like this. And this voice she heard asked her: Are you prepared for death? I am not prepared for death. I want to live, she answered the Light . . . The Light asked: Can you tell me of any day you lived? She was at a loss, not knowing what day of her life to recount . . . Scrambled events from her life began cavorting before her eyes . . . She tried, at a loss, to catch even one of them, but she could not . . . Again, the Light spoke: Apparently, you cannot tell me about a single event from your life . . . Remember! it said again . . . She remembers, she wants to tell about the events cavorting before her eyes, and she tries ineptly to put words together. What should I talk about? This, or that? she asks, looking carefully through all these events . . . The Light seemed disappointed in her, as if she had nothing she could talk about . . . Then it asked: "Do you ever read books?"

"Me?" she asked. "There is not a single book I have not read."

"What is last book you read?" asked the Light.

The last book? I have no idea now what it was about, that book! Damn! Perdition! It's on the tip of my tongue. A writer left it in my quarters. And the book is called Holy. The Holy Book . . . I remember this writer said that if someone read that book through, he'd end up in the nuthouse and spend all his life in the nuthouse until he rotted away there. How would I have known, then? But he wasn't lying. Yes, that's it, the Holy Book. I met that writer at a beer hall. I liked him from the start. The stars drew me to him, for some reason. When I walked up to him, he just handed me the mug he was holding and said, "Drink! I bought this with the last pennies I had. We'll split it."

I was already drunk as a pigeon, and maybe that's why it happened, but he and I hit it off right away. I swallowed the beer in one swig.

"Good beer?" he asked.

"Hell, no! It's old beer!" I answered, and then I asked him: "Did you like it?"

He answered, "I don't mind. Long as it's called beer. Too bad . . . One more mug would be just the thing! Got any money? And if you do, shall we have another apiece?"

I had one silver ruble. It was all that remained of the hundred from the night before. My friend for the evening had given them to me, the one I'd spent some time with. Could I have gone cheap, pricing myself at a hundred rubles per night? . . . That's because the night before I hadn't been able to find anybody, that's why I went cheap. But anyway, earning a hundred rubles overnight is nothing to sneeze at. And now, you see, just one remained. Half a beer wasn't enough to rinse out your mouth. So I blustered at him, something filthy. I swore to God, even, "Strike me dead if I have even a kopeck!" The stranger's forehead went wrinkly:

"If you don't have any money, what are you doing hanging around me for, you trollop? Blast it all! I'm barely hanging on here myself! Where do you get off? Get out of here!" he shouted.

Angry now, I slapped my silver ruble down on the table.

"Here's what I owe you for that half mug of beer! Take it! Have a ruble, drink your beer, drink some poison, what do I care? Here! Take it!"

"Well, now! So that's how it is! We'll get two mugs for a ruble, all right?" He picked up the empty mug and then gave me a surprised glance.

"You got a husband, lady?"

"A husband?" The question made me laugh. "A husband!" I cracked up. Watching me, he laughed, too. "All the good-looking men are my husbands, got that? Every one of them!"

The stranger stopped laughing and said:

"What about me? Am I good-looking, eh? Look at me, too, you filthy so-and-so! Come on, then!" He swore up a storm and cackled. "You're nice-looking yourself, even now. Your beauty hasn't left you yet, eh? Let's be together today, you and me, what do you say?" He stared at me.

"What about tomorrow? We'll be together tomorrow, too! Remember, once I've caught a man I don't let him go . . . And remember one more thing! I don't do business with people as broke as you. How much will you pay for a night? A hundred? Hmm??"

The stranger frowned. "Know what? Instead of paying a hundred and being with you, I'd rather use the money to buy three bottles and get good and high. I've had enough women like you. You're all alike." He spat on the ground, and, cursing me with foul words, he left to get his beer. A little while later, eyes sparkling with joy, he brought back two mugs of beer and, just as if he'd spent his own money on them, put them down on the table with a flourish.

"Drink up, O living soul! It's the only thing that makes this world a good place!"

I burst out laughing. I laughed like a boor. I felt like somebody was tickling me inside. I liked this man more all the time. Every other word he said was a curse. But you can't shock me with those words. I got used to them long ago. I've always liked the scallywags and pottymouths the best. I've seen very polite men, too. They sleep with you for a night, then they begin to pray and beg, "Just don't tell anyone you were with me, please don't tell!" They're always so cautious. But a scallywag like this doesn't care. He doesn't know anything but bad words. We drained those two mugs in a flash. "So, what do you say?" he asked gruffly. "Will we be together? I'm here today, gone tomorrow, say what you will. People like me don't make ourselves available to every woman. Because we don't want any hurt feelings." He roared with laughter and swore some more. I was not pleased by that. "Who do you think you are to act so high and mighty?" I asked. "Me?" he asked. "I'm a writer. A writer!" I laughed when I heard that. If all the men like him called themselves writers, it would be the end of us all. "You're a chump like anyone else. Only your voice doesn't quite suit you. Do you know that? A woman with a man's voice has no shame, and a man with a woman's voice has no strength." I laughed. His voice truly did sound like a woman's. And he didn't look a thing like a writer. Bald! If all writers were like that, we'd all drop dead. I didn't think there were any writers left in the world. I stifled my laughing and put on a serious expression. "What book have you written? If you even have a book. Maybe I could read it sometime?" I asked him. "Me?" he asked. "I wrote the Holy Book. The Holy Book." I was surprised. "What Holy Book? I've never read it," I admitted. "It's a book people tuck into their jackets to read. Somebody sees it, and bam! The slammer! Or the nuthouse, the loony bin! Walls up, walls down, walls all around! An iron door. Nobody comes out of there whole . . ." Suddenly, I shuddered, for some reason. "What did you write about in your book? Something feels fishy about it. There's some devilish trick to it."

"You call it a book, but do you have any idea what kind of book this is? The first five words were sent down from heaven. They descended on me and wrote themselves. The rest, I filled in. This book might be the salvation of man, the salvation of the world! It contains the formula for salvation. We need to bring it to the people, and if we don't, the end of the world will be upon us. So many places I've gone, trying to explain it. Nobody understood. Forget understanding: they tossed me in the loony bin. You think I'm hanging out here for the fun of it? Don't believe me? This is a mental patient's uniform. You know what the Russians say: 'The world is one huge mental hospital, and we are all patients!' They shove pills down our throats, ply us with medicines, and if we disobey, it's time for electric shocks! Yes!" he said and lifted one finger in the air.

"See here?" He showed me the striped shirt that peeked out from beneath his jacket. "Anyone who manages to figure this world out, to see what life is, he goes psycho, and that's because people who don't know the riddles of the world and secrets of life, people who don't want to know, they make him wear a psycho's mask. The stupid can't be psychos. All they can do is deceive. They don't have enough brains for anything else.

"You know every person has his own personal end of the world arranged for him? So . . . you disappear here, you pop up there, but there's never a finale! Life! What a plague!" he said in his unnaturally feminine voice. "Even Tsiolkovsky, the father of modern rocketry, was a psycho! The real deal!" He made the crazy sign with one finger near his temple. "He thought that when somebody dies, his atoms get spread across the universe, then land in some other being and begin a second life . . . If the dying being was happy, his atoms are happy, too, and the new being's life will be a happy one . . . That's what he said . . . If the atoms are unhappy, then it's the opposite. A human being's job," he said, "is to eliminate all unhappy life on Earth . . . Have you heard about that? Tsiolkovsky said that all those unhappy lives needed to be destroyed . . . And who's that, you might ask? . . . Sick men who are barely alive, cripples, weak-minded fools, and wild animals . . . Who can say? A psycho and a schizo! That's your father of rocketry! He had six sons, and two of them hung themselves, suicides! There you have it! Think about that! But if that psychopath had read my Holy Book, he never would have been like that . . . He aimed his rockets at human heads, not just the heavens! Right at human brains, he aimed them! What do you think happened, eh? You think demons drove Tolstoy into the desert before he died? No and no! Just before he died, he finally grasped my formula, he figured it out, he solved the mystery of this false and bottomless world, the Almighty took him and his heart up to heaven, the Almighty didn't want his special intellect to die—his special intellect had the right to be born again. An intellect can't sort out black from white in this world. The Lord doesn't need the souls of people like that. People's souls don't die. They go on and live a second life . . . Pythagoras was reincarnated exactly 216 years after his death, wasn't he? . . . But the gods don't give men immortality . . . They told Pythagoras: 'Ask for anything but immortality, don't ask for immortality.' Then he said, in immense grief: 'I ask you, in my life and in my death, do not part my soul and my intellect's memory!' In the end, he got what he asked for, even though he died: No matter how often his soul transformed, it never did part ways with the memory of his intellect. His intellect stored all the information it had taken in, like it had been snapping pictures. His soul was in both Euphorbus and Hermotimus. After Hermotimus died, his soul became the soul of a fisherman named Pyrrhus, who had prophetic dreams when he slept. After Pyrrhus died, after spending time in all those bodies, his soul returned to the breast of the newly born Pythagoras . . . After exactly 216 years . . . Pythagoras retained all those events, like he'd strung them like beads on the string of his intellect, saved them in his memory down to the finest particles, like he'd carved them in stone . . . And I'm a cosmic intellect, too! I'm a demiurge who grants eternal motion around the universe to the human soul! . . . Half my heart was born of heaven, and the other half was born of Earth. The Holy Book starts with words sent down from heaven. People like me don't die. We dissolve and go invisible. Soon I'll be invisible, too. Only one thing bothers me: How do I escape and get free of these psychos? . . . They'll find me in the heavens and on earth, in the grave, even as ashes. They'll find me and pack me away in the nuthouse again . . . I just can't get free of that nuthouse . . . As soon as I get free of it, the angels swoop down and carry me away, up there."

I couldn't tell if I believed what he told me. Not to mention the beer was making my head spin. I was already afloat. Together, the two of us went to my house. All the way there, I kept right on nagging him: "Show me your Holy Book." He never did show me. When I asked him why he wouldn't show me, he said: "You're a sinful woman, so I won't show it to you. No sinner ought to read even a word of that book . . . Soon as you open it, everything written there will vanish in a flash." That's what he said. The writer and I were together till morning. I was incredibly tired; I collapsed and fell asleep, and he left, but left behind his Holy Book. I don't know if he forgot it or left it on purpose. Suddenly, I saw something poking out from under the mattress. All kinds of thoughts crossed my head at once. I went on lying there, thinking: "What could that be?" To be honest, I was just too lazy to pick it up, and besides that, I nodded off. And, also, I thought that everything around the place was mine in any event. It would be better to have a snooze. I lay there for a long time, thinking I'd pick it up later. But I couldn't really fall asleep, and I couldn't get up either. I didn't even know what time it was. I just lay there . . . I was really pooped. If not for that tiredness, wouldn't anyone have gotten up and had a look? Up to then, as God is my witness, I'd never met a man like that. He wouldn't let me sleep, wouldn't let me at all . . . And two or three times he even whispered to me: "I've never met a woman like you." How many men have I been with, and not one of them has ever said that to me. Not one! But he said the words. Tell you the truth, I was glad to be the kind of woman he'd never seen the likes of, to think of myself that I could give somebody a few minutes of happiness. I was glad that I'd given one person in this world, at least, a thing like happiness. Happiness, you know, it's not riches, it's not clothing, it's not life . . . I thought it was something like a kiss, like a hot embrace, like sweating floods . . . It's true, that's what I was thinking then. It was daylight outside, and I was still lying there. As if I'd put a sweet in my mouth for the first time ever and was getting so much pleasure sucking on it, and I'd promised myself I'd never get up again in this lifetime. It's true, that's what I was telling myself. I felt like as soon as I got up, I'd lose this sweet moment forever. That night, the writer had said he was lying on the Holy Book, lying on a book . . . Strange! Soon as I close my eyes, I hear the words he whispered in my ear, I remember his words as if he's whispering to me again: "You set me on fire, you set me on fire . . . Nobody's ever set me on fire like this. But you did!" When he was mauling my soft breasts, when I couldn't get enough air, those words he whispered in my ear, the kind I'd never heard before, seemed uniquely sweet . . . Then I tasted all the sweetness of those words, and they made me melt. He asked: "What is beauty?" Like a fool, I started telling him this and that, everything I thought about beauty. And him? He said: "Beauty? Here it is." He ripped the blanket off me, almost tearing it, and he ogled my body like he wanted to eat it up. Plus, he turned on the light, and he said, "Here it is." When I tried to pull the blanket back to cover up, he ripped it off again. I felt embarrassed, ashamed of my nakedness. But he started massaging my calves, my legs, gently, and then not just my legs, my whole bare body, and it started seeming gorgeous even to me. I could feel there was beauty alongside me, inside me. "There it is! An unfinished Rembrandt!" he said, pointing at me . . . Later, this bald writer of mine had a hard time remembering who I reminded him of, and then he remembered, and he was so happy about it he clapped his hands. "I remember! You know who you look like? You look like Thaïs the Athenian! You know who she was? Alexander the Great's mistress! And also the wife of the King of Egypt."

"What was she, Alexander's mistress and the wife of the King of Egypt at the same time? . . . What a thought . . . I wouldn't say no to that . . ." I said.

"The devil can't do what a woman will! For example, Eleanor of Aquitaine was the wife of two kings at once . . . the English king and the French one," said the know-it-all writer. "I've never met a woman like you before," he said, enraptured. What about me? I've seen plenty of chumps like him. Before, I thought there was nothing in men that interested me. But I found this one interesting. He seemed interesting. I went on lying there and lying there . . . Suddenly, somebody knocked on the door. Somebody knocked hard on the door. I thought it was probably the writer. To be honest, when I heard the knock at the door, I was glad. Usually, men only spent one night with me . . . So had I made this old dope come back? . . . "I've still got fire in my body," I thought. There was still that banging on the door. It was him. "He could just come in and quit showing off," I thought. I felt like getting up and going to the door. I think, Soon as he walks in I'll drag him into my still-warm bed. But then I thought, "Well, I'm a woman, aren't I, and if I do that I'll lose all worth." And I went on lying there practically senseless. I stuck the calves that had so enraptured him that night out of the blanket, and went on lying there, unaware of anything. That thing was sticking up under me, I could feel it in my back. But I had no desire to pull it out from under me. Then the door opened, and two people walked in. They were dressed in completely identical clothing. The only difference between them was that one was tall and the other was tiny. Black gloves on their hands, black glasses over their eyes. I was frightened. I pulled the blanket over myself and tensed up. Who were they? The question drilled through my brain.

"Hey, Lady!" said the overgrown one. "Who was here to see you today?"

"First of all, my name isn't Lady, and second of all, my name is Thaïs the Athenian."

"The Plebian?" The undergrown one couldn't hear right, and couldn't talk right, like he was chewing his tongue.

"Clean out your ears, ugly! Not Plebian, Athenian!"

"Fancy that, fancy that . . . six of one, half dozen of what have you . . ." The runty one snickered, and he looked like an overstuffed sack. "Athenian, then!" said the undergrown one, all puffed up again. "Why don't you tell us who came to see you?"

"Who could possibly come visit a woman?" I asked him, hiding myself under my slippery blanket again. "Somebody."

"And who is this somebody of yours? A dog? A bird? A man?" asked the undergrown one in an ugly, whining voice. "Do you spread your legs for everyone who walks in here? Do you do any picking at all?"

"What's the difference if you pick them or don't." I was starting to get mad, too. "Some man! All men are alike. Even you, heh! What are you just standing there for, you lonely little bugger?"

"He's on duty," said the overgrown one. "He's busy."

"Why don't you tell us . . ." said the stumpy one again. "Was it a suspicious man who came to visit you? With a certain something tucked inside his jacket?"

"What?" I asked, surprised. "Vodka, was it?"

"Is vodka all you need, then?" asked the tall one meanly as he searched my room. "Vodka! You ever think about anything other than vodka?"

"Sure I do," I said, offended. "I think about a good man. If only you'd come by just for kicks! God save me from chumps like you!"

"Hush, you! We're on duty."

"There's no duty of yours at my house! Get out, get out of here!" I said, really angry now. "I'll start screaming rape! Shoo now!"

"Listen, lady, you watch your mouth, you hear me? Do you hear me? Sit down, shut up, and answer my questions! We're here on duty."

"What about a little of *this* while you're on duty, eh?"

"He can't get it up," the overgrown one said sharply. "He's on duty. If you don't believe me, take a look," he said, and he showed me some official document. "Why don't you tell us . . . Who were you with last night? Who was he?"

"Who do you think I was with? Who I sleep with, who I don't sleep with, that's my business, got it? You want me to tell you who I was with?"

"Yes!" they both answered at once.

"Only I bet you were with the king of Spain, right?" The runty one was teasing me. "Tell us!"

"I was with the spy you're looking for! He had something under his jacket. He tried to scare me right off the bat: 'If you don't let me in I'll blow up your whole House of Sodom!' he says. 'I blew up three skyscrapers in New York,' he says. Then I was scared, and I went to bed with him, held him close, hugged him and kissed him just like he wanted . . . Oh, he was a passionate one, and poor, as it turned out. Probably a spy who'd come from Africa . . ."

"Don't you change the subject," said the overgrown one. "Did he have a book under his jacket?"

"A book? I don't like people who read a lot of books." I said it like a tease, but my soul was shaking inside me. "Once, I slept with one of those bookaholics, and he spent all night trying to remodel my brain. You know what he told me?"

"What?" asked the runty one, who was nodding along with my story, intrigued. "What did he say?"

"He said, 'I need solitude.' Then I got angry, and I told him, 'What kind of man are you? Who needs your blabbering!' Since then, I haven't let any of those scholars get a piece of me. Know what I mean?"

"Answer the question. Did the man yesterday have a book with him? Did you see a book?" demanded the runt.

"No!"

"Try to remember," said the overgrown one. "Think hard! The Holy Book is missing. A psycho stole it . . . and we think he wants to give it to the people . . . If you see it, let us know immediately. Got that?"

"Yes, sir!" I shouted like a soldier, and I jumped up to stand at attention. Then I took a look at myself. I was buck naked.

"Oopsy-daisy, now who do we have here, Ave Maria? Check out the figure on her," said the shorty, mocking me, ogling me. "Who were you again, before? Taisya the Plebian?" The shorty wrinkled his nose in disdain and guffawed. "What a girl!"

Anger bubbled up inside me. I'd make him regret that, I thought. I turned my big fat bottom to them and started to chant:

"O-pa! O-pa! America! Euro-pa!" And I wiggled my butt in front of them, and I roared, "Get out! Get out of here! Help! Rape!"

"Oh, you think you're so smart, do you? Just look at her! . . . All right, let's go, before this crazy bitch tries to show us anything else," said the overgrown one, and he moved to leave. The shorty followed him, but then he turned around and gave me a jeer and spat on the floor. "Shameless woman!" he said.

While the runty one closed the door, I shouted so he could hear me: "No, I've got no shame! Only nerves! Get out of here!"

They vanished at the same instant.

Either they walked out the door or slipped through the keyhole, but, anyway, they disappeared like the ground had swallowed them up . . . I didn't feel like budging. I'd never been so tired. That thing under my mattress was poking me painfully in the back. I turned over, stuck a hand under the mattress, and felt for it. It really was a book. Written on the cover: "Holy Book." I thought, naively: "He must have left his Holy Book here." I picked up the book and opened it . . . I couldn't read a single letter . . . I closed it . . . When I went to open it again, some woman appeared before me. I have no idea where she came from. I thought maybe I was seeing things. I closed my eyes and opened them . . . The image was still there before me, not going away. And this woman. I'd seen her before . . . I think: "I've seen her somewhere." I couldn't remember a thing, and I was really terrified. I think: "Who brought her here?" At any rate, I finally recognized her. It was my third husband's wife. I recognized her . . . Sure, I recognized her, but I was really terrified, because how much time had passed now since she'd died? She was dead but was always following me around, like walking in my footsteps. I see her out in town during the day, and I dream of her at night. She is dressed in a long dress made of white calico. I suppose I'll never be rid of that woman. What is she, still jealous of her old husband even in death? Day and night I see her, enough already, how long is she going to follow me everywhere I go?! It was true, I'd married her husband without any ceremonies or licenses. At first, I was jealous of her, too, and I made them remove all her photographs from the house. I'm a woman, aren't I, and jealousy is in a woman's nature . . . I was jealous . . . And if that's not enough, I was even jealous of her baby. It wasn't a week before I told him: "Make your choice: either me or the kid. When I see that child, I think your wife isn't dead, I feel like she'll come back to life tomorrow and come right over." Then he answered: "What could I do with him? He's what I have left of my wife! What could I do with him?" And then he hugged the child and wept bitterly. It's true, he wept just like that child, that little baby, was wrecking his life, ruining his future. I also thought, then, that the kid was the only thing in the way of us being a happy family. We decided together: "We'll get rid of him." But how? Who would we give him to? Who could we trust him to? That bothered us both more than anything. It seemed like the most bothersome question in the world. Not to mention that the kid never let us sleep at night. Soon as we close our eyes, he starts screaming, and it's deafening. I didn't have a day of a peaceful, happy life with that husband. Soon as we go in another room and start to embrace, here comes that little scallywag, howling his lungs out! Soon I was really fed up. And my husband was fed up. "Let's get rid of him," we decided together. "Who's going to do the getting rid of?" I asked. "You do it," he said. "I mean, it's my kid, so how can I get rid of him?" In the end, we decided I would be the one to get rid of him . . . and my husband wouldn't raise a finger to help. Not to mention that he had a dream about his wife that night. He dreams of her telling him: "My child never stops crying. Every day, the earth conveys his weeping to me." After that dream, he was too scared to fall asleep the rest of the night, shuddering at every little noise, as if his wife would open the door and walk into the bedroom any minute. A little while later, a big mole, the size of a fingernail, appeared under his son's ear, the same kind his wife had. And that was after he saw her—maybe he was awake, maybe asleep—hugging the child close, feeding him from her breast. When he saw that, my husband was terrified. Soon as he opened his eyes, he saw his wife, quietly humming a tune, nursing the baby, giving him motherly pats, whispering to him. Then his wife gave the kid a loud kiss under the ear and laid him in his bed. My husband, stunned and terrified, stared at the kid for a long time, not breathing, not looking away. His heart was pounding like crazy, and, terrified that his wife might notice him, he didn't move, didn't even blink. Soon as his wife laid the kid in the bed, he started to cry. Bitterly, he cried. The father paid no attention to his son's crying, just sat there shaking from that wave of fear. For me, that baby's crying was impossible to bear, impossible. I was furious, and I started to shout curses: "Drop dead, you! Shut up, damn you! Stupid spawn of a stupid woman!" "Don't yell at the child!" That was my husband at the time, sticking up for him. "I just dreamed of his mother. She was right here. I saw her with my own eyes." That made me even more furious. "You and that son of yours should both drop dead! Dead, dead!" I shouted, all out of patience. "Get rid of him. Got that? If you don't get rid of him, I'm leaving!" So we decided to get rid of the kid . . .

Christmas was coming . . . That winter was a harsh one . . .

In the dead of night, we snuck out of the village together and walked toward the railroad, which was two kilometers away. My husband, who was dead set against killing the kid, shouting at me that he'd sooner lose me than ever give up his child, had dreamed about three Travelers . . . They told my husband they'd come by the will of God, and they asked him, "Do you love God?" To which he immediately answered, "I do." They told him: "Then take your only son, and carry him to the Sacred Mountain, and give him as a sacrifice." He could not reconcile himself to the death of his son, and he was tormented, because after all, he did love the boy very much. Not to mention this was the only child he had from his deceased wife . . . My husband told all this to the Travelers who had come to him. He made them understand that his love for the Creator had no bounds, and he would not stand in His way, and, in the end, he agreed to do it. At dawn, he would go to the Sacred Mountain the angels had told him about through those Travelers, bearing his son in his arms, and he would climb to the peak of that mountain. From the mountaintop, you can see the whole valley, plain as the palms of your hands . . . Once he climbs to the mountaintop, he kisses his son firmly, with enormous love, and after he binds the boy's little wrists and ankles, he prepares to sacrifice him. When he takes out the knife for the sacrifice and raises it over the child, suddenly those same Travelers appear beside him and grab his arm that's holding the knife. "Do not raise this knife over your son! Do not sacrifice him. Now we know that you fear God, and you would have exercised His will . . . and so you love God, and love for God, for you, means more than the life of your only son . . . We were only trying to judge your love for the Creator," the Travelers told him, and they vanished just like they'd appeared, dissolving into thin air . . . My husband, still dreaming, hugs his son close and kisses him in joy, feeling happy . . . and, thinking that, just like in that dream, the Creator was testing his love for Him, he agrees to really and truly rid us of his son. He agrees because he figures that if God truly loves him, he'll save his son at the last minute again, but in real life this time, not in a dream. As it turns out, he thought I wouldn't be able to lay a finger on a child saved by God . . .

That night, we came to the edge of the forest that the railroad crosses through. A freight train was supposed to be passing soon. The child started to cry, loudly . . . My husband laid the child on the rails but immediately cried out and picked him up again . . . He didn't have the strength to deliver the child to death . . . A light flashed in the distance, and we heard the sound of the approaching train. Here it came, enormous, shaking the earth, its wheels thundering ever louder and louder. The train's clattering set everything around us shaking, and it was even closer now . . . We started fighting over the child . . . Finally, I grabbed the boy and laid him on the rails, and when I grabbed my husband's arm again, we flew into the ditch to hide . . . The whole time my husband desperately wanted to climb out of that ditch and crawl over to the railroad tracks . . . but again and again he slid back down . . . He clutched at clumps of snow, his blood-shot eyes flashed, again and again he scrambled madly upward . . . He bellowed and roared, his whole body shaking, sobbing . . . The train was racing at a breakneck speed ever closer to the kid, ever closer . . . Its head-light illuminated the child lying on the tracks . . . The man couldn't look at the terrible sight, and he covered his eyes with his hands and howled. Time was growing shorter, any second now this speeding train would slice the child in half . . . Time was growing short . . . My husband clawed at his own face, clawed at his breast, and prayed: "Lord, you know how much I love You! . . . Forgive me, forgive me . . . Stop this horror, if you have the power, I beg of You . . . Make it stop! Make it stop!" He buried his face in the snow and kept on expecting that, any second, angels sent by God would show up and stop it all, just like in his dream . . . He expected a lot of the Creator . . . And then the blinding lights of the train whooshing down the tracks fell on a woman in a white dress next to the child. She picked up the boy lying on the tracks and held up her left hand in front of the train flying through the dark night as if ordering it to stop. And the fast-moving train, thundering and panting, slowed and stopped . . . It stopped, breathing heavily . . . When the woman, pressing the child close to her breast, walked off the tracks, the train lurched into motion again, rasping and groaning, and rolled on by . . . We both watched, not believing our eyes, just whispering, stunned: "God forgive us!" . . . "That's my wife, my wife who's passed on! My dead wife! She's come back to life! I recognized her right away!" shouted my husband, either rejoicing or mourning or both, still feverishly trying to scramble back up to the railroad tracks, and always tumbling back down . . . After the train passed, it was completely dark again, you couldn't see a thing . . . Pushing and pulling at each other, we finally made it up to the tracks. The woman in the white dress was nowhere to be seen . . . Five or six steps later my husband saw the child lying on the rails and was overjoyed beyond measure . . . He ran up to the kid, whispering in joy, "My boy, my only son!" But once he'd run up to him, he froze, not believing his eyes, like he'd turned to stone . . . His eyes popped out of their sockets. Then I ran up behind him . . . All that was lying on the tracks was the kid's warm blanket and clothing, and he himself was gone! "Oh, God, forgive me! What is this?" My husband collapsed on the tracks, knocking his head against the ground, writhing in pain, clawing at his breast . . . The two of us spent a long time there . . . For a long time, we looked for tracks in the snow left by the woman in white, but we didn't find anything . . . Dawn came, it got light . . . In the morning, the two of us started back, my husband was burning up inside, he groaned as he walked . . . Groaning in grief . . . After that, things between us cooled, we couldn't look at each other for a long time, we grew apart, day by day . . . Then, after a while, my husband's heart stopped beating, and he left for the next world . . . I remember that on the baby's blanket and clothing, near his head, there was just this same kind of book, with the same cover on it, same as this one. It was brown on the outside . . . and so was this book . . . As soon as I opened this one, like a demon in the night, right away, I remembered that time . . . and when I sat down heavy with those burdensome memories and was living through it all again, in walked that writer, out of the blue.

"The door was locked. How'd you get in?" The writer answered cheer-fully: "Your door is open to me now, as are all the doors of the world!" I asked him: "Where'd you come from, the loony bin?" To which he answered, "The whole world is one big loony bin! You live in it, too!" Then he added: "But I'm leaving you today. I'll vanish." I say: "Two people came looking for you. Turned the whole house upside down." The writer laughed out loud. "They did a search? One long and tall like a sapling, the other one like a little marmot?" asked the writer mockingly. "They're the devil's valets. My book isn't for people who pray to the devil. But the Holy Book isn't for you, either. You're a street rat! One of the reasons I called you Thaïs the Athenian is that she was the queen of fallen women like you. She was the mistress of a great emperor. For the pleasure she gave him, a whole city was destroyed in ancient times. The city was burned to the ground, its ashes spread around the world. Because of one wanton woman, a whole city destroyed! . . . That's what the queen of fallen women did! . . . You're just like her. As soon as you opened the Great Book, you remembered how you tried to leave a baby on the railroad tracks, and his mother saved him, your lover's former wife, your lover who died of a heart attack, isn't that right?" asked the writer, looking me straight in the eye. In the hour he'd been gone, he'd changed so much I barely recognized him. But I was glad when he first walked in again, thinking we'd make love . . . Now the dog only made me sad . . . "You laid your hands on my Holy Book, your sinning hands . . . A curse be upon you! . . . You will lose your mind, and your blood will be fluid as water . . . And the souls of every dead fallen woman in the world will come to you, a new one all the time, and you will fall sick with incurable hysteria of the womb . . . A curse on you for your wickedness, a curse for the sins of women!" This writer handed down sentence like a judge, convicting me of all womanly sins . . . "Do you know why the world is falling apart? A bad womb, a stinking womb, births evil people, and it births evil itself along with them," said the writer, reaching the very peak of his thoughts. A silence like the grave hung between us for a time. I broke it with a question: "But who on Earth are you? God's toady? A prophet? Who are you?" I shouted at him. He pondered that, staring at some single spot . . . then he looked up at the ceiling instead, then walked to the window . . . and looked quietly outside, where it was getting dark . . .

He whispered something I couldn't hear, got all agitated suddenly, and then, just like a clump of dandelion fluff slowly drifts off in the breeze, he smiled a pure, childlike smile, took one deep breath, sighed out all the air he had in him, picked up the book in its brown cover that was lying before me, pressed it carefully to his chest . . . and started to speak, quickly, full of feeling, in a voice like the rustling of leaves in fall, like a light gust of wind, like a babbling brook . . . He started to speak quietly and calmly, but his voice, like ocean waves racing to the shore, like waves beating ever more furiously one after the other against the cliffs, became more threatening, more majestic as he spoke . . . Anyway, he started to talk.

"A weight fell upon me . . . My body felt crushed, squeezed hard from all sides. I was being dragged into the dark hole of some weird sack of coal. I heard a clattering, merging into one simply unbearable noise. Suddenly, the darkness began to be illuminated, and a light appeared before me. I realized I was soaring down a tunnel of light. The clattering turned into singing, something like Rachmaninoff's 'Vigil.' I saw myself below me, spread-eagled on a hospital bed.

"A doctor bent over me and covered my face with a sheet. Then I experienced an extremely unusual sensation. I could feel nothing except peace, relief, and quiet. I discovered that all my worries had disappeared, and I thought to myself: 'How peaceful this is, now, and there is no pain . . .' I realized that I had died, and I didn't regret being dead, but I also had no idea where I was supposed to go. My thoughts and consciousness felt just like they had when I was alive. And the whole time, I kept thinking: 'Where am I supposed to go? What am I supposed to do? My God! I'm dead! I can't believe it!' I started moving through the darkness into some long space. Similar to a pipe, or something like that. I can't describe it. It was very dark . . .

"And at that moment, I felt myself separating from my body, slipping through the mattress and rails on one side of the bed—I truly did think I was slipping through that railing—down, onto the floor. Then I slowly rose up. While I was moving, I could see nurses running into the room . . . I moved over to the light in the ceiling and looked at one person, the doctor, in profile, it was a very clear view, and there I stayed, hovering right under the ceiling, looking down . . . I felt like a sheet of paper somebody had blown all the way to the ceiling . . . I saw them trying to bring me back to life. My body was spread on that bed, and they were all standing around it . . . I watched them massage my chest, shake my arms and legs, and I wondered what they were so upset about. I was fine, now, after all . . . I watched my body, all wrecked, among the people who had gathered around it, but, you know, it didn't arouse a single feeling in me. Like it was somebody else, or some object. I knew it was my body, but I didn't feel anything for it . . .

"At some point I started to feel sorry for myself, and I wanted to go back, but there was a light glowing, in front of me, at the end of the tunnel. A woman was waiting for me there, someone long dead whom I'd loved very much. I hurried toward her . . . She smiled mysteriously, and in a single second my whole life flashed before me, birth to death. I relived it all, down to the slightest detail. I wept over past griefs and I rejoiced over past joys, just like in life, but differently, somehow. The woman gestured for me to go back, and I understood my work on Earth wasn't done, and I returned. I opened my eyes to see a white sheet. I tried to shout and moaned. The doctor yanked the sheet off my face in astonishment, and said, 'He's alive!'

"Yes, I died, and then I was reborn!" There, he stopped and fell silent, sad.

"You ask me who I am? I'm not a Prophet, nor the right hand of God . . . I am a man who was reborn . . . if you want to know . . . I sensed what death was, then after that death I was resurrected, and I brought with me this Holy Book . . . The Holy Book is the book of immortality, and I brought it here . . . I wrote down all the words . . . Now everyone is looking for this Holy Book . . . khans and emperors and presidents and kings, rich men and poor men, devils and demons . . . Nobody wants to die. Everybody wants to rule the world! . . . But greed rules the world . . . Greed makes people want to eat each other up, and through their greed they try to seize power and wealth and status, money, women, destiny, life, happiness, love . . . Out of greed, people want it all, everything except their own death, but out of greed they can't discern the doors to death, flung wide open, so close by . . . And people have stopped sensing the majesty of death . . . And other people, who consider themselves great prophets, have started to scorn them . . . This age is a disaster . . . God gave man life, but not predestination . . . The Creator does not designate a destiny for everyone, but he never expected Man, whom He created of His love, to have such a wretched fate, such a stupid human fate . . . He gave Man faith, love, hope, and life . . . But fate has only one master: Man himself! . . . Today I'll dissolve, vanish, become the ether, be absorbed into space . . . I've found the secret of the world! Nobody knows it but me. But me remaining in this world would be a worldwide disaster. A man who knows the secret of the world has no right to live on Earth . . . Today is my last day," he said, and stopped.

His words sent a shudder through my body. I was coated in sweat, my forehead felt like ice, and something was wrapped around my neck like a snake . . . That set off a storm of memories inside me, like getting whacked with a saber . . . Before my eyes they marched, one after the other: how I wept, how I raged, how I cursed, my whole unlucky fate, and my whole pallid life . . . It was like I was sensing the end of my life, and I almost burst out in tears . . . My arms and legs trembled, my heart pounded madly . . . I felt something cold, like a snake around my neck, I touched it—yes, there was snake around my neck, wrapped three times. Its mean little head dodging this way and that, it stared straight at me with it fiery red eyes . . . like piercing me through with its gaze . . . From that gaze, I thought I could hear a quiet, hissing voice . . . Before me, as I stood trans-fixed by the snake's eyes, in a single moment, my whole life flashed before me . . . It flowed like sand between my fingers . . . In my confusion, I tried to remember something . . . but not one of those past events racing before me with a thunderous roar, like the wagons of that train, hammering my brains, was anything I could see; it all blended together, rushing past at a terrifying speed . . . nothing I could catch with my mind . . .

That day, a meteorite fell to Earth from the sky.

It was the first sign sent by the Creator . . .[1] The end of the world was supposed to come with fire . . . And, as he'd said, he dissolved into thin air,

---

1. TIBETAN MONK NOTIFIES NASA ABOUT END OF WORLD. A monk known as the Oracle of Shambhala, from the Gyandrak monastery near Mount Kailash, has notified NASA that the end of the world is near. His message states that on December 21, 2012, the Earth

into the infinite blue space I could see from my window . . . He vanished like a candle snuffed . . .

The snake that was wrapped around me bit me right in the neck . . . When the snake sank its fangs into me, my eyes flew wide open . . . I fell

---

and the rest of the solar system will pass through a galactic "null band," according to a report by Earth-chronicles.ru. The Oracle says complete darkness and silence will fall over nearly the entire planet at around ten o'clock in the morning, Moscow time, on December 21, 2012. There will be no light, electricity, lines of communication, or sound. At that moment, the Earth will pass through the galactic null band. "This is a state of space in which all energy is quelled and it cannot spread, where no object has an electromagnetic field. There is no need to worry or fear," writes the monk. The darkness will come with cosmic auroras and deceptive flashes of light and will last for three or four days. Then the light of the sun will appear again. "Earth's animals will sense the coming of the cosmic darkness early, and will hide in their burrows," says the monk. "People in cities will not sense it and will fall victim to madness. Ten percent of the Earth's population may die." The Oracle of Shambhala also offered some practical advice for the people of Earth:

1. You must prepare for this cyclic shift in advance. Wrap up your affairs for 2012 and do not launch new activities. Pay your debts.

2. On December 20, 2012, collect your children, important documents, and cash, and leave the city for the countryside. Prepare stores of food for two months, because electricity may not function for a long time.

3. You must have stores of water, firewood for heat, and candles for light at home. Keep a wood or coal stove in your house, because electricity will not travel over wires starting on December 21, 2012.

4. Telephone and television service will be interrupted. During the "dark days," cover the windows with dark drapes; do not look through them, do not believe your eyes and ears, and do not go outside. If you must go outside, do not go far. You may become disoriented, because you will not even be able to see your hand before your face.

5. When the light reappears, do not hurry back to the cities. Stay in the countryside until spring.

According to the Tibetan monk, the Earth will fully emerge from the "null band" on approximately February 7, 2013. Electricity and public transportation will be partially restored. By the end of March, the world will be fully up and running again.

The end of the illuminated world will fundamentally alter people's worldview, says the Oracle of Shambhala. People will become more spiritual. Both developed and developing countries will see a blossoming of various teachings encompassing both science and spirituality, and systems for improving health and personal development. "This will be the most important impetus toward human progress in a very long time," he concludes.

over and lay there like a tree with its roots chopped off . . . Everything that used to seem murky and unclear snapped into focus for me that very minute. Two nuthouse orderlies put rubber handcuffs on my wrists and started looking for a vein to give me a shot . . . I lay there, weak, sprawled on my back, like my soul had flown out of my body, and my breath and voice had no power and no volume, but I begged them: "No shots! No shots!" The icy needle first cooled my body, then set a fire in my veins, it set me on fire . . . My soul was burning, my blood was boiling . . .

That night, I met the person who had written the Holy Book, and all night long in my dream, he and I strolled around a garden, talking . . .

In the nuthouse, you're not allowed to say "God," not even in your sleep. You're not allowed to utter that name . . .

Thaïs the Athenian was finished talking, and that was the end of her tale for the Light. When she got an injection, she always went away into some uncanny world where everything was unthinkable, and she herself changed and saw mysterious changes . . .

This time, she was talking with the Light.

The Seven

By the middle of the night, these seven somehow made their way to the great desert, where they collapsed in exhaustion and slept like the dead. Soon it began to get light. Dawn was approaching. When the rays of the rising sun touched the eyelids of Thaïs the Athenian, she awoke in a fright, instantly remembering both her conversation in the psychiatric hospital with the Light and the injection. She opened her eyes and saw the Great Desert . . .

"Where are we?!" she shouted, loudly, again.

Genghis Khan raised a hand, calming her. "Hush!" Then he nodded at the Emperor, who was lying still.

"The Emperor is in a trance . . . He'll tell us what they're saying up above . . . *Hos natura modus primum dedit* . . ." said Thaïs the Athenian in some incomprehensible language. "Did you understand what I said?" For some reason, Thaïs the Athenian was staring at Kozuchak alone.

"I don't know," said Kozuchak, scratching his head.

"Judging by the pronunciation, it's nothing like either English or French . . . It's not even quite like Spanish," said Cleopatra, thoughtfully. Then she jumped and gave a happy yelp. She must have remembered. "Is it Latin?"

"Bravo!" said Thaïs the Athenian, lifting one long index finger in the air. "That is correct! Latin! It means: 'These people were made by the hands of the gods.' Got it?"

"Got it," said Kozuchak, and he laughed, then added, more seriously: "So . . . does that mean the gods made us with their own hands?"

28

"Not their hands, their will," chuckled Alexander the Great. Genghis Khan, who was keeping a close eye on the Emperor, still lying there with his eyes fixed on the sky, said again:

"Hush!"

Only then did the rest of them notice that something unusual was happening to the Emperor.

They all stared at him lying on his back, muttering to himself like a crazy person, rolling his eyes. After all, it had been the Emperor who had first started talking them into a nighttime escape from the mental hospital; he was the one who made the preparations, he was the one who guided them, leading them to some kind of Holy Land, where he promised to grant them paradisaical happiness. His strength had drained away lately, so much so it seemed he could no longer lift even his own shadow . . .

While they watched the Emperor in this strange state, very quiet, Thaïs the Athenian suddenly screamed, hopped up, and slapped herself on her own great big bottom:

"A snake!"

When they heard that, the first to reach her were Kozuchak and Cleopatra. Soon they all saw the snake wriggling across the ground, thick as a woman's black braid . . . Its head held high, the snake slipped easily across the sand, like a fish through water, and it seemed to pay no attention to Thaïs the Athenian's heart-rending howl. The appearance of the creeping serpent shocked them all like a dousing with cold water. Genghis Khan and Alexander the Great and King Lear all ogled the thing in fear, unable to look away as it writhed and wriggled across the sand. Powerless even to chase it, they all just watched, silently, in a stupor.

Usually, desert snakes launch the first strike against anything that moves—animals, people; once they're close enough, they strike at their victim like lightning. Their venom is deadly. Everyone went stone still, watching that snake. When Cleopatra saw it, she couldn't take her eyes off it, she had no strength to control her trembling, and she pressed close to Kozuchak, who was standing next to her, also consumed by fear . . . The snake terrified Genghis Khan as well, and Alexander the Great, and Cleopatra, and they all felt the snake had looped itself around them and was squeezing their bodies tight . . . (All three of them felt, mystically, that they were people who had died of snake bites long ago. Nobody knew when that had happened to them, or whether it was real life or a dream . . . but a deep, black, visceral fear of snakes had made a home in their blood . . .)

Exhausted as they were after their long walk, the sudden appearance of this snake simply laid the six of them flat in a very strange way.

"Nobody make a sound! Nobody move! Not even your shadows!" shouted the Emperor. "That is the snake that is pursuing me. It will murder me with its poison, eventually," he said, his voice shaking, his whole body trembling. "Nobody move! The vile beast has come for me . . ."

The snake crept to the Emperor's feet and lay there, coiled. Genghis Khan wanted to strike it with a stick he held, but the Emperor gestured to him to refrain . . . The other six stared at them, wild-eyed, frantic. The snake began to slowly wind itself around the Emperor's leg, the way people bind their legs for warmth. The Emperor's eyes rolled up in his head, and he froze as if carved of stone . . . If he so much as raised an eyebrow, the snake would sink its fangs into him, he thought . . . And the higher the snake slithered up the Emperor's leg, the less the rest of them understood what was happening, or knew what they should do.

The great snakes ruled this whole empty steppe, the whole sandy desert . . . These snakes were vengeful creatures . . . If you raised a hand against any of them, a thousand more would rise up to take revenge . . . Hunting everything that lived, the snakes of this desert had felled multitudes of people, camels, horses, and every other living species with their venom . . . Was there any creature whose bones they hadn't set to rot here? This place had a name. The Emperor must have known it. From ancient times, this empty plain, this endless desert full of sand, had been called the Valley of Death . . .

The snake did not wrap itself around the Emperor's leg for long. Soon it went slack, like a rope untied, and fell to the ground . . . The Emperor went on staring at the sky and praying quietly . . . Little by little, the serpent crept away from the people standing there, and when it reached its burrow under the saxaul shrubs, it vanished, it melted away . . . As soon as the snake disappeared, the Emperor, still staring intently at the heavens and mumbling his prayers, collapsed to the ground like a chopped-down tree . . . His whole body broke out in a cold sweat. His hands trembled, his teeth chattered, he shook like a man with a terrible fever, shaking all over with fear . . . They all huddled around the Emperor, trying to help . . .

(That night, the Emperor dreamed of a snake.)

This was the snake he'd dreamed of . . . this very one . . .

The coiled snake slowly uncurled and darted like a burning flame over the Emperor's body, as his muscles tensed, as he shook feverishly in fear, every limb seized by terror. Slowly, the snake approached the Emperor, hissing like the wind. It crept toward him there in the complete darkness, as if the two of them were the only living beings left in this world. When a kind of hole appeared in that impenetrable dark, the kind of hole a tiny Emperor might have been able to creep through, and it grew a little lighter, then both the night and the dying light sensed the man's heart stop. It seemed the last weak breath before death flew out of him for good, as if he had given his soul up to God, as if he might be trying to die like the dying night, still sensing this world, so that then this cold terror could not penetrate into him and make him shiver. Then death would not tarry, either, and this man, who had spent his whole life afraid, could tear his own life from his chest and flee, far away, holding his soul in his fist like a songbird. The sense of fear made his soul tremble like a leaf in the wind, cold terror streamed over his body like an icy snake, and the one, actual snake slowly crept along, coming closer, ever closer. In that cursed darkness, the whole universe screamed, trying to drill through his chest. He wants to die, but he is not strong enough; he wants to succumb to nothingness, but he cannot . . . The world has constricted to the size of a cow's hide, as if only these two living beings remained inside it, only two living creatures of this world, drawing closer to one another and detesting one another . . . An icy trembling seized him. He tensed his arms, intending to crush the snake's head, but his body did not obey him. Only his eyes followed the snake, stuck to it. The snake had tensed, it was firm as wood, and it hissed, making clear it needed nobody else . . . The Emperor knew he would die of snake venom, he would have no other death . . . And the night before, in his dreams, he had fallen into a nest of snakes, the sticky, ice-cold snakes wrapped around his neck, and he lay there unmoving, waiting for the snakes to plunge their poisonous fangs into him . . . The snakes crawled over him, making him shake anxiously, they crept inside his shirt . . . Not one snake dared to bite him . . . He prayed relentlessly, to God, the Creator . . . about snake venom . . . wanting to die from that venom . . . Finally, he seized a snake, and squeezed it, to force it to spit venom into his hand . . . He wanted to swallow that venom . . . But wouldn't you know it, even the snake did not consider him worthy of its venom . . . And now, today, this vile creature had appeared with its forked tongue . . . Was it the snake that was making his heart feel so cramped and cold? "Have you come to kill me?" No sooner did he pronounce those words than the snake vanished, as suddenly as it had appeared . . . Yet, even then, soaked in sweat, he screamed . . . That wasn't the first time he had dreamed of that snake . . . If you dream of a snake, you should expect bad news, some terror . . . The movements of an undulating snake speak of someone disappointed in themselves, with an unfulfilled destiny . . . From the snakes that frequented the Emperor's dreams, bringing woe, his everyday doubts were distorted into burdensome thoughts . . . and one thought hounded him: "Even after I die, I'll be tied to that snake . . . My God, even now, when almost nothing of life remains, here in this Valley of Death, this snake has come back and wrapped around my leg like a rope! But why?" That led the Emperor to a deep melancholy, a torment that tore at his heart . . .

"Everything changes in this world. Only Supreme Wisdom and Supreme Stupidity remain the same!" Thaïs the Athenian boldly declared. "Who said that? Updike? Kierkegaard? Churchill? Spinoza? Sartre? Was it that nutter Nietzsche? Or that idiot Freud? Who was it? Huh?"

"Who would ever say that . . . except you! . . . It's one of your own ridiculous phrases!" argued Lear, shaking his long gray locks. "Who said it? Who said it? Pushkin!" he shouted angrily.

"The hell it was Pushkin! Confucius said it, you walking speck of dandruff!" Thaïs the Athenian shot back. "You're the one with ridiculous phrases!"

"Enough! Knock that off!"

"I. Will. Knock. Nothing!" said Thaïs, mouth clenched tight. "You hear me, you parasite?" She flew at Lear, drilling her thin fingers into his hair. "Parasite! Bacterium! Dandruff!"

"Let go . . . let go, I said!" Lear was losing patience, and he struggled to resist Thaïs the Athenian's furious attack and rabid sense of morals, only weakly holding her off as he tried to extract his long gray locks from her hands. "Let go of my hair, you witch! Dirty bitch!"

The woman's fingernails, long a stranger to clippers, scratched across Lear's face: "Turd! Judas! Bacterium! Germ!"

Thaïs the Athenian, seized by madness, fingers hooked into Lear's hair, harassed him and beat him. As he backed up, Lear tripped on a root and fell. Just like a witch, the crazed woman sat astride him and started pounding. Thaïs's crotch sank onto Lear's face. The stench of dirty underwear struck him in the nose.

"Turd! Bacterium! Germ!" Thaïs the Athenian kept on ranting.

Finally, the rest dove into the scuffle and separated the two of them. Only the gentle Cleopatra, not knowing what to do, stood to the side and wept, because the whole journey so far, the hatred between Lear and Thaïs had never cooled . . . Everyone was fed up with them barking at each other like dogs, their endless, irreconcilable enmity . . .

"Both of you, shut up!" shouted the angry Emperor. "Shut up, I say! Curse the both of you! What an ass I am to lead you all to the Holy Land! Keep that up, and you'll never see it!" The Emperor was shaking all over. "Cursed of God, both of you! Stop it, I tell you!" The Emperor's eyes shot lightning, and he frowned like thunderclouds.

His shouting expelled a false iron tooth from his mouth . . . When he saw that, Kozuchak picked up the iron tooth lying in the sand, quickly rinsed it with water from his canteen, and handed it to the raging Emperor. The Emperor put the tooth in place and said, through clenched teeth:

"What a fool I am to have led you on this journey!"

They all went still in the face of the Emperor's rage . . .

"Do you even know what this place is called?" The furious Emperor's blood was boiling.

Everyone froze silent, holding their breath, as if to answer, "No!"

Only Thaïs the Athenian went on quietly muttering, tossing away strands of Lear's hair that had gotten wrapped around her hand:

"Turd! Ballless billygoat! Tried to rape me just yesterday!"

"Shut up, you idiotic whore!" said Alexander the Great to Thaïs the Athenian. "Shut up, you hear me?"

Nobody made a sound.

Lately, the Emperor had become very weak, and he had a heavy cough. Now he coughed that dry, barking cough, and when he'd coughed himself out, he said hoarsely:

"You don't know? I'll tell you. This place is called the Valley of Death." The Emperor's body was struck by shivering.

"The Valley of Death?" Everyone was shocked.

"Didn't you promise to take us to the Holy Land, not some Valley of Death?" said Alexander the Great, scowling at the Emperor. "We're not a bunch of Jews to follow you around like Moses for forty years in the bare steppe and sandy desert, are we? Where is the Holy Land?" he shouted, he who had barely spoken before. "I'd rather have rotted alive in the Nation of Nutters than feed the worms here!" Alexander the Great spat on the ground with relish. "Goddamn! We don't even know where we're going . . ."

"Moses guided the people so they would know the truth . . . Forty years, he led them, but you can't hold out for forty days!" said Kozuchak, standing up for the Emperor. "Did you think cleansing ourselves of sin would be easy? We can make it, Emperor! We have to make it."

"You must persevere . . . Not long remains . . . till the Holy Land." The Emperor sank heavily to the ground, slowly leaning to one side. "Persevere . . ."

Cleopatra, who hadn't interfered up till then in the dispute between the older men, sat down next to the Emperor and laid his head in her lap. It was hard for him to breathe; he could not inhale deeply; there was pressure on his chest . . . Kozuchak gave him some water from his canteen. In the heat of noon, which can boil your brains, the water was even hotter . . . The Emperor took a gulp, then spat it out.

Hot tears ran from Kozuchak's eyes. The whole journey so far, he had supported the Emperor and come to love him.

"What are you doing, crying?" asked the Emperor.

"No!" Kozuchak sniffled and wiped away a tear.

"Don't cry." The Emperor saw that Cleopatra's eyes were gleaming wet, too. "I'm not feeling so well right now . . . It will pass . . . Then we'll set out again . . . It's not far now to the Holy Land . . . I'll just . . . just nap a little . . ." The Emperor dropped off, but not to sleep; he dropped into the infinite expanse of his tangled, heavy memories . . .

"Who was Mary Magdalene?" asked Thaïs the Athenian, breaking the silence. "Who was she?" she asked Genghis Khan.

Genghis Khan frowned.

"Nobody I know . . . There was nobody called that in my harem!" he answered stupidly.

"Do you know?" she asked Alexander the Great.

"How would I know?" he snapped at her.

"Idiot! But it's true, how would you know?" Thaïs the Athenian snapped back. "Since you've never read a word . . . But I don't want to ask this speck of dandruff, germ, bacterium anything," she said, turning quickly away from Lear and screwing up her face in disgust.

"But I know!" said Lear, mockingly, staring at Thaïs the Athenian. "I know who she was."

"Nobody's asking you," Thaïs the Athenian told Lear.

"Don't ask if you don't want to . . . But I know who she was . . ."

"Well, I'll be. A guy like you, you know?" Thaïs the Athenian said meanly. "Tell us what you know, dandruff!"

"Mary Magdalene was a whore! A whore."

"Gimme a break! . . . Get a load of this . . . What does a louse know about whores?" Thaïs the Athenian cackled at him. "Get a load of you! That's a good one!"

"She was a whore, just like you!"

"If you ask me, a whore like me is a thousand times better than a ballless billygoat like you! Tra-la-laaaa!" Thaïs the Athenian turned her back to Lear and shook her great big bottom at him. Then, shooting him a sideways glance, she added: "And if you want to know, Mary Magdalene stopped being a whore and became a Great Woman! Got that, you speck of dandruff?" She turned back toward Lear and went on. "What a fool I was, hoping you'd be any use! My lovers were Seneca, Montaigne,

Plutarch, Diogenes, and Freud, you know . . . My lover Basho wrote a poem for me:

> *Spring is departing!*
> *The birds and fish are weeping,*
> *Their eyes fill with tears."*

"Quit bragging about your lovers! You're no Mary Magdalene!" Lear spat out the words with disdain.

"Easy now, your highness," Thaïs the Athenian retorted with a click of her tongue. "You're not a king, you're a stinking stable boy! A mangy horse is a poor match even for a blind mare!"

The unspeaking steppe. Dusk descends on the desert wilderness. The flaming sun sinks below the horizon . . . Genghis Khan noticed the sun was setting strangely. When the sun reached its lowest point, it looked just like an apple a dragon had taken a bite from. Its lovely light radiated in all directions . . .

"Look at the sun! The sun!" Genghis Khan pointed a finger at the sky in fright. "The sun has gone dark . . . There's a solar eclipse . . ." he started shouting mindlessly.

When he heard the shouting, Alexander the Great, who had been breaking a bottle lying nearby against a rock, looked at the eclipse through a shard of glass. Then everyone picked up pieces of the broken bottle, and they also examined the sun. Only Lear was frozen in bewilderment, like he'd bitten a rock, and suddenly, when he came to, he attacked the others angrily . . .

"A solar eclipse? A solar eclipse?" Lear grabbed his own head. His hands were shaking, his veins were pulsing. "How I detest all this! The sun! The night! Women! Infidels! Unpicked poppies! Josef Stalin! Reagan! Chikatilo! I hate them all . . . Earthly hope has to be beaten to death; only then will there be salvation in genuine hope . . . That's what Kierkegaard said, that's what Mierkegaard said . . . That's what I say!" Lear's illness overcame him then, and he ground his teeth, foamed at the mouth, shook all over so that nobody was able to hold him up, just like he was having an epileptic attack, and then he collapsed on the sand. He scooped up sand by the handful and flung it in every direction . . .

"Spout, rain! Spout a rain of sand! Strike, thunderbolts, meteorites, cleave my very brain! Let the dragon devour the sun! Let there be darkness! I desire the darkness, now, complete darkness! . . . We are mortal men!" In his ecstatic state, Lear cried out every thought that entered his head. His eyes were burning. "Mortal men choose the path of darkness and violence, even if they hate to admit it. Savages! You have to speak with them in their own language!" Lear went deeper into his fit all the time. "There are more of them that hate . . . They're easier to control . . . The more destructive the goal, the more eagerly they work for it. I'll use their hands to build the worldwide revolution . . . Yes! . . . Revolution? I'll build a party of debauchers and sinners; they will rise up against God! My party will gradually amass ever more power and step boldly onto the political stage! The world will be debauched, and the debauchers will triumph! They will usher in the Apocalypse!" Lear's hands shook, and his whole body was seized by trembling. He stopped talking for a while, looking all around, then went on, quietly, at half the volume. "I remember it all . . . I was mortal . . . I was an angel . . . I played . . . I lost . . . I forced women . . . I washed the bodies of the dead . . . And now I am dead myself . . . Who will wash me?"

This kind of insanity had seized him, sometimes, before. When it happened, he always shouted out whatever came to mind, words impossible to understand, and foam frothed from his mouth like a rabid dog. He was in that same state now.

Lear could not get himself back to normal and went on muttering and raving . . .

"Opus . . . Mopus . . . Puss . . . Muss . . . Mussolini . . . Insolini . . . Sorrini . . . Besorry . . ." he muttered, grinding what remained of his teeth, writhing like a dragon was eating him from the inside.

The other six, used to his fits by then, waited impatiently for the moment the light would dawn on him again. Once he began the monologue from

King Lear, he would transform completely, nostrils flaring, forehead flat-
tening, and he always recited like he was playing the role at the Globe in
London . . . That's what happened to him this time, too:

> Blow, winds, and crack your cheeks! Spout, rain,
> Till you have drench'd our steeples, drowned the cocks!
> You sulph'rous and thought-executing fires,
> Vaunt-couriers to oak-cleaving thunderbolts,
> Singe my white head! And thou, all-shaking thunder,
> Strike flat the thick rotundity of the world
> Crack Nature's moulds, all germains spill at once,
> That makes ingrateful man!

Every time he reached the end of his monologue, as if he'd poured
out all his torment into a boiling vat of poison, he shut down with a snap
and fell senseless to the ground. This time, too, he fell backward as if he'd
dropped dead . . .

"Bravo! Encore! Bellissimo!" This turn of events always made Thaïs
the Athenian ecstatic. Sweeping away everything in her path, chattering
up a storm, she ran to the prone, motionless Lear. She lifted her skirt up
over him and farted loudly. "There you go! Gas for dessert!" she said and
shook her skirt over his body.

There truly was an eclipse of the sun that day . . .

The Emperor, still being propped up by Cleopatra and Kozuchak,
deep in his thoughts, slowly sank into them, like sinking into a well.

"In the end, this had to happen . . ." The Emperor felt he had foreseen
all this, and had been preparing all his life to say those words. But what to
say? . . . At some moment, the sorrow that had been lodged like a needle
in his heart all his life, deep in his breast, would suddenly explode, and an
end would come to this senseless life.

Was he expecting that? Or did he sense it with the coming of the
snake? He did not know, did not understand . . . The Emperor was tired.
Tired? He truly was tired of all this. As soon as he closed his eyes, that
snake appeared to him. Many years ago, a gypsy woman had told his fortune: "Death will come to you from a snake." Those words and that snake

had pursued him all his life . . . What a cursed world! . . . The unbearable alienation of humankind, the leaden silence . . . And this minute, so long awaited, this day, this year: it all came to a complete void. And what did he need with this coming of the snake? . . .

He had one reason for fleeing the nuthouse and traveling to the Holy Land. True, he did not know where this Holy Land was located; he simply did not want to be among the rank, dirty linens of the nuthouse when death came, he wanted to die in the open desert, in the untamed steppe; basically, he did not want to die in that home for nutters . . . He dreamed of the Holy Land, where people are made pure and released of everything foul and then depart for the other world . . . Only now did the Emperor sense that the crazy people following him also wanted to cleanse themselves before death . . . But he could not reveal to them that he was going there to die . . . He had no idea why the Creator had resolved to send him death by snake venom . . . or was he destined for that from birth? . . . The Emperor sank again into his somber thoughts . . .

The world flew before his mental gaze . . . It tormented him, this sinking into bottomless thoughts . . . He sank and sank, ever deeper, into an impenetrable darkness, into a senseless, grievous fog . . . Billowing, murky, confused samples of memories . . . With a clatter, a racket, pictures from his life rushed past him and vanished in the endlessness . . .

He could not remember . . . could not remember how it all began . . .

The Emperor

He could not remember. He could not remember anything. All the thoughts were mixed together in his head, and he did not know who he was or what was wrong with him. The worst thing was that he simply could not understand what this fist-sized thing on his neck was; he strained to understand but could not. *Forgive me, God!* This fist-sized thing that looked like a brain: Did it come from his head, or had somebody cut it out of some other place and stuck it to the back of his neck last night? Now, when that thought drifted into his head, he felt at his neck, and unable to trust a thing, he went to the mirror. But he couldn't see his head in the mirror. All he saw in the pitch dark was his own two eyes, which glowed like cat eyes. Only today had he seen that his eyes could glow like that, never before, and he was astonished. It frightened him. He was frightened of his own eyes. Not just his eyes: himself, too, and the idea of trusting himself now terrified him. Dark blue veins swelled on his thin, bony hands, and when he touched them to his face, he felt the icy cold of that touch. He thought he could feel a glacial sea inside him that turned everything he touched to ice. Even these hands, it seemed, were not his hands at all; somebody must have chopped them off a corpse and stuck them onto him. He didn't know what was wrong with him. Or maybe his soul had already left his body, flown off to who knows where? This was all a mystery to him. There is only one thought pounding in his head, and in anger, he clenches his teeth, and the clenching of teeth only makes him angrier, and he could feel himself going insane, as if he'd already gone, as if he no longer understood a thing, as if he were deprived of all reason, and when he lost the power to reason, he'd lost himself, completely, too. Did he truly feel this, or did the thought come from his powerlessness?

He did not understand even that. And what was going on? His two eyes peering at him from the mirror glowed, like a wolf's eyes in the night. Not bold enough to gaze for long at the reflection of his eyes, he reached out his thin, bony hands and touched the mirror. The most curious thing was that where the mirror stood, there was no sunlight, and the mirror, as far as he could judge by touch, seemed to be made of ice rather than glass, so badly did the cold burn his fingers when he touched it. Though not even a weak hint of sunlight could penetrate this dark room, the mirror's smooth surface gave off a weak glow; no, not so much light as a weak, wavering, barely noticeable luminescence, and that seemed strange to him. Tearing his gaze away from the mirror, he looked around in trepidation. A great darkness was covering the universe, and the wind whistled through it, and dust rose in a tall column. He was in a strange state that nobody could understand or explain. He just could not remember how he had come to be there. Just then, he heard the knocking of falling drops . . . clop . . . clop . . . coming from he didn't know where. But as soon as he felt ready to concentrate on that sound, it stopped, and a dead silence set in all around again. A *dead* silence. That dead silence was willing to kill him. And again, maybe out of fear, he listened, tense.

It was as if some invisible force had given him an order, and he had no will or reason of his own; his thoughts were drawn out in an endless string that wound tightly around his chest, and now he obeyed that order completely, the one from nobody knew where. In no state to do anything his reason told him, he subordinated himself to that cursed mysterious force, becoming its slave. He had given his whole life to that force, streaming into his mind on a current of air, and he, the mute executor, waited for its instructions. Now it passed around his brain on the current of air, and again that mysterious thing, a thing, or a feeling?—that was something he could not explain—his head could no longer make sense of anything, his thoughts had fled away. And to this mysterious invasion, pouring like a stream of air into his brain, he surrendered his soul, and not just his soul, but his entire internal world, all of him. *We died, we're all dead!* he thought. Sorrowful thinking leads to death. And he arrived at this idea, invisible to the eyes, impalpable to the touch, terrifying to all that lives. A person cannot die of solitude; he seemed to sense the solitude of death,

superiority over death; he did not want to die, and mentally he was trying to separate death from himself; but here the air, and darkness, and
everything spoke only of death. And on that day, he recognized his own
powerlessness before death. His weeping was proof of that. But, strangely,
along with this weeping, and the air—as if this world had been born of
air, and of the human voice—a question arose in his thoughts: *Who are
you?* It struck him so powerfully that he could not answer. Then, again,
he heard that crazy knocking of drops, and the drops pounded out clearly
again and again: clop . . . clop . . . They tormented him as if they were
falling directly on his brain, not on the floor. If you want to kill a person,
he thought, you should do it by dripping water into his brain: kill him
with droplets, the end of the world will come from water, but even without knowing how far we are today from the end of the world, he felt sure
that in this present drought, water would triumph over man. He didn't
know if he was thinking this himself, or if the power hidden inside him
was saying it. How would he know? That thought flooded his brain like
molten lead. Water would triumph over all humankind, over the dead, the
great water would triumph . . . or darkness. Solitude, like the dark, would
triumph over it all. Damn them both, the water and the dark! Solitude,
like an abscess in the soul, like a worm—it digs in, harries you, causes
pain, blurs the vision with impenetrable darkness. Ideas borne on air penetrated his brain. He had almost forgotten about the drops, for some reason, but then he suddenly remembered, and started thinking about them.
The darkness took on the guise of death, and the light had dwindled to
nothing. This world without light felt orphaned, the whole universe felt
orphaned, and then the man burst out in tears, his whole body racked
with weeping. It was a long time before he could stifle his sobs, and finally
he approached the mirror again, resolving to look into it once more. Here
was the mirror before him again. Steam rose on the icy surface from his
breath. On the mirror's smooth surface, the ice began to melt, and he, this
man who wanted to see his reflection—the reflection and not a man, not
a phantom—was glad. He had not talked with anyone for years, and now
he could talk with himself, with his reflection. From the human breath,
from the warmth of his breath, the surface of the mirror was covered with
drops, no, no, they didn't look like drops at first, the fine dew his breath

left on the surface of the mirror glazed over into drops, but the murky water froze that same instant, and so he could not see himself. It seemed to him that all humankind had vanished from the world, or been completely eliminated, and he alone remained; and though he wished to, he simply could not see himself in the mirror. He very much wanted to see himself, but again, all he could see were eyes looking directly at him, floating in fire, like the eyes of a prophet . . . *Oh, Creator, what ill fortune is this, what sin is loose in this world?! Humankind has existed for so long. For what sins do you now castigate us?* . . . But the world responded with a dead silence, as if the world heard nothing, as if it had died of its own deafness. His yearning soul keened, and there in the corners of his eyes, burning with no brilliance, teardrops swelled. And those tears, born of his eyes, showed that his eyes were still alive, and they seemed to be the last light breath of his strength. Not letting those tears drop to the ground, he squeezed his eyes shut; he caught them in his powerless, thin hands, which he held at his chin, and he brought his hands to his mouth. That was because he was thirsty; thirst tormented him as badly as in the heat of noon. He brought his hands holding his two small tears to his mouth and licked them, tasting their salt, but that made him remember the dryness in his mouth and his thirst, and he felt thirstier than before. Now he was genuinely thirsty, and his eyes went dry; it was some kind of curse, the water's curse for what he had just said, that water could kill a man. Again, he walked to the mirror and tried to melt the ice on its surface with his hot breath. On the surface of the mirror, sweat appeared, just like on a human body, a fine sheen of droplets. And as he looked into that sweating mirror, this man, for some reason, remembered the drops of sweat on the sweating body of a naked woman with whom he had spent the whole night, long ago, making love. Maybe the wind had blown in the memory of that woman, maybe it had arisen unnoticed like some mysterious feeling, but it splashed into his tangled thoughts, and now he thought of that woman as someone God himself had sent to him. Just look at how he, having fled the nuthouse, had given this woman he'd met at a beer hall the Holy Book, as a night's payment, in which there were written seven holy words sent down from heaven; he, cursed by those holy words, was shut in a darkness from which there was no way out, and this was the punishment. Curse that sin! This castigation had fallen to him, sinner that he was, for one reason: he had not brought the Holy Word to the people but traded it for a night in a woman's embrace! He stood guilty before those Holy Words, and for that guilt he ought to spend the rest of his life lying prone beneath a stinking female crotch, but that would be too small a recompense; he ought to spend the last days of his life under drops of water falling on his head. That punishment was supposed to have come to him, if not this day, then the next . . . But this day, he decided to flee the darkness . . .

Flee what darkness? What darkness do you mean? When he thought that, he shuddered, as if a snake had crept across his chest. Everything felt strange, maybe because he was in the complete dark, or maybe because of his solitude, or because he often had been afraid of the dark, honestly, in the past (but let's set aside this talk of the darkness; he had decided not to think of it)—being in the complete dark, he wanted to forget about the dark, but perhaps that was just his foolish attempt to distract himself. Just slightly standing up, he moved forward in tiny steps, his arms extended before him like a blind man, hands spread, as if searching for some item he could touch with his fingers, but he was not searching for an item, actually, but a wall. There, he took a step, then one more, but his eager fingers found nothing, though if they had, he might have been able to determine, then, by running his fingers over it, whether it was alive or dead, but he could not feel a thing in that darkness, not even the mirror. The mirror frightened him. It frightened him because he had heard, somewhere, that a mirror was a door to the other world. Once, long ago, he had heard that in a mirror like that, you could see who you were, what kind of person you were. Maybe that was the reason he did not want to find the mirror he had seen. After that, he moved forward a little more, wiggling his fingers, spreading his hands, but he couldn't find a thing, and it seemed that there was nothing at all left in this world that anyone could touch. How could it be that every object had vanished completely in this darkness, dissolved into this darkness? Then he took another step, and immediately he heard the falling drops again, and he heard the voice of those drops . . . clop . . . clop . . . and it seemed to him that it was a complete unknown, that not a soul could possibly know, where those drops were falling from and where they were landing. And was it in fact those drops doing the knocking, or his fist-sized heart thumping: Dook . . . dook . . . ? And about that heart: Was it still there, in the man's chest? And if it was there in his chest, that meant he was alive and hadn't departed to join the dead. There, another step, then a second, a third. His fingers struck something in the darkness. What was it? He started in fright and jerked back his hand as if he'd been burned. The thing he'd touched seemed to radiate life and proximity, and that meant that his soul, which had seemed to be hanging by a thread, must still be in place. Now he resolved to feel it and discover what it was, and he moved his hands forward, and walked. His hands hit a wall, an ordinary wall, but why was it so cold? The cold made his hands turn blue. Yet, despite all that, he thought that if this was a wall, there must be a door in it somewhere, and he started feeling and patting the wall all over, yes, he went on running his hands over it, searching for a door. Searching for the door, he happened to recall blind men he had often seen outside. The blind spend all their lives in darkness like this, he thought, and now he was experiencing in the flesh what it was like to be blind. He had found a wall, and now that he'd found it, the desire that had long been smoldering inside him to flee from that darkness flared up with new force, taking over everything. Where to run? And who had brought him here, only for him to desperately want to flee? One day, without any special ceremony, he had suddenly found himself here, locked up, and that meant he had come here himself, and if he'd come himself, then he would have to find a way to leave himself, and if he couldn't, then he would rot and die in this darkness. Then he stepped on something. By feeling around on the ground to find it, he realized it was a box of matches. He opened it and felt it. No matches! Panicked, he felt all around on the ground, looking for matches, and he felt one, and that match rescued him from thoughts of death. He decided to light it and have a look around, to find out where he was, where he'd been stuck, and whether there might be an end to this great darkness. He calmed his rapid breathing and carefully, very carefully, drew the match across the box. A tiny flame, like a bird's tongue, sprang from the match. He looked around. Before him was a mud wall, which looked to be many years old. In the light of the flame like a bird's tongue, he read a sign which stated, in big letters, NATION OF NUTTERS. As soon as he read the last letter of that sign, the match went out . . . and again the great darkness reigned . . . He could not remember anything about the existence of a country with the strange name "Nation of Nutters." And again there flew into his mind (damn his mind!), like the wandering wind, the thought of death . . . No sooner had the thought of death come to him than an icy cold descended over his entire body, head to foot, spreading through every blood vessel, not from fear, and nor was the cold made of solitude; it reminded him stubbornly, once again, that he was still alive, and this turned into a feeling that always turned him back to life. When he thought of death, in order to distract himself, he always thought back to the most curious things he'd experienced in the life he'd lived, and when he began to remember, that woman always came straight to his mind, the one he'd met when he ran away from the psychiatric hospital, and how the two of them had spent all night naked as the day they were born, making love nonstop, damp with sweat. She had told him then: "I've never seen a man like you before," to which he responded: "And I've never met any women like you." So the night flew by, but their passion never waned, their embraces never cooled, and suddenly, he was frightened. He was frightened because he had fled the nuthouse that night, and there was probably already a search party after him, and if they found him, they'd lock him up in that triangular yellow building again, and his previous life, the nutter's life, would begin again. "You're a nutter," the huge black mustached orderly will say, and he will answer, hanging his head meekly and looking at the ground: "I'm a nutter." When they heard that, all the nutters in the ward would cackle with their senseless laughter. Laughter doesn't become nutters. They don't know that this type of laughter for no reason is their biggest humiliation in life, and, not sensing that, they laugh as if they want to split the universe clean through. Damn their laughter! They fall over laughing. In this world, the nutters are only afraid of one man, the big mustached orderly, and they don't bother with anyone else. There is only one person whom nobody can make laugh, who doesn't laugh even if he makes you laugh, and that is the Holy Man. Not a soul knows whether he named himself that or the nutters did, or if the head of the nuthouse gave him that name. The local nutters even tried asking the man where he got a name like that. He said nothing for a long time, then came closer to them, and said: "I want to give you your minds back, bring you back into

the world. If I do that, only then, then I'll accept the name Holy Man."
Then he said that if he couldn't do it, a flood would threaten the universe,
and the snakes would creep out and destroy every living thing on Earth
with their venom. Paying no heed to that, the nutters got up, babbling and
laughing, and made a dogpile on top of him, and then, under so many
people toppling over and sitting on him, he nearly passed away. When
nutters like that do that kind of thing, whoever they pile on top of they
could kill, just like that. If it hadn't been for that huge, black man, who
knows what would have happened . . . what would have happened to the
Holy Man . . . Now he remembered the Holy Man . . . He remembered
and tried to unreel the whole spool of memories that stuck like tape to the
Holy Man he remembered . . . That time, back in the nuthouse, they had
a clear night, and in the barred windows, through the cracked glass, countless twinkling stars could be seen, strewn across the sky . . . That night, the
Holy Man came to the table that stood in the center of the small ward and
took a book from his pocket, and he whispered the opening prayer inaudibly, moving his lips, then started to read it in a chanting voice . . . in the
middle of everyone sleeping in the ward . . . Only one nutter had insomnia
at the time, and only one eavesdropped on the gentle voice of the Holy
Man whispering, observing his every move . . . The Holy Man, as if sensing nothing, paid no attention to the nutter who stealthily stuck his head
out from the blanket and observed him with great attention. He seemed to
think everyone had long been asleep . . . The Holy Man chanted from his
book. The words of that book seemed to be flowing like molten lead into
the ears of the eavesdropping nutter . . . The Holy Man read: "The wrath
of God falls from heaven onto the impiety and injustice of those who stifle
truth with injustice . . . This is because they have learned everything that
can be known about God; God has given them all knowledge . . . This is
because God is the invisible foundation, His everlasting strength and
Divinity has been known since ancient times through His appearance in
everything born, and therefore these people are left with no answer . . ."
The Holy Man read that part especially melodically, then smacked his lips
and fell silent for a time, lifting his gaze upward . . . "These people, who
know everything about God, think the opposite, driven by empty
thoughts . . ." The dancing tongue of flame from the lantern lighting the

hospital ward cast the Holy Man's shadow on the wall, and the shadow was enough to reveal that he was submerged in difficult thoughts. "The darkness blanketed their mad hearts . . ." The tongue of flame in the lantern shuddered in the Holy Man's breath with every word he uttered. The Holy Man gazed upward and fell quiet for a long time. His shadow on the wall seemed turned to stone, for a while, frozen and motionless. Then, returning to life, mumbling something to himself, whispering words impossible to understand, he went back to reading. "Considering themselves intelligent, they were deprived of reason . . . and they held the immutable sacred glory of the Lord God equivalent to the bones of men, and birds, and animals, and reptiles, fated to putrefy with time . . . and therefore God gave them the putrid desires of their own hearts, and so they soiled their bodies . . . They perverted God's Truth into a lie, and instead of worshiping the Creator, they began worshiping created things, and they began serving the devil . . ." The Holy Man sighed heavily. "Eternal glory to the holiness of the Creator!" he said, speaking in a heavy, colorless voice; he was one of a kind. "They paid no heed to God's impending Judgment Day." He ran his palms across his face, and added, in a livelier voice, as if experiencing a new strength: "At Judgment Day, everyone will be rewarded as they deserve!" After that, the Holy Man closed the book.

Outside the window, the night was thick and mute. Again, he ran his palms across his face . . . Why was it now that this moment had drifted into the nutter's memory? Because nobody ever did find out how the Holy Man disappeared from the nuthouse. The nutter said that during that deep night, the whole sky suddenly glowed with a bright light, as if lightning was flashing, and just then, like in a dream, the sun seemed to fall from the sky, and the whole world was illuminated with a blinding light and trembled. When the nutter saw all that and gave a piercing scream in fear, nobody heard him; they were all sleeping like the dead. And then he saw them, flying into the cramped hospital ward on a ray of light shooting through the window: three angels . . . (He saw an angel descend from the heavens, his shoulders draped in a cloud, a blue turban on his head; his face was radiant like the sun, his feet burned with bright fire, and in his hands he held an open book. The angel planted his right foot in the sea and his left on dry land, and raised his right hand to the sky, and from

there a deafening voice boomed out, like a lion's roar. And for some reason, this voice spoke to me: "Go and take the book from the hands of the
angel who stands with his right foot in the sea and his left foot on dry
land." I went to the angel, as the voice from heaven instructed me, and
asked him: "Please give me the book." This is how he answered: "Take this
book and eat it. When you eat this book, it will be sweeter than honey in
your stomach, but you will taste an acrid bitterness in your mouth. This is
because such is the taste of truth. The taste of truth is bitter, so not everyone is fond of it. This book is the Book of Truth; it is a book of salvation
from God; do not keep the words hidden under seals, for the Day of All
Reckoning draws nigh." With those words, the angel put the book in my
hands. When I took it in my hands, I began to look through it. But I did
not find in it a single word, a single letter, because this book was a collec-
tion of blank pages . . .) The three angels, dressed in white, raised up the
Holy Man. The nutter did not quite see how they looked; he was wincing
in fear, holding his breath, and besides that, he could barely keep from
crying out in fear. Before he left, the Holy Man kissed the forehead of
every sleeping person, and not only them; he also kissed the nutter who lay
awake, shaking in fear, on the cheek. As he took his leave, he began to
weep. Why did he weep? Perhaps he felt sorry for them, or sensed he
would never see them again, because he was taking a path of no return; or
was it because he had been unable to give reason to these people, or
because his Holy human plans had failed? . . . Anyway, it was a mystery
both for the nutter who saw the Holy Man's tears and for the Holy Man
himself . . . The last words the Holy Man said, the nutter heard clearly. All
he said was this: "I will be back soon . . . How blessed are the words of that
book!" And after he said that, he kissed the book he held in his hands with
obvious love . . . But to whom had he spoken those words? The sleeping
nutters? The four walls of that cramped ward? Or the nutter hiding under
his blanket, watching him on the sly? The nutter had no idea at all . . .
Before he left, the Holy Man took out the book he had tucked under his
jacket and laid it under that nutter's pillow. Nobody else saw the Holy Man
lift his head and put the Book under his pillow. He was the only one who
knew it happened. After the Holy Man put the Book under his pillow, he
vanished without a trace. It was only when he looked at the cover of that

Book, with its golden lettering, that he realized the Book was a miracle sent down from heaven, and he considered it a legacy left to him. For a long time, he hid the Book away from people, hesitant to open it . . . And besides, if the huge bushy-browed orderly caught him with that book, he would vanish just like the Holy Man vanished, like something dropped in the water. Shaking in fear constantly before that bushy-browed one, unable to say a word in his presence, he lost what was left of his mind, then, and went completely insane with fear. Earlier, during the first days, when he'd only just gotten into the nuthouse, he was always thinking of running away, looking for an opening. Once he arrived in that nation of nutters, he sensed immediately that what they called "education" could kill a person. And once he realized that, he was angry through and through, thinking: "What do nutters need with rules and regulations? A nutter is a nutter." But everyone who caught the wrath of the bushy-browed orderly who kept order in the nation of nutters shook at the very sight of him, and even at the memory of him. Anyone who caught his eye felt like a criminal being led to execution. The attendant told them: "I'll squeeze the yellow water from your hearts and drink it. I'll drink it mixed with your blood. If there is no order in this nation, not a single nutter will have a successful treatment and become like normal people!" Then, the nutters had been astounded to discover that the world wasn't full of nutters alone, but there were normal people, too, and the subject was of intense interest to the nutters for a long time after that. So what would happen, now, if a person like that were to get his hands on the Book the Holy Man had left behind? It would probably be the end of humankind. The bushy-browed one had imposed a strict ban on reading books. Anyone found with a book faced the same punishment: the death penalty. Only now did he realize that, frightened by that word "death," he had not read a single book here. Even aside from those apprehensions, he knew for certain when his own death would come. Long, long ago, he could no longer remember when, a gypsy woman had approached him at the market gate. She read the palm of everyone at that market every day. "You will live through a great deal. Your life will be long, but you will die a death that isn't your own; you will die of a snakebite," she said. When he heard that, he pulled his hand out of the gypsy's hands, quickly, as if she'd given him an electric shock. A lot of time had passed since then. That event stayed in his memory for a long time. He sensed that even now, in this pitch darkness, he was not alone, that there were two living creatures in that darkness: one was he himself, and the other, lying coiled up in a corner, was a black snake. For now, it was sleeping, but not even he knew when it would awake. Thinking about that snake, he remembered what the vanished Holy Man had said: "Do not wake the snake. As soon as it wakes, the end of the world will come." And now here they are. He is afraid even to look at it, much less touch it. He waits for the snake to open its eyes. Waiting, while the snake sleeps in the dark, a question begins to plague him: he feels he is dreaming everything that is affecting him so immensely right now, including that when the snake lying coiled in the darkness wakes up, it will strike and sink its poisonous fangs into his body, and he will know the gypsy woman's long-ago words were true when she said, "You will die of a snakebite," and including the fact that he'd always believed that was the way his life would end, and including the idea that his current goal was to get out of this darkness . . . What dream is he talking about? Which dream? He wants to have his way, but he is powerless to do anything, and so he must think that this is a dream, and so he wants to call all this a dream, rely on this being simply a dream, but what kind of dream could this possibly be? Now he's pinched himself, hard, he's touched the mirror, and he sees that this is all the plain truth, the waking world, not a dream. Yes, it's true that he slept today, woke up as usual in his ward, and when he got out of bed he even noticed how completely dark it was; he simply got up as always, thinking he'd start an ordinary day, but then he couldn't find the door or even the walls of his room. He tried to feel something with his hands, holding them before him, but nothing worked; around him it was fully dark, and there was a mute, dead silence. He froze for a moment, calculating where he might be: he remembered, he thought, that once he was in a mental hospital, but this place did not resemble his home, nor even his latest place of residence, the nuthouse; there were only walls of darkness with no doors everywhere around him, plus a mirror that had appeared out of nowhere, and also a black snake, lying in the corner, coiled in a ring. Maybe it was his fear of that snake that made him remember one long-ago event . . . Clearly and distinctly there came before his eyes a vision of that ancient, unremembered time when he had been the Emperor . . . Back then, nobody had asked him if he wanted to be the Emperor, or maybe they had, but his raggedy memory couldn't retain a thing; anyway, back then, he had felt like a real Emperor, and he could even recall snippets of his coronation ceremony. He had made a sweeping speech, then, which began with the words: "I, the Great Emperor . . ." and the whole court bowed low before him, shielding their eyes from him, like from the umbra of God, and recording his every word in the chronicles. That day, triumphant music blared from every bugle, and he handed down countless promises, and pardoned everyone who asked for clemency, and that day he announced that he would lead every subject bowing at his feet to the Holy Land, located at the center of the world, where all their sins would be forgiven . . . Perhaps it was because the local jewelers had made the crown they put on his head at the coronation ceremony that day one size too small (it was made of gold and platinum, decorated with diamonds and gemstones . . .) Anyway, that day, it took all his strength to force that symbol of power onto his head, and even though the tight crown squeezed his head that day, he put up with it, and delivered his entire triumphant imperial speech, and promised to personally lead all the people bowing at his feet to a better place . . . Even now, the people's shouting rang in his ears: "All hail the Emperor!" . . . Over the years he wore it, the imperial crown shriveled up half his brain and finally merged with his skull . . . Once it had grown fast to his head, nobody could take the imperial crown from him. Wearing that crown, he slept, walked, spoke, drank wine, took amusement, and abandoned himself to hot, fiery games of love—wherever he was, he always wore that symbol of power, and he even forgot all about his headache . . . It's stunning, but by then the Emperor considered himself an equal to God, and he found he could not remember the last time he'd mentioned the name of God. Inside this man who tried to make himself an equal to God, the certainty arose, over time, that he was absolutely no worse than the Creator . . . Overly proud, no longer sensing anything human inside himself, as if he were as magnificent by then as the Prophet, he began, apparently, to forget who he really was . . . No, no, he didn't forget . . . He simply felt he'd achieved the same sainthood as the Prophet . . . and now that he'd reached that magnificence . . . a sickness of the brain set in, where that crown was eating into it . . . After they tied his arms and legs to the bed, making him thrash and twist like a sheep on the block before a sacrifice, the mental hospital doctors stuck their needle into the fat vein of his right arm, and then he, who a second ago had felt like an Emperor, an equal to the Creator, hollered with all his might, spraying saliva, shouting so loudly every person in the mental hospital got to their feet: "Emperors! Presidents! . . . Communists! Cops! Dictators! . . . Secret police! False patriots! Heretics! . . . Prosecutors! Misanthropes! Ideologues! Idiots! . . . Political prostitutes! . . . Bureaucrats!. . Shitocrats! Blasphemers! . . . Judases! Apostates! Infidels! Antichrists! How holy am I? This is all a lie! This is all a betrayal! You sold out God! You've summoned false witnesses, shown yourselves guilty beyond all redemption! . . . You betrayed the Lord, sold him out for thirty pieces of silver! You did not heed the wailing of the man on his knees: 'Guilty I am before God the Merciful, I have betrayed Him.' You cursed him! . . . And then what?! . . . Then the crowd called out: 'Nail the Lord to the cross!' . . . It shouted, and spat in His face, it beat Him and harried Him! And then . . . it asked, humiliated: 'Will you have mercy, Lord, on us who beat you?' . . . You are all accursed of Heaven! All the sins of man began with that betrayal of the Lord . . . Not the Creator . . . You always prayed devoutly to creation, bowing before creation like before a holy shrine!

"No . . . No! . . . No, I tell you! . . . No shots! You are divine retribution! . . . No shots!" Out of strength by then, he whispered those last words quietly, pitifully, through his frothy lips, and his eyes looked like the eyes of a sacrificial victim after the sacrifice . . . Exhausted by his great thoughts, the Emperor sank into a deep sleep . . . Like microbes absorbed into his brain, the crown soaked into his skin . . . As he slept, he always dreamed of the same scorching deserts of the distant Holy Land, the blue waves of the Sea of Paradise, and that Holy Land he had so long yearned for appeared in the distance, like the magical bird Simurgh . . . In his dream, he went on walking toward the Holy Land . . . Not just in his imagination, but in real life, too, he had always wanted to go to the Holy Land, and had dedicated himself to that, the sweetest of ideas . . . and now here he was, walking to the Holy Land . . . He walked, having left behind all the sins that had once stuck to him, as if he'd washed all the dirt off in the bath, and he felt light and transparent, like a priceless vessel; he walked, submerged in the great waves of his imagination . . . He drifted, unhurried, like a pregnant camel drifts across the sandy desert . . .

The Emperor woke up . . . with difficulty . . .

Coughing hoarsely, the Emperor propped himself up on his wrinkled hands, rose with difficulty from his bed, and walked to the barred window, where the light was coming in . . .

The people were gathering outside in a crowd . . . He could hear the sound of the motor on the old yellow psychomobile with the big cross on the side . . . Two orderlies in black gowns opened the back door of the yellow vehicle, brought out a stretcher, and carried it to the morgue in the comfy nest, which was outside the Emperor's window . . . The Emperor, thinking somebody else must have died, went on watching the door to the morgue . . . Kozuchak and King Lear paced back and forth nearby . . . Though he didn't feel very well after that injection, the Emperor walked outside into the fresh air, too . . . Kozuchak ran up to him. Kozuchak, anxious, started spitting out words, rushing and stuttering:

"Emperor, Emperor! The Holy Man died, the Holy Man," he repeated. "The Holy Man . . ."

The Emperor broke out in a cold sweat. He had dreamed of the Holy Man that night.

"His heart gave out after an injection," said King Lear, and he took a deep drag from his hand-rolled cigarette.

"We thought he was a Holy Man, but it turns out, he was just like us, a batshit nutter!" Lear coughed from the cheap tobacco smoke. "They're carrying him out now . . . We'll say goodbye . . ."

Tears gleamed in Kozuchak's eyes.

"Don't cry. He was a nutter, just like us . . . Nutters don't cry over nutters. What, did you believe he really was a Holy Man?" asked King Lear. "There's a reason they say that even a frog looks like a stallion to a dry lake. What would a Holy Man be doing in a place like this nuthouse?"

Just then two orderlies came out of the morgue, carrying the stretcher.

"No!" one of them shouted, the one wearing glasses. "What the hell! No! He was just lying here . . . He was just lying here dead!"

The Emperor, Lear, and Kozuchak all froze still. When they recovered, they rushed to the morgue and saw a white sheet on the ground, the kind they use to cover corpses. But on the shelf where the corpse ought to be, there was nothing but a gleaming aluminum wristband with the Holy Man's name on it. Every patient in this hospital had that kind of wristband fastened to his arm.

A siren burst out in a deafening wail . . .

The patients began gathering in the central yard of their comfy nest. All the nutters always gathered in that central yard when the siren sounded. The first ones to the yard were the Emperor, Kozuchak and Lear, and then Genghis Khan and Alexander the Great appeared, and then all the rest trickled in: Freud, Mussolini, Hitler, Aesop, Epicurus, Picasso, Kant, Thaïs the Athenian, Sophia Loren, Cleopatra, Chaplin, Van Gogh, and more. All those names had been given to them in the nuthouse.

The nuthouse's head physician addressed those who had assembled.

"Starting today, discipline around here is going to be much stricter!" His whole body was shaking, as if he were struck by fever. "Anyone violating the rules will be given an injection. Every book found in this nuthouse will be burned, on my orders! Do you hear me?"

"We hear you, Your Excellency!" answered all the nutters in unison.

According to the rules, that was the only way to answer in a situation like this one.

They burned the books in the nuthouse, and, among the ashes, the Emperor found the unburned cover of the Holy Book, and one of its pages. On that page, miraculously preserved, there was text about the Day of the Lord's Coming . . . The Emperor hid it under his jacket immediately.

That day, when he returned to his own ward without letting on to anyone what he was holding under his jacket, his entire body could feel the warmth radiating from the book's cover. The Emperor decided to hide it under his bed, in the most secret place, where nobody would be able to find it and read it in the night. That idea swallowed him whole . . . The Emperor got out the Holy Book, kissed it, and touched it to his forehead. Immediately, he smelled the scent of burning, the sour aroma of ashes. He wrapped it in a few layers of an old rag and hid it under his bed . . .

The death of the Holy Man made the Emperor think deeply. In his thoughts, he tried to sort out exactly who the Holy Man had been, and what kind of person he was . . . Was he just like the Emperor, a poor unfortunate fellow locked up here and diagnosed as a nutter? Or was he actually a holy man, a great man? . . . Then a strange and wild idea came into the Emperor's head, and he felt like rejecting this world, full of temptations, and running away.

That night, the Emperor did not sleep . . .

He paced back and forth across the crowded ward and just could not rid himself of those haunting thoughts. One insane idea had been pounded like a nail into his brain . . . The mysterious vanishing of the Holy Man, into thin air . . . that extraordinary departure of his into the next world . . . it had sunk its claws into the Emperor's chest, which had already ached badly enough before . . .

O unfortunate night! When the number of human beings on Earth reaches six billion, six hundred six million, six hundred thousand sixty-six, the dark demon will awake . . . and the End of the World will begin . . . and people will start being born dead . . . and the feelings of the demon will stir in their breasts, and we will give up this world to be governed by the devil! . . . Awake! . . . Those words echoed and repeated right in his ear. The words repeated and repeated, roaring on, deafeningly close. He could find no way to rid himself of the words that haunted him. The Emperor— who had previously said that we are all the servants of God, that our bodies and breath and souls all came from God, and who firmly believed that himself—now argued against his own past thoughts. He argued against them because the Lord considered the tortured life he was living to be what he deserved, because God's mercy, God's love, and God's light had not been given unto him, he who had patiently borne all the torments of his fate. Clearly, people bereft of God's love, those who were unfortunate and downtrodden in life, were completely on their own . . . The difficult thoughts of those recent days lead the Emperor to that conclusion . . . And he decided to commit suicide . . .

On the very first day he spent there in the nuthouse, the Emperor had decided to commit suicide, and looking around his crowded ward for the easiest place to hang himself, he settled on the window grate. It seemed to him, then, that those bars on the window would end his life. Now, too, that strange thought awoke in his head. He tied one end of his belt to the grate on the window and the other end around his neck . . . but he couldn't make up his mind to go any further, couldn't do it, because he was scared of death. The Emperor asked himself: Well? Was he leaving this world? The fact he had sentenced himself to death made it clear there was no other way out for him. The fact that he would be handing himself over, giving himself up, to the Lord . . . all that triggered a mass of contradictions in the Emperor's chaotic world . . . Deciding on death, he started sensing more acutely the sweetness of life . . . But people, and the intolerable lowness of life, had become impossible for him to bear . . . Between this destiny the Creator had assigned him and the hopelessness of his soul, he couldn't believe that all might end well . . . Even if he stepped back now from death, the same restless thoughts would rise again to harry his soul . . . They were tormenting him . . . When he lay down yet again in the procedure room to get yet another shot, all the unbearable torment made him vow: "That's it! I'll kill myself!" . . . But now, thinking about the sweetness of life, the sweetness of his own soul, his own destiny, he began to retreat from his previous thoughts of suicide, and hesitate. In the end, he decided to tie the belt more tightly to the window grate, put a little stool under his feet, and leave for the next world. He greased the noose, made of the belt, with some laundry soap, and hung it around his neck. He'd read, somewhere, that a well-soaped noose didn't hurt too much and the person would die quickly . . . His hands shook at the sight of the noose, and when he tugged at the knot, he grew short of breath . . . He squeezed his eyes shut and decided to kick the little stool away . . . For a while, his hands held the noose, so it didn't tighten right away . . . He prayed to the Creator, begged Him for forgiveness . . . "I am Your servant, I am Your servant," he repeated humbly . . . Hot tears flowed from his eyes . . . Forgive my sins, he prayed . . . Suffering, he put all his pain into those complaints he directed to the Lord, and prayed and prayed to God with his disobedient tongue . . . He would sacrifice himself to the Creator . . . Saying, in the end, that he was grateful to God even now, he pushed the stool he was standing on away with a foot, and then the noose tightened instantly around his neck, but when he was hanging there, the belt failed

under his weight, and snapped and broke . . . The Emperor dropped . . .
He lay face down without moving for a long time . . . Under the bed,
he caught sight of the cover of that Book that hadn't burned in the fire,
with the one whole, last page . . . The Emperor wrapped his arms firmly
around the Holy Book and, all in tears, began kissing and caressing it with
great excitement and enormous relief . . . He felt his salvation had come
not from the belt breaking, but from God's love . . . All the pages of the
book had burned away, and only this one was unharmed . . . He read the
heading on the page . . . The Day of the Lord's Coming . . . Is that where
the meaning resided in how he, resolved to die, had remained alive? He'd
found a page of the Great Book . . .

That night, the Holy Man had said to him, in parting, "The Day of
the Lord's Coming draws nigh . . . If humankind does not rid itself of sin,
does not purify itself, then Judgment Day will come." Now the Emperor
remembered those words. The thought appeared in his head that no matter what, he had to escape, he had to somehow get to the Holy Land, to
ask the Creator for forgiveness, to rid himself of all sin . . . That thought
lit up his soul . . . The Emperor decided to put that idea in action, no
matter what happened . . . He vowed to himself he would do it . . . But,
so as not to ask for God's forgiveness just for himself, he decided to take
Kozuchak, Alexander the Great, Genghis Khan, and Lear with him on
the long journey, and also Thaïs the Athenian, whom he knew well from
the nuthouse, as an interpreter. He spoke with them all in secret, and it
was decided they would flee the very next morning . . . Now Kozuchak
started to stubbornly demand they take with them a young woman by the
name of Cleopatra . . . The Emperor gave his consent, after a struggle.
He finally consented because Kozuchak said Cleopatra would be a good
female companion for Thaïs the Athenian on their journey . . .

Early that morning, the seven of them fled the nuthouse . . . five men
and two women.

The Seven

The scorching rays of the early sun gradually began to wake the travelers, sleeping side by side in the very middle of the desert . . . The first to wake was Genghis Khan, who had always been a light sleeper . . . His eyes, struggling to open after a nice morning dream, instantly bulged in surprise at what he saw . . . Jumping up, he stood staring, bug-eyed, at the old man standing in front of him, a man who resembled an ancient, dried-out tree. The morning breeze played with the hem of the old man's white robe, and mussed the hairs of his beard, so long it came to his waist, and his deeply sunken, small, elderly eyes flashed frequently, and the tip of the old man's long shadow lay almost at Genghis Khan's feet . . .

It was that shadow that Genghis Khan had first seen when he woke up, and it startled him . . . At first he didn't notice, but the man was standing on one foot. It was only when his tired eyes focused clearly that he saw the old man was standing on one foot there before him, and his second leg hovered over the ground, like his foot had been chopped off . . . At first, Genghis Khan thought the old man was naturally that way, that he had been born that way. And he thought it strange: Where could this man, thin as a dried-out tree, have come from, to stand here before him in the desert, where the heat can boil your brains? . . . By the knobby veins in his arms, by the fact that he seemed to feel no pain, even though his foot was planted in the burning sand, it was clear that he had long since grown accustomed to the heat of the desert . . . The previous day, when the seven of them, exhausted by the long day's walk, had collapsed in a row willy-nilly to sleep, nobody had so much as thought about this old man . . . Not even Genghis Khan, who had lain down a little off to the side from the other six, ever suspected the man existed . . . But he, Genghis Khan, was the one who saw him first, he who hadn't had the slightest inkling the previous day that this one-legged man, straight as a nail, existed. He carefully examined the mysterious figure . . . Then he started poking and shaking the Emperor, who was sleeping to his left, to wake him up . . . The Emperor was startled, too, to see the man standing before him . . . Truly, the sight of that old man, who looked just like a dried-out thousand-year-old tree, would have astounded anyone . . .

When the Emperor and Genghis Khan walked up to the mysterious man, the other five woke up in the row where they'd been sleeping, and rubbing the long sleep out of their eyes, they stared at him without a word . . . The Emperor went closer to the ancient old man and stood next to him, wondering what he would say to the travelers. Genghis Khan watched him closely, looking glum . . . Then the grim Alexander the Great also approached . . . In this limitless wilderness, where danger constantly threatened people and animals alike from every direction, the appearance of this old man, motionless as a stake driven into the earth, gave rise to different thoughts and suspicions in each of the seven travelers . . . Today was the first time they had seen a living human being in this untamed steppe . . . On the one hand, his appearance gave all seven hope, exhausted as they were by this lifeless desert; it gave them hope because they assumed the one-legged old man standing before them must live somewhere nearby, in some village which had to be close . . . Each of the seven, thinking about the old man, had their own theory about how he appeared.

"Good traveling to you, pilgrim," said the Emperor, the first to break the silence. "Where are you heading?"

The old man did not answer the Emperor's question but stared silently straight ahead.

That surprised everyone.

"Hey, maybe he can't speak," said Thaïs the Athenian, walking closer.

"No, he's probably just a little deaf. Or totally deaf." Kozuchak peered curiously at the old man's face.

"Might he be a demon in human form?" asked King Lear, hesitantly taking the conversation in a new direction.

"But why is he standing on one foot? Maybe he's doing yoga," mused Cleopatra, giving the old man a kind look. "People who do yoga often stand on one foot like that while they meditate."

"In the desert . . . completely alone . . . What sort of idiot would do yoga here?" asked Alexander the Great. "But what if he owns this desert?"

"He's an imp. What language does he speak?" asked Thaïs the Athenian, boring into the old man with her eyes. "Look! His eyes seem alive . . . I think he's one of those tongue-tied people who don't understand our language . . . You speaka Inglish? You speaka Arabian?" asked Thaïs the Athenian. The old man stayed silent as the grave. "Oh! Maybe he's one of the forty Jews who Moses took with him? Hee-hee-hee!" Thaïs the Athenian cackled at her own joke.

The old man said nothing, staring straight ahead, as if waiting for something, his eyes gleaming.

"Perhaps he's a nutter who escaped from the nuthouse before us. He reminds me of somebody," King Lear said suspiciously. "Look, he's holding some kind of letter . . ." And, truly, a small piece of thin leather, no bigger than the palm of his hand, hung from the old man's left hand, and there was writing on it.

"What does he look like?" asked Thaïs the Athenian, turning to the other six. "A Hindu? A Greek? A Mongol? A Kyrgyz?"

"A Bedouin," said Genghis Khan.

"A Jew," said King Lear.

"A Greek," said Alexander the Great.

"You could say he's African, but his skin's not black. You could say he's French, but his skin's not white. His eyes are narrow, but he doesn't look Japanese. So what exactly is he?" Kozuchak wondered out loud.

"A human being. He looks like a human being!" said Cleopatra.

"I didn't hear anyone calling him a monkey or a crocodile," said Genghis Khan. "But what language does this man speak, scourged by God? We should ask him how to get to the Holy Land."

The Emperor stepped right up to the old man and examined his sunburned face and small but lively eyes. The white shirt, scorched by the sun, was so worn out on the old man's body that it looked like it might disintegrate to a handful of dust at the slightest touch. The Emperor paid special attention to the note on the scrap of leather, which hung from the hand of the motionless one-legged old man . . . The Emperor bent down to read the note.

"My name is . . . Devani Burhu," said the Emperor, sounding out the syllables from left to right.

"Devani Burhu," repeated the stupefied Alexander the Great. "So he's a dervish? . . . A seer? . . . A man of God?"

"For forty years, I have been standing on one foot in this endless desert as a protest against the Creator," the Emperor read out loud from the scrap of leather. "We are all born of the Creator's mercy, love, and respect . . . We are the children of the Creator . . . If the Lord created the son of man with love, then why did he also create Hell for mankind? . . . I am opposed to any man going to Hell, for man is not only God's servant, but also God's love . . . Therefore, he deserves only to live in Heaven, to taste the sweetness of Heaven . . . I used to pray to the Creator to forgive the ignoramuses, but those same ignoramuses cast stones at me and tortured me . . . They led me into this desert and abandoned me here, alone . . . I do not take their ignorance for a sin. There are no sins upon them . . . If God truly created them, then why did He create them in such cruel ignorance? . . . It is not the fault of those people. It is the fault of the Creator Himself . . . I have come to block your path, because your path leads to Hell . . . I am blocking the road to Hell." The Emperor read the last words and stopped, feeling sad.

The old man did not even twitch, just stared silently straight ahead.

"He says he's protesting God?" asked Genghis Khan angrily, giving the old man a sideways look. "I suppose that's why they say a blasphemer always pursues those who love God."

"He says he's blocking the road to Hell?" asked Alexander the Great. "Now that's interesting! But who is he, huh?"

"He said he asked the Creator to forgive the ignoramuses . . . but the ignoramuses threw stones at him?" asked Kozuchak. "Why wouldn't they throw stones? Who do you think God is, some buddy of yours? Demanding things of God is ungodly . . . He's just some poor guy with a defective brain, the kind whose bell is missing its clapper . . ."

"Poor man . . . Can't you see what kind of life he's led, looking at his face? Can't you see the sorrow in his eyes? . . . Why are you all piling on to pick on him, like vultures on carrion?" Cleopatra, distraught, stepped into the center of their circle, right behind the old man. "Why are you pecking at him like that?"

"Shamelessly he praises his own self, he sees no others! Elevates himself with the angels, he hints the prophets were his brothers! Poor old Rumi wrote that once," said Thaïs the Athenian, with a click of her tongue. "Do you know who Rumi was?" She directed the question, meanly, to Genghis Khan, as usual.

"You're asking who a ruble was?" Genghis Khan responded, confused.

"All he understands is rubles," said Alexander the Great dismissively.

"Ach, damn you all . . . Who said anything about a ruble?" Thaïs the Athenian was hopping mad. "I'm talking about that old man! He says he's protesting God? Who can be against God? Only the Devil, that's who! . . . So isn't he a devil in disguise? Look! Isn't he standing on his left foot? Only devils ride with their left hand and stand on their left foot . . ."

"Maybe we should knock him over with a rock? Then . . ." Something childlike stirred inside Kozuchak. "If he's the devil . . ."

"No!" The Emperor stopped Kozuchak even while he was aiming a rock at the old man. "Drop that rock, you spawn of a serpent!"

The old man truly was standing on his left foot. Everyone got excited by Thaïs the Athenian's idea.

"He says he's blocking the road to Hell? So what, Emperor, are we going to Hell?" Thaïs the Athenian put her hands on her hips like a crow putting on parakeet feathers and spoke in her sharp, chattering, whiny voice. "Where's this Paradise, eh? Where are the luscious orchids, cypresses, palm trees, Syrian roses, figs, grapes, peaches, and almond blossoms? Where are the sky-blue vistas, the precious gems, the paradisaical gardens for God-fearing people? . . . There's nothing anywhere around here except this endless desert! . . . Wasteland everywhere you look! . . . Sand! . . . Sand!! Hell, he says . . . I don't want to go to Hell!"

"I don't want to, either!" shouted King Lear, like a crazy man. "I'm afraid of Hell!"

"Oy!" Cleopatra yelped in fear. That was because she had seen Lear step on a snake's tail. The coiled snake twisted its body and slowly unwound. The tense gazes of those six pairs of eyes, which had just been nailed to the old man, turned to Lear's foot, the foot that had stepped on the snake's tail. "Look! A snake! Move your foot, move it! It'll bite!" Cleopatra squealed.

When King Lear lifted his right foot, the snake twisted its body and slowly slithered toward the bare foot of the still old man and began to coil around it. An instant stunned silence dropped onto each one of them, after all their noisy fuss, and, despite themselves, they watched the snake move. It lifted its tiny head and flicked its forked tongue, and then the snake coiled around the old man's leg and began slowly climbing it, higher and higher . . . It crept relentlessly ever higher, like climbing a rotten tree, up to his knee, then his thigh . . . The old man did not even tremble, as if he had known that snake for forty years. He went on standing motionless as a stake driven into the earth . . . Its tail twitching, the snake crawled as far as the old man's wrinkled neck, wrapped around it twice, and lifted its tiny head where it hung before the old man's face, staring straight into his small eyes . . . The snake's forked tongue had been in constant motion, but now it pulled in its tongue and peered into the old man's eyes for a long time, without looking away . . . All of this stunned the Emperor, and his forehead was coated with sweat, and a slight trembling shook his body. The Emperor had always been especially terrified of snakes, but he tried not to let the others see his fear . . . The snake now coiling around the old man was not the one that was pursuing the Emperor . . . This snake was different, much longer, much more terrifying, much more mysterious . . . It seemed as if the old man and the snake, staring into each other's eyes, eyeball to eyeball, were conversing, were speaking to each other without words, with only their eyes . . . As if the old man understood the snake's language, and the snake understood his . . . the complete silence persisted for a long time . . . A tremor went through Lear's foot, the one that had stepped on the snake, as if it had been shocked . . . He was frightened, but not for the old man peering into the snakes' eyes; he was frightened because his whole body had started to shake severely . . . Everyone waited in horror for the snake to sink its poisonous fangs into the old man's face . . . The old man moved his dry lips, just like he was speaking to the snake, but they could not understand him . . . The snake tensed, then lowered its head with its eagle's beak before the old man's face, swayed slowly side to side, relaxed its embrace, and, just as it had crept up the old man, began creeping down again . . . When they saw that, everyone sighed in relief. The snake flung itself to the ground and, twisting its body, began to slither away, leaving a faint trail in the sand behind it. The snake's oily skin, reflecting the gleaming sun, was blinding, and seemed especially beautiful . . . All seven, frozen like statues, watched attentively to see whose direction the snake would move in next. The snake was heading for King Lear, who was already trembling, and now his trembling grew to a spasm. As it slithered between Lear's parted feet, the snake paused for a moment . . . and slowly slithered on across the sand . . . The moment the snake stopped, Lear thought the end had come, his death had come for him.

Fear emptied King Lear's bladder . . .

When the snake left the old man, who was barely alive, with his sunken eyes and overgrown beard, everyone except Lear sighed in relief, as if they had personally cast off the snake. The Emperor stepped closer to the old man and noticed that the man's eyes, blinking and darting, seemed to be asking him to look at the other side of the scrap of leather where the note was written. When he saw there was also something written on the other side, the Emperor turned over the scrap of leather and started to read. On this side, the message was far shorter, and he read it quickly to himself. Alexander the Great saw him do it, and nodded his head, encouraging him to read it out loud.

"The snake," read the Emperor, aloud this time, "is the sentinel of Hell. The gates of Hell begin at the serpent's nest."

"The snake is the sentinel of Hell?" Genghis Khan immediately echoed him. "So this is Hell, not Heaven, is that it?"

As if in response, the old man nodded his head.

"There you go! The gates of Heaven are open unto you! Welcome, honored psychos! . . . Everything you've done wrong, down to your bone marrow, down to your every cell, down to your smallest veins—it's all redeemed! Congratulations! You've rid yourselves of sin! . . . Now nobody can give you injections and shoot you up with sulfozin! Take a load off, relax, enjoy the sweetness of Paradise, drink nectar from the flowers like bees, may honey drip from your lips! Drink the dew like the snakes, may poison drip from your lips! . . . You must have seen it! You all saw it!" Thaïs the Athenian scolded them all, and she started to dance wickedly.

"Run away, speak with scorn, waste your love—Repentance will catch up with you! I won't ask you who wrote those lines! It's Goethe, you idiots! Goethe must have been writing about losers just like us! Good Lord, we're just outside Hell! Prepare to repent!"

"Hell? What are you talking about?" The clear-eyed Cleopatra went pale, confused. "Emperor, is it true?"

"It's true, it's true!" shouted Lear, eyes flashing, shouting curses. "You, Emperor, you've been torturing us for forty days now! You promised to lead us to the Holy Land! This desert has no end! There's not the slightest bit of greenery or shade anywhere to be seen! . . . You wanted to devour us, and you did. You wanted to swallow us whole, and you did! . . . Curses and more curses upon you! . . . This bloody dervish says Hell begins with snakes? . . . There are snakes ahead of us, snakes behind us . . . We're in a viper's nest! . . . How stupid must we be, not to see it! . . . Here! Take it!" Lear tore off his belt and held it out to everyone around him. "Strangle me with this, right here! Strangle me!" he said and tried to shove his belt into the hands of Alexander the Great, then Genghis Khan, then Kozuchak. "Strangle me with this belt! Stop humiliating me! Yes, Emperor, take it. Accepting death at your hand will be no sin for me. Take my belt . . . Strangle me to death!" Lear said those words and fell on his knees before the Emperor.

The Emperor took the belt, grabbed Lear by one shoulder, and shoved him hard to the ground.

"Son of a bitch! Spawn of a dog!" He began lashing Lear's bent back with the belt. "Do you call yourselves people? You're anything but people! . . . And that's why I'm bringing you to the Holy Land, so that even if you never reach Paradise, you'll finally realize that you are human beings. Until you realize you're a person, the gates of Paradise will never open to you! . . . God didn't send you Hell. You created Hell all by yourselves! And that's because you, all of you, forgot that you are people! . . . Insolence and abomination! . . . Idiots! Hell is castigation, castigation for those who have forgotten their humanity! . . . If you remember you're a person, then the road to Hell is closed to you, but if you forget, then the road to Hell is right there . . . and the snake, the sentinel of the gates of Hell, will open those gates for you! . . . Go on in, you scoundrel! Make yourself at home!"

Lashing Lear's back with the belt made the Emperor short of breath, and made his hand go numb. All the anger he had stored up at them all, he delivered directly to Lear . . . The Emperor's anger stormed inside him because these endless, constant questions about when they'd reach the Holy Land, when they'd reach Paradise, had driven him truly mad, driven him into a white-hot rage . . .

Lear said nothing, face down in the sand . . . Like a leaf torn from a branch, all his fury flew away, it went up in smoke . . . For a long time, he lay there, breathing the scent of the sand . . . Suddenly, he remembered the sinful words he had once spoken: "I don't give a damn about Hell or about God's punishment! It's all a lie. If He has a Hell, if He castigates us, then why doesn't the Creator smite me for this? I'm my own master! I'm my own God!" . . . The Emperor had been right to chastise him: "Son of a bitch!" . . . He was born a human being, but he lived like a barnyard animal, and it seemed there was nothing sacred for him in this world . . .

The sun squatted over the distant edges of the desert . . . And these seven again set out on their long journey to the Holy Land . . . Long ago, they had left behind them the tiny dervish, Devani Burhu, waging his protest against God, who had created Hell, by standing on one foot in the middle of the desert for forty years . . . Although they had walked far beyond him, they still looked back, from time to time . . . And they continued their journey to the Holy Land . . .

Once Lear had boasted that he was not afraid of Hell or the punishment of God . . . But now he walked in fear, both of Hell, and of God's castigation . . .

King Lear

The old man's wrinkled hands dug into the young woman's white breasts.

The girl surely found the old man repulsive, but the opaque darkness had locked these two within the same four walls, a tiny space in the infinite universe . . . When the old man's hands pried open the front of the girl's dress, her full white breasts emerged, like two bright moons from behind dark clouds, illuminating everything around them with the light of dawn parting the darkness of night . . . The young woman bristled with disgust when the old man's twitching whiskers and his beard, prickly as straw, poked into her . . . Like a man dying of thirst in the desert, when his throat is all dryness and his lungs creak, and a swallow of water seems more valuable than life, the old man knew he could die happily once he made his way to this young female body and dedicated the last remaining days of his life to passionate pleasure in her arms . . . A death like that would be only fair, after his whole cursed life . . . His wrinkled hands caressed her breasts carefully, as if he were looking for something there . . . The old man had seen much of life, and sampled much of what female passion could offer him, in his time, and now, as if deprived of reason at the height of sexual arousal, he wanted to arouse her, too, like he had in his long-ago, younger years, arouse a powerful desire in her to respond, to own her fully . . . His tugging at the hem of the soft fabric of her skirt revealed her glowing white body, and he caught her scent, the maddening scent of a young woman. This poor, destitute age of ours, for which all people are identical, had brought these two into the same bed . . . For her, perhaps, it was simple: the night would pass and the dawn would break, but the old man would have liked to put all the days and nights he had lived into this one night and make it last forever . . . The girl lay there like she had just been born into the world, and the old man, who had long ago forgotten how lovely a girl's beauty could be, shook like an adolescent beholding a woman's body for the first time . . . One more instant, he thought, and the fire in his blood would burn him up till nothing remained. The old man's dry mouth touched the girl's lips. The girl had not pulled away; her difficult life long ago taught her enough, and giving in to her own growing arousal, she wrapped her arms around the old man. The old man's whole body trembled, his legs shook like a newborn calf's legs . . . It was difficult to believe that this girl lying beside him would soon, truly and wholly, belong to him, and that is why he trembled. His whole body trembled, as if he were a man discovering this particular joy for the first time. For the first time, he was feeling this . . . The girl sighed deeply, and he could tell her sigh was not from passion and not from arousal; it was a sigh of unmet desire . . . The naked girl removed the old man's shirt, stinking of sweat, and she took off everything else, too, baring him fully. That made the old man perspire some more . . . He understood why he was bathed in sweat and what was bothering him, and it was that although the girl was attractive, although she wanted him, his whole body remained insensate, deprived of all virility, afflicted by a lack of vitality . . . "Curses!" thought the old man. "The curse of old age! Here it is!" He tried tugging on his member, but it shriveled and slipped from his fingers. The passion that had seized her sent the girl into a frenzy, and she started sobbing and tearing at her hair . . . She grabbed a pillow and flung it away, and flung off the blanket, too . . . Passion stormed within her . . . The old man wanted to display his own passion . . . But his dying body just would not come alive . . . He had seen his own pitiful death in this lovely female body, and, understanding that this was the worst torment in a torturous world, that no calamity could compare with this torment, the old man started to weep . . .

Human passion had brought out the weeping of both of these people . . . Suffering had brought out their cries . . .

In the nuthouse, they called the old man King Lear.

A former actor, he had never stepped outside the fate assigned to him, neither in life, nor on the stage . . . When he considered his destiny, he had never wanted to leave the flowering gardens or the paradisaical pleasure

of his life. As an actor, he played no major roles, and it was almost an acci-
dent that he ever entered a theater, but he did understand the language
of women extremely well, and he knew all the whims and desires of the
female mind, and he was willing to sacrifice everything for their sake, and
nothing else of value in this world held any importance for him. He led
a squalid life with a squalid fate . . . However many women he one way
or another made his wife, he let just as many of them go, and so many
came into and out of his bed as he flitted constantly, like a butterfly, from
woman to woman . . . Once, when he read something about curses on
a page in the Holy Book, he ripped that page into tiny shreds, shouting:
"Yes, I'm truly a filthy man, I spit at destiny, I laugh at it . . . I don't want to
hear a thing about sinning and salvation! Where is this Creator of yours?
If he truly exists, then why doesn't he curse me? I've ruined and sullied
so many girls, stolen their virginity, taken my pleasure from them, and
then tossed them out like old gloves into the garbage! Where's my curse?
Where's my punishment sent down by the Creator? No, it doesn't exist! It's
all empty words! Nonsense!" Truly, nobody's curses could have stopped
him . . . The only respectable thing he did in his life was to play the role
of King Lear. He remembered Lear's monologue, the one about the wind:

> Blow, winds, and crack your cheeks! Spout, rain,
> Till you have drench'd our steeples, drowned the cocks!
> You sulph'rous and thought-executing fires,
> Vaunt-couriers to oak-cleaving thunderbolts,
> Singe my white head! And thou, all-shaking thunder,
> Strike flat the thick rotundity of the world
> Crack Nature's moulds, all germains spill at once,
> That makes ingrateful man!

He always delivered King Lear's monologue, his Shakespeare by way
of Pasternak, with immense inspiration, applying all his strength to it, as
if he were living Lear's unfortunate life, as if he were cursed with Lear's
madness . . . Other talented actors in his theater could not play the role any
better than him . . . And there was plenty to say about his romantic adventures at the theater . . . He never let a single pretty actress slip by and always

swooped down on them like a bee to a flower, and when he exercised his extraordinary talent for seduction, and sweet words, none of them could ever resist him. There was one time he fell in love with an actress, and, bursting with that love, he stirred up such chaos in her life, and harassed her so badly where her husband could see it, that the woman's life was destroyed, thanks to that God-denying man, and she finally had to get a divorce . . . Later, the actress ended up on the street . . . Lear had an illness that had afflicted him since he was a boy . . . When a fit of madness seized him, nobody could contain him or calm him . . . Like a raging storm, seeing nothing, forgetting all shame and conscience, he used to march right out in public, holding high his banner as a male and a madman . . .

Lear was tall and handsome, a slim, well-built man . . . He also had one special gift: he was eloquent and sharp-witted, always joking, and that quickly won him the hearts of everyone who heard him speak . . . And now that old age had come, now that he had outlived his stormy youth and was living quietly and calmly, he remembered his younger years and wanted more luxurious moments with a young girl . . . But who would agree to sacrifice herself to an old man like him? Who would go where he said to go, or do what he said to do? . . . Lear collected all the money he had saved and decided to spend it all, invest it all, in one night of pleasure before he died . . . He brought a girl he bought for the night into his small room, and she was not just a girl but a beauty, slender as a cherry sapling . . . And what would the girl care? As long as he paid, the rest was none of her concern. It didn't matter who he was—old or young, black or white, a professor or a gangster—the important thing was that he paid well for that night . . . He knew his money didn't stink . . .

Now, powerless over his decrepit body, Lear lay and looked, longingly, at the moonlit body of this gorgeous girl, who had turned away from him in disdain . . . Surely, the night would be a long one . . .

Feeling the weight of his inadequacy, Lear lay there and swore quietly, curse upon curse, for all his helplessness, his dead body, his flaccid virility . . . As usual, in cases like this, the night lasted forever, and it seemed the dawn would never come . . . At that cursed moment, he recalled, sadly, the time when his manhood was inexhaustible, when he was overflowing with virility, the time of his own blossoming . . . He remembered that time, and was furious at his helplessness, and his dwindling penis . . . They paraded before his eyes, the days when he used to forget everything else while thinking about women, when his eyes flashed and the end of the world wouldn't have bothered him a bit . . . When he recalled those times of excess and potency, today's powerlessness, like a shred of old meat stuck between his teeth, disgusted him . . . The young woman lay there turned away from him, thinking her own thoughts . . . She couldn't understand why she had started weeping, why she had sighed so sadly . . . But perhaps she was thinking of the inexorability of fate, and by cursing her own bitter fate, she was railing against this night? Such was the life of a prostitute; such was her daily existence . . . She shouldn't blame herself . . . Lovely dreams, sweetly cherished images . . . This time, she dreamed of her mother . . . She only remembered her mother in snatches, in pieces . . . And because of how she remembered her in snatches, she never could paint herself the whole image, but could only imagine how her mother looked in pieces, flashing clearly one by one like jumping flames, pieces of early memories she could stitch together into an overall portrait . . .

Lear . . . that was not his real name . . . After they fired him from the theater, he beat around doing odd jobs . . . sweeping the streets . . . working as a guard . . . hiring himself out as a gardener . . . But, no matter where he worked or what he did, he always kept a pretty woman nearby . . . One time, while sweeping the street, he found the torn cover of a book with a single unharmed page . . . On that page, there was something about Hell . . . Skimming through that description of Hell, while remembering the time of his own male potency, he exclaimed: "Where I am, there is no God, and where there is God, there is no me!" He tore that page out angrily, and added with fury, "Where are the ones who mete out punishment? When will they castigate me? Let them just try . . . No . . . They don't exist! Even if they did, they couldn't do anything! It's all a bluff! It's all a lie!" he shouted, bursting with awareness of his own manly omnipotence . . . Truly, if you gathered in one place all the women he had slept with, there would be such a crowd they wouldn't fit in a city square . . .

On the page he had read, there was a description of Hell . . .

On the cover of the book, from which only one page remained, he read: "Holy Book." He picked up the cover and held it in his hands for a long time, examining that title. Then he tossed it into the autumn leaves and swept it all up into a pile of trash, where it remained. But the page he had read, with the description of Hell, he could not toss into the trash pile. Folding it neatly, he tucked it away in his breast pocket . . . This man did not fear God's wrath; he had lived through many difficult days, being squeezed through the sieve of life, but of all the difficulties he had born in his lifetime up till then, he had never suffered at women's hands, or because of women . . .

. . . But now Lear was lying next to this naked, available young woman like a desiccated old bean pole . . .

The breath of the woman lying there intoxicated him, like the scent of blossoming oleaster in the mountains . . . The girl said nothing for a long time . . . Privately, she was impatiently waiting for dawn, while Lear, the elderly philanderer and ladies' man who had long since lost his potency and vim, prayed that this night would never end . . . He kept waiting for his body to suddenly stir, come alive, exert some effort, so he could leap up and finally take this delicacy of a girl, and after that, he'd happily agree even to the fires of hell . . . But Lear was like dry old wood: you can water it all you like, but it will never put out a green shoot . . . Maybe it was to make the long night shorter that he decided to start a conversation . . . And the conversation he started was awkward and uneasy . . . Without noticing that awkwardness, he made a request to which the girl did not respond, holding her tongue, for a long time . . .

He told the girl:

"Tell me about your parents."

For a long time, the girl didn't speak. Lying with her back to him, she sighed deeply, with regret, and asked ruefully:

"Why do you want to know?"

"I was just asking," said Lear, grasping the awkwardness. "I'm sorry if I offended you . . ." And he politely shut up.

"With people like me, you can offend us or not offend us. It's all the same. We don't care." The girl propped herself up a little in bed. "But I know that if I ask you how old you are, that would be insulting to you. I know that . . . So I'm not asking. See?" The girl was getting drawn into the conversation. "We don't do this so we can go around asking people their age . . . You don't really care who my parents are, do you? To be honest, you're not the only one! I don't care, either."

"Well, I . . . I was just asking." Lear was confused, and did not know what to say.

"It's fine . . . You're not the first, and you won't be the last." The girl pouted her little lips, chronically sick of such annoying questions. "Only clients who can't get it up ask questions like that, just to make things last till morning . . . And they're always preaching at us, not that they have any idea if it does us any good. We're born this way! Prostitutes!" she said, sharply. "Prostitutes have no parents. If you must know."

"I was only asking . . ." Lear muttered.

"So you were just asking. I was just answering." She turned away unhappily.

Lear regretted, deep in his soul, that he had asked such a stupid, inappropriate question.

"I do know a little about them, actually," said the girl, sighing heavily. "They worked in a theater, apparently, both my mom and my dad. That's all I know."

She stopped talking. She gave another deep sigh . . . Now Lear thought the girl looked much older than her age. He had thought of her as a little Parisian street urchin up till then, but now Lear sensed, in her sigh, some of her rueful, difficult life.

"I've heard my mom was a famous actress. But I don't know anything about my dad."

"Do you remember your mother's name?" Lear asked, with a hint of premonition.

"No," she answered succinctly.

She had kept her back to him, but now the girl turned toward Lear.

Despite the dark that reigned in that room, her body was dimly lit by a dull light. Lear's wrinkled hands touched the girl's breast. While Lear's hands came to rest on the full breasts, round as ripe apples, she took his wrinkled hands in her own long fingers, and removed them from her breasts, and brought them to her lips for a gentle kiss . . .

Lear was intoxicated by her scent, catching a hint of a barely noticeable aroma of mountain flowers coming from her body . . . The girl discarded her initial caution and used her slender hands to gently caress Lear's neck, his earlobes . . . She felt slightly bad that, lying there next to him, she hadn't been capable, hadn't been able, to excite him quite enough . . . The smell of cold sweat covering Lear's elderly body repelled her . . . Lear had retreated into memories of his long-ago youth, his dashing, reckless days, which were now so far in the past . . . When there's a fast stallion under you, raring to go, you can do anything . . . Lear had begun to realize his stallion had galloped away for good, long ago . . .

"You have big, strong hands. The hands of a real man," she said.

"My hands?" Lear was surprised to hear her say that . . .

Those words sprouted confusing feelings for Lear, making various thoughts stumble, whining, into his head, scraps of memories . . . There was a woman, many years ago, who had said those same words to him. He remembered her for a long time; after her, there were a lot of other women in his life, but none of them ever spoke about his hands the way she had, that actress . . . She had also said, back then: "You have big, strong hands. The hands of a real man." And now this young woman was saying the same thing? . . .

Back then, working in the theater, he had started seeing one actress who was much older than he was . . . She was at the peak of her fame at the time, but even so, just like hundreds of other women who ended up in his arms, she melted for him like wax in a fire . . . And after that, nothing could separate them, not the judgmental conversations and rumors all around them, and not even their constant passionate betrayals of one another . . . It was only many years later that Lear left her for someone new, setting off after the next female specimen . . .

Even losing both his home and his job at once, and ending up on the street, wasn't something he considered a punishment. There was a time when he worked for a couple years in a morgue . . . He used to bathe the corpses, then plunk down all the money he earned at the bawdy houses he frequented . . .

Then, something devastating and unforgettable happened to him.

The mere recollection of what happened, what he saw then, made his whole soul feel soaked in blood . . . The thing that so shook him was that the great actress he had loved, the one he had chased after, bathing in the sweetness of her love—she was there, lying dead, on the table in his morgue . . . She'd been hit by a car . . . That actress, so disfigured that nobody would have recognized her, had already been in the morgue for a week . . . Lear only just happened to recognize her, after taking her for just another unidentified body . . . That evening, the director of the morgue did his big evening inspection, examining the unidentified bodies and telling the assistants which ones to put in the common grave.

At the morgue, unidentified bodies like this one didn't get ritually washed; the assistants loaded them into a truck, and buried them two or three to a pit . . . The assistants called those bodies "unserviced" . . . When the director told them to bury this female body in the same pit with two unidentified male bodies, he joked rudely, "Those two can monkey around with her in the next life!"

The two big assistants guffawed at his joke: "We'll lay her down between two men! Ha-ha-ha!"

Lear was surprised to recognize the woman, and, not believing his eyes, he stood there for a minute, staring at her . . . The director's words shook him out of his trance: "What, do you recognize the dame?" . . . That night, under the cover of darkness, Lear returned to the morgue, turned on the light, and went to the room where that woman lay . . . Getting hit by the car tore the skin all over her face, and no part of her body looked unharmed . . . But Lear recognized her . . . This woman was his actress . . . a woman he had loved . . . Tears sprang up in Lear's eyes . . . Her arms . . . legs . . . neck . . . her heavy, thick braid, with strands of gray . . . the mole under her earlobe . . . Lear knew all of it . . .

Visions of the happy days they'd spent loving one another appeared before his eyes . . .

Lear, a man with no God or devil in his head, had so loved that actress that he lost his last shred of reason; he played many roles, and all the roses the adoring audiences cast at his feet, he collected, so he could shower the woman he loved with them . . . He never thought they'd meet like this . . . A weakness overcame Lear, and he could barely stay upright, so he leaned against the table on which the woman lay . . . He wished he could say something to her . . . Then Lear felt, quite clearly, that their

spirits were speaking without words . . . They were talking without uttering a sound . . .

"Who brought you here?" Lear asked her.

"Who do you think? The wind," answered the actress.

"The wind?" Lear was surprised.

"Yes, the wind . . . a strong wind . . . You remember King Lear's monologue about the wind?" she asked.

"Yes . . . I remember . . ." said Lear.

"They told me you were in the insane asylum, but here you are . . ."
she said. "What is this place?"

"This place? . . . The morgue . . . a morgue for great people."

"A morgue? . . . A morgue for great people, you say?" she asked.

"Yes . . . a morgue for great people."

"A morgue for great people . . . That doesn't sound good. I remember
your monologue about the wind . . . Nobody could deliver it like you . . .
Recite it for me. I want to hear it one more time," she told him.

"Should I?" Lear wondered, giving the actress a questioning look.

"All right, I will," he said out loud.

He felt like he was back on the big stage with the actress. He'd started
to forget that monologue. There were pauses, as he recited it, as he recalled
forgotten words . . .

"Wind!" Lear pronounced that word, and the rest of them, clinging to
each other in a chain, followed in order. "Whence do you come? Whence
do you blow? Come and sweep the whole universe clean. Drown it all! . . .
Come now, if you can, and sweep the whole world clean . . . Come now,
come now, let's see what you're made of! Blow your heart out, winds! Spit,
fire! Spout, rain! Spout, rain, strike flat the thick rotundity of the world,
crack Nature's moulds, all germains spill at once . . . Come on! Come
on! . . . O maddened winds! . . . Stop! Furious as you are, stop! Sweep me
away from here like a tiny leaf, if you are able! . . . Give me your worst,
hurricane! Carry me beyond the clouds! . . . Take me, carry me away!"
Lear recited with inspiration, but gradually his recitation transformed into
a lament, and trailed away into fitful sobs . . .

In the dark morgue, Lear sobbed, striking his chest . . .

He wept, embracing one leg of the table where the actress lay . . .

Had he perhaps driven her to this? . . . Lear had toyed with the fates of many people, not just one, and only now did he feel any guilt, and so he wept bitterly . . .

His strong, broad hands—which had once grasped at beautiful women's ankles, which had passionately embraced the slender waists and massaged the breasts of many a girl—now grasped the leg of that table for dead bodies in the morgue, trembling, drained of strength . . .

"Now I'll wash your body," Lear said.

He remembered what the actress used to say: "You have big, strong hands. The hands of a real man." And his whole body shook as he wept and wept.

He buried the actress himself . . . and erected a sign over her grave with her name and title on it . . . He did not invite anyone to the funeral. How could anyone appreciate her after death, when they hadn't appreciated her in life? The thought that nobody had even looked for the actress, the whole seven days she had been at the morgue, made his bones ache . . .

Now, lying in bed with the girl, and hearing her say: "You have big, strong hands . . . the hands of a real man . . ." Lear started to think . . . He remembered that long-ago love affair, that torturous love, that tragic love . . . She had said that, once, too . . .

"Why so quiet?" asked the girl.

"I was thinking," said Lear.

"Do you know," she said, "that in ancient times, in Japan, they had places called 'Assuage your sorrow' . . . Only very rich men went there . . . crazy old farts . . . and they spent the night with young girls." She told the tale with zest, turning to face him, shoving off the blanket that hid her lovely body, letting her breasts, round as apples, press fluidly to his elderly chest. "And not even those young girls knew who they were spending the night with, who they were getting it on with . . . Know why?" The girl gave Lear a questioning stare.

Intrigued, Lear asked, "Why?"

"They didn't know because they gave them sleeping potions made from plants' roots . . . And they slept through the whole thing . . . slept like the dead! . . . But their bodies were hot and their hearts were healthy . . .

In the morning, they never remembered what those old guys did with them, they had no idea . . . Once, one of the girls went to bed with one senile old fart . . . Don't feel bad about me saying 'old fart' . . . You're much younger, right?" she asked, sucking up to him. "This old fart couldn't do a thing to her all night long, and when morning came he fell asleep, exhausted . . . So he's sleeping, right . . . And then all of a sudden . . . he jumps out of bed like someone dropped a cold snake down his shirt . . . Know why?" she asked, giving him a meaningful look. "It turns out . . . the poor girl died . . . They gave her too much sleeping potion . . . Why did they put the girls to sleep, you ask? . . . That was how they did it, so that the girls . . . never knew . . . what rich guy . . . what old man they slept with that night . . . But none of that has anything to do with us . . . I just felt like telling you the story . . . And we do still have a long night ahead of us, don't we?"

She had been curled up in a ball until then, but now the girl straightened out and pressed herself to him, caressing his whole elderly body. She wanted her caresses to stir the desire inside his old, impotent body. She breathed her hot breath on Lear's cheek and started tickling his ear with her thin tongue . . .

But the girl's completely bare, hot body, lying on top of Lear and caressing him, could not stir a responding desire in the dried-up wood of his old body . . .

Lear severely regretted hiring the girl for the night . . .

He wished morning would come quicker, or, failing that, an earthquake, even . . . Apparently, this night would never end . . .

Annoyed that all her efforts were failing, the girl yanked the blanket back up, wrapped herself up in it, turned away from Lear, and broke out in tears for some reason, her whole body shuddering . . . And in her weeping, there was sorrow for her lot as a woman, and there was disgust for the life she was living. The girl truly seemed to be mourning her fate, her lot in life . . . this particular female fate, all torment and difficulty . . .

The girl wept, her whole body shuddering . . .

Her powerless, soundless weeping was her complaint to the Creator, who had handed her such a lot, and her parents, whom she had never known, and who had left her in this infinite, untamed desert of a life; she wept for her unhappy, humiliating fate . . . Gradually, she calmed, and her eyes closed . . .

Lear knew the girl lying next to him was breathing, but, sensing his own powerlessness, he didn't know what to do . . . Looking at her, turned away from him, Lear suddenly noticed, in the weak moonlight, a little black mole under her earlobe . . . Strange . . . his actress had had the same kind of mole . . . Back then, in the morgue, Lear had recognized her because of that mole . . . The mole was the thing he recognized . . . and now this girl had the very same mole, in the very same place . . . That mole steered Lear to a particular thought . . . He had loved to kiss the actress right there . . . When Lear kissed her there, the actress had always felt particular pleasure . . .

Lear had always thought that the actress's whole allure, as a woman, seemed concentrated specifically in that little black spot . . . And the girl had a mole in the exact same place . . . The full moon was framed right in the window . . . Its glow poured milk into the dark room . . . The girl looked at the moon for a while, without speaking, then said quietly:

"I heard there would be a lunar eclipse tonight."

Lear changed the subject. "The mole under your ear . . . it's very pretty," he said. "I knew a woman with a mole just like that, once . . ."

"Was she an actress?" the girl asked out of the blue.

"She was," said Lear.

"Someone told me my mom had a mole there, too," the girl said. "I should tell you . . . it's sort of an erogenous zone," she said flirtatiously.

Looking the girl over, Lear tried to find similarities to the actress . . . Her face . . . eyes . . . brows . . . her smile . . . the dimples in her cheeks . . . her forehead . . . hair . . . only now did he notice that she very much resembled the actress . . . He noticed that, and, immediately, he plunged into uneasy thoughts . . .

He felt heat swelling inside him . . . His whole body was on fire and trembling . . .

"No, no," he thought. "Nooo . . ."

In his mind, he carefully analyzed everything that had happened . . . He remembered—curse a memory like his!—how could he have forgotten?! . . . He had gotten the actress pregnant . . . The news of it sent the theater, all those gossip-lovers, into a frenzy, and all the actors were talking about it . . . Then Lear was fired from the theater, the actress and her husband divorced, and later, a little girl was born . . . Rumor had it she gave the girl up to the orphanage . . . Snatches of memories of that sad event . . . Later, Lear lost interest in what became of that actress . . . Other people occasionally told him about the little girl born of their love . . . That was it . . . Fate tossed them in opposite directions . . . And now . . . now . . . this . . . The girl's words were taking on more meaning all the time, and they pierced his heart, tore it apart . . . How? How could this be? . . . In what possible way . . . ? O merciful God! The word "God" also plunged like a knife into his suffering heart . . .

The night outside his window made Lear feel cold and comfortless. But the flight of fancy born of that feeling was carrying him now, like a bird, over the uncharted reaches of the ocean of the endless blue sky, to an island, dark in the distance, like a black mole.

No, no! . . . Nooo . . .

Ponderous, leaden thoughts break the wings of his fantasy, pull him toward the ground . . .

No, no! . . . Nooo . . .

Panic and terror force his heart to beat madly.

No, no! . . . Nooo . . .

Probably, great people forged their great thoughts in total solitude, thought Lear.

No, no! . . . Nooo . . .

What about him? . . .

No, no! . . . Nooo . . .

Now, when his soul laughs at his solitude, what great discovery could he make that would be worth shouting the news to all humankind? Or, pursued relentlessly by these thoughts, would he seek out a way to rid himself of them?

No, no! . . . Nooo . . .

For some reason, Lear now felt like a match burning out. His life would be snuffed like the trembling flame of a dying match. Why was he comparing the whole life he'd lived to a burning match? What need did he have of that, and was there even any similarity?

No, no! . . . Nooo . . .

Why would he rather not burn too long, why did he want to spark out and smolder out like a match, disappear into the earth?

No, no! . . . Nooo . . .

Was Lear exhausted of life so soon?

No, no! . . . Nooo . . .

Or was this leaden, suffocating silence, this dull, wordless night, which had settled into the room with him, were these pained thoughts, strained and draped across his brain like an old spider web . . . were they forcing him to look more closely at himself, weigh everything on his conscience?

No, no! . . . Nooo . . .

Or perhaps none of this was a coincidence? Life is a kindling. This is an extinguishing. Without this, where is the mystery in life?

No, no! . . . Nooo . . .

Life brings only one kindling, only one extinguishing. Is that the idiotic law of the universe?

No, no! . . . Nooo . . .

Recently, Lear had been having long conversations with himself at night, staring at the ceiling. He had gotten into the habit of repeating those words, ones he'd read in some book, every morning. Lear thought about those words constantly, and suffered, unable to pull himself out of this deep well of thoughts . . .

But the truly agonizing problem was the young girl lying next to him . . .

No, no! . . . Nooo . . .

Why this cursed night, why now? . . .

The wait for the endless night to end, the night that stretched on like rubber, was such an unbearable torment to his soul—the night tore up his heart, and it ached as if it had been soaked in pickling brine all night long. Now the night seemed plainly simple, now so complex that all his thoughts were ground into a fine sand, and, aside from all that, even if you raced to the ends of the earth, even there, this night would never end, it was infinity itself, stretching on and on.

No, no! . . . Nooo . . .

Strange . . .

No, no! . . . Nooo . . .

Either the human world was created of a thousand varieties of complexity and a thousand secrets, or our souls are the most complicated things in this world, or we've transformed ourselves into complicated souls. Finding wise answers to those questions, I think, will never be simple, even if we dive into the debris of thoughts and shovel through everyone's brains.

No, no! . . . Nooo . . .

On one side of this dilemma there loomed an enormous abyss, a black hole. How was Lear to know that this was the way a night overflowing with thoughts and feelings would come, that the night would stop the motion of the universe just for him? And that, when it came, the Night would be in the guise of a girl? . . .

No, no! . . . Nooo . . .

Before, Lear had disavowed the Creator, once he didn't care whether He existed or not, and he had laughed at Hell: "Where there is God, there is no me, and where I am, there is no God!" he had shouted, thumping his chest . . . Is that why he had crumpled up the page with the description of Hell and swept the Holy Book into the pile of trash? "If the Creator castigates his servants, then where is my castigation?! I will live like a bee drinking nectar from the flowers of life, and I will toss out women like gloves, as many and as often as I want! Don't lecture me, don't preach to me, don't douse me with venom like the creeping beasts! . . . What are life's sins, life's crimes, to me?" That is what the madcap Lear had once said . . . And now? . . .

No, no! . . . Nooo . . .

And he and this girl were imprisoned here in the dark together, and they were supposed to be drowning in lust . . .

No, no! . . . Nooo . . .

Was his actress this girl's mother?! . . . He who had denied the castigation of God, he, the tomcat, the debaucher of women, the foulmouthed man accursed of God, could he have known he would end up in bed with his own daughter? . . . Had he foreseen it? . . . Could it be that the day had come when he would answer for all his sins, now, with the pleasure he took in the arms of his own daughter?! . . .

No, no! . . . Nooo . . . No, no! . . . Nooo . . .

And this cry of "No!" sliced through his body like a dagger, and pressed down upon him with a weight no one could bear. Could this girl . . . born of his and the actress's love . . . have come into his arms as a punishment, as a castigation? . . .

Now he was stuck between two fires: he had laid the actress's body in the earth with his own hands, and he had lain in bed with the daughter born of their love affair . . . He never would have guessed that this cursed, miserable fate would have brought him together with his past . . . His boastful impiety and intemperance had locked him into the cold, dead world . . .

It grew light in the east . . . A new day was being born . . .

The girl got out of bed and began to get dressed . . . Once she was dressed, she turned to Lear and asked,

"Where is my pay for the night?"

Lear got up without a word, and in the morning light, he looked more closely at the girl's face . . . He felt convinced that she very much resembled the actress . . . Lear tossed at the girl's feet all the money he had with him . . . The girl's eyes flew wide open at the sight of all that money scattered across the floor . . .

"Is that all for me?" she asked.

"Yes, it's all yours," said Lear, too shy to look her in the eye.

"Don't you worry that we didn't actually do it . . . It happens . . . I understand . . . Next time . . . No big deal . . ." she kept saying as she picked up the money, giving him sideways glances. "So . . . did you know my mom?"

Lear could not answer. Just then he had no sense of himself . . . He didn't know what was wrong with him . . . Was he alive, or was he dead? . . .

"Sorry, can I ask you one question?" Lear said to her. "If you ever found your father or your mother, what would you do?" Lear had to force himself to utter each word.

"Me?" she asked on her way out of the room.

"Mmm-hmm . . ." Lear muttered, as if he'd gone mute, and nodded.

"I would . . ." the girl answered. "I'd kill them both with my own hands. Death is all they deserve," she said, and she walked out of the room and slammed the door.

Lear froze in place, turned to stone . . .

His eyes bulged from their sockets, and a frenzied energy began to rise from his toes up, filling him all the way to his scalp . . . And, suffused with that frenzied energy, he roared loud enough to make the universe tremble . . . "O Creator! Is this Your punishment?! . . . All my life, You hunted me, and now You've decided to chastise me?"

Lear's cry was deafening and full of grief . . .

He beat his head against the wall . . . Madness overtook him, and his epilepsy twisted his body and threw him to the floor . . . The senseless world transformed before his eyes . . . And now, hungrily, passionately, screaming, he began shouting his monologue, putting into his recitation everything that pierced his soul, all his grief, all his madness, all his despair . . .

"Wind! Whence do you come? Whence do you blow? Come and sweep the whole universe clean, drown it all! . . . Come now, if you can, and sweep the whole world clean . . . Come now, come now, let's see what you're made of! Blow your heart out, winds! Spit, fire! Spout, rain! Spout, rain, strike flat the thick rotundity of the world, crack Nature's moulds, all germains spill at once . . . Come on! Come on! . . . O maddened winds! . . . Stop! Furious as you are, stop! Sweep me away from here like a tiny leaf, if you are able! . . . Give me your worst, hurricane! Carry me beyond the clouds! . . . Take me, carry me away!

> Blow, winds, and crack your cheeks! Spout, rain,
> Till you have drench'd our steeples, drowned the cocks!
> You sulph'rous and thought-executing fires,
> Vaunt-couriers to oak-cleaving thunderbolts,
> Singe my white head!
> Strike flat the thick rotundity of the world,
> Crack Nature's moulds, all germains spill at once,
> That makes ingrateful man!

That day, they took Lear to the mental hospital.

The Seven

The scorching rays of the morning sun poured over the sandy desert . . .

The desert was resting, uttering not a word . . .

A light morning breeze raked sand into a small hill, and the smooth slope of a great dune froze in the relentless silence . . . It looked as if the enormous cooking pot of the domed sky had been overturned atop this desert, and one portion of the rim of that pot of clear blue endlessness was smack against the desert's surface, very close by . . . And if you were to walk toward it, keeping your eye on the mirage, then the edge of the pot that seemed so close would begin moving away from you, farther and farther, and your path would grow ever longer, like an afternoon shadow, while the desert would stretch on endlessly . . .

Within that limitlessness, which exhausted the eyes, there was a countless number of identical camel-humped sand dunes, and you might pass the same place a thousand times and never notice . . . the sandy ocean of the great desert . . . The desert has its own law . . . The bones of many people who had perished in this Valley of Death, whose corpses had been food for the desert's inhabitants, lie among the hills of sand, terrifying as sleeping dragons . . .

Yesterday's solar eclipse had been astounding . . .

The seven had amused themselves with it for a long time . . . The fire-breathing dragon in the sky swallowed down the sun, after which the sun was invisible for a while, and then it suddenly reappeared, with a bite taken out of its side . . . Aware of the approaching solar eclipse, all the life of the desert—which was constantly hopping here and there and running across the sands—it all seemed to hide and disappear . . .

Even that snake from yesterday, it seemed, the one that had wound around the Emperor's leg, had known that the sun would soon go into hiding . . . Like a length of hacked-off rope, the snake had dropped from the Emperor's leg, and then, without looking left or right, it crawled straight under a saxaul shrub and hid there . . . And Genghis Khan, who sensed the dragon was just about to swallow the sun's face, shouted to the others: "Look, a solar eclipse!" . . . On the day of a solar eclipse, on the day the curse came to bear, he had been delivered to the mental hospital . . . Among the seven of them, only the taciturn Genghis Khan had a different name in the nuthouse . . . He wasn't exactly sure how the name "Genghis Khan" had stuck to him, except that he did have a strong resemblance to the real Genghis Khan, in the face . . . People said that on the day of that other solar eclipse, a snake had bitten him, and he started going around seized by madness, and they sent him to the mental hospital . . . That was only one small part of what could be told about him . . .

After the snakebite, having lost his reason, this man spent a week or more between two worlds . . . When he found himself between the door to this world and the door to the next, he lost all hope and did not know what to do, and he was overtaken by a very long dream, and in that dream he saw the real Genghis Khan . . . He told everyone, later, that in that dream, Genghis Khan took a handful of earth from his own grave, walked up to him, stuffed it into his mouth, and made him eat it . . . And he ate the earth like ground corn, his mouth stuffed with it . . .

Ever since then, the taste of the earth from Genghis Khan's grave had never left his mouth . . .

Genghis Khan

Genghis Khan lay in the pitch dark with his last breath in his lungs, and memories of the days he had lived streamed before his eyes like tiny grains in a stream of flowing sand . . . He had dreamed a terrible dream in the night . . . In that dream he had died . . . After they had given him to the ground, put him in his place, a crowd assembled at his grave—madmen, blind men, lame men, children, wolves, jackals—and all of them surrounded his grave and ate the earth from his burial mound like ground corn, chomping through it by the handful and stuffing their mouths with it . . . That dream reminded him of something a shaman had told him long ago: "Your soul is eternal, but after you die, people will eat the earth from your grave like flour . . . If you do not want that to happen, nobody must know where you are buried. When the time comes, you will rise, and give earth from your grave to one man, who will eat it like ground corn . . . and your soul will go over into that person along with the earth . . . and your soul will enter him not to prolong his life, but to bring castigation . . . That man will be insane. And he will bear the punishment for your sins . . . He will be one of your many distant descendants . . ." In this dream before death, Genghis Khan had seen that shaman . . . The dream gave rise to various thoughts inside him . . . As if the clump of days he had lived was dissolving in the palm of his hand, those days flashed quickly before his eyes, which were preparing to close for the last time, and he, grasping at other events from torn-out pages of memories, felt as if he were trying to string them like beads on a single thread . . . A multitude of thoughts tore at his brain, and it seemed his flagging breath might stop at any moment. He lay still in a heavy silence, too weak to resist the senseless thoughts that agonized his soul, haunting him, pushing him closer to the void between life and death. They were born of all the sorrows he had survived, and all his ideas about life. He who had vanquished the entire world for the sake of two words he could no longer find, to unify his thoughts; he who belched forth insatiability like a dragon belches fire, clawing the moon from the sky by night and the sun by day; he who had turned the world upside down, seizing herd upon herd of horses to fill the world; he whose hands had gathered great quantities of treasure, taking life from the weak, severing the hands of the strong, subjugating all Creation to himself; he who had deprived men of their tribes and nations of their nationhood while his countless soldiers overturned all the Earth with their saber blades; he, Genghis Khan, now, by the grace of God, lying on a multitude of blankets in the place of honor in his commander's tent, was deep in thought, sensing his imminent departure from this world . . . Once, he had disgorged blasts of implacable fury, but now Genghis Khan lay like a dry, withered bone, helpless, feeling caged in a powerless body . . . His eyelids, glued together, barely parted, and only rarely did his thin, tattered beard tremble, and he began to talk to himself in words nobody could understand. Like an autumn leaf, his once inexhaustible body was wilting and going dry . . . The irresistible gale of his thoughts swept up brief scraps of memories of days past, and he tried to remember the events that stood behind them. Gradually, crumb by crumb, he recalled something having to do with his past battles . . . His thoughts flew like a lost sheet of paper chased by the wind across the naked steppe, now swooping up, now dropping down, now slapped and plastered against a tree's branch, where only the edges of the page remain trembling . . . Among the countless memories, one event—like that sheet of paper stuck to the tree—stood out among the swarm of other multihued thoughts . . .

. . . He had just turned twelve years old . . .

That was the age when hair had just begun to sprout in his armpits, and every time he put on his wolfskin cloak, there was a terrible smell: his armpits had started to stink . . . Before, he had only met that scent coming from older people, and now he had it . . . He tried to wash it away, but the stink remained, and the more hair appeared in his armpits, the more they stank . . . One day, a limping old blind woman sat Temujin in a wooden tub and bathed him with hot water . . . The old woman scrubbed his whole body, and lathered him with Chinese soap . . . Temujin remembered the smell of that soap, a miraculous, gentle smell . . . He never encountered such a miraculous smell anywhere, ever again, though he longed for it. It could be that the aroma of that soap, which so astounded his sense of smell, was simply one of his first childhood memories . . . The old woman had wrinkled, twisted hands, and her face, covered with count-less deep wrinkles, seemed to have nothing human about it . . . This old woman had spent her whole life bathing people, and she always bathed them thoroughly, like her own children . . . Temujin's father had invited her to their home and asked her to scrub his son clean in the tub . . . When the old woman grabbed Temujin firmly in his private places and started to bathe him, he had been embarrassed and tried to use his hands to hide his penis from her. She paid no attention to that, and rubbed and lathered his penis with both hands, and right away it filled with blood and sprang out erect . . . When she mixed hot water from the kettle with cold water and poured that clean, warm water over Temujin, he felt amazingly light, free, and pure. After that, when the old woman wasn't looking, he stole a piece of the Chinese soap, whose scent was all over his body now, and several times he inhaled that astounding aroma, with pleasure. After she rubbed Temujin dry, the old woman led him into the light that fell through the opening in the top of their yurt . . . She sat him before her under that light falling from above, and used a sharp blade to shave the coarse hair from his head, leaving just a clump of it over his forehead, and then she started shaving the new growth under his arms . . . That is when he learned that armpits could be shaved . . . After that, the old woman used a small knife to trim his toenails, and she mixed the clippings with green trimmings from a dry juniper branch that hung on the wall, and she threw the mixture into the fire under the rumbling cooking pot. Why she did that, Temujin did not know. He put on the short robe of light silk his father had bought him from the Chinese merchants and walked outside, feeling as fresh as if he'd just been born again into the world . . . As soon as he stepped out of the yurt, a noisy gaggle of boys his age crowded around him . . . At that moment, the world seemed especially exquisite to Temu-jin, and he felt more significant, more important, even taller and older than his peers, as if, in that instant, he'd become an adult . . . and, that day, the girls started looking at him differently, expecting him to treat them differently, and for them and their girlish imaginations, he became more attractive, more handsome, and they all seemed to fall in love with him at once . . . Temujin's father lifted him up onto the horse he was leading . . . As soon as he was on its back, he made the horse rear up, and they set off at a gallop . . . The wind whistled in his ears, and that hotblooded horse galloped uphill, flying fast as a snowstorm, carrying him free and easy . . . He raced through gullies and ravines, he crossed streams and forest groves, he soared into the hills, and Temujin showed everyone what a true Mongol he was by the way he raced that horse and guided it . . . From the lowlands he'd left behind, the echo of the younger boys' happy shouts followed him . . . He aimed and launched an arrow into the sky, into the endless, heavenly blue . . . Forever afterward, Genghis Khan thought of that day as the first page in his book of life . . . It lay open before him . . . Temujin had often heard his parents speaking about him, still a bit dismissively: "Look how big he is already." . . . And he heard it again that day, annoyingly enough . . . His father said it to that crooked-legged old woman, as if to remind everyone, and he also told her that he and Temujin's mother were planning to go visit some relatives who lived two mountain passes away, and they wanted to leave Temujin under her supervision . . . That evening, before the sun settled into its nest, Temujin's father and mother saddled their horses, packed their things, and set off to visit their relatives, leaving Temujin at home, and they told him to obey the lame old woman in all things . . .

Night came, and stars glittered in the clear sky . . .

The dim glow of the moonlight streaming through the opening in the top of the yurt seemed to bathe everything inside with a new meaning, a new significance . . . Temujin, whom everybody was treating differently now, tucked himself into several layers of down blankets for a bed, and he felt light as down himself, and these new blankets, which had come from who knows where, had a wonderful smell . . . Now it was late at night, and silent . . . Only the sounds of snorting and scratching came from the horses, in the distance; there was an occasional dog barking, and the barely audible rumble of the river a horse-ride away, and all of that seemed to reveal the night's true beauty . . . The nighttime hush was disturbed by the sound of the lame old woman limping to the door of the yurt . . . When the old woman opened the door and came inside, Temujin heard that she wasn't alone . . . Judging by the voice, the person who came with her was a woman . . . Every move the old woman made was accompanied by the tinkling of silver jewelry the other woman had woven into her hair . . . Panting, out of breath, the old woman lit a lamp and placed it in the middle of the yurt. The camel-hair wick burned in a small dish of oil, giving off a weak, flickering light . . . She was whispering in the woman's ear, the woman she had brought with her, but the woman didn't respond, other than to mumble, "Mmm . . . ," and nod in agreement with her every word . . .

Hidden in his high bed, Temujin lifts his head carefully and tries to catch what they are saying . . . But he can't make out anything very clearly . . . The old woman is about to leave the yurt, leaving the second woman behind, and as she walks out, she tells her: "I will come back when the sun rises." The woman says: "I should leave before sunrise." The old woman nods in agreement: "He's little, yet, a gosling. You teach him everything." And, saying that, she walks out of the yurt. Temujin has not understood a thing . . .

The same night, the same snorts and scratches from the horses, the barking of dogs . . . the noise of the river . . . Temujin goes on hearing all those things. He is waiting. What will this woman say? . . . A dead silence inside the yurt . . . Temujin lies stiff on his downy blankets, holding his breath . . . The woman has walked to the head of Temujin's bed, removed her robe, and hung it on the wall . . . Temujin detects on her the scent of that Chinese soap . . . A mysterious feeling rose in Temujin's chest, making him feel a genuine heat . . . He had never experienced anything like this before . . . Then the woman walked to the center of the yurt, up to the lamp . . . a young, pretty woman, maybe twenty years old . . . The yurt smelled like her scent . . . She began to get undressed . . . As he watched her, Temujin, bare naked, felt this heat, and excitement, a fire in his veins . . . While the woman was getting undressed, he lay there, pressed ever more firmly into his bed, wrapped in a blanket, hiding his head, eyes squeezed shut, pretending to be asleep . . . Though he tried, the eyes he forced shut opened of their own accord, and when he caught sight of the naked woman, they opened wide, bulging from their sockets, and a fire he could no longer control, capable of carrying him to unknown places, swept through his veins . . . His unruly penis, swelling between his legs, felt strange, and now it came to life, thrusting out long and firm like the neck of a bellicose rooster . . . The completely naked woman was standing there, bathing her bright-white body in the pale light falling from the top of the yurt . . . Temujin had often heard people use words like "luscious" and "gorgeous" when talking about women, but now he saw it himself . . . She was just two steps away, and he could see her beauty and smell her aroma. Gradually, his entire body flushed red and glowed hotter, like a dung chip thrown in the fire . . . Without uttering a word, the woman walked, light as down, to his bed, and lifted the right edge of the blanket that covered him. Now the woman's scent was even clearer. Her long, thick braid, her bright-white body, her breath, her round breasts protruding like two hills in the endless steppe—it was all so stunning, so striking . . . Temujin lay there, bewildered . . . The woman's full legs touched his thin ones, only just beginning to grow muscular. Temujin's body was already burning hot with arousal, and now it felt the fiery heat from the touch of the woman's legs, like the touch of a sword tip heated over the flames . . . The crooked-legged old woman must have lathered them with the same soap, because both Temujin and the female stranger bore its aromatic Chinese scent . . . The woman's voice interrupted the temporary silence:

"Aren't you sleeping?" she asked, gently. Not only was she beautiful, she also had a gorgeous voice.

Temujin said nothing at first, but then answered succinctly:

"No." He simply lacked the strength to answer in more detail or say anything else.

"I have come to teach you," she said. "You are of age . . ."

Saying that, the woman began to gently stroke the forelock on Temujin's newly shaven head. The palm of her hand was as hot as the rest of her body. Partly out of childish innocence, and partly only pretending to understand nothing, Temujin asked:

"Teach me what?"

"What, you ask?" Her laughter was like the sound of thousands of silver bells. Transparent, and somehow mysterious. "I have come to make you a jigit," she replied, and she gave Temujin a gentle pinch.

"I'm already a jigit," Temujin answered, his voice trembling.

"You say you're a jigit? Would a jigit lie here all huddled up? . . . Your whole body is trembling . . ." she cooed, and her palms massaged Temujin's chest. She realized he would not take the initiative, so she had begun her attack.

"What's your name?" Temujin asked. Truly, he had never seen this woman anywhere before, and he had the feeling she was from somewhere else, some other tribe . . .

"I am a Tangut," she answered.

Temujin had been right to think she was from a different clan, a different tribe. She did not speak the way people spoke here.

The woman kissed Temujin's neck, under his ear, and at first her plump, warm lips sent a tremor through him, and then the intoxicating scent of her body and her breath brought him pleasure. She pressed closer to Temujin. The woman was much older than him, and taller, too, and her body was fuller, and smelled like a ripe pear . . . Temujin's little lips sank between the woman's two ripe breasts, and all the scent of her body seemed to be concentrated there, and the luscious aroma only increased his desire . . . Embracing Temujin hungrily, her breasts hung at his lips, and she tickled his face with her nipples, letting them peck at him like quail's beaks, playing with him. When her nipples touched his lips, she said, her voice full of passion:

"Kiss them." When Temujin, his mouth dripping saliva, awkwardly kissed those sweet-smelling nipples, she laughed as if it tickled.

"You don't even know how to kiss . . . What kind of a jigit are you?"

She hugged Temujin more tightly, and each touch was like a bolt of lightning to him, and she rolled onto her back and opened her legs, pulling him toward her. When he found himself on top of her, Temujin's head went foggy; he was drunk with passion, and while until then he had held out, controlling his mind, trying to keep in check his excitement at the way she moved, now, when he was just about to enter her, he could no longer hold back, and his semen came shooting out. That was the first time Temujin felt how his seed could flow even despite himself, till he ran dry . . . The sight of the slimy liquid upset him, and he rolled off the woman's body like an arrow had pierced his back . . . He felt light as down . . . and he was embarrassed . . . He wanted to flee the yurt and run away, anywhere . . . The woman sighed and said:

"Don't feel bad. It's not easy to become a jigit." Quickly, she got up, walked to the hearth, and washed away Temujin's seed with water from the stone basin next to the fire. Temujin lay there guiltily, saying nothing. He felt as if someone had poured cold water over his hot, rabid feelings, but he also felt unbelievable relief, as if he'd tossed a camel off his shoulders. After washing, the woman came back and lay down in the bed next to him. Again, Temujin smelled that thick scent.

"Will you clean yourself?" she asked.

He misunderstood her question, and answered,

"I had a bath earlier today."

"Go and wash . . . After that, both men and women must wash," she said. "Can I pour the water for you?" she asked.

"N-nooo . . . I can do it," he said, stuttering and ashamed.

He got out of bed and walked through the dark to the hearth, picked up the brass jug sitting near the fire, thought for a minute, and poured the water in it over everything he had below the navel, and then he yelped. The water from the jug was too hot . . . He splashed some more over himself, more or less, and went back to bed. There were small, hard tidbits of something under his body. He picked up one of them and examined it in the light. It was a coral bead from the woman's broken necklace. They both started searching the folds of the bed for more red droplets of coral. The woman counted every bead . . . When they finally found the last bead, the thirty-third, they sat down together near the hearth in the center of the yurt and started to thread them onto a string of silk. The work brought them together, and now Temujin felt less shy with her. When Temujin walked to the doorway and looked outside, he saw that the sky had grown lighter in the east, and dawn was approaching. Now the horses weren't snorting and the dogs weren't barking, and only the sound of the distant river seemed to reign in this silence before sunrise . . . He returned to the hearth and looked at the woman, and only now, in the light, did he see how beautiful she was . . . She was uniquely beautiful, and as shapely as a peri, and the knowledge of it kindled a new energy inside him. Temujin leaned over her and started kissing her neck and face, noisily . . . and now, inside this awkward Temujin, who did not even know how to kiss, a genuine masculine passion began to stir. He wanted this woman, right here at the hearth . . . They both fell onto the bed . . . This time, Temujin satisfied all his senses, and felt he was truly a man. The woman under him could only moan, helpless.

"Now you are a jigit . . . You are a big, strong man now . . ."

When dawn came, she got dressed, pulled on her robe, kissed the exhausted Temujin gently on the cheek, and vanished from the yurt like a current of air . . .

He did feel like a genuine man . . . He dreamed of gathering a huge army to conquer all the earth, and giving every woman love, pleasure, the sweetest passion . . . and he remembered what his father said: "A Mongol does not fight a Mongol over a woman. Anyone who fights over a woman is not a true Mongol!" He remembered that, and . . . in his mind, he argued back: "I will fight over women! I will go to war over women, and, if I need to, I will vanquish the whole world for the sake of a woman!" . . . That day, the day Temujin became a man, he wanted to shout those words to the world, and make sure the whole world heard his cry.

. . . Now the mighty Genghis Khan, who had wanted to conquer the world for those words, lay immobilized, trying to seize upon individual memories that swirled before his eyes in a whirlwind, forcing him to recall things that happened long ago. . . . Suddenly a hard shudder shook him. . . . He was frightened, distracted from his mournful thoughts, by a nöker serving as a guard who had walked into the yurt . . . Genghis Khan, at the far edge of life, swallowed the uncountable thoughts that filled his mind and twisted his soul . . . The nöker had brought in the magicians who opened his veins to speed his blood . . . He felt a small influx of strength, began to feel just slightly like himself . . . The snake's venom, which had spread throughout his body, gradually lost strength thanks to the healers' potions, and he began to come back to life . . . After he asked his nökers to gather all the healers and wise men, fearing the future, he was weighed down by heavy thoughts. He told himself that if the strength of the poison in his blood waned, if he was able to get to his feet, if the Creator gave him healing and he became like he was before, then, Genghis Khan vowed to himself, he would begin a new life entirely . . . Instead of dying meekly in an empty yurt, he thought of various things that warmed his soul. He understood that this was only a distraction, a way to calm himself, and he thought about what might be sweeter to a man than his soul or his life, when that man so loves his life . . . A nöker brought in another saintly healer . . . This one said nothing, to be sure no evil spirits or demons overheard him, and he blew on the coals to rouse the flames, so that a large fire burned in the center of this, the khan's main tent, to thoroughly smoke the khan and everything around him, chasing away all the evil spirits and demons. He jumped and stamped on the ground, he beat a drum, he spun in circles, and only then did he begin to speak in riddles, in hints, about what would be or what might be. Spells like this had once brought Genghis Khan relief, and made it easier for him to breathe . . . After that, the healer who had revived and invigorated Genghis Khan began speaking in his special way, and revealed everything the khan had been thinking . . . But now the time of the lunar eclipse was near. At these times, spirits and demons gather strength, and they wait impatiently for the occasion. They do not obey the spells anyone recites; they make use of all the evil that people have within them; they seize the weak, they suffocate the strong in the night, both old men and infants who still have long lives ahead of them and much water left to drink— they want to steal it all for themselves, and they roam the earth, hunting for it . . . They walk from house to house, sometimes crying like children, sometimes howling like jackals, sometimes in the guise of witches with hoarfrost in their hair, sometimes giggling like playful young girls; they take all kinds of faces, and try to imbue complete evil into the sons of men . . . An eclipse is a holiday for spirits and demons . . . And if someone only half alive, someone ill, falls into their hands, that is the end . . . They can easily drag him to the other side, to their own abode . . . Only this particular magician, people said, could cope with them. That is why the nöker brought this one to Genghis Khan. The magician pointed his thin beard high as he lifted his face to the light falling from the opening at the top of the yurt; he closed his eyes tightly and began to speak with the world above . . . Everything he heard from the world above, he began to relate, without skipping or hiding a word, to the suffering Genghis Khan, laden with his heavy thoughts . . .

"O, Tengri!" His trembling voice fluttered, and he stooped like a humpbacked old woman. "May this eclipse bring us good things!" Suddenly, he collapsed to the ground and froze, pressing an ear to the earth, listening to the beating of the earth's heart. He spoke furiously, tossing the words before him, his voice accenting certain words, thickening certain expressions; he smacked his lips and pressed his hands over his ears. "The senses are numb . . . The earth has shivered . . . Hatred intensifies . . . The day of slaughter draws nigh, the son against father, older brother against younger brother, older sister against younger sister . . ." Here, he trembled. His voice lost its power, and the words that flew rasping from his throat became ever less coherent, and the seer's whole body was seized by trembling, from head to toe. "Cities burned, order overthrown, a people destroyed . . . A rushing river of blood comes this way . . ." The healer stood in the ray of light from the opening at the top of the yurt, like a man watching the steppe burn in blood: "The coldhearted grasp for power . . . Betrayal and corruption grow by the hour . . ." He closed his eyes and went on in a whisper: "The day will come when men will rarely die their own deaths, and man's wickedness will multiply, and Tengri will grow weary of the beastliness of his human descendants and push them to destruction and deviation. Yes, Judgment Day is nigh . . ." The healer's whole body shook, like a man touched by demons, and his blue veins popped out. "O, Tengri! The day of vengeance is drawing nigh, not just for your spirit, but also your own mortal body, and all your descendants . . ." The healer collapsed, helpless, at the foot of the khan's throne in the middle of the yurt. "The day draws nigh," his voice rasped out, and tears rolled from under his pale blue eyelids . . . "It draws nigh . . ." He lay on the floor, unable to lift his heavy, trembling hands to wipe away his tears.

"It draws nigh . . . It draws nigh . . ." Genghis Khan repeated through his own dry lips. "Draws nigh . . . draws nigh . . ." He sighed with grief.

There was a reason Genghis Khan repeated those words. That night, he'd had an astonishing dream . . . In the dream, he saw thousands and thousands of ravens, covering the sky . . . They looked like people all in black, returning from a graveyard, and they flew under the cold, cloudy sky like the countless soldiers of Genghis Khan's army, flapping their wings and shouting: "Draws nigh . . . draws nigh . . . draws nigh!" and covering the whole sky with their bodies . . . The countless ravens crowed with human voices and swept over the earth . . . As they soared over Genghis Khan, they cast their droppings on him . . . He felt completely covered in raven shit . . . From the west, following the blackness of the ravens, raising clouds of dust, a chaotic flood of white donkeys came rushing toward Genghis Khan's camp, the kind that usually only fools and dervishes ride, and healers and magicians and wandering lunatic bards . . . In the sky were the ravens screaming with human voices, and on the ground were the white donkeys raising dust with their hooves . . . a whole deluge of white donkeys wearing saddles . . . And those donkeys, their saddles slipping sideways, their ears poking out, did not bray as usual, but shouted out loud, just like the ravens in the sky, so loudly their cry echoed in the heavens: "Draws nigh . . . draws nigh . . . draws nigh!" . . . The Mongols believed that dreaming of ravens or donkeys was a dire omen, meaning the terrible day of God's wrath was approaching . . . The thousands and thousands of ravens soared over Genghis Khan's head, and the thousands and thousands of donkeys raced alongside him . . . The dust they stirred up swirled in cyclones that overtook the whole earth, and that cyclone was laced with flames, one great fire . . . And the fire transformed into a raging inferno that left nothing living on the face of the earth, not a single sapling, not a single living beast . . . And the cry coming from that inferno, the prayers to God for salvation, was piercing enough to reach the heavens, and it seemed those cries were wafting up from the cauldron of Hell, from the people boiling inside it . . . Dervishes, healers, and seers, their garments in flames from this hellish inferno, their staffs shattering to pieces and burning, their hair and beards smoldering, prayed tirelessly, meekly resolved to surrender their own souls to this great force . . . They burned in the fire, repeating, like the ravens and donkeys: "Draws nigh . . . draws nigh . . . draws nigh!" . . . And then some kind of vital force descended on Genghis Khan, from he didn't know where, and he lifted his head and propped himself up in bed, and wrath twisted his spotted face: "Be gone from here! Be gone!" he shouted. The healer had communed with the higher powers, he had conveyed everything that had come from them, and now he went silent in an instant, gazing glumly at the half-dead Genghis Khan . . . This was the effect of his spells and prayers: he had begun to heal Genghis

Khan, who had lain motionless for forty days, too weak to utter a word or lift his head; he had poured strength into him, given him the ability to speak . . . The spark of life appeared in Genghis Khan's slanting eyes, and a weak flush crept across his cheeks . . . Genghis Khan nodded to his nöker, signaling him to take the healer away.

"Draws nigh . . ." Those words were like a knife in his heart. Genghis Khan, who had drunk all the water poured for him in his time, who no longer thought of anything other than death, who could feel the earth pulling him in, was tormented by the seeming endlessness of this final journey to the other world. Shreds of grievous thoughts clung to his belea-guered soul. Genghis Khan knew he was ready for death . . . But the dis-tance from life to death, the long lengths to which his torturous twilight thoughts had been stretched, pressed heavily on him . . . He thought his time in this sad world had already gone on far too long—he could not be among the living, but he was not yet among the dead . . . Anyone would have thought the snake's venom would have quit him in those forty days, but the venom still rode his blood around his body and did not want to leave . . .

. . . They had brought a girl to Genghis Khan that night and put her in his bed. She was the captured daughter of a Tangut khan, a tribe of which every last family had been destroyed . . . They always brought a pretty girl into the khan's tent, for his pleasure, bare as the day she was born, when her turn came . . . Genghis Khan used those girls only once each, taking their virginity. That night, the soldiers brought Genghis Khan the daughter of the Tangut khan, whose tribe he had ordered torn out by the roots. She was lovelier than the moon and more blinding than the sun . . . News of the beauty of the khan's daughter had once spread through all the land. The rulers of strong peoples wanted to win her, and the rulers of weak peoples cursed themselves for their poverty. So many ambassadors from khans and padishahs, and even from the Chinese emperor, brought luxurious presents in hopes of a marriage with the Tanguts, but this young woman arrogantly turned away the ambassadors and messengers without a word . . . Genghis Khan heard that the khan's daughter was more than merely beautiful: she was a warrior skilled as any man . . . The Tang-uts did not surrender to Genghis Khan's forces, and stubbornly fought, to their last man, on the field of battle. And this girl, the one who was now set to rest in Genghis Khan's embrace, had also been in that last battle, dressed as a warrior, and she slew many Mongolian heroes in that bloody slaughter. It had not been easy taking her captive . . . Genghis Khan, who had vowed to destroy the entire Tangut line, decreed that mercy should be shown to her alone, and that she should be sent to join the flock of his female prisoners . . .

This flock of prisoners was watched over by specially trained, castrated guards, eunuchs who served the women. All the servants who served, fed, and catered to them dawn to dusk were Chinese men. It was in their blood to obey every order without fail. When these castrated servants prepared a woman for the khan's nightly amusements, they bathed her body in steaming cow's milk from the morning milking, and rinsed her in aromatic water provided by Arabian merchants, and decorated her hair with Chinese henna, twisting every lock, and dressed her in a silk gown; then they covered her face with a light veil and waited for the khan's order to deliver her to where he would take his rest, and once they received that order, they placed her on a delicate litter and carried her on their shoulders to the khan. The Tangut khan's daughter was washed in camel's milk, and they rubbed her body with honey from the Altai and made a ravishing beauty out of the already gorgeous daughter of the Tangut khan and carried her to where Genghis Khan was taking his rest. There, too, there were rules to follow. When the women had been carried to the carved walnut doors, made by craftsmen from Bukhara, they were supposed to strip bare, and then they were led inside and tucked naked into the khan's bed. This was done out of concern for his safety. That night, Genghis Khan was waiting for the daughter of the Tangut khan, in the place where he would rest, in his bed made of a multitude of blankets . . . Genghis Khan had never waited for a prisoner before. They always arrived first, and waited for him to arrive . . . But this time, he waited for the daughter of the Tangut khan, and he had his reasons. To win her embrace, Genghis Khan had arranged the bloodiest of slaughters, all for the sake of this girl; for her charms, Genghis Khan had annihilated the entire Tangut line. And now Genghis Khan lay there, in the grip of his masculine desires, in order to know the bliss of the Tangut girl's embrace, and take his pleasure in it, there on that towering pile of downy blankets . . . The eunuchs undressed the girl in the doorway, leaving her in only a flimsy skirt of Chinese silk . . . Only girls with their virginity intact could claim such a privilege. The daughter of the khan of the Tanguts was still a virgin . . . Not a single living soul knew how carefully the girl had prepared for this night. Under her short wrap of Chinese silk, she had hidden a snake she had wrapped around her body. When two servants opened the door, the daughter of the Tangut khan walked in, carrying with her a haze of scent, sparkling with the luminescence of the moon, and word of her had spread far and wide, through every land . . . Nobody noticed that while the beautiful girl crawled into Genghis Khan's bed, while she lay there turned away from him, her fingers kept a tight grip on the small head of that snake . . . Genghis Khan had tasted many samples of female honey, but he was pleased by the girl's behavior . . . Carefully stroking her body, breathing in the aroma of her loose, flowing hair, he kissed her neck under her earlobe, and his lips brushed against a coral necklace . . . That coral necklace stirred an ancient memory within him . . . The first woman who had shared his bed had been a Tangut, too . . . Burning with desire, Genghis Khan let the memory carry him far into the past, long ago . . . "Your necklace is beautiful," said Genghis Khan. The daughter of the Tanguts said nothing. After some time, she responded: "My mother left me this necklace." And with those words, she began to weep bitterly, her tears flowing . . . "Her mother," Genghis Khan repeated to himself. He thought for some time . . . Genghis Khan's passion burned cooler, and he remembered that first woman, the one who had made him a man . . . She had also worn a coral necklace . . . The girl was choking on her sobs . . . To Genghis Khan, they were only a girl's tears . . . Still weeping, she began to speak . . . "You are so bloodthirsty! You are so cruel . . . You murdered all the Tanguts, as if taking revenge for something, you cut them down, to the last child! What did they ever do to you?" Genghis Khan had never heard such a thing from a prisoner, and he was stunned . . . The stupefied Genghis Khan listened to the girl weep . . . "I despise you! I came here to kill you!" she said through her sobs. Genghis Khan decided to hear her out. For him, a man who did not know the meaning of sympathy, the girl's weeping was like a blast of thunder in a clear sky . . . Her whole body trembling, the girl sobbed and sobbed . . . Then she froze, silent . . . Genghis Khan did not understand his own feelings . . . The cruel Genghis Khan, who had men beheaded like hens for the slightest impropriety, now lay there at a loss for words . . . "How many coral beads are in your necklace?" he asked her, suddenly, not thinking. The girl paused for a moment, and then answered, "Thirty-three." Surprised, Genghis Khan repeated: "Thirty-three?" . . . A profound quiet settled in between them again . . . Before the daughter of the Tangut khan knew what was happening, Genghis Khan was between her legs . . . The girl resisted desperately, but Genghis Khan's heavy-boned body, lying with its full weight on top of her, did not even feel her fighting . . . His belt was untied, his pants slipped down, he leaned into her with his whole sinewy body, which had seen so many bloody battles, which was nowhere unblemished by scars from saber blades and spear points, and he used his body, its skin a scratched, worn, dented suit of armor, to press and scrape, like a file against iron, the girl's body, smooth as a ripe peach . . . Genghis Khan's powerful hands lifted the Tangut girl's legs, and his organ pierced through her like a sharpened sword . . . Despite her struggling, his raging organ found its target, and the girl howled and bit Genghis Khan in the shoulder as hard as she could . . . Paying that no attention, Genghis Khan went on relishing the honey he had found, like a bee who had landed amid the sweetest nectar of any flower . . . and that was when the girl released the snake that was tied to her waist, and let its tiny head go free, which she had been squeezing between her fingers until then, and she pressed its venomous fangs to Genghis Khan's stomach, all while he labored, coated in sweat, between her legs that were raised to the sky . . . "I despise you! I despise you! . . ." Genghis Khan was caught by surprise, and frightened at the sight of the snake that had bitten him, he screamed . . . As if they'd been waiting for that scream, the guards at the door immediately burst in . . . They grabbed the Tangut girl by the hair and dragged her from the room . . . The snake's venom had already begun spreading through Genghis Khan's body, and he collapsed onto his back . . .

When soldiers came to the khan, expecting to receive their orders to execute the Tangut girl by splitting her apart between two trees, in punishment for bringing a snake to bite the khan in revenge for the whole Tangut tribe, he thought hard for a long time, and then issued an order nobody had expected: "Bring the daughter of the Tangut khan here!" The body-guards brought him the Tangut girl, tied up in camel-hair ropes. Though the guards had beaten her cruelly, maiming her for her attempt on the khan's life, her beautiful eyes had not lost their courage, and they blazed bright with fire and hatred . . . So badly did she wish for vengeance for all her kin, for every Tangut, that she was ready to face death, in any form God chose for her, and she stood tall before Genghis Khan, gazing upon him with scorn . . . There was little Genghis Khan had not experienced in his life, little he had not seen before that moment . . . But this, this hatred, was a surprise . . . Then the words he had spoken to the crooked-legged old woman, long ago when he was the boy Temujin, came drifting back to him . . . He had told that old woman with the creased face: "I will fight over women, I will fight because of women, and if I need to, I will conquer all the world for the sake of a woman!" And when the old woman heard those words from Temujin, she responded: "You will die because of a woman!" That was her curse on him. Genghis Khan had never thought her curse had any meaning, but now, dying, he remembered it . . . Those words tore at his soul . . . He looked for a long time at the brave daughter of the Tanguts . . . When he had ordered her brought to him, he had thought she would fall at his feet, cringing and begging for mercy, calling on God to save her . . . But, when he saw her, Genghis Khan set those thoughts aside. He realized the woman standing before him was stronger than most men. Genghis Khan looked at the girl attentively for a long time, then lifted one weak hand, and ordered, succinctly, "Release her. Give her a horse to ride, clothes to wear, and a handful of silver in a purse." Genghis Khan's words made the people around him mutter unhappily. Dissatisfied voices rose all around him. The guards frowned, too, at this strange decision by the khan. The lordly men around him had partially drawn their sabers, but a look from Genghis Khan was enough to prompt them to sheathe their weapons again. They were not about to oblige the khan to issue the order a second time. Though the snake's venom had already begun to act, Genghis Khan rose from his seat, and spoke to the daughter of the Tangut khan, who stood glaring at him in open hatred:

"I have split many warriors' skulls. I have torn my enemies' tribes from the earth by the roots, razed them to the ground, destroyed entire peoples.

But I have never sent one worthy adversary to death. A true warrior must appreciate his adversary. Only a man who appreciates his adversary can conquer that adversary. This girl proved a worthy adversary to me. Only a true warrior, a worthy adversary, can go to her death to avenge her people, to avenge them all. To someone so prepared to sacrifice themselves, I can offer only honor and my deepest respect. Let this act demonstrate my respect for her! Release her!" Genghis Khan fell silent, waiting for his order to be carried out.

The people around him, who had listened carefully to the khan's words, began to mutter again. Only great men could make as sober a speech as that; the simple people jumped to their feet as if they had been touched by fire.

"O, Tengri! This is not the right thing to do!" said Genghis Khan's son, who stood beside him, furious.

"I am not the kind of man to repeat my words, my son!" said Genghis Khan, piercing him with his gaze. Hearing those words, everyone quieted at once, and silence reigned. "Instead, hang those grovelers, whose eyes have gone dry, and let them see no more!" he added angrily, with a frown; he meant that the guards who had not noticed the snake the girl carried on her body were to be put to death.

The next morning, as Genghis Khan had ordered, the girl was let go, and they gave her a horse to ride, clothes to wear, and some silver in a purse; but nobody noticed which direction she rode in, north, south, east, or west . . . Nobody knew, except the khan himself, that many years previously, some time very long ago, that girl's mother had made a jigit out of the young Temujin, and the two of them had spent the whole night alone together, like two strings playing a single melody. Nobody knew that Genghis Khan still held the Tangut girl's necklace, the one that had belonged to her mother, the one with thirty-three beads. And so Genghis Khan's wish to be rid of his very last sorrow was granted . . .

Genghis Khan's condition grew worse from day to day. The venom stole his last strength and slowly steered him toward the grave . . . As he lost hope of recovery, he gradually lost hold of the last remnants of his life . . . When the inner circle learned the news of the khan's hopeless situation, rumors, doubts, and predictions about the future of the khanate began to circulate. But Genghis Khan did not lose courage, and he hid the pain that filled him inside his cruel heart, not mentioning it to anyone, to avoid giving strength to his enemies or dampening the morale of his soldiers, with whom he had survived many bloody battles; he gave no indication and kept it all secret, so the rumors of his illness did not spread far among the people, and the ordinary men and women knew nothing about it . . . In those days, people believed a cruel word was a lash, and a warm word was a halter rope . . .

The weakening Genghis Khan remained in the twilight of his dusky, vague thoughts, and those thoughts were his only confidants; he could share his sorrows and secrets with them alone . . . His forehead was damp with perspiration, his body was covered in sweat, and he took fright at every sudden, unexpected thought . . . Then a sharp, draining feeling emerged in his heart. That sort of feeling can only lead a person to one thought, which is the thought of Life and Death, and the more his health deteriorated, the more frequently he returned to that thought . . . He saw many things, both awake and asleep . . . In his dreams, he saw countless numbers of black ravens, covering the sky with their wings . . . and donkeys burning in a fire, screaming like human beings . . . Would that he had never had such dreams! . . . He felt Death was stealing up on him through that dream . . . And there were the healers, dervishes, seers, and interpreters of dream, with the robes they wore in flames . . . Within this great, filthy torrent he caught sight of the crooked-legged old woman, who once foresaw that he would have his death at a woman's hands, and he was frightened even to consider what that dream might prophesy . . . The old woman had appeared to him frequently in these last days . . . Look at what fate dictated, look at this thread of life . . . Bogged down inside these torturous thoughts, as if in the cauldrons of Hell, he quietly prayed to the Creator for mercy . . . Once, he had the strength to survive anything; once, nothing had been too much . . . Genghis Khan was now fully in thrall to the supreme, absolute law of life. He felt the words "he was born, and he died" pelting the hide of the great Genghis Khan, under the beating rays of the sun, his own hide, he, who in his time had rivaled Heaven in his might . . . His worries grew, his sorrows multiplied . . . He was losing confidence in himself, with these thoughts of the inevitability of death, the inevitability of Judgment Day, which had sliced like a sharp blade into his withering brain . . .

Once, full of fury and cruelty, he had shattered human lives to pieces, destroying everything, turning cities to wastelands, murdering whole peoples down to the last clan, bringing terror to the whole universe . . . But now the great Genghis Khan was occupied solely with his own problems, thinking, in the last minutes of his life, only of the meaning of death and the meaning of life, the meaning of pleasure and the meaning of suffering, and what it meant to simply live. He thought he must have been born under false pretenses, and he prepared to give up his soul to the hands of death . . . Just as many people had given their souls and perished because of the terrible Genghis Khan, because of his blade, dripping blood . . . Now, despite his grave condition, he thought about the fate of all those people who had perished, with a bitter sigh . . . Had they had time to feel the way Genghis Khan felt now, to sense the meaning of life and death? . . . Or hadn't they? . . . Those questions tormented him . . . Once, Genghis Khan's eyes could not get their fill of death, nor his blade of blood, but now these ceaseless thoughts tore at his soul . . . Perhaps Genghis Khan had thought before about life and death, and he had believed that life was beautiful . . . As someone who had never sensed death or known the value of life, what bothered Genghis Khan now was not the thought of his own death looming over him, but thoughts about the deaths of the people whom he had caused to perish . . . That bothered him, because he had begun to forget about the holiness of God and Death . . . This tormented him . . . These thoughts made him shudder . . .

As Genghis Khan lost strength from day to day, his time grew thin, and there was less and less water left for him to drink . . .

They could find no cure for the snake's venom . . .

When the healer saw the droplets of sweat on Genghis Khan's brow, he knew the khan's days were numbered . . . Only rarely did his wan face suddenly come back to life, and then he plunged again into his ceaseless, restless dream . . . Genghis Khan asked the healer: "As soon as I close my eyes, I see my ancestors. What does it mean?" The healer answered him firmly: "Repent! Repent!" Genghis Khan did not understand, but he repented, devoting his last strength to the act. Again, that cursed crooked-legged old woman stood before him, as if she had come back from the dead . . . Her face was creased with deep wrinkles, and her arms hung lifeless, like dry twigs . . . Genghis Khan thought: "Maybe Nunkur and Mankur, the angels of the grave that visit dead men, have given my soul to this crooked-legged old woman, or told the blasted woman to tear my heart from my breast?" . . . Such were the thoughts that emerged from his bleary mind . . . The old woman spat the water she held in her mouth into Genghis Khan's face and said: "Do not go into the great sleep. When you close your eyes before you depart for the other world, hear my words on your deathbed." . . . The old woman's long speech came to him in fragments, like clumps of wool, and it was not a curse, nor God's judgment, nor obeisance to His Holiness; he felt as if he were hearing her words through a veil of wool . . . "O unfortunate man, who wanted to steal the throne of God, soon you will be split in two, and your soul will quit your body . . . By the favor of those up above, I overheard some dire news for you: dark forces arrayed against you want to feed your flesh to the ravens, and toss your bones to the rats and fieldmice, and curse you with an eternal curse of God . . . The time has come to count out your final hours . . . Your loved ones will come to you, and you will speak to them, but they will not hear your voice or see your face, which they find repulsive . . . As you see your loved ones complain and lament, you will repeat, again and again, 'I'm dead! I'm dead!' . . . You will be deaf to the weeping of death. You will not sense the pain of death, nor the grief of death, nor the terrible sickness of death. You will ascend very easily to the sky . . . Do not fear this, do not fret about it, do not mourn over it. Pray to the Great God of the Sky and beg for His forgiveness! . . . Under you, over you, all around you, everything will plunge into a deep darkness . . . Fear will propel you from behind, and your whole body will be seized by a tremor . . . Do not fear this, because it is all a deception, an illusion . . . From the wordless hush of that great darkness, voices you cannot understand will emerge, and fearful screams, and deafening cries: 'Strike! Kill!' . . . This means that you are drawing near to the fires of Hell . . . but do not fear that, either . . . Move onward, on to the last trial of death . . . First, give Death your body, and then it will demand your soul, both your God-given body and your soul . . . Do not give up your soul. Your soul was created to be eternal, and its life does not expire . . . You must not punish your soul . . . If you give it up, the doors will be shut to your soul forever, and it will never be reborn or come back to life. Your soul will not be able to enter the world of the gods or the world of the demonic giants, but only the world of the beasts of the earth; the way is closed to unfortunate souls, leaving them only two paths: one filled with a bright golden light, showing the world of human beings, and the other lit with a blue light, showing the world of animals. The only thing your God-given soul can find, the only place it can go, will be the human world or the animal world . . . Souls live inside people and beasts, and a soul can change a man to an animal or an animal to a man . . . Your soul is eternal, but do not forget that there is also castigation of the soul, and your soul will bear that castigation. Many hundreds of years after the great Genghis Khan, it will settle in the breast of a man who will be bitten by a snake and lose his mind . . . Your soul will be castigated for the people you destroyed, the ones you annihilated down to the last clan. Take no joy in dying from snakebite: the castigation will never end, and it will emerge as tears of blood in all the descendants who come after you . . . For all the bitter sins their ancestors commit-ted, your grandchildren and great-grandchildren will answer, down to the seventh generation and more! The punishment will be on their heads! The curse will be on the head of your last descendant!" That is how the crooked-legged old woman, who stood before his eyes as if she were still alive, finished her bewildering speech. Genghis Khan's eyelids twitched, and only now that the terrible thing called Death was pressing him to the ground did he feel bereft and inconsequential before the Creator . . . His previous ideas, equating himself with God, collapsed to dust, and he was left empty. The great Genghis Khan, who had once ridden his visions of glory to the moon, likening himself to God, fell to earth like a bird shot in flight . . . There was a reason for his tearing torment . . . How could it all turn to the ash of an old campfire, all the astounding days of his victory, when he conquered all the land under Heaven, won all the riches of the world, and reveled in the pleasure of countless women? . . . He would go deaf, unable to hear the ring of golden coins and the rustling of silk; he would go blind, unable to see the pale glow of gemstones, or sumptuous virgins who moaned all night in his arms, whose playful ways stirred the stallion's heat in his breast. Could it be that the source of all sensation, in his soul, was running dry? Could it be that he would no longer rest from his labors in the gardens of delight and drain the cup of pleasure dry? God forbid! Would his world soon turn so shrunken and poor? Could it be that the Joy of Life would vanish, the force that had always come in song, giving him nights to rest and a virile strength? . . . The cup of his life had been poured out, the world had gotten too small, like a glass of water for a camel, and the life measured out for the great Genghis Khan was being surrounded by demons from every direction . . . Was this the human lot? . . . Why was no buttress created for this world? Why was there no Eternity in this world? Could not human beings have been immortal, with drops of water from the spring of life sprinkled on their lips? . . . Who in this world had ever lived holding pleasure by the bit, joyfully living life so that no matter how much they served up, they never served it all, and it flowed without stopping, without end? . . . What a blind, wretched, lying world, full of deception! . . . Now what was he to do?! . . . A deep sleep overcame him, his half-dead body exhausted . . . All his strength, all his resourcefulness, deserted him in this most difficult time . . . Genghis Khan remembered that he had once sent riders across the world, up and down, to look into every corner and do whatever it took to find for him the elixir of immortality . . . After forty days and forty nights, the riders found a silver-bearded Scholar, living in the distant mountains, who knew the secrets of the universe. They brought this man with his hands and feet bound, and his eyes covered with a black rag . . . Genghis Khan took one look at the ugly old man with the small head standing before him, stroking his long silver beard, and turned his piercing, dissatisfied gaze to the riders. Was this all they were able to find after searching all the earth? The Scholar was short of stature and all dried up, and he did not drop to his knees before Genghis Khan, but stood there looking at him, unmoved, studying him with his cold eyes.

"Do you know why you have been brought here?"

"Yes, I do," said the Scholar, nodding.

"Tell me, if you know!" said Genghis Khan. "They say there is nothing in the world you do not know?" he added, stressing the last words.

"I do know a thing or two . . . But there is much I haven't yet learned . . ." said the Scholar thoughtfully.

"Brew me an elixir of immortality. I want to live forever," said Genghis Khan, getting straight to the point.

"There is no elixir of eternal life, but there is a way to live forever!" said the Scholar.

"What is this way?" asked Genghis Khan.

"A rule for life . . ." said the Scholar.

"Which is?"

"A man must remain a man," said the Scholar.

"That's it?!" Genghis Khan was furious.

"You will have a long life, a second life . . ." the Scholar answered, puzzling him.

"A second life? What do you mean?" asked Genghis Khan.

"Your second life will be the life of your soul, the life of your spirit," said the Scholar. "You will have a long life of the soul. But when it comes to the fortieth generation, it will be interrupted . . . A descendant of yours will be insane," the Scholar said, and then he fell silent.

"Insane?" The blood rushed to Genghis Khan's face, and he felt like twisting the Scholar's head on his neck, like a tiny partridge. But instead of surrendering to his wrath, he let the Scholar finish. He listened because, long ago, the crooked-legged old woman seer had said something similar. The Scholar repeated her prophecy, word for word. Rather than chop off his head, Genghis Khan ordered that the Scholar be stripped bare and sent outside in the nude. The people who saw the Scholar emerge from the khan's tent started to laugh and tease him, and they threw everything they could find—rocks, refuse, animal dung—and they spat in his face and set their ferocious dogs on him as they chased him out of town . . . That night, the crooked-legged old woman again appeared to Genghis Khan in a dream, and scolded him severely: "You stand at God's threshold and search for the elixir of immortality? Why? Why did you tear off his clothes and let your people mock him, spit in his face, and set their dogs on him? He will curse you, and your descendants will pay the price!" . . . Genghis Khan only vaguely recalled this episode from the past, and he began to furiously pray to God for forgiveness, sensing that until his dreams improved, his health would never recover. He prayed for forgiveness . . .

The snake's venom circulated through his body . . .

The healer who had banished all the evil demons and spirits from the khan's yurt, all the black spells, everything that flew at Genghis Khan's head and wished him ill, trying to return him to spiritual balance and good health, now tried to strengthen his body . . . Genghis Khan did not want anyone to know that only hours remained to him . . . So Genghis Khan sent the healer to his death. For easing his journey to the other world, for opening the gates of Paradise to him, for saving him from the fires of Hell, for protecting and defending him, he sliced off the healer's head with his saber . . .

Having sent the healer on his eternal way before his own departure, the khan summoned a commander, a noyon who had served him faithfully, at his right hand, for many years . . . They spoke at length, and there were no witnesses . . . Genghis Khan, at the threshold of Death, told this noyon his dying wishes . . . His sons were whiling away the time, waiting for their father to die, so they could then seize the khan's throne and divide up all their inheritance . . . Genghis Khan did not summon his sons or his nökers to convey to them his last request. He knew when the day of his death would come, the day of his departure, but he did not hurry to express his will . . . Something unprecedented had befallen him—he who had conquered the deserts and untamed steppes, the highest passes and mountain peaks, he who had forded so many rivers and streams, and let loose torrents of blood, he who had razed the entire world: he tried amusing himself with a girl, and now he was near death. What could be worse? The thought was maddening, and it twisted his soul in knots . . . Who could have thought the great Genghis Khan would meet his end like this? . . . He lay still as a bale of straw, and his life was like a dying fire . . . If he had given his soul up to God on a bloody battlefield, if he had fallen in a blood-drenched battle, if he had been cut open by a spear or mortally wounded by an arrow, or if a sword had pierced his heart, then there would be no shame in accepting death before his soldiers, who had conquered all the world like an avalanche crushing everything in their path. Wasn't it shameful to meet death in the embrace of a Tangut girl, and stifling his masculine pride, to hide from his people and slowly fade into death? If the great Genghis Khan were to die a hero's death, a lion's death, his soldiers would lower their banners and kneel, his wives would shout their piercing cries of mourning to the heavens, making every heart tremble, and his sons would mourn their father with the deepest sorrow. Mourning as a tribute, out of respect for death . . . But like this? . . . What shame was this?! . . . A great man facing a death that was not great at all, but rather unheeded, unhappy, and humiliating? . . . As death advanced, Genghis Khan hid his helpless, motionless body from the people . . . The earth gives solace to a dead man . . . And God knew he had one secret he had never told a living soul, one he did not wish to tell anyone . . . Genghis Khan knew that his soul would leave his body on the night of a lunar eclipse, and he sensed that he was surrounded by evil eyes, constantly following him, jinns and peris, evil spirits, demons with horns, seductive wraiths with copper talons, the lowest of cursed men, the souls of the dead, and aside from them there were the cawing ravens and white donkeys, the evil omens, the dervishes and the ogres and the possessed, all circling constantly around him, invisible to the eye . . . They pursued the great khan's soul and his body, to drag his soul away, to feed his body to the worms and bugs, and that thought gave him no rest . . . A lion should not have a rat's death, nor a falcon a raven's death . . . Genghis Khan wanted to forget those thoughts . . . There was nobody strong enough to sully him, mock him, shame him! . . . For days and days, the hope of survival lingered, warming Genghis Khan's soul; death was frightening, but hope inspired him . . . When death came grasping, it was important to fight back and extend the snowy flurry of life, even by a little; his thoughts about life, for which he so thirsted, like for water in the desert, stood before him then like so many shadows: when you chase them, they flee, and when you run from them, they pursue you . . . These wandering thoughts from places unknown seemed to have no end, and even if he were to drown in water or burn in fire, he could not rid himself of them . . . Or was it that a man with an ugly life was supposed to have an ugly death? In that case, why did this misfortune gnaw at him like a worm, instead of snatching his soul away at once? Why did it continue to torment him? . . . It preyed on the weakened Genghis Khan, aggravating him . . . and so, once he had summoned his loyal noyon, he ordered a big fire lit outside his central tent, and he ordered that sacrifices be made to the God of the Sky, so that the aroma of the sacrificial meats would spread, and he could sit undisturbed with his noyon, free of all outside observers; the smoke would unravel even the demons who had come for his soul . . .

Genghis Khan told the noyon that he had surrendered to an imminent death, that the water of his life had run dry . . . The traces of days gone by and the stamp of the past were being rubbed out, and now there was nobody closer to him than this noyon . . . Genghis Khan knew there was no person more loyal to him, in his heart, than this devoted man . . . "I am dying, and I am entrusting my last wishes to you for safekeeping. Not another living soul knows of them . . . Let nobody know of them other than you. Not my sons, not my wives. You must keep my words a deeply buried secret, and you must do everything I tell you, without fail. When I die, dig my grave deep . . . This is what I want to ask you . . . I will give you six cloth sacks, each one different from the others. Seven days and seven nights after my death, open the white sack, and follow all the instructions you find written there, no matter what they say; follow them word for word, my noyon. But I want to tell you, now, that in the last, sixth, sack, you will find a message in which I express my wish to make you the heir of my throne after I am gone. But before that, you must do everything written in the first, white sack, and then everything written in the second, yellow sack, then the third, green one, and then the other sacks, black and red. Here before my death, I have lost faith in my sons, who will fight one another to inherit my throne. None of them would give me a look if I collapsed on the road, and they will not give me a proper burial when I die . . . You have always served me loyally, you have always been beside me, and all my faith and hope resides in you, and you alone." This is what Genghis Khan said as he lay dying . . .

The night of the lunar eclipse was approaching . . .

Not seven days passed before the great Genghis Khan surrendered to the Death that had bound him and departed on the long road to eternity . . . His dying world, his vanishing world, flew off into endless space . . . Who can argue against fickle fate, or contend against it? . . . O unfortunate life, fragile as a sheet of glass, you fall into the abyss, you struggle to beat out your path, you fall and take off in flight . . . Is this the rule of human life? . . . Once the soul soars from the body, there is no bringing it back . . .

Seven days and seven nights passed, and the noyon opened the first sack that Genghis Khan had left him, the white sack. Inside, he found a scroll. So that nobody would see him, the noyon found a hidden, empty spot, and read everything written there by lamplight . . .

My faithful noyon! May the Great Sky be a guide to your spirit! Just as, in life, I considered you my most trusted noyon, now that I have closed my eyes forever, I offer only you my trust. Why have I told you to keep hold of me, and not deliver me to the earth for seven days and seven nights? . . . I thought that by distracting the jinns and evil spirits before my burial and my funeral, I might cheat this persistent death, and be resurrected . . . But it was no use, and as you can see, I am still sleeping the eternal sleep . . . My soul, spreading its wings like a silver falcon, has flown into the sky. Starting today, it will fly through the sky and watch you carry out my wishes . . . If you see a silver falcon in the sky, know that it is me, and feel that it is me! . . . My soul will be flying alongside that falcon, watching you, a cloud white as wool . . . Know that these are the tears of my soul . . .

My faithful noyon! Wash my body in the waters of the river, anoint it with honey, wrap it in seven layers of camelhair felt, and between the layers, place leaves of walnut and freshly mowed young clover . . . The road is long, my burial place is far away . . . Send a troop of forty nök-ers before you and bridle forty horses and load the seven chests from my tent onto seven camels, but do not open those chests; what is inside them, you must not know. These are my terms . . . Along with the forty fast horses and forty nökers, take with you seven loyal soldiers, and a she-camel with a calf . . . After seven days and seven nights on the road north, you will come to a single, ancient walnut tree, growing at the foot of a mountain . . . Only then may you open the yellow sack . . . Do everything that is written there and continue on your way . . . My loyal noyon, as soon as the first star appears on the seventh night of your journey, you must turn your company—bearing my body in a hand-made shroud—toward the Polar Star . . . Whoever you meet on your way, whether man or wild beast, destroy them all, leaving none among the living . . . No man, no bird, no fish, no beast must know where your company is taking my body, where it halts for rest, which direction it is moving! . . . A long journey is ahead of you. Prepare well! I trust you to the Great Sky, my faithful noyon!

That was the end of the scroll from the first sack . . .

Under cover of night, when the first star appeared in the sky, the noyon rode from the camp accompanied by forty soldiers and seven nök-ers, herding before them forty fast horses, thirty-nine male camels, and one light gray female camel with a calf . . . Throughout their journey, they were prepared to slay every living thing they encountered, whether human being, wild beast, or bird in flight . . . The noyon was a taciturn person by nature, spare with his words. He issued orders to his men silently, with gestures of his hands, and only barked out or grunted exclamations when absolutely necessary . . . The light gray female camel with the calf carried the tightly wrapped Genghis Khan, and she plodded slowly at the head of the caravan . . . The caravan walked for three days and three nights, rais-ing dust, never tiring. The untamed desert, where only the wind reigned, rolled past, and there was not a single living soul around, until, finally, the edge of a mountain range appeared in the distance, in the direction where he was leading them . . . Suddenly, they saw silhouettes of men approaching . . . When he noticed, the noyon rode to meet them, taking with him seven guards and ordering the rest of the soldiers and nökers to form a tight ring around the camel carrying Genghis Khan's body, and not let anyone come near it . . . The seven soldiers had taken arrows from their quivers and laid them on their bows, and they had drawn their sabers from their sheaths, ready to ride to meet the strangers and engage them in battle, when the noyon riding at the head of the column stopped them by raising his right hand. This was the sign to be in no hurry . . . Soon, the noyon's men and the strangers descending the slope were within a lariat's length of each other . . . The noyon looked them over, and the sight made him shudder . . . Riding in the lead was an unarmed old man, dressed like a Tibetan, and he was followed by perhaps a hundred people in ragged clothing, whose faces, black from the sun, were covered in oozing sores, and whose heads were topped with dirty hair, and they were hunched under the weight of the wooden stocks around their necks, using their last strength to drag their feet through each step . . . "Stop! Where do these beggars come from?" called the noyon, giving them a threatening glare. The old man, who had been riding half asleep on a bony horse that could barely lift its hooves, gave a start when he heard the noyon's shout. Even before the body of the old man napping on the horse awoke, it trembled in fear at the sight of the armed troop of soldiers ahead. The noyon did not understand a word of what the frightened old man began sputtering out in response, mixing Chinese and Mongolian speech . . . "Where do these good-for-nothings come from? Who are you?" the noyon asked again. "Who are these people?"

"Who are they?" The old man stared at the noyon, uncomprehending.

"That's what I asked you!" shouted the noyon, his face flushed with anger.

"I am leading them to the far-off, untamed steppe," said the old man, his slanting eyes glinting. "They are all damned!"

"Damned?" The noyon's eyebrows shot up in surprise. "For what sins?"

"Oh, their sins are massive . . . they are doomed . . . They're all insane . . . This one," he said, pointing a finger at a hump-backed old man at the front of the column, "acted against God, and that one with the braid is neither a man nor a woman, but he thinks he's a girl, and that one there raped his own daughter, and there's a blood drinker, and the cross-eyed one is a poet who won't write about anything but love, and that one with the crooked mouth was the khan's wife's lover, and that one said the world is round instead of flat. He's a *mudaris* who teaches at the madrassa . . . Everyone you see here, they're all damned, all doomed, the wrong fit for their own graves!" He glared with hatred at one of them, who had a face covered in blisters and eyes sheathed in white. "And this one, if you want to know—he's a genuine man-eater . . . The whole way, he's been crying to me that he misses blood, blowing bubbles with his spit . . ."

"You're bringing them away to the untamed steppe? Then what are you going to do with them?" asked the noyon. "For the doomed, there is no death, is there?"

"No . . . These types have no place in the ground, honorable warrior, and nobody who kills them will see any favor for it . . . God created them all to be hapless . . . I'll make them food for the vultures and jackals, I'll treat the rats and bugs of the untamed steppe to their bones. You know, my fine fellow, if a wolf eats a human body, the bones remain. If a fox chews those bones, the joints remain. If a jackal gets at them, the biggest ones remain, shin bones and thigh bones . . . But after the bugs come, nothing is left . . ." The old man kept prattling on. "There's no higher punishment than a cursed death . . ."

The noyon had gotten distracted by his conversation with these people who had so unexpectedly appeared on the road, but he knew they still had far to travel. Sensing that nothing but death awaited these worn-out beings, he decided not to waste any arrows on them and ride on by; but just then a cloud appeared in the empty sky, and from that cloud, rain began to pour.

"I can smell it, I can smell it! You are going to bury a corpse! Before your corpse starts to stink, give it to me, and I'll gnaw on its bones!" The one shouting was the one the old man had called a cannibal, a man with a stock on his neck and chains on his feet, pale-faced, with protruding upper teeth and thin cheekbones. "Give me the bones to chew!"

The cannibal's sudden cry infuriated the noyon. The louder the cannibal shouted, the harder the rain poured down, as if the heavens had simply torn open with a roar; lightning flashed and thunder roared. "Me! Give him to me! I'll eat him up and pick his bones bare! Bare, bare, bare!" shouted the cannibal, foaming at the mouth. "Bare! Bare!"

The noyon believed the rain was the soul of Genghis Khan, traveling with his body, and he gave the signal to his soldiers: "Slay them all, sparing no one!" Immediately an arrow flew at the crazed, shouting, hungry man, the cannibal who had completely lost his mind. The arrow shot through his mouth, through his brain, and out the back of his head . . . The arrows the warriors let loose, quick as lightning, mowed them all down in an instant, leaving none among the living . . .

This left a dark mark on the soul of the noyon, who until then had not met even a creeping beast or a bird, to say nothing of other human beings, on the first three days of the journey. Who were those people? What clan and tribe were they from? Where had they come from, and where were they going? If the noyon had given in to his feelings and rode on, paying no attention to them, he might have disobeyed the orders of the late khan . . . He could feel the Great Sky watching him closely, using the eyes of the khan's soul . . .

At dawn on the seventh day of their journey, the noyon's men, driving the horses and camels before them, came to a great, ancient walnut tree growing at the foot of a cliff. The noyon told the caravan to rest, dismount, and have something to eat, and he rode closer to the tree. They did not know he intended to burn the white sack and read the scroll from the yellow sack. Away from prying eyes, the noyon took the scroll from the yellow sack and began to read.

My compliments to you, my loyal noyon! In good speed, and without delay, you have reached the tree. I hope you arrived here at dawn. Now, keep to the trail in the direction where the old walnut tree's shadow lies when the sun is one lariat length high. By noon, you will arrive at a full, fast-flowing stream. Travel half a day along its banks, against the current, and by then night will fall. Follow the star Mizar . . . At dawn, after you pass two steep bluffs, you will come to the place where the river forks in two . . . From there, you will again travel west . . . Going in that direction, you will reach a hump-backed mountain . . . Go along the foot of that mountain, and you will come to a narrow, hilly ravine . . . Be wary in the ravine, for old vultures nest there, and they can smell a dead body from a great distance. The whole flock of them could attack me, my loyal noyon . . . Cross through that narrow ravine, and you will emerge onto a plateau of bare rock . . . When you come to the broad, flat foot of the mountain, you will see a great hearth made of stones. When you come to that hearth, my noyon, open the third of the sacks I gave you . . . A long journey lies ahead of you. Mount your horse, but before you do, cut down the old walnut tree, uproot it entirely, and burn it completely, down to the last twig!

The noyon finished reading, then waited until the sun was at the height of a lariat length, and after he marked the direction they would travel in, he told his soldiers to fell the tree, root it up, and burn it . . . After the last twig burned to nothing, the caravan set off in the direction chosen for them . . . The journey was arduous, and they left behind the two bluffs, and the place where the river split in two, and the humpbacked mountain, and came to the narrow, hilly ravine . . . When they reached the ravine, they saw hordes of bald vultures perched on the massive, rocky cliffs . . . The noyon ordered his warriors to ready their bows, and to shoot as soon as the vultures attacked . . . The vultures watched from above as the men rode along the trail, frozen motionless where they sat . . . Their stomachs were full, and although they smelled the scent of dead flesh, they did not move to attack. The vultures had already thoroughly pecked over the bodies of the doomed, the ones the old man had been leading, the ones the noyon had ordered killed, and now they had neither the strength nor the desire to so much as flap their wings . . . The noyon recalled what Genghis Khan had told him: "Destroy every breathing thing in your path." He was not eager to shoot those vultures, so languid and full, but then a silver falcon appeared in the sky overhead. It was the bird whose wings protected the soul of Genghis Kahn. As soon as the noyon saw the falcon, he ordered his soldiers to shoot all the vultures perched at the top of those steep cliffs. The vultures pierced by their arrows dropped like rocks from above . . . The ravine filled with the desperate cries of wounded vultures, trying to save themselves . . . When the last vulture fell to the earth, a wordless silence settled all around them . . .

With the horses and camels in the lead, the noyon and his seven guards in the middle, and the forty strong young soldiers in rows in the rear, the caravan soon emerged onto an expanse of bare rock. When the noyon arrived at the broad, flat foot of the mountain, he saw an enormous hearth, just as it was written in the scroll . . . As they neared the hearth of stone, the noyon again rode far from prying eyes, and he burned the yellow sack and took the next scroll from the green one . . .

My compliments to you, my loyal noyon! I welcome you and bless you! You have reached the hearth, but you will not linger here for long; you will continue your journey. This place is called the "wrathful place," and is not a place you can spend the night; dragons who sleep by day come out by night to hunt, and they devour everything that moves; they roam these bare rock cliffs by night in search of prey . . . On the sunlit side of the hearth, the Tibetan monks have carved a sign, and nobody but you must read it; after you read it, carve it out. The Tibetan monks call that sign the Seal of God. I may have passed away, but my spirit still lives, and that means that I am God of all the universe! There is no God above me! My seal is set in human hearts; while these false Gods leave traces of their seals on stone, I set my seal on the hearts of men like you. He who is strong contains the might of God! . . . Destroy that cursed seal of the false God, my loyal noyon! . . . Wipe it clean, then take the route to the east. You are now just a day and a night from your goal. I know, I feel, your love, your loyalty to your God . . . Go east, my noyon! . . . By dawn you will reach the Great Mountains, whose majesty is beyond all comparison, and at the base of those mountains, you will see a single, mighty juniper tree. Go to the tree, burn the green sack, and read the scroll from the black sack . . . Everything you must do will be written there . . . Be on your way, my loyal noyon!

The noyon read everything written on the scroll from the green sack, took out his sharp dagger, and carefully carved away everything carved into the rocks of the hearth.

When he had chipped out the last letter of the inscription on the stone, the noyon led them all onward . . .

Moving east, they traveled for one day and one night, and then emerged at the foot of the great mountain range extending from that place in two long ridges, and they found a tall, solitary juniper . . . At the place where the two ridges of the great mountain met, there was a foothill, as beautiful as a woman's sleep. There, centered between those two mountain ridges, grew the juniper tree . . . The noyon rode to the tree, took the scroll from the black sack, and moved some distance away from his servants, as usual. Then he began to read what was written there . . .

My loyal noyon, carefully read everything that is written on this scroll from the black sack and carry out every word you read. By the way, have you burned the scroll from the green sack?

(When he read these words, the noyon hopped up in fright and hurried to burn the scroll from the green sack.)

Now, my noyon, read each word carefully. You have come to the tall juniper. It is a thousand years old. This is the place you will bury my body. Dig the grave for my eternal slumber as deep as the roots of the juniper tree and as wide as the reach of the juniper's roots . . . Over a thousand years, the juniper has softened and moistened the earth, and it will be soft as down to me. Dig under its roots as deep as they go. Begin digging my grave at dusk, when the evening Cholpon appears in the sky, and finish before the morning Cholpon fades. As you dig, be sure nobody utters a word, and so that nobody hears the horses snort and camels groan, lead them from here one horse ride away and keep them there all night . . . Pile the earth you dig from my grave carefully to one side, and give water to the juniper you have cut down, from time to time, so that its trunk does not go dry and hard. Pay special attention to this as you dig, my noyon. Before you finish digging my grave, before the morning Cholpon fades in the sky, sacrifice your fortieth soldier, and water the bottom of my grave with his blood, and then cut from the juniper tree the seventh branch from the bottom and the seventh branch from the top, and call forth my spirit, pray to God, and burn the whole juniper to ashes, and spread the ashes at the bottom of my grave, on top of the blood of the sacrificed fortieth warrior. After that, bury the body of that warrior, with all the honors, at the bottom of my grave, after you dress him in my garments, and lay his body head to the east, feet to the west. In the other world, soon after he is buried, two angels will come, from the east and the west, to interrogate the spirit of the dead man about the affairs of the earth, and we will deceive the angels, and place on that warrior's soul the inquiry meant for me . . . Make the warrior's grave marker the height of a horse; and after that, on top of it, make me a khan's throne from the branches of the juniper tree, and lay the branches of the thousand-year-old juniper above me and below me, and weave the juniper branches tightly around my body, leaving no gaps; seat me facing the west, and what I did not manage to finish in life, where I did not set my feet, I will conquer after I die. Dress me in the clothing of the Scholar who knows the secrets of the universe, and perhaps the dark forces of the other world, who fear the Scholar, will not dare attack me in his clothing. Before you bury me, anoint me with blood with one hand, and honey with the other, and as you recite the funeral prayers, when the morning Cholpon fades in the sky, cover my eyes with clay, and then begin to fill in my grave . . . When you have filled the grave over my head, so that my body cannot be seen, take the gold, gemstones, diamonds, and jewelry from the seven trunks the camels carried here and spread it all on my grave; as she guards these treasures, the white snake who is the ruler of these lands will also guard my body from those who might wish to wreak vengeance upon me, or dig up and desecrate my burial place . . . Arrange the thirty-nine brave soldiers in a circle around my grave, my noyon, and bind their eyes with black rags, and then stand with your face to the vanishing morning star and recite the burial prayer for me, in its entirety. After the morning star fades, no jinns or evil spirits can find a buried body. With your prayer, call forth my spirit, and cleave it from my body; only when you hear the horses neighing in the distance, and the crazed camels lowing, and the cry of the falcon that has accompanied you all this time, will you know that my soul has separated from my body, but nobody must see this, my loyal noyon. Not even you . . . After you send my spirit to the sky, your seven nökers must recite the funeral prayer over my grave, and then they must push each of the thirty-nine warriors, one at a time, into my grave alive. After they have pushed them all into the grave, your seven nökers will bury them beneath earth the depth of a man. After that, herd the forty horses to my grave, the ones at pasture far away, and drive them into the grave alive, as well, on top of the soldiers. Bury the horses alive, then cover the rest of the grave with large boulders, lying them close to one another, but no higher than the surface of the earth, and then seal all the cracks with white clay so that neither rain nor groundwater can seep into the grave. When you have done all this, my noyon, take the female camel you brought with her calf, and out of sight of the camel, slaughter the calf with your own hands so that its blood all flows onto my grave, and then lead the mother camel to this place so she can know the place where her infant died, and smell the scent of his blood. This is because you must bring this she-camel back to this place in one year, to perform the commemorative funeral rituals on the anniversary of my death. Before the sun rises, drive all forty camels over my grave many times, to level it with the earth; the grave must be no higher and no lower than all the rest of the ground. After each pass of the camels, soak the earth with water. Before the sun rises, the camels must level the grave; when a camel walks a hundred times over the same place, until his mind goes hazy and his eyes dim, he will begin to urinate copiously, and this is also good, for hungry rats avoid places where camels have urinated, and so do polecats, weasels, and all the creeping beasts . . .

After the camels tread the grave until it is level with the ground, your seven nökers must lead the camel who came with her calf to one side, and then they must shoot all the rest of the camels, with their bows, over my grave. Remember, you will return on that she-camel in one year. She will not fail to find the place where her calf's blood was spilled, even after a year. Very soon, a flock of vultures will swoop down on the slain camels, and they will peck and tear greedily at their flesh. You and your seven warriors must step aside and wait until the vultures peck the camels' bones clean and white, and then shoot them all, as well, then gather the remaining camel bones into a heap and burn them . . . My loyal noyon, there are many words on the scroll from the black sack, and you must carry out every one of them, carefully and precisely. Only when you have finished everything written here may you open the red sack and learn what you will do next. May God preserve you!

That was the end of the writing on the scroll from the black sack . . .

From nightfall to sunrise, the noyon followed all the instructions, down to the smallest detail, as written on the scroll from the black sack . . . The great Genghis Khan was given to the cold earth to begin his eternal slumber . . .

They dug an enormous grave, the size of a pit used to store grain, and piled the earth into a hill . . . After arranging the thirty-nine young soldiers around the grave, their eyes covered with black rags, the noyon began chanting the burial prayers to God, and like a shaman in a trance, he thumped on a camel-skin drum, the sweat pouring from his body, his voice rising ever higher, his feet stomping as he spun in a dance, tilting this way, then that way, his body shaking all over like a man who'd lost his mind . . . Shouting all the time, grieving as hot as molten iron, praying now for the hides of the nökers circling the grave, then for their bodies, then for their souls, then for their hearts, he swept them all up in his frenzy, too, and they began dancing to his rhythm . . . With the rhythm of his drum and the motion of his body—now he fell with an ear pressed to the earth, as if listening to the world, now he leapt up as if listening to the sky—he bewitched and enchanted them all, just like a snake . . . He was not himself. Everything inside him raged and boiled in madness . . . Thumping his breast as hard as he could, the noyon called out: "O Great

God who rules us, have mercy, take us with you!" The soldiers, in all their ecstasy, joined the call of the frenzied noyon. "Take us with you! Take us with you!" They also gazed at the heavens, reaching their arms skyward, and shouted in grief, just like the noyon, as if their voices could reach all the way to God: "Take us with you! Take us with you! Take us with you!" . . . Their call soared over the land. Roused up and out of their minds, the soldiers began leaping, one after another, into Genghis Khan's deep grave, and the noyon's plan to push them in, one at a time, came to nothing; the warriors threw themselves in all together . . . They fell to the bottom of the grave like apples dropping from a tree . . .

The noyon and his seven nökers leveled the grave with the earth and drove the forty camels across it many times. He looked at the sky and frowned; there was not a cloud in the clear sky, not a single bird flying past . . . At the very bottom of Genghis Khan's grave, there was the first of the forty sacrificed warriors, and over him sat Genghis Khan on his juniper throne, and above him were the gold, silver, gemstones, diamonds, and riches that the white snake who owned this place would guard, which she would not surrender to anyone, defending Genghis Khan's body in her protective zeal, and she would come to live here; there were the forty fast horses, and Genghis Khan's thirty-nine warriors who had summoned his spirit . . . It was a thousand-fold mystery, to the noyon, how the blessed Genghis Khan had found this place, and conceived a plan that never would have occurred to any ordinary, mortal man . . . After he had done nearly everything written in the scroll, the noyon breathed a sigh of relief, and slaughtered the camel calf right in front of its mother, in the light of day . . . The female camel roared as if possessed, the foam flowing from her mouth and the tears from her eyes . . . She shrieked, her two humps lurching, her long legs kicking, and would obey nobody; she pounded with her front hooves at the place where her calf had died, out of her mind, flinging froth from her muzzle . . . This gray she-camel, who had seen the blood splash on the ground from her sweet, clear-eyed calf, the little one who had just been merrily hopping about, who had leaned against her flanks and then gone leaping around her . . . she wept, and the hot tears sparkled in her eyes . . . The gray she-camel wept for a long time . . . The noyon let the calf's blood spill over Genghis Khan's grave . . . The seven nökers did their best to drive the bellowing camel from the place, but she kept returning with a shriek to the place where her calf's blood had been spilled . . . The warriors finally caught the elusive camel, threw a rope around her long, thin neck, and tied her to a sharp outcropping in a mass of rock . . . It was late morning, and the heat of noon was already in the air, when the noyon waved his hand to signal for the seven nökers to shoot the male camels . . . They fell, one after the other, to the earth . . . The surface of the grave, just recently leveled with the ground, was now heaped with camels felled by arrows . . . The slow, peaceful camels lay, legs reaching to the sky, while the blood gushed noisily from their enormous bellies . . .

The noyon and the nökers came down from the foothills to where the she-camel was tethered . . . After a very short time, a countless multitude of buzzards and vultures appeared in the sky . . . The sight of the feathered predators was terrible to behold . . . The buzzards and vultures swooped down onto the camels' spasming legs, where the blood had not yet dried, and began tearing away their flesh . . . their numbers grew and grew, and they came flying from all directions . . . Vultures have a special sense for the smell of death, and for them, this was a holiday sent down from heaven . . . When the feathered predators had pecked the camels' bones clean, when their bellies were full to bursting so they could no longer fly, the noyon's nökers surrounded them and let their arrows rain down, leaving not a single vulture alive . . . The seven nökers followed the noyon's orders and collected all the scattered bones into one pile, laid juniper branches on top, and set them on fire . . . The fire burned brightly, giving off thick black smoke, and it swallowed up the remains of the camels and vultures and buzzards . . .

Even after the bones had turned to ashes, the sharp, ugly smell of burned fat hovered all around . . .

The noyon took out the red sack, which he had carried with him for so long, and took the scroll from it and began to read.

My faithful noyon!

So began Genghis Khan's final message. Tears sprang to the noyon's eyes, unbidden, as he read the words . . . This was his Master, he of the great name, he who now lay in the black earth; but when Genghis Khan was alive, when he had worn the name Genghis Khan, at the very sound of that name, the earth trembled, the winds rose, blizzards roared, mountains crumbled, landslides converged, rivers boiled, the steppe groaned, the sea heaved, the heavens gaped open, and he took lightning in his hands, and no mortal man had found it easy to speak his name . . . The noyon felt all this . . . Everything could now fall apart, nothing now remained, as if it had all vanished; his soul, God knew, sobbed in grief, and the noyon felt like an orphaned child . . . He went on reading the scroll from the red sack . . .

My faithful noyon! I have left this faithless world and departed for the world everlasting. I know your value. With you, I never needed to repeat myself; you always carried out my every word. Now read this scroll from the red sack carefully and carry out everything written here with precision. Today, after midnight, you will set out. On your return trip, you will meet nobody: no nests of vultures, no solitary walnut trees, no birds in the sky . . . You are alone with your seven nökers. I am leaving to you my khan's throne, all the wealth I have amassed, all the property I have collected, my armies, the lands I have conquered where the Mongol banner flies, and even my female prisoners . . . I ask you to return to my grave once every year and conduct the memorial rites, and to make sure not a single soul, not a single person, knows the way here. Let me rest in peace . . . Set out after midnight. Have the most loyal of the seven nökers travel at the end of the line, and as he travels, tell him to kill the others, one at a time . . . On the way home, you will each ride with one day of distance between you; the last man will rid you of the others, in turn, and nobody will discover this or guess it is happening. You must ride in front, leading the gray she-camel. A road of seven days and seven nights lies before you . . . Riding last, in the course of those seven days and nights, your nöker must eliminate the others riding behind you . . . You will meet him when a distance of seven shouting voices remains until the khan's camp, and before that, your nöker must eliminate all the rest . . . At a distance of seven shouting voices from the khan's camp, there is a raging mountain river, and there you will wait to meet your last nöker; you will meet him, and then shoot the gray she-camel with your bow and throw her body in the rough water . . . Kill that camel . . . I do not want the beast to be your guide. You are an intelligent man . . . You will be able to find my grave without the camel's help . . . My noyon, tell your nöker that you need to kill the horses you have been riding, and kill your own horse with a dagger . . . Throw your horse's body in the river . . . Tell your nöker to kill his horse and throw it in the river, too . . . At a distance of seven shouting voices from the khan's camp, at the place two rivers meet, you will conduct a memorial rite for me, you will recite a prayer for my soul as it soars to the sky, and, my noyon, you will kill your last nöker with a knife to the back; there is no other way. Nobody other than you must know the location of my grave. I trust you will not share the secret with anyone . . . On the morning of the seventh day, after you travel on foot the distance of seven shouting voices, you will arrive at the khan's camp, and at that time, everyone will still be asleep . . . Enter the camp and drink all the kumys in the leather flask that will be hanging at the highest place in my yurt, down to the bottom of the flask . . . At the bottom of that leather flask, you will find a small pouch of cured leather. Inside that leather pouch is a scroll bearing my order to appoint you the heir of my throne. Take that decree and rouse up all the people; gather them all at the center of my camp and read it to them, taking all power in your hands . . . Please, do not place much trust in my sons, and do not let my wives near the camp . . . Be a righteous khan, and protect the people, my noyon!

The noyon had always carried out Genghis Khan's every instruction faithfully, and now he had a talk with the nöker most loyal to him, telling him everything except what directly concerned him, and he took a pouch full of golden coins from his pocket and slipped it into the pocket of that loyal nöker. This was to signify his consent and his silence . . . That night, after midnight, they set off on their return journey . . . The noyon rode in front of them all, one horse ride ahead of the rest, and the other solitary soldiers rode behind him, each one horse ride away from one before him . . . The nöker who came last of all murdered one of them every night . . . Finally, where the two rivers met, the nöker and the noyon met. They killed the gray she-camel and their horses, and tossed their bodies into the raging river . . . After the two of them held the memorial rites and recited the memorial prayer, after they agreed to continue on foot, together, to the khan's camp, the noyon sunk his short dagger into the nöker's back . . . So had Genghis Khan decreed.

Before dawn, the noyon, now alone, walked into the khan's camp . . . Everyone was still asleep, and it was deadly quiet . . . When the noyon walked into the khan's tent, he immediately saw the leather flask of kumys hanging in plain sight . . . Tired after his long journey, the noyon decided to drink it all, take out the leather pouch with Genghis Khan's decree, and read it out loud to everyone . . . When the noyon had greedily drunk up all the kumys from the flask, he saw the little leather pouch . . . He grabbed the pouch and hurried to open it . . . He felt a fire in his stomach, his eyes clouded over, and he swayed where he stood as if the earth had shifted under his feet . . . Desperately trying to keep his balance, he took the tiny scroll from the pouch, but when he tried to read it, his eyes seemed to be blindfolded, and he could not make out a word . . . The noyon knew the kumys had been poisoned. The poison closed his throat, he began to suffocate, and, unable to breathe, he swayed, the ground slipping away underfoot . . . But even in that condition, before his heart stopped beating and his body died, he made one last despairing effort and opened the scroll . . . He opened it and his eyes bulged from their sockets . . . He saw that Genghis Khan had written just two phrases on this small scrap of paper. His eyes were growing dim, he was losing his sight, and he could not read, only stare frantically at the words . . . They danced before his eyes, and on the paper he saw a splotch of blood, and he thought that there must be something written there to calm him . . . There were only a few words on the paper, words written by Genghis Khan . . . The noyon recognized Genghis Khan's slanted handwriting even as he died of that poison. Now his eyes were ceasing to see, but the noyon realized that everything written on the scrolls from the seven sacks, and everything written on this small scrap of paper, was tightly connected . . .

My faithful noyon! With this I arrived. With this I depart.

The noyon only just managed to read those brief phrases, and when his soul took off from his body, he grabbed for the wall, but the blood quit his veins, and with his mouth and eyes open wide, the noyon died . . . He knew he had faithfully done everything Genghis Khan had ordered him to do; his conscience was clean, and he died the death of a saint . . . For the noyon, the last words Genghis Khan wrote to him stung more bitterly than any poison . . . "With this I arrived, with this I depart." What was the truth behind those words? Why had he left a splotch of blood and a riddle on the scrap of paper? The spot of blood on the scrap of paper was proof she had been a virgin, the young woman whose tribe Genghis Khan had destroyed, the one who had come to him with a poisonous snake wrapped around her waist . . . That night, as Genghis Khan listened to the girl weep, and listened to her threaten him, saying she'd come to kill him, and as he saw how implacable she was, his attraction to her grew and grew . . . When Genghis Khan saw a meek, motionless beauty in his bed, he felt no joy from her embrace . . . But the Tangut girl awoke his desire, and the more she spat and shouted in fury, the quicker the blood ran through Genghis Khan's veins. He had grown used to picking listlessly through the most beautiful of the beautiful, and he had stopped noticing any difference between them, but this girl, fragrant as a flower, planted a seed in his aging sense of passion, and restored his sense of desire, endowing him with a mighty strength . . . Genghis Khan's heart had begun to harden toward women, but then it stirred and began once more to beat powerfully with arousal, and in the arms of that young, beautiful girl, he felt he was in a garden of delights . . . His lungs could not hold enough breath when he kissed her plump lips . . . when he tasted her tears . . . Yet the Tangut girl's thoughts contained nothing but hatred for Genghis Khan, and she disdained him, and was filled with disgust . . . He kissed her lips, breathed in her scent, tickled her neck under her ear with his beard, and pressed her pelvis tightly to him, and although Genghis Khan was no longer young, the strength of passion churned within him. The opposite feeling churned within the girl . . . When he gave himself over to that embrace, when unbridled passion stormed inside him, when he had reached the peak of his passion and begun blissfully descending, when his whole body was suffused with pleasure, the serpent's cold, venomous fangs sank into Genghis Khan's body, but, with his arms still around the girl, he barely felt them. It was a minute before he realized what had happened, and then he tossed aside the blanket, grabbed the naked Tangut girl by the hair, and tossed her out of his bed . . . That was when he saw the spot of blood on the rumpled bedding, and instead of giving in to the rage that seized him, he took a small piece of Chinese paper from its hiding place under the pillow and used it to blot up the blood. Genghis Khan had always collected the virginal blood of the women brought to him for the night, and to save proof of their virginity, he always used Chinese paper to soak up their blood. He did the same this time . . . Not another soul knew of his habit . . . He considered taking a woman's virginity to be akin to taking a major city with a massive army . . . Countless little bundles of that paper had accumulated in his chest . . . This piece of paper, where those few short words were written alongside the virginal blood, was the last of them . . . Genghis Khan's secret was one he entrusted to nobody else, and with him, it departed this cursed world . . . She had been the daughter of the Tangut khan, and the daughter of the woman who had made Temujin a man; though not the khan's daughter by blood, but his adopted daughter, and nobody in the world, not one living soul, other than Genghis Khan, knew that the woman who had put Temujin in the saddle as a real jigit, the one who made him a man, had also received his seed and born him a daughter. The sorry fate of this sorry world, the sorry secret that Genghis Khan carried like a stone in his heart . . .

. . . The death of Genghis Khan, who had once said he would go to war over a woman and vanquish the whole universe for the sake of a woman—that death came to him from a woman's embrace. The noyon was ignorant of all of this, and in his ignorance, he passed away . . .

The noyon took with him, into eternity, the secret of where the great Genghis Khan lay buried in the grave . . .

That night, there was a lunar eclipse.

The Seven

There was no visible end or edge to that all-encompassing desert.

The seven travelers had no food left . . . Their water had run out, and they all longed for just one sip to drink . . . The heat, enough to drive them out of their minds, hung all around . . . They searched for the slightest shred of shade, but there was nothing but the naked desert . . . The Emperor's condition was growing worse all the time. His soul was barely holding on, and as his last strength slipped away, he shuffled along weakly, barely moving his feet . . . The sun's heat was still intensifying, and now not even the usual denizens of the desert could be seen; they had all hidden away in their burrows . . . The Emperor split Alexander the Great, Genghis Khan, Thaïs the Athenian, Kozuchak, and Lear into two groups, and without knowing where they were starting from or what direction to go in, he sent them off to search for shade and respite from the broiling heat . . . The sunburned blisters on the Emperor's neck were starting to fester . . . The travelers searched for shade and shelter until dusk fell, and found nothing but sand in that naked desert, and then they collapsed on the ground, out of strength . . . The worse the Emperor's condition grew, the worse the prospects for all of them. And this desert, cursed of God, showed no signs of ending . . . It stretched and stretched into the endless distance . . .

They left Cleopatra to watch over the Emperor. He divided them into two groups and sent them to look either for a person, someone who lived nearby, or a source of water, and he instructed them not to walk too far, so they wouldn't get lost . . . The Emperor wanted to nap, even briefly, in the scant shade of a dune, just to have some rest . . . Cleopatra, who could not go far from the Emperor, scrambled to the top of the biggest sand dune in the area and gazed far into the endless desert, trying to catch sight of some living being . . . After she surveyed the desert, she returned, disappointed, to the Emperor . . . There was no visible end or edge to that desert . . . Cleopatra walked back to the Emperor, then bent over him to tell him what she had seen and what she had thought, but she saw he had fallen sound asleep . . . At that moment, the sleeping Emperor was dreaming of eternity . . . His dream, wrapped in memories, seemed to lead him by the hand to distant, unknown places . . .

Was the Emperor dreaming, or was he traveling to his eternal rest?

The Emperor's fragile body and his soul were splitting apart. Now, so close to the Holy Land, the Emperor's soul has split from his body, and it has taken on the look of a human being, and there in the very center of the desert it has frozen motionless, while the Emperor's body wants to move forward, but cannot . . . A human being, split in two . . . Which of them would keep the Emperor's crown? The soul, disguised as a Man with a saddlebag over his shoulders who wants to throw stones at Satan? Or the Emperor, who has the face of a Man? Tired as they both were after their long journey, and difficult as they both found it to move their feet, they began a heated argument:

"I suppose you're also walking to the Holy Land?" the Emperor's soul demanded of the Emperor's body, and it held one index finger high in the air. "Well? Are you?"

"I am, me too . . ." The Emperor's body muttered haltingly. "Me, too . . ."

"What a wretched day this is! What a pointless day! Unhappy, unheeding, unseeing wretch! . . . You're a mad, unhappy wretch who doesn't know, doesn't sense, doesn't see what time is bringing closer. It's sad," said the Emperor's soul, regretfully. "Are you still planning to defeat the devil?"

"I don't know," said the Emperor's body, forcing out the words through a nervous tremor. "I don't know . . ."

"You don't know?" asked the Emperor's soul. "If you don't know, I'll tell you. You were born in filth, and the devil, the one you want to throw stones at, will tell you: 'I was born of a ray of light,' and he's been collecting curses from the son of man since time immemorial . . . Did you know that?"

"I didn't know . . . No, I suppose I don't know . . ." answered the Emperor's body.

"Take a look at yourself," said the Emperor's soul. "Look at your chest. Do you even have the strength to cast stones at the devil, when you also have to strangle the devil who's sitting on your chest? You don't, and that's because all you people want is to compete over everything, but you can't deceive the Creator much longer! He sees everything . . . He sees everything . . ." The Emperor's soul took him by the hand.

"Gimme a break! I'm the one you've been searching for!" His soul was getting angry again. "I'm here, right in front of you! Don't walk to the Holy Land. You don't need to trudge through harsh wastelands, ford raging rivers, and cross mountains that scrape the sky. Come here. I'm right here with you."

"You're my soul!" The Emperor's body was seized with trembling. "You're my soul!"

"O blind man, o unhappy wretch, what a mad, miserable wretch you are!" The Emperor's soul shook all over in anger and frustration. "You all speak holy words, but you don't realize the fire in your breast went out long ago, all of you blind, evildoing men! The Creator said, in his Holy Word: 'Love the person, respect the person, treat him kindly, do good deeds!' You all want to hold two hot coals at once; you wipe your mouths with the Holy Word, and at the same time, you live under Satan's curse! You do not fear the curse of God, but you do fear the braggarts who claw their way to power. You do not fear Him! You speak with Him as if you're equals! You are kindling for the fires of Hell, you've forgotten the Creator who gave you life and raised you with love, and you've surrounded yourselves with people who love the seductions and temptations of demons. Where is your faith in the Creator? Because God himself is faith, and the name of God is faith!"

"God himself is faith?" asked the Emperor's body.

"You wretch, why are you looking for the Holy Land in this broiling desert?" asked the Emperor's soul. "Why are you, a man too weak to handle the demon on your own chest, going there, as if you've been invited? To mock the place? To cheapen it and dirty it? Don't go to the Holy Land. It isn't there. It's here before you."

"You're my soul! You're my soul!"

"I am your soul."

"You said you would lead me to the Holy Land," said the Emperor's body, and it burst out in tears. "You promised you'd rid us of our sins! You promised us!"

"That's a lie! It's all a lie! The Holy Land is here. It is me . . . You all would rather live like beasts and worthless men than die like the righteous and saintly!"

"You promised! You're my soul!" said the Emperor's body.

"Yes, you dried-out old stick. I'm your soul! I'm your soul! I am eternal! But you, you who never learned to appreciate and cherish me while you were alive, you're about to die and rot in the sand! You traded me to the devil for a leaky bucket, like old junk at the bazaar, and now you want to pelt him with stones! But he's had the flames of Hell ready for you for a long time, and soon everything will be burning hot! The day is coming! God's day is nigh," said the Emperor's soul, menacingly. "And on that day . . . on that very day," said the Emperor's soul, "on that very day . . ."

"That day will come, and on that day, the Lord will come to Earth," said the Emperor's body, with a trace of hope. "Our Lord God will come to Earth . . . We will die on Judgment Day, on Doomsday," muttered the Emperor's body, stumbling over the words.

"Oh, stop! Prepare for your journey," said the Emperor's soul. "Prepare for your journey!"

"What journey?" asked the Emperor's body.

"What do you think? The journey to eternity," answered the Emperor's soul.

The Emperor was submerged in a long, deep sleep . . .

He dreamed of his soul, ready to depart . . .

The snake, the one that had been following him so closely, crept up to where the Emperor lay huddled in the shade of the dune, and coiled into a ring . . .

The snake felt sorry for the person lying before it. It sensed that the world was small and time was running out, but it sensed that for a reason: there was something that tied and bound these two living souls, something that was right in front of one of them and in the very heart of the other; the person is unaware of it, but the snake, which may be a creature of the earth but is quite perceptive, and listens to the earth—the snake knows. Before the snake lies the snake's son, who has no idea that his father resides in the body of that snake, and who anyway lacks the strength to know it. This person would rather be rid of all snakes. The snake moves slowly toward the person, and the person has only one thought: Kill the snake, but how? . . . There was no rock or stick anywhere around . . . This tormented him, like being fried in a pan without oil . . . The person was in torment . . . Is there any torture worse than this in the world? For a person . . . The Emperor lacked the strength even to startle the snake . . . In his bloodless arms, there was no strength . . . In his thoughts, he wants to kill the snake, and how would he know that his father's spirit has come to him in this snake? . . . His father's spirit has come to the Emperor wrapped in snakeskin, in a snake's form . . . The snake crept close to the Emperor, lying with his head in the shade of the dune, and coiled into a ring . . . It gazed unceasingly at the Emperor . . . While his father's soul was approaching him in the guise of a snake, the Emperor's soul was ready to burst from his chest and flee, anywhere, far away, without a backward glance . . . It was ready to fly . . . The snake gazed for a long time, unceasingly, at the Emperor . . . The Emperor's soul backed away in fear, and his eyes bulged from their sockets . . . His soul, light as down, flew from his body and rose toward the sky . . . Only now, after rising up easy and weightless, did it feel that it had kept an endless torment hidden in its chest its whole life long . . . The snake watched the Emperor's soul flying into the sky, watched his son's soul leave his body, watched it rise toward the sky . . . The Emperor's bulging eyes stared at the endless sky . . . Having his eyes open reminded him of a great secret: if a person dies that way, it means he has not solved the mystery of life . . . The Holy Man had told him that, the one who died in the psychiatric hospital . . . Why, the Emperor wondered, in this last hour of his life, was he having a conversation with his own soul? . . . Seven days after the Holy Man died in the psychiatric hospital, he had come back to see the Emperor. He remembered that vaguely, in pieces, and was not actually sure if he had come or not. Maybe experiencing this torture was what made it seem that right there, right at his ear, one phrase the Holy Man had said was constantly being repeated. He had said:

"My Body is my prison, the cell which locks up my soul. It is waiting out its prison term in my body. It is Me, myself."

"Emperor! . . . Emperor! Wake up, they're coming back! They're coming back happy . . ." Cleopatra's voice made the Emperor give a start. "They're coming back happy, like they've found the way to the Holy Land! Get up!" said Cleopatra.

Soon they had all arrived and surrounded him in a noisy crowd.

"We saw the silhouette of a man, even from a distance . . . he was walking in our direction, Emperor!" Kozuchak told him hastily. "He was coming right toward us . . ."

"We all saw him . . ." said the others, talking over one another.

The Emperor's lips were dry and his eyes felt sticky; his lashes had started to gum together . . .

"Hush for a minute. Listen to me." The Emperor cast his eyes over the six of them, standing all around him, and sighed heavily. "I might be speaking to you for the last time . . . I've stopped feeling even this hellish heat that has seared all our brains and blistered our skin . . . Look, the sun's rays are passing through me. They don't hurt. And those rays of light no longer blind my eyes . . . You cursed ones are all turning your faces away from me . . . even the sun . . . There is utter chaos in my head, everything is all mixed up . . . What can I draw out of this heap? . . . It's all mixed up together, the night and the day, the clouds, birds' cries, crickets' chirps, and the echo of an empty bucket, and a donkey braying, and the taste of colostrum, and dandelion fluff, and horses neighing, and girls giggling, and the scent of a woman's breast, and a torn-up diary, and a puppy's rollicking bark, and the light of falling stars, and a blinding burst of lightning, and the belch of a man who drank too much ale, and a yellow autumn leaf, and the sad words of an ancient old woman, and the creaking of a cart, and the rattling of a train that shakes the earth, and the thunder of a fast horse's hooves, and the reflection of the moon in a mud puddle, and the noise of a mountain stream, and people weeping over the dearly departed, and majestic, unbearable silence . . . and a life grown hateful . . . and the endless, great desert, and the hot, shifting sand underfoot . . . everything . . . everything . . . and this whole unhappy world with its blizzards and hurricanes . . . it's all mixed up together . . . All of this has worn me out, and I'm exhausted . . . My soul is exhausted, too . . . I think the voice of exhaustion is ringing in my ears, like a glimmering melody, like a sorrowful prayer . . . but now I can no longer hear that voice, either . . . I can no longer feel the heat of the sun, or the melody of prayer . . . My soul has been stuck to the earth . . . I promised to bring you to the Holy Land . . . You haven't gotten there yet . . . but I don't think I'm going to make it . . . You can only get to the Holy Land when you catch the whole truth of this deceptive world, its whole actuality . . . I've realized that and found it . . . but you are still looking . . . Forty days, I walked . . . and what I found—what turned out to be my truth, what turns out to be the truth I was searching for—it was in me, all along, and without understanding ourselves, without knowing ourselves, without peering into ourselves, we will never find that truth . . . It turns out that it is in our humanity, in our hearts, which have forgotten that we are human. We are people to whom God gave a soul, every one of us, and we have destroyed the path lying from heart to heart . . . It turns out that holiness resides in each one of our hearts . . . We need to search for it inside ourselves . . . I am breathing for the last time . . . soon my breath will cease . . . But you all go and prepare for your journey . . . This journey leads from heart to heart."

The Emperor released his soul, once and for all, and his eyes glazed over . . . When the snake crept across them, his eyelids shut . . . Cleopatra shuddered at the sight of the Emperor's closed eyes . . . The Emperor had died with his eyes open . . .

Only the snake who had accompanied the Emperor knew . . . The snake believed that a great mystery you do not understand in this world is one you will grasp in the next . . . It crawled over the Emperor's face . . . When the snake slithered over his eyes, staring at the sky, then they closed for good . . .

When Cleopatra saw the snake who had pursued them from the start of their journey slithering over the Emperor's sandy deathbed, she shook with fear. Immediately, she imagined the hulking nuthouse orderlies, and their needles like the fangs of snakes . . . She had always desperately resisted those orderlies who held her arms tight when they gave her a shot, howling at them:

"No shots! . . . No shots! I can't stand sulfozin! No shots!" . . .

Cleopatra

"No shots! . . . No shots! I can't stand sulfozin! No shots!" The young woman resisted desperately, not giving in to the two enormous men whose powerful hands had held down many a nutter in their long careers . . . The people they get their hands on often sob, burst free, fight back, bite, and curse them out with dirty words . . . They're used to all that . . . They do what the head doctor tells them . . . This time the one who had landed in their outsized grip was a skinny young woman, and pretty, whose sweet face could make any man's heart beat faster . . . The woman who had been kicking and lashing out so desperately just a moment before went limp as a flower blossom when the needle entered her vein, and her eyes closed meekly. A paleness descended over her face, previously flushed pink, and the sweet cherries of her lips went dry. Her tongue was the only part of her left moving, and it was babbling disjointed phrases . . . The woman fell into a hopeless sleep . . . Her long lashes lowered, and her hands lay still as death, like the hands of a corpse . . . She had just been frantically fighting off the two giant hulks in white scrubs, but now she lay quiet, in the nutter ward that stank of sweat, wrapped in a sheet. The woman had only arrived in the hospital recently. The staff was aware that the terrifying place was an awkward match for such a lovely young woman, so they gave her special care . . . The mental hospital's head physician even issued strict orders to handle the sweet young lady with sensitivity, demanding they provide her a few special privileges and never take their eyes off her . . . Everyone who saw the woman got the impression she was perfectly healthy, with a clear mind, and one look from her glorious eyes made all the men pant quietly . . . Rumor had it that the son of some king or other had fallen in love with her and declared that either he'd marry her or his life would be over . . . The king and queen didn't consider this daughter of a poor beggar worthy of their son, so they betrothed him by force to the daughter of the king of a neighboring country, and made him marry her, and after trying everything they could think of to remove the first woman from the picture for good, they finally decided to hide her away there in the nuthouse . . . And there was a reason they'd given her a shot today. Soon a man in a black trench coat, black hat, and dark glasses would come to see how the woman was doing and what she was up to, and he'd call her into the chief physician's office and make her recite a Japanese poem about the moon . . . Last time he came, the man had harsh words for the head doctor: "We brought you a mental patient, not a healthy young woman! Is this a nuthouse or a resort you're keeping her in?" The doctors knew that if they didn't give her an injection before he arrived, if they didn't dull her mind, they'd all be in for it. So that was the reason they tied her up and gave her that shot of drugs . . . For some reason, when the woman recited Japanese verse to him, the man in the black hat always turned on the chief physician, cursing him and calling him all kinds of foul words, as if a black dog and a white dog were fighting in his mouth . . . The woman could not make herself forget the one time, during a long winter's night, when she and her lover had driven to a solitary little house on the banks of a mountain stream, where they lit a big fire, and she gave herself to him, that young prince, for the first time . . . When she remembered that moonlit night, she always repeated the lines from that poem . . . And the poem seemed to her to be the only way to preserve all the wondrous moments of that night . . . The man in black listened to her poem, and every time, the last lines of it drove him absolutely mad, and he started to stomp his feet and shout out curses . . . Once the woman began to forget the other lines, when she could no longer recite all four of them, he came alive, and rubbed his hands in glee . . . He wanted to erase every line of that poem from the woman's memory, and, along with them, the memory of the prince she had loved, and there were plenty of documented cases in which injections such as the ones she was receiving caused people to forget lines of poetry, and often even their own names . . . By then, everyone had started calling her Cleopatra . . . Soon enough, she did forget her own name, and got used to the name Cleopatra . . . And as if that weren't enough, by now even the last lines of the Japanese poem had vanished from her memory . . . The young woman had only just been furiously resisting the two huge brutes of orderlies, but now she sank into a deep sleep . . . As her eyes closed, she fell even deeper into an endless dark . . . Before her eyes, all kinds of visions rushed past, like grains of sand . . . Her thoughts sped ever faster, on the wings of those images, things she had never thought of in her life, racing across the pages of the past, and this feeling, while she was neither asleep nor awake, put her astride the slender back of a tiny bird, and carried her deep into the endless dark, to the very bottom of the abyss . . . Before her eyes, like pictures on an endless reel of film, events flashed by from long ago, and she felt as if she were a part of those events, as if she had actually lived in that ancient world . . . In the nuthouse, they'd started calling her Cleopatra, and she'd forgotten her own name, too, and before she knew what was happening, she'd gotten used to her nickname, and started to think it was her real name, given to her at birth . . . That needle, which could kill off all feeling even in a healthy person, driving him insane, caused her unbearable pain with every prick, pain that made her muscles go hard and toppled everything inside her upside down, a pain that shook her and made her foam at the mouth . . . After an injection, she suffers, falling into oblivion . . . Her head cracks open, her heart feels squeezed . . . She thrashes from side to side and grinds her teeth as if she's having an epileptic fit, and tears out her hair . . . This only happens to her at night . . . Later, much later, she begins to feel calmer, and lies there, out of strength, remembering nothing of what happened . . . And this beautiful, stubborn woman, who has only just been raging like a storm at sea, like the maddened wind casting one furious, towering wave after another against the cliffs—now she lies meekly on the old, torn sheets of the nuthouse mattress, like the sea becalmed after a storm, its even surface sparkling in the light of the sun . . . Incapable of assessing what kind of state she was in, too weak to make sense of anything around her, the young woman felt she was sinking into some kind of impenetrable darkness, into the wide-open arms of eternity . . . As if she's been puffed full of air—although, to be honest, she didn't look like it—some mysterious force was carrying her away into the unknown . . . A moment came when she thought she might have left behind the nuthouse and its torments, and she experienced an unbelievable relief, feeling light as down . . . It seemed to her that some spirit, with a hand as invisible and impalpable as air, had revived the real Cleopatra, the one long gone, and that real Cleopatra had entered her body . . . Now she felt like the real Cleopatra . . . This woman had gone into the body of that Cleopatra, the real Cleopatra, and Cleopatra had come into her when she went into the other one, and so they'd basically switched souls . . .

. . . On nights when there is a lunar eclipse, male leopards start fighting over females, driven by an acute desire to mate.

One leopard was cursed by Osiris, and, carrying that curse all his life, he finally turned into a house cat, a dwarf among leopards . . . Cleopatra couldn't sleep from the incessant, loud howling of cats . . . Cleopatra was insatiable in terms of all things amorous, and she had played all her feline games that night, as usual, romping like a cat in heat in her feathery bed with an African bodyguard all the way till morning. The previous day, Cleopatra had gotten her eyes on the black man from Sudan who guarded the Egyptian imperial palace, and during her morning ablutions, she'd followed him and used her little dagger to carve a half-moon shape, which meant that when the moon appeared in the sky, he was to come to her. (There was supposed to be an eclipse of the moon that night . . .) Night fell . . . Darkness began to creep over the moon, and the Sudanese man arrived in Cleopatra's chamber. He knew the punishment that would follow: he knew that, at dawn, he'd be beheaded like a baby bird, and he'd depart life for the next world, with no complaints. After a night with the queen, he would happily accept death . . . In the morning, on Cleopatra's orders, Syrian eunuchs from the palace sliced off the man's penis with a knife and tossed it to the leopard that had been thrashing around its cage all night, demanding a female, longing badly for a mate. (On the night of a lunar eclipse, leopards go stark raving mad with lust . . .) As Cleopatra satisfied her own passionate thirst for sex, she ate up yet another man . . . (What can you say when the Holy Book ends up with a nutter! . . . Even the Prophets make mistakes. The book containing the Holy Words ended up at the head of the bed, under the pillow, of a nutter, the night the cats fought, when Cleopatra ordered the Sudanese man's penis cut off in the morning.) Cleopatra had dictated her terms to him—"If you can do the deed forty times before the night is over, I will spare your life"—but she and her caresses wore him out, and forty orgasms was beyond his strength. The man saw that Cleopatra was not even all that pretty . . . Many men dreamed of her, falling at her feet. Some of them lost their minds, some of them lost their heads, all because of her, blinded by their masculine lust, and many excellent men had fought duels, and many had died, with her name on their lips. This woman gave herself over to passion with condemned slaves, then watched them die in pain. She found it entertaining.

There was a lunar eclipse . . .

. . . The young woman's dry lips occasionally gaped open, and she moaned, and for a long time she couldn't figure out where she was, or even what century she was in, and how she had ended up like this, but her soul—letting her know she was still alive—kept showing her perplexing pictures. Her gaze picked up only a great darkness ahead of her, but she sensed she'd penetrated into a land of distant images, and was now there in the middle of some long-ago life in a foreign world . . . After the thin, sharp needle pierced her vein, her world disappeared, and her eager soul dove into that mysterious world, full of all kinds of events and images . . . Eras and occasions passed before her eyes and spun around as they paraded by, and she felt like a ray of starlight soaring into the endless distance . . . Now and then, her mind reminded her she was still alive. The drug her blood was carrying through her body caused her excruciating pain . . . but the pain gradually faded . . . They injected her, even though she'd desperately resisted the gigantic orderlies who held her down, even though she'd begged them not to give her a shot and cried hot tears . . . Now she lay lifeless . . . She lay on a mattress stinking of sweat in the nuthouse . . . Needles sharp as serpent's fangs kept piercing the woman's veins . . .

. . . Its forked tongue flicking, the serpent carefully crept across Cleopatra's yielding body, onto her stomach, then between her breasts, full as ripe pears, and then around her neck. The snake moved like it owned the place, as if she were its property, and it roamed unrestricted over her body . . . Among snakes, there have always been two inviolable laws . . . First, an animalistic devotion to what you own, and, second, a merciless sense of revenge . . . The snake had especially strong feelings for Cleopatra . . . And Cleopatra coddled that snake, and took it with her wherever she went, keeping it safe, feeding it, watching over it . . . Cleopatra kept that snake hidden from everyone . . .

When the snake slithered over Cleopatra's breasts, toward her fragrant, protruding nipples, it took a sniff of their pleasing aroma, wrapped itself around her neck, lifted its head in front of her face, and stared into Cleopatra's eyes with its own glass-bead eyes . . . The snake saw an abyss in Cleopatra's eyes . . . This wordless exchange, eye to eye, which nobody in the world knew about—and even if they had known, they wouldn't have understood—generated a transfixing eternity of thought and images neither one could quite grasp. The woman and the snake seemed to have entranced one another, and they had a long conversation, the two of them, without uttering a sound . . . (The snake had been a gift to Cleopatra.) The Egyptians called it a Great Serpent. Snakes like this one had been found on the banks of the Nile, and only there, since ancient times, and the local people, who called it the Nile cobra, had always worshiped it . . . Cleopatra took better care of her Nile cobra than her own children, never entrusting its care or supervision to anyone else, and she always personally served it fresh buffalo milk in the morning and took it to bed with her at night. The snake took pleasure in slithering across Cleopatra's body, and it brought Cleopatra pleasure, too, and helped cure her of certain illnesses and painful thoughts and protected her from the evil eye of her rivals and cleansed her of the curses of her enemies. This snake had its own history. Once, Egypt had been in the throes of an epidemic, and people had died by the thousands. The illness struck everyone, from newborn babies to the very old, sparing nobody . . . Egypt's cemeteries were bursting with new graves. The Egyptians rushed to flee the disease, running in random directions. They tried praying to God, and they made sacrifices, but the illness would not retreat, and it started to seem the people would face total extermination. Neither their prayers nor the many sacrificial victims did any good. Concluding that God had cursed them, the Egyptians wept tears of blood. Finally, the infection spread as far as the King of Egypt. Doctors, healers, and dervishes were brought in from all corners of the world, and they lit enormous fires to chase away evil spirits and jinns, and scholars came to mix medicines and potions to fight the disease, but nothing helped. One morning, when the king's servant girl was milking a buffalo, a cobra from the den of snakes on the banks of the Nile (the Egyptians called them Gai) came creeping to the dish of warm morning milk and lapped it up, spraying its venom into the milk. Just as the bewildered servant girl came to her senses and moved to dump out the milk, someone in the palace shouted: "Milk for the king!" Hearing the order, the servant grabbed her milk pail and ran straight inside, without another thought. The milk could extend the dying king's life, even if only a little, so instead of pouring it out, she handed the pail to his servants. Terrified of being punished, she told nobody what had happened that morning, and she shook all over, afraid of hearing that the king might be dead. The next day, when she was still shuddering at the thought that the snake's venom might have harmed the king, some palace guards came to see her. The servant girl thought they must have come to punish her, but no—the king had taken a drink of that milk and immediately recovered his health and sat up in his bed . . . When they asked the girl for the secret that had healed him, she told them all about what had happened with the snake. After news of the king's recovery spread like lightning across Egypt, the people all brought troughs full of milk to the banks of the Nile and left them near the serpents' lairs, and then they drank the milk with the snake venom in it. The terrible disease that had killed so many stopped spreading. Ever since then, Egyptians have prayed to snakes and considered them sacred. The king issued a decree: anyone who killed a snake would have their hand cut off. Egyptians thought of snakes as spiritual teachers . . . When they married off their daughters, Egyptians included a snake in the dowry . . . The snake crept across Cleopatra's glowing white body, reveling in her scent, sweet as figs . . . So many hands had caressed this miraculous body, and while those hands and their owners were long gone, now, the snake could smell the traces they had left on the woman's body . . . Cleopatra didn't shudder at the cold touch of the snake's skin; in fact, it aroused her, and brought her pleasure . . . For a while, she could ignore the sorrowful thoughts that lay over her heart like a black storm cloud: the so recently departed spirit of Caesar, object of her soul's desire; Mark Antony, whom she grieved over, whom she'd given an army and sent off to die; and then there was her worry about what would happen to her children, held hostage by Octavian, and the horrible fate of Caesarion, who they were sure to punish soon—all this retreated in the face of her overwhelming arousal . . . Once she caught the sweet scent of a fleeting escape from life, she gave herself over to weighing and evaluating days gone by, reviewing all the pages of her life, one by one . . . There was her cunning, there were all her plans . . . Now the plans and the cunning both seemed to have drifted far from the great queen's reach . . . She was looking straight into the face of death, and she was ready to prove she'd never be a plaything for that hateful Octavian. Octavian's desire to celebrate his victory in the streets of Rome, to make the great queen parade barefoot there so the people could abuse her and shower her with curses—that would never happen. What could possibly be worse? . . . Death would be better. Death was the highest court! That thought drew her in . . . Rome would never see her shame. Cleopatra was preparing herself for the long trip to the next world, where she'd meet both Caesar and Antony again . . . She wants to pause right here, for a moment . . . She wants to get a better grip on all these loose threads of thoughts . . . Right this instant . . . right this instant . . . Thoughts of loosening garments swarmed through her head . . . thoughts like that only come to someone who's not afraid of death . . .

Then there was the snake . . . On her body, it sniffed out traces left by the hands of Caesar, favorite of the Moon, and Antony, favorite of the Sun, and her worthless brother Ptolemy, and the slaves who appeared day after day and met their deaths in her embrace, and the eunuchs who would stop at nothing to satisfy her untamed lust . . . The snake stuck out its forked tongue, and there, on Cleopatra's body, it felt like it was in paradise . . .

The queen's crown on Cleopatra's head, her golden bed, her pillow stuffed with priceless, milk-washed down, and the light breeze washing over her like a blessing from the Nile . . . It was all heaven on Earth . . . Her servants Charmion and Eiras, never more than a step away from Cleopatra's golden bed, loyally awaited her mercy and kindness . . .

As Cleopatra lay there without speaking, one more thought emerged among all the others in her head: the thought of one slave she'd spent a night with . . . and the thought of her Syrian eunuchs . . . When she remembered them, she realized they were the only ones who had been able to satisfy her untamed lust, and she gave herself over fully to remembering that night of passion and pleasure . . . And the more she thought about that untamed lust of hers, the more powerful was her desire to satisfy it. In that, she felt no different from any wild animal . . . Cleopatra knew women were capable of deceiving the entire world, that there was no force in the world powerful enough to overwhelm a woman's brain and ingenuity . . . She had realized, a long time ago, how powerless rational thought was before a woman like her . . . Given how she could spend the afternoon lounging with Antony in a bathtub full of goat's milk and Colchian honey, giving herself over to every possible pleasure, and then steal more satisfaction from her slaves in the night, she figured there must not be a single force in the world more powerful than her own cunning . . . Cleopatra had Syrian eunuchs for bodyguards, too, whom she put to work assuaging her unbridled desires, bringing her pleasure . . . She had her own magical ways of achieving bliss. No woman but Cleopatra had discovered the secret to that particular satisfaction. At night, she used to personally lock five Syrian eunuchs in the lions' cage in the palace, to make sure the eunuchs understood that pain and suffering followed pleasure, and then she simply enjoyed the sight of the eunuchs' tortured death as the lions tore apart their bloodied bodies . . . Cleopatra had sent Antony to certain death, but she was not yet broken. She knew, she was certain, that Octavian's cruel plans to celebrate his victory would never come to pass . . . Now she spent no time thinking about Octavian's vow to parade her barefoot through the streets of Rome, mocking the beauty which had driven so many men out of their minds, and bringing out all the people of Rome to rain dirty words down on Cleopatra and spit in her face. No, she had decided to meet her death with dignity, and now she lay there paying no attention to her abbreviated thoughts and minor terrors, submerging herself in the memory of the pleasures and satisfactions of days gone by, remembering nights of lust and loveplay, wishing she could relive them all, wrapped in the embrace of the sweetest daydreams . . . She was wandering in a paradisaical garden of perfect moments, swimming free in the paradisaical sea of the past. So many people had given their lives for the sake of Cleopatra's embrace. So many had enslaved themselves, lost their minds, kissing every inch of her body. When she remembered all the men who had kissed her so passionately, losing all semblance of humanity

and transforming into beasts, and when she remembered the feeling of
revulsion and disgust she felt when she regarded them from the peaks of
her own passion, she had to smirk a little . . . Cleopatra saw herself as the
empress of human senses, no, more than that, a goddess, and now she was
lying completely undressed in her bed of gold, with her lover, a venomous serpent. . . . Truly, she had a gorgeous body. Her body had the scent
of almonds, as if she were simply made for love, as if every lovely bend of
her perfect toes, her waist, her bouncing breasts, her swagger, her gaze
(which made men melt like snow in the sun) . . . Nobody could resist a
woman like her, and anyone would happily die for merely a glance from
her; what was death compared to red-hot, untamed lust? . . . Her servant
Charmion brought her a small piece of pressed silver, shaped like a leaf,
where somebody had written a vow of love. The servant didn't know where
it had come from. She'd found it that morning when she was tidying up
the queen's golden bed. Cleopatra had taken it off the neck of the man
from Sudan. She'd asked him about the writing on that silver leaf, and he
told her that, back home, he had once loved the daughter of a chieftain,
and she felt the same, and love blazed up between them, but when some
servants found out, they told their master. The chieftain, furious, gave the
order to have the man's head cut off, but his daughter fell at his feet and
begged him, in tears, to spare her lover's life. So the chieftain had him sold
into slavery, instead, to some merchants from Egypt . . . The chieftain's
daughter wrote those words of love on the silver leaf, and hung it around
his neck like an amulet, telling him never to take it off . . .

Cleopatra drifted smoothly along on the wings of those memories,
which passed, one after another, through her mind . . . For some reason, she especially remembered that black-skinned man from Sudan . . .
Spending the night with him revealed to her what a true man could do.
She had never experienced a virility like that, stamina like that, not in
Caesar, who had conquered half the world, nor in Antony, who had been
out of his mind with love, nor from her effeminate brother Ptolemy . . .
That night, she reached the very apex of bliss, and the sheer pleasure of
it made her head spin, like she'd sipped the intoxicating wine of unre-
strained lust, like she'd submerged herself in the sweetness of the highest
form of pleasure, and she stopped even being aware of the male body

penetrating her own, so far above the clouds was she then, seemingly far beyond all worldly senses . . . Yes, she shot up to the heavens, leaving the whole pointless world behind, all the palace intrigues, and at the peak of pleasure she crossed over from the mortal world to a paradisaical garden . . . In that garden, she met the god Ra, and when she conversed with him she discovered the secrets of this world. She learned that you could walk right up to the gods and speak with them, once you climbed the ladder of ecstasy; she already thought of herself as a peer of the Creator, thinking she might as well call herself a goddess . . . But this utter bliss was too fleeting, and that amazing world shattered under the huffing and puffing of the Sudanese man. Her world of pleasure collapsed, the mighty, ebullient wings of her feelings broke down and stalled, and she felt like a snuffed-out bonfire . . . But still, he'd managed to lift her to those heights on the strength of his passion, and he'd helped her sip that honey, so she didn't have him executed, and he lived another day . . . The following night that bonfire of love was lit again, and they rode that passion, light as air, off through the seas of pleasure once more . . . It was so unfortunate that anyone who ended up in Cleopatra's embrace seemed to have their head chopped off the very next day, and after that, those heads were displayed for public view . . .

There was a lunar eclipse . . .

(They say that the Holy Book was sent down from Heaven that night. They say the Holy Book was sent down to save the world from certain death. That night, there was a lunar eclipse . . . Have you ever heard of anything so ironic? . . .) As the queen's final minute approached, the tearful Charmion and Eiras, feeling as if their souls had gone up in flame a thousand times and been reborn, did everything they could to hang on to Cleopatra, refusing to surrender her and her unearthly beauty to the other world . . . The sound of the bloody battle raging outside the palace gates came closer and closer . . . Any time now, Octavian's soldiers would burst inside, chain the queen's lovely arms and legs, drag her from the palace by her hair onto the war-torn streets of the city, and shove her through them like human garbage . . .

The terror was drawing near, but Cleopatra went back to peruse the volumes of her astonishing memories and was soon fully absorbed in one of them. She remembered the pleasures the Syrian eunuchs had brought her, the ones who'd done their utmost to banish Cleopatra's ever-present ennui. No earthly pleasure could compare with those fantastic nights. They satisfied every side of her lust! . . . The pleasure they brought her was the reason Cleopatra always kept them at hand, like pets, like fancy birds in a cage . . . Once, one of those fantastical nights went farther . . . That night, the eunuchs whisked Cleopatra to the climactic peak of paradise and pleasure, where her every desire came true. No person before her had ever visited that place, or even sensed it existed . . . Those feelings of satisfied passion carried her to seventh heaven, where, once again, she met the god Ra . . . This time, Ra was not pleased to see her, as he'd been before. He was in a grim and disapproving mood, and the leaves fell from the trees and the flowers wilted all over paradise; the sweet scents and sing-ing birds all disappeared, and it seemed every living thing had dropped dead . . . Ra's divine crown was coated in rust, and he seemed to have lost his joyful radiance . . .

Ra told Cleopatra how displeased he was: "Here you are in seventh heaven, where no mortal has ever set foot, and you experienced no suf-fering or deprivation to reach this place . . . I know that you climbed to the peak of human bliss, so you think you're my equal, but this is the road to nowhere, a false path! . . . Eventually the day will come when you will know the torment of true penance. Take no pleasure in today's good for-tune. Think about what is coming," he said. He said that, and vanished. Waking from that trance, Cleopatra felt as if she'd plunged straight from seventh heaven down to the cold, hard ground . . . Now, suddenly, one radiant thought, light as air, consoled her . . . That thought intrigued her and settled firmly into her mind. The thought was there, but expressing it in words was vexingly difficult . . . (Let us recall the words of Akutagawa, whose story "Faint Smiles of the Gods," for all its style, was obtuse, and who said: "Much to their misfortune, and unlike us, the gods cannot commit suicide.") She realized that even if she died, her soul would be immortal. She did not want her soul to suffer. She might have been able to plunge a dagger into her heart, or slip a noose around her neck and hang herself, but she could not do it . . . She couldn't, because what she needed was a way to embrace death without any pain and weeping . . .

She didn't want to remain among the living until Octavian came for her! She did not want to become a toy for him, and die a shameful death; she did not want to walk the streets of Rome with chains on her arms and legs, listening to the Roman catcalls . . . She decided to die with dignity . . . Realizing how close death was, now, completely changed her view of the world. She hadn't used her brains, or her cunning, or her beauty to take the golden throne of the monarchy, and perhaps that had been a mistake; she had brains and cunning and beauty, after all . . . but she also had a special understanding, a view of the world, and her striking feminine charisma. Long ago, she had dreamed of the day when she would declare herself queen and goddess of all Egypt, an equal to Ra . . . But she did not know, then, that only sheer purity could deliver that to her . . . Cleopatra had replaced the human feeling for love with an animalistic feeling for copulation, heartfelt adoration with artifice and lust. She thought she was the Goddess of Love, but she was enslaved to her own instincts, believing she could use sex to solve all the world's problems . . . Her jealousy and thirst for power had driven her to drown her brother Ptolemy, poison her other brother, kill her younger sister Arsinoë . . . In Cleopatra's hands, life and death resided together, and always in competition . . .

The snake crept along her calves and thighs, and when it reached her most delicate place, it bit. She never felt the snake's slender fangs penetrate her white, white body . . . A wave of heat washed over her, the venom, hot as fire . . . The venom spread throughout Cleopatra's body, and soon its power hit her small, throbbing heart. For the woman who had called herself the Goddess of Love, who'd kindled lust in men, who'd driven many of them to their graves and torn others out of their graves, those two drops of serpent's venom reminded her that she was no different from any other woman. Cleopatra had yearned not for love, but for wealth and power, for the satisfaction of all her desires, and now her false, vengeful, unforgiving soul was sputtering out . . .

This particular female of the species did not depart for the next world at the peak of feeling; she did not die like a great woman, or like the mistress of magnificent passions, but rather like a slave to the filthiest, basest feelings and desires . . . Oh, yes, Cleopatra realized she was only a lowly female, and she only realized it now, as the flickering light in her eyes went dim, and her long lashes slowly lowered to cover, forever, her dying eyes . . . She departed this world, in which she had striven so insatiably not for the sake of genuine feelings, not for love, but for wealth, the wealth of a saccharine life . . .

. . . The snake's fangs pierced into Cleopatra . . .

. . . The snake's fangs pierced into Cleopatra . . .

"No shots! No shots! . . . I can't stand sulfozin! No shots! . . . No shots! No shots!" . . .

She slept . . .

. . . She dreamed . . .

In that dream, she was deep in the limitless universe of sleep . . . She understood nothing. The vicious heat injected by the needle seized her whole body, broke it, and made her sweat, and while she had just been shouting like a madwoman, trying to escape the pain that pierced her entire body, now she felt light as down, like a peri flying, wings outspread, across the sky, her mind empty, and before her, paying her no attention, a whole parade of dreams marched by . . . She couldn't make out the insignia fluttering along before her, she couldn't get a good look at the procession, and soon the sheer speed of it all made her tired . . . Suddenly, she heard human shouts and roars, and saw herself, barefoot, in a thin white dress, on a wide road . . . It was a Roman road . . . The majestic Capitolium rose before her . . . There were chains on her arms and legs, and people thronging both sides of the street . . . "Hail Octavian! Death to Cleopatra!" came the shouts, deafening, from the right and the left . . . She realized she was on a street in Ancient Rome. Before her and behind her were columns of guards, leading Cleopatra down those Roman streets. And on both sides, there were the shouted curses and hateful eyes, as if the people wanted to eat Cleopatra alive . . . Where her crown should be, her head bore a tin plate, and sometimes the pebbles they threw at her hit the plate, making it ding . . . Women made terrible faces at her, their fingers pulling their eyes and mouths askew, and the men grabbed their crotches and pointed at her and mocked her . . . Other people ran up to spit in her face with glee . . . The young woman wondered what crime she had committed to face such a punishment. Had the Romans confused her with Cleopatra and taken her for that whore of a queen? . . . Her mind just could not process it . . .

The woman had a name, a very pretty name, only ever since she had come to the nuthouse, people had called her Cleopatra (an inner voice whispered: "I am my second Me!") . . . The nuthouse's head doctor had given her the name Cleopatra . . . Had Rome ever seen such a spectacle? Everyone was there, old people and babies, kids and teens . . . They came out on the streets of Rome and flung at her every piece of filth the city could offer, doused her with buckets of it, an endless downpour . . . (You can reach the magnificent city of Rome—and everyone used to dream of going there, emperors, traitors, swindlers, perverts, carnies, politicians, poets, artists, musicians, hooligans, marauders, pickpockets, mafia men, fascists, communists, fancy-pants, Huns, Timurids, dabblers, prostitutes, scandalmongers, devotees, religious fanatics, and victors of all types—you can reach Rome by any road, all roads lead to Rome, paradisaical Rome, the Rome of tricksters and frauds, the Rome of whores and prostitutes, the Rome of powerbrokers and rogues, the Rome of the great and the damned. And here she was, walking down a famous street of the famous city, walking down a Roman avenue. She walked, subjected to filth, through the city of filth. It wasn't supposed to be her, walking there. It should have been Cleopatra, who had outsmarted her humiliation, shed it and escaped for the next world. Sometimes even Death leads to Victory! . . .)

The sharp rocks made the young woman's bare feet bleed. What had she done to incur the wrath of all these Romans who hated Cleopatra? . . . It seemed this Roman street of shame would never end. A luxurious-looking carriage decked out in gold was coming her way. (This was Octavian's carriage. Octavian, in his victory, was enjoying Cleopatra's shame on the streets of Rome.) And suddenly, in that carriage, she saw the ruler of the Nation of Nutters, and his wife sitting next to him. She didn't see any sign of their son, the man she loved, sitting with them. It was because their boy had already been married to the daughter of the ruler of a neighboring realm that his father, the king, ordered the unfortunate young woman locked in the nuthouse. She'd been there ever since. They hounded her, not leaving her alone even in her dreams, where they perched in the triumphant Octavian's golden carriage and looked down haughtily, disdainfully, as the girl suffered, shaming her before all of Rome. Drums beat, louder and louder. And the crowd howled along with them: "Death to

Cleopatra! Death to Cleopatra! Death to the whore!" Their jeers presaged some catastrophe, and the street seethed and writhed with excitement till it was unrecognizable. Such was the punishment, for this young woman, for holding on so tight to her love, for not surrendering her love for the king's son. On both sides of the street, the throngs of Romans roared louder, which meant the death sentence had now been handed down . . . The eyes of the multitudes gathered here were full of cruelty, vicious. Rome bellowed like a dragon released: "Death to Cleopatra! Death to the prostitute! Death to the whore!" The girl began going deaf from their shouts. The king of the Nation of Nutters and his wife might as well have been beating the devil's drum, and their encouragement added energy to the people's fury against her, the young woman walking barefoot, feed bloodied, across the thorns and garbage they tossed before her . . . They'd decided to hang Cleopatra on the square near the Capitolium, in view of the whole buzzing crowd. There was a gallows erected on a dais in the square before the Capitolium, and they led her there to the intensifying thunder of the drums, surrounded by the countless excited throngs . . . The multitudes crowded around the king of the Nation of Nutters and his queen, who had descended from their golden carriage and taken up places of honor under a canopy, and the crowd went on shouting relentlessly: "Hail Octavian! Hail the emperor!" It was exceedingly strange that the Romans never realized it wasn't Emperor Octavian sitting there in the place of honor, but the king of the Nation of Nutters, and they went on screaming and hailing him like crazy. There was a laurel wreath ringing the golden crown atop the king's bald head, and in his hands, he held a golden staff, and there was a chain of diamonds around his neck. When the accused woman was led to the gallows they had erected on the dais in the square in front of the Capitolium, the hate-filled crowd exploded with shouts that rent the sky. The Romans had yearned for this moment for a long time, and now their excitement hit its peak. The hatred they all felt for Cleopatra stank of the blood that fueled human predators . . . They led the young woman across the dais to the gallows that stood in the center . . .

In an instant, the banging of the drums and the roaring of the crowd stopped, and it was so quiet you could have heard a fly's wings beating the air. The bodice of Cleopatra's dress was torn, her thick black braid,

gleaming in the sun, had come unraveled, the mischievous wind played
with her loose, wild hair, and she covered her pale face, where not a drop
of blood remained, with her hands . . . She felt no shame before the multitudes surrounding her on all sides. She could only think of how this was
all because of her love for the son of the King of Nutters, her burning love,
in punishment for which they'd shut her away in the nuthouse. There in
that country of nutters, they thought an ordinary girl falling in love with a
prince was as terrible as a man acting against God. Now they were delight-
ing in her agony, relishing the chance to punish the girl and her feelings.
Her eyes searched and searched, but the young woman could not find the
man she loved in the multitudinous crowd. She could bear being punished for true love, for her feelings, which she considered to be of a higher
order than death, but these Romans didn't mean to execute her! She was
here in Cleopatra's place, and she had no desire to take Cleopatra's punishment. The young woman did not want to answer for Cleopatra's faults,
even if she was willing to bear any punishment for the sake of her own
love. So, instead of trembling in fear, she held her head and eyes high,
her eyes full of love and sadness, burning with the fire of love, and looked
death straight in the face. She would sacrifice her life for love by slipping
her head into the noose . . . This fit the rules of this deceptive world, where
black was made white and white was made black . . . As she put the noose
around her pale, white neck, the young woman froze, straight as an arrow.
The noose against her smooth, pale skin felt like a cold snake coiling
around her neck, and she felt revulsion . . . When the executioner gave the
rope a tug, she started to choke, there wasn't enough air . . . The Romans
must have gone blind, they couldn't see who was who, they mistook the
king of the Nation of Nutters sitting on the elevated golden throne for
Octavian, who burned with hatred, and mistook the young woman for
the real Cleopatra, not the one whom the nuthouse inmates all called
Cleopatra. That was all there was. Was this her punishment, her castigation? The young woman closed her eyes . . . And she saw the clear blue
sky . . . In the sky was the man she loved, the one who'd awakened love
inside her, the one for whose love she had given her life . . . He was rushing
toward her, like a falcon in a dive, wings folded back . . . Any moment now
he would reach her, embrace her, and carry her high into the blue sky . . .

The young woman whispered weakly: "It's me . . . me . . . I'm not Cleopatra . . . I'm here . . ." She repeated those phrases, barely moving her dry, dying lips, barely shifting her tongue . . . The young woman remembered the long winter night she'd spent with her lover . . . That night, in a thin white dress, her hair loose and wild, she'd recited Japanese poetry in her quiet, gentle voice:

Oh, how light, light
Oh, how light, light, light
Oh, how light, light
Oh, how light, light, light, light
Is the moon!

The young man drew closer, and she caught the scent of his breath, any second now and he'd kiss her neck . . . Closer, closer, and the distance between them kept dwindling . . . Now the young man stood before her . . . When she lifted her eyes, framed by their long lashes, she saw this young man before her . . . but he looked nothing like her lover . . . Before her stood Kozuchak, who lived in the nuthouse, just like her . . . When the film cleared from her eyes, she recognized Kozuchak . . . She said, "I am not Cleopatra," and he whispered back, "No, no, you are Cleopatra . . . You are the real Cleopatra! But even more beautiful!" The girl shuddered, and could feel every broken place in her body, so broken, so broken . . . The sulfozin injected with that sharp needle had spread throughout her body, her lips trembled, she felt like her bones were shattering, and she shook . . . Kozuchak handed her some cold tea . . . She drank it all up thirstily . . . Kozuchak was the youngest patient in the nuthouse, and so the people there called him Kozuchak, the sacrificial lamb . . . He was always saying he had to save people, save them from the devil's claws, and he had to burn Satan on a bonfire . . . Kozuchak moved his lips close to the young woman's ear, and whispered.

"You know," he said, peering stealthily left, then right, "today is the day of the coming of God . . . That's what the Emperor said . . . He left us the Holy Book and he said to read it, he's coming to see us . . . He said he'd take us to the Holy Land and rid us of all our sins . . . Here's the cover of the Holy Book." Kozuchak took a book cover out of his pocket and handed it to the young woman. "That guy, the one with the black hat, who came to see you . . ."

"A black hat?" she shouted and sat up in bed. "A man in a black hat? No, don't give me any sulfozin! . . . No shots! . . . No shots, I said!" She collapsed to the floor, screaming, and rolled over the ground, banging her head, scratching with her fingernails, as wild as if she'd lost her mind. "No shots!"

Kozuchak wrapped both arms around the raving woman and held her close. They sat there like that for a long time. Her whole body was trembling, even her lips were trembling . . . Gradually, the fit lost its grip on her, and the young woman began to be herself again, calmer. For a while, she said nothing, lying motionless, but then she pushed herself up on her weak arms.

"A man in a black hat," she said dully, abruptly. "And then what happened?"

"What happened?" Kozuchak did not continue his tale until she spoke those words, afraid to mention the man in the black hat again. "He started searching the whole nuthouse, gathering up all the books . . . and he burned up the Holy Book, along with all the other books he found in his search . . . right in front of everyone . . . burned them up and made us all watch . . . Only this cover from the Holy Book is left, the only thing left from all the burned books, and this one page from it." Kozuchak put a finger to his lips. "Shhh . . . This page is about the coming of God . . . I read it . . . Want me to tell you what it says?" Weak, exhausted, the young woman nodded.

Kozuchak went to stand in the light falling from the window, and started to speak . . .

"'The day of the Lord, the day of His coming is nigh . . . He comes like a thief in the night, comes quietly . . . The sky will boom with thunder and flash with lightning, and everything that exists on the Earth and under the ground will burn in a great fire . . .'" Kozuchak looked at her, waiting for her reaction. She listened, unmoved. When a strange madness seizes the world, how pure, honorable, and righteous must they be who await the coming of the Lord? . . . "'On that day, the sky will disintegrate and fall, and the whole world will be turned to ash . . . And us? . . . We people, we wait for what we've been promised, a new sky, a new sun . . . Because that's where Truth, Justice, and Faith live. The Lord said that those who wait and believe in truth, justice, and faith are his favorites, and the dishonest people with bad intentions, who don't understand justice, will burn in a great fire . . . God's wrath will spare the honest people who thirst for justice . . . Do not stray off the path of justice, or succumb to the devil's temptations, but see and accept the Lord and the Great Savior! Live and grow in God's mercy!' That's what that page says . . . It's a Holy Page, so it didn't even burn in the fire . . ." At that moment, Kozuchak froze, distracted, and started whispering a prayer, like a madman. "Do you fear the castigation of God?" he asked, suddenly, staring at the young woman.

"Yes," she said, her voice unsteady.

For a while, neither one of them spoke.

"You know," said Kozuchak, his eyes gleaming, "on the Day of the Lord's Coming, we should be in the Holy Land!" She could feel the faith in his words.

"The Holy Land?" she asked, confused. "Where is that? Rome? Egypt? . . . Babylon? Where?"

"It's called the Holy Land! It's not Rome or 'Egypt or Babylon," Kozuchak answered with confidence. "If we arrive in the Holy Land on the Day of the Lord's Coming . . . then all our sins will be washed away . . . The Emperor said that, too . . . Early in the morning, tomorrow, we're going to run away from here and go to the Holy Land . . . Will you come with us? The Emperor said he knows the way there . . ." Kozuchak's voice was almost inaudible.

For a while, the young woman did not answer. She didn't know where she was, and her thoughts were running amok somewhere far away. (The voice in the young woman's head whispered softly: "I am my second me!") Her imagination carried her off to another world . . . It was as if only her body, left behind in that hospital ward, could hear Kozuchak talking about God . . . Her soul, feeling light as the lightest down, soared high into the sky and flew far, far away, deep into a great darkness . . . And events in this world opened like the pages of a book before her flying soul, and the higher it flew, the deeper into history she seemed to dive . . . The ashes of the entire world swirled up into the sky, and she could see the universe seized by the great flames of a fire, the planet melting like wax in the heat of it, and a deafening, piercing cry rose up over the whole mass of humanity; a dust cloud darkened the sun, and the ashes that rose from the earth disappeared into the great darkness, and hung in it like the stars of the Milky Way. The young woman no longer knew what century's air she was breathing or where she was. The merciless, massive extermination of peoples, the unbridled criminality reigning in the world, the rivers of blood and oceans of desperate tears—everything that had accrued over the whole history of humankind—it was all there for her to see . . . The young woman felt as broken, as beaten, as if somewhere in this mad, cruel world she'd been crushed and ground between millstones, then pushed through the eye of a needle . . . Carried that way in a whirlwind of time, she found herself in the palace of the actual, great Cleopatra, Queen of Egypt. What wind had brought her there? She had no idea . . . and she had shown up just as Cleopatra, lying naked in her bed, had presented her white, white body for the snake to bite. The young woman gave a wild cry. The snake's fangs pierced into Cleopatra's body. The young woman, and Cleopatra's servants Charmion and Eiras, screamed in chorus: "Cleopatra!" The young woman saw everything that happened, but nobody—neither the dying Cleopatra nor her servants, who killed themselves immediately after their mistress's death—could see her now . . . Cleopatra's brilliant eyes flashed one last time and went dim forever, and just then, something like a gust of air, something that could neither be touched nor seen, separated itself from her breast, rose up like a light breeze, drifted straight to the young woman's chest—the young woman whom the people in the nuthouse called Cleopatra—and slipped inside her, and it felt at home there, settling in and settling down. The universe froze silent . . . The young woman felt that invisible something, and she shuddered. Until recently, all she could hear had been the ringing in her ears, but now she felt a strange sensation . . . "I am my second me," the girl the people in the nuthouse called Cleopatra whispered, almost inaudibly. If it hadn't been for Kozuchak, they would have hanged her there, in Rome, on the square before the Capitolium. Kozuchak saved her from the gallows, from death. Or had it all been a dream? A vision? She found it to be quite the riddle. Truth and dreams had merged and mingled in her head . . . She had been sitting there, aloof, up till that moment, but now the girl gave a start and answered quickly:

"I'm going to the Holy Land, too!"

The Seven

Kozuchak cried bitterly for a long time, clutching the Emperor's stinking, sweat-soaked tunic in his hands . . . The grief of his loss, and his anger at the dead man, whom the others had never understood—all of that could be heard in his cries . . . His was the weeping of someone who had spent his whole unlucky life downtrodden, and he was beset by the feeling of how quickly life comes and goes, how fragile it is, and all his childlike serenity had flown away. Not knowing, not understanding, what sort of power this was, what sort of feeling this was, and why it kept reviving everything that pained his soul and poisoned it, awakening thoughts that suffocated him and split his chest open, he sat and wept bitterly . . . He felt the whole sorrow and grief of loss. Lips clenched, short of breath, he sobbed . . . He could not speak, only mutter, moan, and roar with that inner sadness, with everything deep inside . . . Who had brought him into this life, who had tossed him into the cauldron of this inescapable fate, to pound everything good out of him, like unwanted fat? On what unlucky day had they found this untamed steppe, this lifeless wasteland, among all the variety of life, and abandoned him here, driving him out of his mind? . . . He wept because he had no answer to questions about the bitter Truth of Life, about his bitter Fate . . . Now Kozuchak was weeping in grief not just for the late Emperor, whose life had been cut short, but also for his own lowly fate, for himself . . . The Emperor had been a riddle to him, when he still lived, like an uncrackable walnut, and he had died a riddle, too . . . Kozuchak had never known kindness or human mercy in this vast and endless world, and he had always been alone with his soul and his sadness, but he had sensed human warmth in the Emperor . . . Now it weighed on him bitterly that he had never dared speak of that to

161

the Emperor while he could . . . That vague thought sank amid the other thoughts, and remained there, like that, in his adolescent breast . . .

"We shall search for the Holy Land, and there in the Holy Land, we shall pray to the Creator for forgiveness, for the absolution of our sins." Kozuchak had heard the Emperor speak those words early one morning, standing next to the old tree that grew in the center of the hospital yard, staring up to the top of that tree . . . He remembered that now. The Emperor's voice still hovered in his ears. But whom had he been talking to? Kozuchak didn't know. That time, he remembered, he stood still, hiding, trying to catch everything the Emperor was saying.

"Both man and the universe are great mysteries . . . The Creator gave us life, not sins; we people—knowing that the Creator exists, that he is watching us—we commit sins all on our own, and we will ask God's forgiveness for the sins we have committed . . . God is merciful, and we are born of God's love," said the Emperor thoughtfully, and then he stood there glumly, saying nothing, for a time. Kozuchak saw tears gleaming in his eyes. He took a moment to catch his breath, and then, as if suddenly recovering the gift of speech, the Emperor began talking again, quietly. "O Creator, you cannot strip us of our guilt, or forgive us our sins, and so you must send us a Great Day of interrogation, for which we must provide answers . . . Are we prepared? Are we worthy?"

His thoughts about the Holy Land were interrupted by the Emperor's sweat-soaked tunic . . .

Kozuchak was surprised to feel something inside that garment's inner breast pocket: a small piece of stiff paper, folded importantly in half. The Emperor himself had written words on that paper. The writing began with the words "O Lord!" Kozuchak started to read the even lines of letters on the page . . . The Emperor had jotted down his unruly, scattered thoughts over the day or two before he died . . .

O

Lord! . . .

O God!

You created the son of man to be Great

in this universe . . . you gave greatness to your slave,

and instilled this greatness in his breast, this greatness, my Creator,
you instilled in his heart, you created his soul
to be immortal and eternal . . .
on the day that we, your slaves, your creations, subject our souls to
misfortune, subject our souls to pain, when we commit crimes that the
earth cannot endure . . . he will subject us to inquiry, draw the soul from
each breast, and collect, collect, collect . . . mercy has been uprooted . . .
the time has come . . . the time has come . . . the time has come . . . the
time of the inquiry has come . . . here I stand before you . . . how I would
like to escape the nuthouse and rinse myself in dewdrops . . . to hold a
dandelion in a mischievous breeze and run after its tiny parachuting seeds,
to listen to the chattering songbirds and splash in cold water . . . to wash
my face in the pink light of the sunset, catch and hold a moment of life . . .
I wanted . . . to submerge myself in this glorious world, yes, in this
pleasure, in this wizardry . . . Yes, and if I should surrender my
soul for that moment, for that miracle . . . to feel . . . this bliss . . .
to revel in it, bathe in it . . . Then, yes! . . . Then, yes, as I drown
in that comfort, even death would be nothing to fear . . .
I recognized none of this . . . I did not sense it . . .
the light in my eyes has gone out . . . gone out, sputtering,
like an old lantern . . . darkness has captured the world . . .
O night! O pain of my heart! . . . Cursed day of misfortune!
Ohh . . . a wasteland, extinguishing the glow of my eyes . . .
O cursed night, despised . . .
Ohh! . . . Lord!
Forgive . . . me
I beg of you . . .
Ask me Your questions!
Me, your slave . . .
I am prepared . . .
God! . . .
Oh!

These were the words the Emperor wrote the day before his death.
And Kozuchak was the one who read them.

Kozuchak

It had been six days since the angels descended to earth . . .

They had worked hard all those six days, flying across the entire earth in search of the child born 665 days before, to deliver to him the golden words of God. Day and night they searched, flying all around our spherical Earth. On the 665th day of his life, the cries of this child, who had been provided the soul of a great human being, changed to resemble a wolf-like howl, as if he'd been born a wolf instead of a person, and he howled while he cried, and that crying reached the ear of the Creator in heaven, and carried an alarm, as if all life in this universe had been compressed into one small ember, and the clairvoyant little boy had sensed, on the 665th day of his life, that a great misfortune would befall every living thing in this world created by the might of the Creator; that night he howled like a wolf . . . He cried like a wolf howls as it gazes at the moon. For six days and six nights, the angels searched for the child.

When the seventh day was approaching, heaven summoned the angels back.

One day and one night remained.

If they did not find the child who had been given divine power by the seventh night, the Earth would be seized by a terrible calamity, vast glaciers would grow, and the whole world would be flooded. Such was the danger threatening the Earth, which looked, from a distance, just like a walnut spinning fast around its axis.

This was a sign of the end of days . . .

(In the chapel, I heard a thunderous voice. This voice told the seven angels: "Go and pour out on the Earth seven cups of God's wrath!"

The **first angel** poured out his cup over the Earth, and all who bore the mark of the beast and worshiped him were covered in revolting, festering ulcers;

The **second angel** poured out his cup into the sea, and all the creatures of the sea perished, and the sea was filled with scarlet blood;

The **third angel** poured out his cup in the rivers, and the rivers transformed into streams of blood;

The **fourth angel** poured out his cup on the Sun, and the Sun was given the power to incinerate the people and destroy them;

The **fifth angel** poured out his cup on the throne of the beast, and his kingdom was covered with impenetrable darkness, and everyone who lived there was overcome with torment, and festering boils, but they did not repent and they railed against God;

The **sixth angel** poured out his cup into the great Euphrates . . . and the river ran dry, opening the way for the kings of the Orient, yearning to attack, conquer, and steal, and from the jaws of the dragon, from the jaws of the beast, and from the jaws of the false prophet, there burst forth three evil spirits who looked like toads, and these evil spirits would deliver calamity and destroy all kings on the Great Day of the Lord;

The **seventh angel** poured out his cup into the air; and from the chapel in the sky, a voice rang out: "It is done!" . . . And thunder boomed, lightning flashed, a terrible storm blew in, and the Earth trembled, and no human being on Earth had ever beheld such an earthquake, not since the Ice Age . . . The great city split in three parts, the idol worshipers' cities were destroyed, and the Creator, remembering mighty Babylon, handed down a cup full of the wine of wrath . . . And God's wrath fell on the city . . . Islands sank in the waters, mountains collapsed into the plains, hail rained from the heavens onto the people's heads, hailstones as big as rocks, and when the hail came, the people railed against God, so severe was the storm . . .

One of the seven angels came to me and said: "Come with me, and I will show you how a sullied woman, sitting above the flooded world, is judged and castigated . . . The earthly kings engaged in indecency with this woman, and lost their minds over her blandishments, and grew intoxicated from her wine . . ."

"And who is she? . . . Who?" I asked. "Thaïs the Athenian? Or Cleopatra?" I could find no answer to my question . . .)

The day of the Holy Man's birth was approaching . . .

That winter was harsher than other winters, with a frost that bit to the bone. Who lies waiting for this moment? The spirits of the dead and all the demons wait impatiently for the day of the Holy Man's birth, not knowing what to do with themselves . . . Invisible, till then, to human eyes, all these creatures come alive and emerge onto the surface of the earth. Only when the roosters crow at night do the dead begin rising from under the earth.

They fear nothing but human eyes.

During this time of year, people begin dreaming of their long-dead relatives and acquaintances. Demon women pester pregnant women, and, invisible to them, they try playing nasty tricks, just for the sake of doing harm. The spirits of the dead rush in circles around the houses where they died, and wander all over until the roosters crow in the morning . . .

The spirits of the dead, who reside forever in a place in the universe tightly sealed with eighteen thousand black curtains, know and feel nothing except a great darkness, but at this time of the year, they come alive, and rise up as the short winter day ends and the long winter night begins. They rise from their places with the roosters' first evening call, when people begin preparing for sleep. The Lord raises all these spirits of the dead from under the ground so that they can rush in circles around the houses where they died, there on the surface of the earth, invisible to everyone, and so they can see how life is going for the living, so they can look in on their friends and loved ones who still reside in this deceptive world.

On this long winter night, the surface of the earth becomes crowded with the spirits of the dead. But they try to remain invisible to people, and that is because if a living human being sees one of them, that spirit will incur the wrath of God, and be cursed, and will never again be able to rise to the surface of the earth.

That is the law in the underworld.

In just the same way, this woman, who died last winter, knew to take advantage of the mercy and might of the Prophet Jesus, and after the roosters crowed that evening, she rose to the surface of the earth and set off for a solitary little house at the edge of a village, to look in on her baby and her husband, whom she had left alone with the child.

Calling no attention to herself, making no sound, she approached the house at the edge of the village.

Night had fallen outside. The windows where a light burned brightly blinded her, and she flew to the window of a room where no light burned and looked inside. You should know that creatures like her see nothing in the light, because they are used to total darkness, where they are expert navigators. This was the spirit of a woman who had died the previous year, who, in her lifetime, had been beautiful, with a shapely figure and pretty face. How many young men had fallen in love with her and chased her everywhere! But, by God's grace, she also met her future husband then, the man who was later left with a motherless child to care for. Her husband was a quiet, modest man, and they lived with mutual respect and intense love for one another.

But look what Fate decreed: this woman died not long after giving birth, and imagine how badly she regrets not being able to nurture her newborn babe, and although she resides in a different world, now, all her thoughts and desires are in this one, and most of her memories revolve around her tiny, pink infant and her husband, whom she left behind in this world.

How could she forget, after all? How could the poor man manage, now, without a wife? How was he going to understand their little chickadee and raise him? Men find it difficult to raise children on their own. God forbid a man bear a woman's burden.

It grew darker, and while circling the house, the spirit-woman stumbled on a piece of iron under the snow, and when it heard the clamor, the chained-up dog raised a terrible clamor of its own, barking, and even though it didn't know what made the sound, and couldn't smell anything, the dog went on yapping.

The woman's spirit passed by the dog. The piece of iron it had struck with its foot was no ordinary piece of metal; it was part of the fence meant to go around the woman's grave, stored away by her husband. He had put off erecting that fence until the spring. Perhaps he had put it off till spring, or perhaps he had completely forgotten about his wife; in any case, one part of that future fence now lay under the snow. The woman could feel it in her gut . . . But the spirit-woman took no offense at her husband's decision; spirits almost never take offense; they don't know the meaning of the word. After all, in the world where they live, they have the Prophet Jesus, who treats everyone the same. Spirits have shed the sorts of feelings we have in this world.

The woman's spirit circled the house and came to a large window. She looked inside and saw a room where there was complete darkness and a deep silence. *Maybe I could go inside,* it thought, feeling tempted. Spirits can move through any crack a breath of air could slip through. So it joined itself to a thin breeze and sailed into the house through a hole the size of a mouse's eye, and then both the breeze and the spirit were inside. It was pitch black in the room, but that kind of darkness is like sunshine for spirits . . . Then the spirit heard some barely audible voices. The woman's spirit realized, with alarm, that there were two people in the house. One of them was her husband's new wife, one he had taken in even before it had been forty days since the passing of his first. The woman's spirit felt jealous of her husband for marrying before those forty days were up. Yes, it was a spirit, but it could feel jealousy; after all, if a husband remarries more than forty days after his wife's death, he is clean and pure, as far as she is concerned, and then all feelings the woman's spirit might have for him would vanish, and he could do whatever he pleased once that time was up; but now this wound would give the woman's spirit no rest, and it was seized by worry and agitation . . . Now the spirit would always moon about in this anxious world of the living, always penetrate into the thoughts of its living relatives in their dreams, appearing to them, and this would mean trouble both for the spirit and for the living . . . Yes, a sorry fate awaited them all. The woman's spirit, moving slowly and quietly, approached a big bed, where the man and his new wife were making love. She could hear their panting, lustful breath, and the constant creaking of the bed frame, and the woman's moaning, pleading voice whispering sweet words to the man on top of her, holding him tightly to her . . . giving herself wholly to him . . .

The bed creaks, and the man's movements intensify the rhythmic creaking of the bed, louder, harder. There they were, the two of them, surrendering themselves solely to that worldly pleasure, completely unaware that the spirit-woman stood half a step away, and that it could see their bodies move and even hear every word they uttered, and their every moan . . .

That night was the spirit's first time visiting that house . . .

Before the birthday of the Prophet Jesus, spirits come alive for seven days. And on the very first of those seven days, the spirit-woman saw her husband in bed with another woman. It may have been only the woman's spirit, but it did, in fact, feel jealousy. The bed's creaking quieted, and after their heated embraces, the exhausted man was drenched in sweat . . . But the woman was unsatisfied and couldn't rest, and still burning with desire, she started to stroke the man's hair, and gaze at him pleadingly, asking for more. The first flame of their lust died down, and they began speaking gently to one another. The spirit-woman remembered having adored whispering with her husband, just like that, as they touched gently, like two dandelion heads. It could remember that now. The memory was salt in the wound . . . And what they spoke of stunned the spirit-woman, partly out of jealousy, partly out of bewilderment, as it succumbed to its old feminine weakness, even though it was a spirit.

"I'm constantly jealous of you," said the woman. "Very jealous."

"Why?" The husband didn't understand, and he stroked the woman's hair. "Who makes you jealous?"

"Your wife," the woman answered. "Lying with you here, I was thinking about how you used to do the same things right here, with your wife, and I felt jealous . . ."

"Stop," said the husband, and turned away onto his other side. "Who can be jealous of a dead woman? You can't be jealous because of the dead . . ."

The woman moved closer to the man and caressed him.

"If your wife came back to life, would you marry her again? Or would you stay with me? Tell me," she said.

"None of that makes any sense!" said the man, unhappily. "How can anyone be jealous over someone who's dead?"

The woman looked offended.

"Then why have you still not taken her picture off the wall?" She pushed away from him, hurt. "What is she, better than me?"

"Why are you going on and on about my wife?" the man demanded.

"Fuck you and your wife! Either tell me you'd choose me, or I'm leaving!" The woman broke out in sobs that shook her whole body. "And get rid of that kid of yours. If you don't . . . I'm not going to live with you anymore! What if I have a baby tomorrow? You wouldn't care about our kids! You'll only fuss over your own. Send him away . . . I'll bear you nice little babies. Will you?"

"Send him where?"

"Where else? The orphanage." At that moment, with her hair black as night, and her gleaming white, bare body, the spirit-woman found her as strikingly beautiful as an angel.

How could the husband walk away from the embrace of such a gorgeous woman? He'd wilt and die . . .

The spirit-woman sensed that life itself was too small a sacrifice for a woman like that. From the next room came the loud cry of a child. Immediately, the spirit-woman darted on a stream of air into the room where it heard the crying. The baby was sobbing, a gut-wrenching wail . . . Not knowing what to do, the spirit-woman stood helplessly and watched him . . . Overflowing with pity for the child, the spirit wanted to pick him up and calm him, but it lacked the strength and even the ability. It fluttered helplessly around the baby, like a moth, desperate to help . . . After a while, as if the child sensed his mother were near, he quieted . . . He babbled something, the incomprehensible sounds aimed straight at the apparition of his mother, before him . . . The child's eyes were carbon copies of his mother's, while she was alive, and now she was a ghost. The spirit-woman looked around at the walls and window curtains. Everything was the same as she had left it. There had been no changes. When the spirit-woman saw the photograph on the wall near the bed where the baby lay, a picture in which that same spirit, as a living woman, was smiling happily at something, it took fright. Seeing a photograph is a bad omen for a spirit. This spirit knew that. Perhaps it was when the spirit jumped in fright that it broke the string on the necklace of ruby-red beads it wore, and the necklace fell to the floor . . . Oh, Lord—her husband had given her that necklace the day the baby was born, as a symbol of their long, happy life to come as a family. Something seemed to startle the baby as he lay in his bed, and he burst out crying loudly again . . . He wailed as plaintively

as if someone had plunged a needle into his little body . . . His crying
intensified, and soon it seemed less like a baby's wail and more like a
wolf's howl . . . His terrible sobs threw the spirit into utter dismay . . . It was
still sailing around the baby's bed like a desperate moth with its wings on
fire, unable to help the baby . . . Finally, the woman burst into the room,
her face twisted in anger, shouting: "Shut up, you! Hush!" The woman
was completely naked . . . The baby went on crying . . . on and on . . .
The woman tried to outscream the baby, boiling over with anger, and she
shouted, "Go to hell! You can't even cry like a human being! You're howling like a she-wolf whelped you! Nasty beast, cursed of God!" The baby
went on crying. A short time later, the husband followed the wife into the
room, also bare naked, except with a towel around his waist. He picked
up the baby and tried to console him . . . The child started wailing even
louder than before . . . It was a voice that seemed able to reach the ears of
angels . . . The spirit-woman floated through the air in that room, which
stank of the baby's urine . . . Nobody here could see her or hear her . . .
Soon, cradled in the man's arms, the child quieted and fell asleep . . . The
man carefully handed the baby to the woman . . .

As soon as she laid the baby in his bed, she started in fright, as if her
naked body had been doused with icy water:

"Oh my God, what is that?" She had stepped on something cold.
"What is this? . . . Beads, I think? I've always wanted some beads like
these!"

"Beads, you say?" The man was intrigued. He was very surprised.
"Where did you find them?"

"Right here," she said. "Right here . . ."

"That's strange. How did they get here?" asked the spirit-woman's
husband.

"Strange . . ."

The man had bought that necklace himself.

He picked it up and even sniffed it. The beads smelled strongly of
camphor. The scent made his nose twitch. The suspicions growing in
his soul started to overcome him. He couldn't stop wondering where this
string of beads had come from. He knew its history well and he had recognized the necklace immediately: his late wife had never taken it off, even

in the bath, and it was still around her neck when she was buried. He'd given his wife that necklace the day their baby was born, the one who had just been hollering so loudly, and had now, finally, calmed down. Beads like rubies, made of stones red as pomegranate seeds. A cold terror seized the man, turning his whole soul upside down. He suddenly realized, with grief, that last year he had forgotten to offer a sacrifice for the birthday of the Prophet Jesus, and had not given any thought to his wife, who at that point had died not very long ago, and the thought made his soul freeze, icy cold. Not to mention that the baby was always muttering something he couldn't understand, as if he were trying but failing to say something important . . . He made incomprehensible noises, and his crying was different from usual. The man had not waited even forty days after his wife's death to bring this new woman into their home, lured by her beauty. Now, fascinated and surprised, she was examining these beads. They had lived together like a married couple for a year and half but had never made their marriage official. Still, they considered themselves husband and wife. The man did not, in fact, know very much about his new wife's past; she never told him anything about who she was, where she was from, where she was born or grew up, other than that she had worked as a teacher somewhere. They both seemed wary of talking about their past. The man was not a completely ordinary person. He had spent seven years drinking to excess, and had seen everything life had to show, and if he hadn't met his late first wife, his life in the world would have been over. There was no point denying it: his late wife had made him a human being. She had dressed him up and set him straight. He was a man who could do a little of any trade. His late wife had grown up in a religious family, the daughter of a pious man, and that was probably the reason she always kept herself spotlessly clean, morally speaking, never breaking any of God's commandments; she was a woman who followed strict rules . . . After she married her husband, she lost touch with her pious parents, who had been against the marriage, and they were all that was left of her family . . . And then she died, following the destiny God had determined for her. But she had left this child behind . . . This sobbing infant was her entire legacy. . . . The husband took a twig of dried juniper that had long been hanging off a nail in the wall, laid it on a tin plate, lit it with a match, and walked all through the house, spreading smoke into every corner. His soul felt on fire over how indifferent he had once been to his wife's suffering and all her difficulties, and since her death, he hadn't even given her a thought . . .

From the other room, he could hear the woman's angry shouting . . . She had gone in there to calm the baby, who had started crying again, and lull him back to sleep. The woman's lulling and scolding techniques were identical: a loud shout and abusive words . . .

The juniper smoke forced the woman flying through the air to leave the house. Spirits can't stand the scent of juniper smoke . . .

The day of the Prophet Jesus's birth was approaching . . .

On that day, the angels descended to Earth. . . .

The spirits rose from under the ground . . .

Pretending to be in a rush to comfort the child, the woman grabbed the string of beads from her husband's hands, and took it into the other room, where there was a mirror . . . She walked up to that mirror, put on the necklace, and peered at her reflection. She stood there turning this way and that before the mirror, looking at herself, to see if the necklace was flattering . . . The woman shrugged out of the robe she was wearing, and stood completely naked before the mirror, looking . . . The man walked over to her . . . Naked, tall, and solid, he stood behind the woman . . . The smell of the woman's body struck his senses. This woman's body was naturally endowed with its own alluring scent. Especially alluring were her two breasts, full as ripe melons, which would catch the attention of any man. It had been those breasts that attracted this particular man, the first day they met, and on their first night together, he hadn't been able to drag his face away from them. When he saw her wearing the necklace, he thought it looked stunning on her, and that made his mood even darker. But he did not make a sound . . . Just then, a feeling was nagging at him that made all his thoughts scatter, that stole his peace, that gave rise to vague suspicions that tormented him and saddened him . . . That nagging feeling would not leave him alone. In this mood, he sank into all kinds of thoughts and speculations . . . Where had that string of beads come from? The thought stabbed through him like a knife through the heart . . . eating him up from the inside out . . .

Today it was 665 days since the birth of his son . . .

666 is the devil's number. The next day, the devil's curse would descend on the child, to mark him with his seal . . . And the angels who had descended to Earth were supposed to come to the child, before the curse of the devil fell on him, and they were supposed to take up his soul and give it the strength of the prophet, and the prophet's holiness . . . The angels descended to Earth with that immense responsibility, and they had flown all over the planet in search of the child who had turned 665 days old, and this was the house where they were to find that child who was meant to have the prophet's holiness, the one a great power would touch . . . They were searching for a New Prophet who would have the power to save the world from utter filth and abomination, where honor and dishonor, humanity and beastliness, mercy and cruelty, wisdom and stupidity, cleanliness and filth had all become entangled, a world on the brink of collapse and self-destruction . . . They flew to Earth to find, in this child, the power, the ability, to save the world . . . The angels were invisible to the eye, and nobody could hear them flying . . .

On this day, the angels flew to this house from Heaven, and the spirits came up from under the Earth . . .

(I saw an angel descending from heaven, carrying a key to the abyss and an immense chain. He caught the dragon, the ancient serpent with the face of the devil and Satan, and bound him in chains for a thousand years. Then he plunged him into the abyss, and hung a lock on his chains, and put his seal upon it, so that he could not plague the people for a thousand years; but after that he would have his freedom, for a short time. And I saw thrones, and seated on those thrones were the ones given the right to judge; and I saw the souls of those who had given their lives for Jesus's teachings, for God's word; they were not those who had bowed to the beast and its likeness, and had not received its mark on their foreheads or hands . . .) (. . . After a thousand years, Satan was released from his chains, and they set out to deceive all the peoples living in the four corners of the earth, Gog and Magog, and he gathered them all for battle; and their numbers were more than the waters in the sea. And they marched all across the world, and surrounded the forces of the righteous, and the city God loved. And then God sent fire down from heaven to destroy them all.

And Satan the deceiver was thrown into a lake of burning sulfur, and the beast and false prophet lie in this lake with him; and they will suffer there day and night for ever.)[2]

"How do I look?" The woman could not take her eyes off the mirror, admiring her reflection. "What do you think?"

"Gorgeous," said the man sadly.

The woman, bare naked, turned to the man standing behind her and pressed herself tightly to him. Embracing him, she pressed him close to her breasts full as melons and kissed him hard, as she glowed all over with glee. Again, the scent of camphor, coming from the beads hanging around her white, white neck, struck his nose.

"Can you smell that?" asked the man, confused.

"Smell what? That's my scent. Don't I smell like a nymph?" said the woman, hugging the man close. She took him by the hand and led him into the other room, and they fell together onto the warm blankets on the old bed.

The woman began moaning, speaking sweet words, which always brought the man pleasure . . .

Again, the rhythmic creaking of the bed could be heard . . .

The baby started to cry violently . . .

The spirit-woman rode another stream of air into the house. By now, the baby was turning blue from his violent sobs . . . Such pity did the spirit feel for its own tiny child! It was full to bursting with that feeling, but it could do nothing . . . The child went on crying, and its cries were enough to tear apart the soul . . . The angels could hear him crying, too, and by then they were not far from the house at the edge of the village . . . The woman was a spirit, but her motherly feelings for her own wailing child filled her entirely . . . The mother felt so terrible for her child, suffered so terribly for him . . . The spirit-woman, rushing in like a gust of air, had never forgotten its feminine origins, and the soul revived the woman's body, giving it blood, and now it was not a spirit, but a real, living woman . . . The spirit-woman, the ghost, took the baby in her arms, pressed him close to her, and

2. Book of Revelation, 20:7–10.

gave him her breast . . . The violently sobbing child quieted instantly and locked his lips on his mother's breast. The child sucked hungrily at the breast of his mother, the ghost . . .

Overcome with a feeling of maternal tenderness, the spirit-woman cradled her child in her arms, nursing him . . . When she saw how similar the baby's face was to her own, she was genuinely glad . . . The woman had given her son a name, even before he was born, and that name was Kozuchak. The name meant "little lamb." For many years, she had no children; on the birthday of the Prophet Jesus, she had sacrificed a lamb and asked the Creator for a child, and then this little boy had been born . . . To show her gratitude to the lamb sacrificed for the mercy of the Creator, they had named the child Kozuchak. But after the Creator gave them a child, he took the woman who bore him away into the other world . . . What grief that the world is arranged in this way, so that something is always lacking! . . .

Very little time was left before the end of the child's 665th day of life . . .

The angels would need to carry away the boy's soul, and soon. They would plant the seeds of a great strength in that soul and give it a magnificent holiness. But the demons also had plans for the boy's soul . . . They had also calculated that the child would soon see his 666th day, and very little time remained till then . . . And the demons wanted to set their seal on the child . . . but for that, he had to live to his 666th day. On that day, Satan's seal would be imprinted straight on the child's soul . . . and then, all his childish purity, all his angelic holiness, all his unspoiled goodness—it would all disappear when Satan's stamp was applied . . . Then the child would grow up, and become another walking, breathing human slave, just another unseeing, uncaring man . . . A slave-like blindness sets in after Satan's seal is set . . . And to keep Satan's plans from coming to fruition, the angels would have to do their duty, perform their sacred obligation, and bathe the child in the holiness of the Prophet . . .

The angels entered the house . . .

They walked through the door . . .

Immediately, they smelled the scent of the coal ash in the iron stove, and the scent of burned juniper. In the middle of the room, on an old bed, lay a man and woman, naked and absolutely exhausted, as if they had just cast off a heavy load . . . The woman was lying on her stomach, and the man on his back . . . Carefully, not giving themselves away, the angels moved into the far room. Quietly, they opened the door and peered into the room, and the angels saw the spirit-woman nursing the child, and they were stunned and astonished . . . When the spirit-woman saw the angels, she started in fear . . . So frightened was she that she barely noticed herself laying the baby in his bed . . . Spirits have a rule that they must not let angels see them; a spirit whom an angel has seen will be punished for all eternity, and even on holy days, it won't be allowed to come to the surface of the earth . . . And then, later, it will also lose its chance of being reborn in the form of some living creature or plant, and it will never have the chance of a new connection to the living . . . In her terrible fright, a silver ring slipped from the spirit-woman's finger and landed on the floor . . . The spirit-woman stole one more look at the baby, then sailed away on a gust of air into the darkness that was now, for her, eternal . . .

The child, its belly full of its mother's milk, lay serenely, babbling something to itself . . . The angels walked up to the baby, and, as if he'd been expecting them, the boy laughed, a pure, childlike laugh, as they came near . . . Standing before the child, the angels didn't know what to do, and they wept in frustration . . . They wept because this child, who had tasted the milk of a ghost, now could never have the Prophet's holiness, nor the power to save the world, and the world would be rotten and filthy again, as it forgot the Creator's holiness, and in this rotten and filthy world, the people like slaves, with indifferent souls, would multiply and multiply all over again, the unseeing slave people, the unhappy slave people, the sinful slave people . . . And the Creator would then be forced to send down a Judgment Day, a Day of Castigation, to his slaves, his creations, into whom he had poured his immeasurable mercy and kindness . . . So full of filth and abomination was the world that there was no other way . . . The son would go against his mother, the father against his daughter, impiety would grow, the conscientious would be shamed, the shameless would flourish, the holy would be slathered with filth, feelings would turn wild, and growing numbers of people would consider themselves equals to God; glaciers would melt, mountains would crumble, the dry steppes would be coated with salt, people would not be able to tell what was improper and reprehensible, they would trample on the holiness God gave to life, they would honor no laws in the world of deception; and here the angels had seen the Great Savior sent down by the Creator, in this child who had lived for 665 days . . . Now this child, who had been suckled by a ghost, was unworthy of that holy charge . . . God's castigation would rain down . . .

The Day of a terrible calamity for the people of Earth was drawing near . . .

The angel's time on Earth ran out, and they were due to return on the day of the Prophet Jesus's birth . . .

Soon the 666th day would dawn . . .[3]

---

3. "And there was a battle. And the angel who was called Satan the Tempter, the Devil, was cast down into the abyss. And with him were several more angels and unclean spirits." (Source unknown.)

I have been collecting tidbits of reliable information about the Devil, and now I have no doubt that the number 666, the Devil's number, is an encoding of his name, and nothing else. Remember the game played with dice, as ancient as the world itself? Three six-sided cubes? The highest score a player can get is three sixes. And what is the sum of all the numbers on the roulette wheel at a casino? 666, again. Temptation is his proper name. Putting it differently, three sixes can be interpreted as a symbol of the absolute maximum, the limit, beyond which nothing can exist. Furthermore, just as in the dice game, this means final, unambiguous victory. There are many numerical and symbolical overlaps between the name of the Devil and the number 666. The essence of the Devil is, in fact, encoded in the coded number of the Beast. He is inseparable from the world, as light is inseparable from darkness. Clearly, this Beast with the name encoded by three sixes will come to rule on Earth. He lurks unseen among us, waiting for his time to come, when all the historical parameters fall into place and all the conditions for his coming will be met. Or he may simply be mustering his allies for the final battle.

The Apostles tell us that the second coming of the Devil will be accompanied by general chaos and the apocalypse. Whatever differences various cultures and religions might have, whatever the names by which they call the Devil, they all agree on one point: a day will come when the Prince of Darkness will arrive, and there will be a battle.

The devil will generously reward those who are faithful to him, playing on human passions and desires. He does not make people any meaner or eviler than they are; he simply reminds them of their genuine, ugly nature. The devil is generous and accepting of all; he takes a person's soul, and in exchange, the person gets everything they want. 666 is the Devil's number.

The devil's seal will be set on this child . . . The woman-spirit bore her punishment that night . . . And now she will never come back to life, neither as a living beast, nor as a plant, and not as a wave, a breeze, a snowstorm, an earthquake, a raging fire, a rockslide, a doomsday, or a great flood! . . .

Late that night, the man walked into the room where the child lay . . .

The baby was sleeping serenely . . . The man sat down on the edge of the baby's bed, and watched him for a while, intently, saying nothing . . . then he stood upright, said a short prayer to the Creator, hoping for His mercy, and started to whisper plaintively: "O Creator, show me mercy . . . I know I have committed a terrible sin, one for which I can never atone in my lifetime, and I'm now in an impossible position . . . My soul has had no peace since I saw that beaded necklace here, the one my late wife took with her when she died . . . What kind of sign is this? Or what kind of illusion? . . . These are difficult times for me . . . I despair . . . Or is this Your way of sending me Your interrogation, of castigating my soul? . . . I will accept any punishment from You. Nobody can escape from You or Your questioning . . . You gave us this life Yourself, and You can take it away . . . You have probably heard my son crying, You have heard him cry; a human child cannot cry like that . . . He cries like a wolf howling . . . What does it mean? . . . I don't understand . . . Truly, yes, I am Your slave, my sins are many, I admit it . . . You cannot forgive them all . . . You are merciful and generous . . . We, Your children, fail to understand, and we are guilty before You . . . Forgive me, Creator, You who castigate the guilty . . . Show me mercy . . ." The man went on whispering plaintively, with no understanding of himself or the state he was in . . . staring hard at his son . . . but the child slept serenely . . . Some of the milk that had filled his mouth appeared on his lips . . . When he saw that, the man jumped up, startled, as if he'd stepped on a cold snake . . . What on Earth was going on? How could his son have milk in his mouth? Who could have nursed him? He looked all around, confused . . . not a sound anywhere . . . Again, he walked over to the baby, and, thinking he must have imagined it, he leaned over him and looked more closely . . . The milk was still there . . . Now a genuine fear seized the man . . . And just then, the man saw the picture hanging on the wall, the one where his late wife had been caught smiling on film . . . That photo made him shudder with fear . . . He was terrified, looking at her, just as if his wife had come back to life and returned . . . At that moment, he stepped on something with his bare foot . . . He bent over and picked it up . . . It was a ring . . . a silver ring . . . That ring made his soul, already charred and blackened as burned wood, turn inside out again; the ring was like somebody shoveling earth onto his grave . . . What terrified him was that he knew with certainty that when they buried his late wife, this ring had still been on her finger . . . What was going on?! The man appealed to the Creator by name and started reciting a prayer of repentance . . . His entire body shook as if he'd plunged headfirst into the snow . . .

The ring smelled of camphor . . .

The man had enough control of his will to take his wife's photograph off the wall and carry it outside . . .

Out in the yard, it was brutally cold . . .

Dogs dropped dead in cold like that . . .

The raised eyebrow of the moon shed heavy, leaden-gray light on the Earth . . .

The stars, sprinkled across the sky like millet seeds, twinkled tirelessly . . . That year, the winter was a harsh one . . .

The man was afraid to even look at the moon in the starry sky . . . He had heard that dangerous forces gather on the moon, in seasons like this, and demons and jinns hang off the horns of the moon and play games there . . . No healthy thoughts even crossed his mind, that night, as his fear bound his feet and deprived him of his reason . . . The man walked behind the house to the tied-up dog. The dog didn't even move, sound asleep, just warm enough in its kennel in this crackling cold . . . The man threw his wife's photograph as far as he could out into the field . . . He thought that everything that had happened that night, all the things that were robbing him of reason, must be because of his wife's spirit, which did not want to leave him in peace . . .

At the spot where his wife's portrait fell, after he flung it with all his might, he thought he saw his wife's ghost appear: it flashed into sight, then dissolved a moment later into the darkness . . .

The man's whole body shook with fear . . .

He could not decide if it had been his wife, or just his terror making him see things . . .

Then he heard the rooster's morning call . . .

With that first call of the rooster, all the spirits, demons, and jinns on the surface of the Earth go home again to their own world.

Trembling in terror, on his way back, he tripped over a piece of iron, and fell into the cold snow . . . Slowly, he used the last of his remaining strength to stand up, and rubbed more cold snow over his face . . . The cold snow dulled the feeling of terror that seared his body . . . The cold snow opened his eyes . . . He realized he had tripped over a piece of metal he'd meant to use to build a fence around his late wife's grave, lying hidden under the snow . . .

On the front porch, the man took off the sheepskin coat he'd flung over his shoulders, then walked inside . . . He went into the room where his son lay . . . His son was still sleeping . . . a deep sleep . . .

That night, the man could not fall back asleep . . . That was the night when all his strength was taken from him, his soul was turned upside down, and he was given a great deal to ponder . . . He lay there for a long time, thinking . . . Thousands of thoughts swirled around his head . . . He tossed and turned in bed, but his thoughts just would not stop . . . When would his Kozuchak grow up and be less of a helpless baby? . . . Or, if they handed him over to an orphanage, as the woman had said, would he be rid of this problem? The thought made him jump as if he'd been burned . . . Kozuchak was the sacred legacy left to him by his late wife, the poor woman who'd given the child life, then departed for the other world! And now he had no choice . . . The only thing he had ever wanted from God was a good life for Kozuchak . . .

But time had passed, and the black night had descended on that house, which angels and a ghost had both visited . . .

When winter was nearing its end, the man had a heart attack and left this world for the next . . .

The woman who had lived in that house with him, unmarried, soon sold the house and vanished, leaving no trace . . .

And Kozuchak was given to an orphanage and transferred from there to a psychiatric hospital.

The Seven

Before dawn, the six of them came to some hills covered with rock and sand. Genghis Khan walked in front, while the rest trailed behind like dogs on a leash, tired from their long journey, barely shuffling their feet. This was a place where the sandy desert adjoined the untamed steppe. Here and there, trees grew to be the height of a man, dry from the constant drought . . . Sparse and unsightly trees popped up in unexpected places, like the hairs of an old man's thin beard . . . The six were thoroughly exhausted from the never-ending sand of the great desert, and when they saw these dry old trees, they rejoiced on the inside, believing that they had finally left the godforsaken desert behind. The dried-out trees seemed to them to be heralds of life, of the end of that bloodless desert . . . Whatever else might happen, they thought the hardships of their desert crossing would be the most grievous part of their whole difficult journey. This place where the desert and hilly steppe came together warmed their hearts like the tempting bird Simurgh, but the difficulties of their journey did not end there. Aside from the solitary wild trees, no other life was visible . . . unless they counted the abandoned old burial mounds, it was as if a snake had come and licked everything bare: there was nothing. Not a single living being to be seen. The travelers had arrived at this place at the time of day when the last morning star was fading in the sky . . . The last to arrive was the disheveled-looking Lear, whom the journey had done little good . . . Thaïs the Athenian may have been a woman, but she was as good as a man at many things, and she walked right behind the one in the front, Genghis Khan . . . This journey to the Holy Land the late Emperor had told them about had been torture for all six of them . . . Their destination stood before their eyes like a green Paradise . . . It seemed to them that as soon as they set foot in that Holy Land, everything bad they had done until then, all their sins, would immediately be washed away, like dirt in a bath, and they would be cleansed, and the doors of Paradise would open wide for them . . . When it was still dark, these six had passed among the ruins of some old tombs, across an abandoned cemetery . . . They walked without any understanding, surprised, wondering what road or gale or devil had brought them here . . . Only in the full light of dawn, when everything grew brighter, did they realize where they were, and take in the whole abandoned feel, the emptiness, of the place . . .

"What devil brought us here?" shouted Thaïs the Athenian, the strongest of them.

"I don't know." Genghis Khan, dumbstruck, scratched the back of his head.

"Me neither," responded Alexander the Great, silently thanking God that they had finally crossed through that desert of sand.

Here, the desert ended, and a place of hills began . . . These old tombs gave them hope that there would be a settlement nearby, where people lived, and that revived their dying hope to rejoin life. They all felt more lively, more cheerful, and they crooned these encouraging thoughts to themselves . . . But it was only blind hope . . . In the pale sky, not a bird could be seen, and not a single cloud. The air all around was lifeless and still . . .

"What about you?" Thaïs the Athenian asked Lear.

"Maybe this is Paradise . . . I can even smell the distant trees of the Garden of Eden," Lear responded, opening his eyes wide and sniffing at the scent of the flowering thorn bushes, growing the height of a man in the distance.

Those thorn bushes were in bloom everywhere, and their gentle scent suffused the clean morning air in all directions . . .

"I can smell it, too!" Cleopatra said happily.

"Oh, come on! That's the scent of the thornbushes," Thaïs the Athenian growled, shooting Cleopatra a venomous sideways glance. "Paradise, you say? What's that, then?" she asked sharply, with a scowl. Thaïs the Athenian stared at five wooden coffins near a half-collapsed wall, and shuddered . . .

"Are those coffins? Or boats, maybe?" Kozuchak asked, puzzled. "They do look a lot like boats . . . Maybe someone put them there on purpose so we could cross the Nile?" Kozuchak felt like joking.

"You're talking nonsense," Alexander the Great scolded Kozuchak. "A boat would have a sharper nose on it . . . In boats like these, all you could do was float the seas of Hell . . ."

"That's right, they don't look like boats," Kozuchak said with a nod, agreeing with Alexander the Great. "One . . . two . . ." He started to count the coffins. "Three . . . four . . . five . . ."

"Why only five? There are six of us," Cleopatra asked.

And there truly were five coffins there, painted black. Lear's nose, which had caught the scent of Paradise, wrinkled.

"What kind of rotten joke is that? We're not here to look for coffins . . . We're looking for the Holy Land," said Genghis Khan.

Just then, a scraping sound came from a jumble of old burial vaults nearby, as if something were being dragged over the ground. Everyone stared, stunned, in that direction . . . The noise came closer and closer, and then, from behind the old tombs, a man appeared, dressed all in black. He had a rope flung over his shoulder, and there was a coffin tied to that rope.

"There's the coffin we were missing . . . They're bringing that last one over now," said Lear, his voice trembling. "That's your coffin, Kozuchak," he joked.

The tall, hefty figure in black clothing wrapped the rope tighter around his hand and kept walking toward them. He lugged his coffin up to the other coffins, and, ignoring the travelers, he went to work, quietly lining up all six coffins, saying nothing. Then he gave the people a grim look. In that look, the anger was obvious; his whole face radiated hostility.

"Excuse me, but I suppose you must make coffins and sell them here?" Kozuchak inquired politely of the man in black.

"Don't be ridiculous . . . What do you think this is, a coffin market?" asked Genghis Khan. When the man in black turned sharply to look at him, his cap, which had sunk to the back of his head, slid off altogether.

They all saw his shaved head, bare as an egg. One glimpse of that bare-as-an-egg head made Alexander the Great shudder. He shuddered because he thought he had seen that man before . . . in a dream, or in real life . . . or he'd met him once, or had he? . . . Anyway, it had been very unpleasant, and it had marked his heart in a lasting way. But the man he remembered, who looked like this one in black, had also shaved his head so that it gleamed, but he had a white film where one of his eyes should have been. Alexander the Great could not quite make out whether this man had the same thing.

"These coffins are not for sale . . . They were made for you . . . free of charge," said the man in black. At that moment, Alexander the Great saw that the man had a cataract in his right eye, and his heart winced mightily at the sight. The man in black bore a strong resemblance to the man Alexander the Great had once seen. Not just a resemblance; it was like the very same man was standing before Alexander the Great right now.

"For us?" Thaïs the Athenian stared at the man in black in surprise, her eyes wide.

"Yeah, you," answered the man in black.

"Beg your pardon, but you can lie in those coffins yourself, because we're off to the Holy Land," said Genghis Khan.

"The Holy Land?" the man in black asked, staring at him uncomprehendingly.

"Yes, yes, the Holy Land," said Cleopatra, hurrying to join the conversation. "The Holy Land . . ."

"And where is that?" asked the man in black, intrigued.

"Where else? . . . Out there . . . to the west . . . That's where we're going," said Kozuchak.

"I didn't know there was a land like that," grumbled the man in black.

"Well, now you do!" said Thaïs the Athenian, as testy as ever. "And we want nothing to do with those coffins of yours."

Now Kozuchak noticed a sign, written on a cut-out sheet of cowhide, stretched between twigs it was stitched to on two sides, attached to the wall of a tomb . . .

"What's that?" Kozuchak asked, mystified.

"An official notice . . . I think . . . in Hebrew," said Thaïs the Athenian.

"Hebrew? That's Cyrillic! It's in Russian," Lear argued.

"That's right, it is Russian . . . It's just that the letters are written to look a lot like Hebrew," said Thaïs the Athenian, and she read the sign, syllable by syllable. "Of-fish-shal no-tice."

"It's not an official notice," said the man in black.

"What is it, then?" asked Alexander the Great, who couldn't stop looking at the white smudge in the man in black's eye.

"It's a record of the structure of Death," said the man in black.

"A record of the structure of Death?" they all asked, bewildered, in chorus.

"Yes. A record of the structure of Death," said the man in black.

"Sorry, but who are you, again?" asked Alexander the Great. "Jesus, maybe? Mohammad? Buddha?"

"No, maybe he's Moses, or Nanak Singh, or Zarathustra!" Thaïs the Athenian hopped like a flea as she spoke. "Who are you?"

"Me?"

"Yes, you!"

"I . . ." The man in black froze for a moment. "I am Death!" he said.

"Death?!" The answer stunned them all. Cleopatra started to shiver slightly.

"We can see that you are Death . . . You sure don't look like Life!" said Thaïs the Athenian.

"If you're Death . . . then where the hell were you when the poor Emperor died? We buried him . . . without a coffin . . . in the naked earth," said Lear, frowning.

"And where is he now? None of us know," said Alexander the Great.

"He's in the other world . . . over on the other side," said the man in black.

"Where? What's that, the Garden of Eden?" asked Genghis Khan.

"Are you going to send us there, too?" asked Thaïs the Athenian. "To the Garden of Eden?"

"First, you all have to prepare yourselves for death . . . The time has come for you to answer for everything," said the man in black.

"Us?" They all stared inquisitively at the man in black.

"We'd better start praying! Death himself has come for us . . . dressed all in black . . . but he must have forgotten his scythe somewhere!" Lear said derisively.

They all fell to their knees sarcastically before the man who called himself Death.

"I'm a God-fearing man who's never done anyone any harm," said Genghis Khan.

"I never told a lie for my own benefit," said Alexander the Great.

"And I . . . I've never been a bother to God, never disturbed his slumber," said Cleopatra.

"I've never stolen anything," declared Kozuchak.

"And I've never raised a rebellion or demanded royal power for myself," said Thaïs the Athenian.

"I never thought I knew better than the king. I never even looked his way," said Lear. "I've never blasphemed . . ."

"All right, gang! Death himself has come to take us away in his embrace," said Thaïs the Athenian with a smirk. "But how can this be? No questions at all? He just up and takes us? . . . But we're still alive . . . We're breathing . . . We're full of energy . . . We're having a blast . . . We're singing . . . La-la, tra-la-la! . . . We're enjoying ourselves . . . and you know what else we're doing?"

"Letting the wind out from under our tails!" said Genghis Khan.

"We're ffffarting!" sang Lear, puffing up his cheeks. "Don't pass gas! Your soul will fly out!"

"What a rotten idea, Mr. Comrade, sir," said Thaïs the Athenian, who could quote anyone. "And do you know what Socrates said about death? He said: 'If death is a transition to a better life, as many people surmise, then death is not an evil, but a blessing.' But by the looks of you, you couldn't do anyone a drop of good . . . So, there you have it, God gave us life, and God will take it away . . ."

"You are correct, respected ghosts!" said the man in black.

"Ghosts?!" Genghis Khan was outraged. "Listen, we don't know if you're a sheikh or a saint . . . But watch your mouth, got that? . . . Unless you want to land in one of your own coffins!"

"My respected ghosts!" repeated the man in black solemnly. "God truly did create human beings, love them, and give them all His love . . . Once I, too, was a person like all of you . . . But I acted against God, and was punished for it severely . . . Bearing God's castigation, I was sent to be a gravedigger for body-souls . . . And ever since then, I've been putting people's long-dead bodies into these coffins and entrusting them to the earth."

"All right, let's see if we can reach an agreement," said Lear. "What's your name, dammit? . . . Oh, yes, Mr. Death, Death . . . You'll have to excuse us, but what did we do wrong?"

"Yeah, what did we do?" they all asked.

"We're not heretics or criminals or scoundrels. We're not the kind of people who slander our ancestors. We're not even nutters." Lear was boiling with anger. "This is utter nonsense! What did we do wrong that we're supposed to lie down in your coffins, hmm? . . . Poppycock, that's what it is! . . . And to tell you the truth, everyone here hates death, we laugh at it, and we're not even interested in knowing who or what it is!" Lear spat juicily on the ground, and then, completely transformed, he began speaking rapidly, as if he were burning up in flames. "We know what we want and we do what we want! We screw . . . We carouse . . . We take our pleasure from life, that's what! . . . We even sleep with our feet pointed at God's house . . . And it's because we were born by His will! Quit pestering us, Mr. Death, if you possibly can, and off you go, fare thee well! . . . I'd rather have a suck-up to God right here than a saint far away! . . . Or, better yet, show us the gates to the Holy Land and open them wide for us! Let us wash away all our sins in the Holy Land and take a deep breath of the air in the Garden of Eden!"

"My respected ghosts! If that's the way it's going to be, then read this official notice. Even the Holy Land can't save you!" After saying that, the man in black pointed to the sign on the sheet of cowhide, hanging on the wall of the tomb.

Thaïs the Athenian, who could put on a very good radio host voice, began to read it out loud.

"Soul Cemetery is designed to assist those who want to formally rid themselves of some item or unpleasant event or phenomenon in their lives by virtually burying it. Everything is eligible for burial here: unsuccessful relationships, silly episodes of life, lost or broken items, or just about anything. Please do not create tombs that may offend others—for example, by containing foul expressions or a photograph labeled with the full name of a living person. Management reserves the right to remove tombs that do not meet public standards of morality or other standards, at its own discretion or at the request of third parties. Please do not bury living people or former friends here. No swearing! Life is hard enough already! Soul Cemetery management." Thaïs the Athenian finished reading the notice and burst out laughing. "My dear Mr. Death! I suppose you're earning overtime, working here . . ."

Everyone shared a laugh.

Apparently disgusted with all of them, the man in black began closing the lids of the empty coffins, hammering them shut. After he had pounded nails into the lids of all six coffins, the tall, hefty, muscular, unsightly man in black tied all the empty coffins to his rope, heaved one end of it up over his shoulder, and prepared to drag them away.

"Sorry, but where are you taking those empty coffins?" asked the perplexed Cleopatra.

"They're not empty coffins. I put your souls inside, the ones that left your bodies long ago, and I'm taking them away to bury them," said the man in black.

"But we're standing right here in front of you," said Cleopatra.

"Well, I can't see you . . . Those are only your bodies . . . only your flesh," said the man in black, and then the rumbling noise of the empty coffins started again, just like before, as he began dragging them away toward the old, ruined tombs . . .

At that moment, Alexander the Great walked over and stopped him.

"I have a question for you," said Alexander the Great. "Can you answer it?"

"Ask. I'll answer," said the man in black.

"I've seen you somewhere before . . . only I can't seem to remember," said Alexander the Great. "But it was definitely you . . . a head shaved bare like an egg . . . a cataract in one eye . . . He looked just like you, and sounded just like you . . ."

"That's right . . . I am that man . . . the one you can't quite remember," said the man in black. "Today, you gave me your soul . . . I've been tracking it for a long time . . . The soul you gave me today has spent time in the bodies of thirty-three living creatures, and it came from the body of the last one, a snake, to be in you . . . I used to come to you in your sleep . . . Who are you? Do you know who you are?"

"No," answered Alexander the Great . . .

Like an antique book baring its pages, a secret feeling that resided in his memory unfolded inside his pounding heart, one that contained events long passed. This mysterious feeling, which had never made itself known before, but whose existence he had guessed, filled him with an entire world of memory previously unknown to him, and this world, like molten lead, spread to fill his entire soul. Once, long ago, he could not have conceived of ever being in this situation, this most difficult position. Now, the bald man with a white haze in one eye, dressed in black clothing, seemed to have untied the knot of this deeply buried feeling which had pestered him for so long with hints and forebodings, but which never resolved itself in his breast . . . Everything he had seen and known before disappeared, like water vanishing into sand . . . A vague recognition of these murky ideas stirred a feeling of fear inside him, and a chill seized his body. These terrible ideas made him cold . . . because it now seemed to him that this man had known him for a long time, and not only that, but was privy to all his thoughts, all the treasured secrets of his soul . . . and now he seemed to be searching, among those ancient ideas and episodes which had faded in his heart, for his own death and damnation. The weakened Alexander the Great, bewildered by these thoughts of the man in black, now suspected that even that name might have been given to him by certain black angels, rather than following the reciting of a prayer . . . Deep in his thoughts, he saw the man who called himself Death, and *that* man's death, and in that same man, the one who had appeared to him as a black angel, he saw his *own* death . . . He understood all this . . . He realized that only with the reason, with the intellect, could one understand a past death . . . That was how one could see it . . .

"That's right . . . You don't know who you are . . . And you don't need to know," said the man in black, looking at Alexander the Great as the latter struggled to extricate himself from the thoughts entangling him. "Some people believe that there is life even after death, and in that life, we go on living in a different body, because we've already been born and said goodbye to this world many times before, and after the death of one person and the birth of another, everything is different: the time, the era, the situation, even destiny . . . Some of us say we don't remember, but some of us do . . . And you don't know who you are . . . And you have no right to know . . . Because this World was born that way."

As he'd said he would, the man in black laid the souls that had parted from the bodies of the six into his black coffins, and he dragged them off to nobody knew where . . .

Alexander the Great

Curious . . .

He'd always known a lot about the real Alexander the Great, though now he couldn't remember what the book was called, or who wrote it, but in that book it said that the only thing Alexander the Great feared, his whole life long, was snakes, and when he remembered that now, he realized how similar he was, in his current guise, to the actual Alexander the Great, with his mortal fear of snakes. It turned out he wasn't the only one afraid of them. So was Alexander the Great, who had conquered the whole world. But it wasn't just their identical names and fears that united them. It was more than their fear of snakes that brought them together . . . Why else would he have declared, out loud, in the psychiatric hospital: "I am Alexander the Great!" . . . Strangely enough, whether from this resemblance or because they both feared snakes, this man, today, was experiencing an inexplicable terror, the kind of terror that made his heart freeze for a moment, and then, bursting from its place in his chest, shoot up into his throat, blocking his breath, poised to burst from his breast. Once his heart had lurched up and gotten lodged in his throat, it finally pushed straight through, and once it had shot out of his body, it got bogged down in the surrounding darkness, and an instant later, both that heart, the size of his fist, and either his own soul or the soul of some long-dead person flew straight back into his mouth, descended into his chest, and set about pounding like mad. And when his soul had flown out of his chest, some other soul entirely had taken him over, and he felt very similar to Alexander the Great, who had been so deathly afraid of snakes, and had died in ancient Babylon . . . And, as he lost consciousness, he sank deeper and deeper into the past, whipped by the blades of the windmill of Time, and

something, like a slip of the untouchable, something light and unknow-
able as air, a substance that had been moving toward him since the time
of that ancient, cursed Holy Book, since Babylon, merging along the way
with other living creatures—that substance entered his chest. What was it?
Just like breathing in air, he swallowed that substance, and began quickly
to sink in the well of time, and he saw and heard the fuzzy silhouettes of
people with the Holy Book in their hands, reading a curse from it: "And
I saw another angel sent down from heaven, and the earth trembled with
its might . . . And with a wrathful voice it shouted: 'Fallen! Fallen is the
mighty city of Babylon, the dwelling of the mad, impure spirits, thieves and
sinners; a den of repulsive vultures, where everyone has drunk the maddening wine of her filth and beastliness and sinned alongside the rulers of
the place, where merchants bleat like sheep as they fall from grace, where
women go about uncovered, copulating in public on every street corner,
where human souls and excrement mix in an intoxication of pleasure and
shame' . . . And in great wrath, the heavens grew dark, and a voice thun-
dered down on those who lived there . . . 'O, my people, take no part in the
foul ways of this city, do not subject yourselves to its filth, come away from
there, leave it!' The faults of that city are as high as the sky, and the Lord
God will unleash His wrath on its sinful ways, and afflict the place with a
plague, and there will be death upon death, cry upon cry, and hunger will
seize it by the throat, and fire will take the city, because the Castigation of
God will fall upon it, and its rulers, who have befouled themselves with
shame and do not know God, will weep bitterly in the midst of the great
conflagration, whose smoke will burn their eyes, and unable to bear this
torture, they will beg in humiliation: 'O black plague of despair, why do
you burden us with suffering? Why have you condemned the great city,
the powerful city, of Babylon? Here, merchants weep, finding no buyers
for their wares, and soon all gold and silver will vanish from this city,
and pearls and precious stones, and silks and fragrant wood, and valuable
ivory bones, and jewelry of copper and silver, and aromatic potions and
sweet-smelling waters, and wine that spins the head and livestock not yet a
year old, and full hives of honeybees and snorting horses, and carts full of
goods and human bodies and souls: none of this will be found here, now,
and the great city of Babylon will fall, cursed!'"

When he heard this curse from the Holy Book, the man thought of himself as more than an equal to Alexander; he felt that he *was* Alexander. Or perhaps the soul of Alexander the Great truly had settled inside him? . . . The soul of the true Alexander the Great, which had left his body for the other world the night of the Babylonian curse, living afterward for many centuries in the bodies of various animals, had found a new home for itself, and, just maybe, it had entered his body along with the venom of the snake that had bitten him one year ago . . . He felt that he was the notorious Alexander the Great . . .

Babylon had fallen . . . The great and sinful city had fallen! . . .

Alexander's warriors filled the city like black smoke and plundered everything they could reach, sacking the riches, drinking the wine, stealing their pleasure from life, raping every woman in turn, until not one was left unharmed. By the time his gleeful warriors rushed in mindless greed to plunder the city, Alexander no longer felt like celebrating his victory. One thought kept plaguing him, one that had long given him no rest: the thought of stomping out the Persian king, Darius, turning him to dust, and releasing that dust on the breeze; and that idea prodded Alexander on to death and blood, capturing his entire being and all his thoughts. This was because Darius, who had not yet crossed the Euphrates, had raised an enormous army from all corners of his kingdom for one terrible, decisive battle. For Alexander, that battle would be more than a clash with the Persian king. It was enormously significant to him, because it meant a cherished opportunity to lay hold of the Gates to Asia. Beyond Darius lay half the Earth. After Alexander leveled the city of Celaenae, he had walked into Zeus's temple. The temple to Zeus, who had smashed rocks to dust with his might, was a temple of seers who could unveil a person's destiny and predict every misfortune that was to befall that person in his lifetime. Alexander had no trust in soothsayers, so he ordered them all to be killed, after having their mouths gagged with rags and their eyes blindfolded. Alexander may have been the only king in the world who so detested soothsayers, and he had his reasons. The day that he took Midas's city, a local seer had told him: "You, tiger, are a man with a bold heart, and you will die not by the hand of man; a snake will kill you." Ever since the great commander had heard those words, he had been ill at ease. Since then, he had dreamed only of a sea of hissing serpents that covered the entire earth, and the snakes were always creeping toward him, chasing him, and this fear, like the snakes he dreamed up, was pursuing him everywhere. He suspected the seer's words would never leave him at peace in the world again. Alexander conquered countless cities, and in every defeated city, he took the most beautiful girl, gorgeous as the sun or the moon, and stripped her of her virginity in his golden covered chariot. Inside the covered chariot was a bed of nine layers of blankets made of precious cloth, topped with snow-white sheets, and under the vehicle there were rows of slaves who held the chariot on their shoulders, and beneath their feet, under the chariot, lay other slaves, whose bodies covered all the ground under the chariot, and around the chariot there stood a squadron of armed soldiers holding flaming torches. Alexander, taking every precaution, had ordered these things done because he figured that snakes would be unable to slither into the chariot through the bodies of the slaves. The beauties in his arms were replaced in every newly conquered city, and from every newly conquered city, a gorgeous new girl lay in the king's bed. This king who ate what slaves never eat, who drank what slaves never drink, made love with a new, beautiful girl every night, from dusk until the morning stars, and the more the chariot shook, the louder the beautiful girl moaned in his embrace, and the slaves' shoulders that supported that chariot from twilight till dawn were thatched with countless scratches . . . Before he seized the city of Celaenae, Alexander had conquered thirty-three other cities, and three hundred sixty girls had spent time in his embrace. Until recently, every time he seized another city, Alexander alone was allowed to spend the night with a woman from the conquered city, while his warriors were under orders not to touch the women. Any man who disobeyed his command was burned alive in front of the people. This was because, after they took the city of Sardis, he had announced that every soldier would be allowed to rape all the women they wanted, and he promised them every woman in the world. The army spent three days and three nights in Sardis, and the warriors, who let no woman escape their attentions, were infected with a group case of syphilis, and in the end more than three thousand soldiers died of it . . . The city's women carried the cursed disease, and it killed Alexander's best soldiers. After that, his army was much reduced in number. Alexander then forbade his soldiers from raping women. But after they conquered Celaenae, Alexander succumbed to his emotions, revoked his previous law, and gave the order permitting the soldiers to rape as many women as they wanted, because everyone believed the women of Celaenae were the cleanest and most beautiful women in the world, and they kept themselves immaculate, washing in the River Marsyas, where the nymphs also bathed. Alexander knew this well, so he allowed his soldiers to rape again. Much earlier, when Alexander had never slept with a woman in his life, his thoughts had been wholly occupied with the battles to come. The important thing was to crush Darius to dust and ashes, and scatter those ashes in the wind, and then the road to Asia would open before him. When Alexander went to the temple of Zeus, it wasn't to get a glimpse of the world-renowned seers and soothsayers. It was to find out who would win the battle for the Gates to Asia. As soon as Alexander walked into the temple, he saw a cart parked by a wall, one that Gordias had once driven. This cart looked no different from any ordinary carriage; the only extraordinary thing was its yoke, secured with a countless number of knots, which would be extremely difficult to untie. The local seers had foretold that the person who untied those knots would conquer all of Asia. The yoke was tied tightly, and nobody had any idea which length of rope led from one knot to the next. Alexander pondered over this tangle of knots for a long time, and then, finally, said, "What does it matter *how* they are untied?" And he drew his sword and sliced through all the knots. Then the seers predicted: "Alexander the Great will conquer the world with his sword, but he will die a beastly death."

So began a worldwide, blood-soaked tragedy . . .

Alexander moved against Darius. Before his great campaign, Alexander had a dream . . .

He dreamed of a coffin . . . The lid of the coffin had been removed, and it was empty . . . Four people were carrying it . . . When Alexander the King asked whose coffin it was, nobody carrying the coffin offered even a word in response . . . The coffin was made of oak planks, and painted with a dark brown paint that glimmered in the sun . . . A boy walked before the coffin-bearers, ringing a small bell . . . Alexander was terrified by this vision, and his terror was because it seemed to him that this was a warning

of coming disaster . . . The boy ringing the bell was blind, as Alexander
noticed when he walked past, and the four people carrying the coffin had
their ears cut off and their heads shaved bare, and their shoulders, which
bore the coffin, were covered in sores . . . They looked like slaves who
constantly carried this empty coffin . . . Sharp cries broke out behind Alexander: "Who died? Whose coffin is that? Why is it empty?" From the thick
masses of people, a throng like a flock of ravens, a decrepit old woman who
had outlived her wits burst to the front, and she started to crow at the jos-
tling crowd: "The fool has been caught in his own trap. He wants to wear
the crown of God, he calls himself the son of Zeus, he wants to destroy all
humankind! He wants to take God's throne away from Him! The power
left him by his ancestors isn't enough for him! . . . May his brains rot! He's
a son of man, or has he forgotten? . . . He's a slave of God! His body will
go unburied, and his soul will know no rest and will bear eternal Castigation! He condemned himself! He'll die a beastly death! And it won't be
the death he's supposed to die, not in a bloody battle, but from the venom
of a snake! A fitting end for a man who claims God's majesty! Only God is
eternal! Only one life is given forever! . . . Only Castigation lasts forever!
His soul has chosen Eternal Castigation! He wanted to take the might of
God for himself! Nobody will mourn his death, this man, and he thinks
he's the equal of God, spilling a sea of human love and a sea of human
blood? He who wields the sword will die of the sword . . . Man loves God,
and God loves man! . . . But this one?" The old woman fell to the ground
and let out a piercing scream. "You're not the pillar of the World! All the
living beings on Earth were not born to feed your belly! Your time has
come, you madman, your time is nearly up, you wretch! O Lord, I bow
only to You, I pray only to You! Hear my voice!" The frail woman gave
one last screech and died, as if she'd been shot with an arrow, clawing her
fingers into the ground. Suddenly, the old woman's ash-colored hair was
in motion, and every strand of hair transformed into one slender snake,
and countless tiny snakes began slithering from the woman's head, as if
slithering from the nest. Soon they filled all the space around, turning
the place into one vast pit of vipers. The snakes lifted their tiny heads
high and hissed menacingly. The flood of snakes surged toward Alexander
the Great . . . Alexander shuddered . . . Fear seized him . . . Alexander's

mother, Olympias, had always kept snakes, snakes she coddled and fed like her own children, and eventually, snakes like that would bite him and he would die . . . Suddenly, his mother herself appeared, splashing milk toward the waves of snakes, and in an instant all the earth seemed washed with milk and the snakes vanished . . . The world froze in silence . . . Alexander could hear nothing but the bell ringing in the blind boy's hands . . . Ding! Ding! Ding! . . . The boy stopped not far from him, and stood as if carved from stone . . . A grave had been dug there, where the coffin was meant to be buried, and the coffin-bearers lowered the empty coffin inside it . . . Without filling in the grave, they started back, the blind boy in the lead, followed by the four coffin-bearers, their heads shaved bare, their ears sliced off, all walking silently past Alexander the Great . . . The only audible sound was the ringing of the bell, which sounded like the beating of his heart. No, that wasn't the bell ringing, but Alexander the Great's heart beating . . . Thump! Thump! . . .

He jumped from his bed as if someone had poured cold water on his head . . . He woke up and looked around. Not a soul . . . In the sky, he could see the young moon, and a sprinkling of stars spotting the space around it . . . In the morning, Alexander summoned two women who interpreted dreams, and he spent a long time retelling his nightmare to them.

"If you dream of a coffin, that's a good omen, my sovereign . . . It means that all your troubles and cares will be consigned to the earth," said the older interpreter of dreams.

"An open, empty coffin means that all your worthless thoughts will leave you, my sovereign," said the younger interpreter of dreams.

"And the blind boy? The bell? The men with the sliced-off ears?" Alexander asked.

"The blind boy, my sovereign . . . that means you must trust not in what your eyes see, but what your heart sees . . . and the bell . . . that is the voice of your heart . . . It is a sign: listen only to your heart, my master," said the old interpreter of dreams. "And the four men with their ears cut off, that too is a sign: do not do what your ears hear, but what your heart hears, my master."

"What about the old woman?" Alexander asked the interpreters of dreams.

Both women fell silent in response. They did not know how to inter-pret the old woman, and they paused.

"You don't know? Well, I do!" Alexander shouted in fury. "Do you know who you both are? You're servants of the devil! . . . The devil sends these dreams, and you interpret them! If you don't know who the old woman is I dreamed of, I'll tell you all about her! It's the devil himself, the one you don't want to mention to me! Only the devil doesn't want men to be equal to the might of God! The devil is the one who plants such thoughts in men!"

Furious, Alexander the Great ordered his soldiers to take both inter-preters of dreams to the chopping block and cut off their heads . . .

Now Alexander the Great was preparing for war with Darius . . .

A Great Battle lay ahead . . . Alexander the Great was readying to open the Gates to Asia . . .

Alexander the Great began his battle against Darius at dawn, when the night's stars began to fade . . . The sun was invisible behind the clouds of flying arrows, and dust obscured the sky. Terrorizing the whole shaken world with the thunder of the crazed battle, the battle that overturned all creation, a relentless current of clashes between mighty powers furiously swept away everything around them . . . The earth stank of blood, and mountains of corpses rose high in the air . . . The merciless Alexander the Great, the man who had set this butchery in motion, showed no pity to anyone, and displayed no mercy; for him, newborn infants and gray-bearded elders were all the same, and in the land of his enemies, everyone was his enemy; he could not find peace until he tore them all out by the roots, transformed into something more beast than man . . . In the fight-ing, swords broke, heads were severed, spears snapped in half . . . The world had never seen such a terrible slaughter, and afterward the vultures, crows, and buzzards, who spent all day pecking at the human bodies in the blood-soaked steppe, were stuffed so fat they could no longer take off in flight. At Cilicia, called the Gates of Asia Minor, Darius's weak-ened army fell, admitting defeat . . . At Issus, the Persians, unable to offer any resistance against Alexander's frenzied assault, retreated, and Darius's prized army quickly fell to pieces and was disgraced. Darius fled the bat-tlefield, leaving his family and children to the whims of fate, searching for salvation for himself alone, a way to save his own life. Issus, soaked in blood, was defeated and completely destroyed. Four commanders close to Darius were taken prisoner, along with his thirteen-year-old son, and they were brought before Alexander the Great. When he saw them, Alexander the Great froze in astonishment. These four prisoners were exact replicas of the coffin-bearers from his dream, their heads shaved bare and their ears sliced off, and the boy was a copy of the blind boy who led their procession, ringing his bell . . . Now, begging for mercy, they all bowed at Alexander's feet, reminding him of the vision given to him before this grand campaign. Alexander the Great, who had always said that the enemy must die either in battle from an arrow or sword, or in captivity in the hangman's noose, who always decapitated the prisoners who beseeched him for mercy, froze still at the sight of these prisoners . . . Why had he dreamed of these people at his feet before this campaign? The question confounded him . . . The thought of it, like water poured on a camp-fire, utterly confused him. He knew that death awaited these captives, but one thing bothered him: What might the connection be between this event and the dream he'd had before the battle? The city of Issus was fully destroyed and burned to the ground; not only the buildings had gone up in smoke, but also the corpses . . . All the captured women, children, and old people were locked in a fortress with high walls in the middle of the burning city of Issus . . . Alexander the Great, who had planned to annihilate them all entirely, was struck by the coincidence, the repetition of his dream here, in real life, and he was overcome by vague, confusing thoughts . . . Then Alexander changed his mind and resolved to put off, for one day, the killing of those who had been shut in the fortress. He warned his soldiers, thirsty for a fight, that if a single hair fell from the head of a prisoner, they would pay the price. Alexander spent one sleepless night in Darius's palace in the city of Issus, and all his thoughts, all his feelings, were occupied with nothing but that cursed dream and its real-life varia-tion. He simply could not escape the thought of it. The dream pursued him everywhere. And then, to rid himself of those churning feelings and ideas, he decided to let loose and relax with some women and drink wine. By then, he was in the habit of giving himself over to pleasure after a big battle, when he wanted to celebrate a victory. What's more, the Persian women's matchless beauty and sweetness attracted him. He remembered telling his advisor Aristotle, after he conquered Gordia, that Persia would be next. He declared then: "There must be only one emperor in this world, and that is me, Alexander the Great!" Then he continued. "Hear this: I want to conquer Persia for three reasons. One: to hang Darius. Two: his wealth. Three: Persian women!" Aristotle, who never concealed the truth from him, responded: "My sovereign, do you know the reason wars begin, empires collapse, and emperors fall?" "You're the advisor. You tell me!" Alexander the Great scoffed at him, annoyed. "Perhaps you will have me decapitated for these words, but I value the truth more highly than my head," said Aristotle. "There are only two causes. The first is riches, and the second is women." To Alexander, those words were like a slap in the face. But he did not express the anger that rose in his heart in any way; he did nothing to Aristotle, who had uttered the words that might have sentenced him to death. Unexpectedly, he recalled that conversation now . . . Alexander the Great was there in the palace of Darius, who had fled . . . The place was scented with the sweet aroma of roses, and lovely birds sang, as if the palace were part of some genuine paradise. But, even so, there was a battle going on in Alexander's soul between untamed passion, which was natural to him, and thoughts about that grim dream. It might have been an attempt to rid himself of the nagging thought of that dream that he ordered his bodyguards: "Bring them in!"

Every time he seized a new city, Alexander enjoyed sampling the joy of all-consuming lust. They brought him seven gorgeous Persian women. Alexander always followed certain rules in lovemaking. After he conquered Troy, when he had felt the same desire to enjoy the pleasure of proximity to a young woman, the girl they brought him had secreted a dagger in her clothing, and she tried to stab him in the chest; it was only his strength and agility that had saved him then. Alexander punished her mercilessly, handing her over for ill treatment to forty of his commanders, and then ordered her hanged before the gates to Troy. After that incident, every girl brought to him was stripped completely bare. That was the Emperor's rule. He prepared to take his pleasure in the seven lovely Persians, to sample joy in this cypress-scented garden of lust. The seven lovely virgins entered the Emperor's spacious bedroom and set about kissing and caressing Alexander the Great. And when, intoxicated by the aroma of their perfumes, the Emperor was as engulfed in pleasure as he would be in the gardens of Paradise, when he was close to the peak of bliss, a small golden bell that lay next to his pillow fell to the floor. The ringing of that bell was a splash of ice-cold water to Alexander. He jumped up as if he'd been stung. He recalled that dream, that vision. All seven women backed away and left the room. Alexander the Great picked up the little bell, and unpleasant thoughts crept back into his mind. He demanded a seer be brought to him immediately. He described his dream in detail and waited for a response . . .

The soothsayer listened, bewildered, and said nothing. Alexander hated seers more than anything else in the world. He summoned them, listened to everything they told him, and had them executed the follow-ing morning. They knew their deaths were imminent, yet they always told him everything, hiding nothing. Nobody knew how many seers Alexander had put to death. Alexander followed a rule: nobody other than he himself could ever hear what a soothsayer told him. Now, a decrepit, lame old man sat before Alexander the Great. The old man knew his hour would come, that Alexander the Great would summon him. He had been expecting it. The seer could feel the sword blade at his neck, and he spoke the truth . . .

"This year is the three hundred thirty-third year," began the elderly seer. His eyes were moist with tears. "Bad tidings . . . your star has set, my lord . . . The men bearing the empty coffin signify those who are waiting for your soul . . . The blind boy . . . that means that you will see nothing . . . I began with the words three hundred thirty-three, my sovereign . . . Before you are thirty-three years old, you will die from the bite of a snake, at the hand of someone close to you . . . They will exter-minate your entire line . . . You will conquer all the world . . . But you, or, more precisely, your soul, will not die . . . After it settles in the souls of thirty-three animals, it will come to reside in a human being, and enter his body . . . The last of those animals will be a snake . . . and only then will your soul bear its Castigation . . . I am the thirty-third seer you have summoned . . . The thirty-third seer you will execute . . . A person spilling another person's blood is a coup of the devil, and a curse on us all . . . You are Emperor to us and a slave to the Devil . . . It is not human reason that rules you, but the Devil. I want to tell you this . . . You must cut off the four prisoners' ears and put out the boy's eyes . . . You must make them into the way you saw them in your dream . . . Put Darius's clothing into an empty coffin . . . Set the procession on its way, with the blind boy in the lead . . . They will walk across the world . . . This is the way you will ward off the evil gathering force around you, and confound the Devil's plans," concluded the lame old seer.

Early the next morning, the thirty-third soothsayer was put to death . . .

The people gathered before the gates of the city of Issus. Darius's four commanders were made to stand on a high platform, along with his thirteen-year-old son. First, they cut off the ears of the four military commanders and shaved their heads bare . . . After that, Alexander came to stand on the platform to remove the boy's eyes himself. Alexander the Great looked into the boy's eyes. Those eyes seemed extraordinary to him . . . Truly, before now, he had never seen such clear, transparent eyes. Alexander had not uttered a sound, before, as he watched the men's ears being sliced off, although his heart pained him. Now the boy was offering him his clear eyes, without fear. The Emperor saw the blue sky reflected in the child's eyes. Those eyes themselves resembled the sky . . . Only now did the Emperor understand how beautiful human eyes could be. Perhaps it was because, before, nobody had ever been able to look him straight in the eye that this child's eyes, now gazing straight at him, looked so clear and supremely beautiful . . . Yes, only now did he realize how beautiful a person's eyes could be . . . When the Emperor heard people speak of human beings, he imagined huge mountains of decapitated heads, and only that kind of victory ever satisfied him; only that gave him strength and a new lease on life and renewed his desire to seize new lands and new cities. But for Alexander the Great, who had ripped the roots of venerable lines from the earth, who had used the rootless to exterminate whole clans, who had made all manner of kings bow before him, who considered himself the strongest of the strong, the words of one lame old man had been a knife to the heart . . . That day, he had heard from the lame soothsayer the pure truth about his own death. Before that, he had declared himself Emperor of the entire world, and equated himself with God, and felt himself the true son of Zeus . . .

The child's clear eyes reminded him of the seer's terrible words about his death . . .

Alexander the Great used his thumbs to push the boy's eyes from their sockets, and he threw those eyes into the crowd . . . The child's warm eyes lay on the ground. The people watched all this and held their breath in silence. Very soon, two birds appeared out of nowhere and flew straight to the boy's eyes, picked them up in their beaks, and carried them into the sky . . .

Alexander watched for a long time as they walked away into the distance: four military commanders with their ears sliced off, barely shuffling their feet, bearing a coffin that held no body, and leading them, a blind boy ringing a little bell, stepping barefoot over the hot, sun-baked sand . . . Even though blood trickled from the boy's empty eye sockets, where his clear eyes once had been, he kept them trained on the path ahead, and rang his little bell . . .

Now Alexander was hot with anger, and he prepared to destroy all the prisoners from the city of Issus whom he had locked in the fortress. As usual, the warriors set arrows in their bows and aimed them at the prisoners, waiting for the Emperor's order to begin the extermination. Alexander the Great loved to watch his men murder his enemies before his eyes. This time, Alexander took up a bow himself and aimed at a boy standing in the first row of prisoners. The boy at which his arrow was aimed looked at the Emperor without fear, as if simply waiting for that arrow. To Alexander the Great, his eyes seemed just as beautiful as those of the boy whose eyes he had just removed. Not only *his* eyes, either; the eyes of every prisoner standing there looked extraordinary . . . The bow was drawn, and any second now the arrow would burst free and pierce the boy's body, but Alexander the Great was lost in thought, and after a short while, he raised his bow higher and shot the arrow into the sky. A thousand more arrows flew skyward after his. The rush of arrows blocked out the sun.

Alexander the Great spoke to his warriors:

"My falcons! You are the soldiers of a great Emperor! Your swords must only be raised against our enemies. My warriors do not aim their arrows at unarmed people and prisoners lying on the ground! . . . Force can only counter force, and those like Darius, who flee before me with

their tails between their legs—I do not consider them enemies! Freedom
to all the prisoners. Let them go! And you, my hawks: rejoice! At ease!"
That was his solemn command. From the cruel Alexander the Great, who
always exterminated everyone he encountered on his campaigns, who
always destroyed entire peoples, this decision came like a thunderclap in
a clear sky . . .

Everyone froze, stunned speechless, quiet enough to hear the sound
of a passing fly . . .

The city of Issus had been consumed for days with a raging fire and
stank of death and corpses, but that night was a holiday . . . Music played,
wine flowed, and, as if somebody had waved a magic wand, the city was
resurrected, and celebrated lustily . . . Alexander's soldiers let no woman
of Issus go untouched, and raped the prettiest of them from dusk to dawn,
and drank until they were drunk . . .

That night, only Alexander the Great did not celebrate . . .

During the siege of Issus, in the heat of the blood-soaked battle, Alexander the Great had been wounded in the thigh with a spear. The pain
from the wound was powerful, but he concealed it from the soldiers fighting by his side. Instead, to inspire them, he led them forward, throwing
himself into the hottest points of battle in a way that would have allowed
nobody to think he was experiencing any pain. But now, after conquering
Issus, when victory rested in his hands, the ache of that wound, which he
could now feel in full measure, grew stronger, making him moan. The
only thing Alexander the Great lacked now was Darius as his prisoner, so
he was eager to set off immediately after him, not letting Darius get too far
away; but his wound would not permit him to stand securely on his feet.
After sufficient time had passed, Alexander resolved to set out again on the
hunt. He would deal one final, crushing blow to the Persian empire and
open the road to India. Paying no attention to the intense summer heat,
Alexander the Great set off for Phoenicia. When they saw Alexander's vast
army, which covered all the earth, many cities on their way surrendered
without a fight, opening their gates to him. But the city of Tyre stopped
Alexander's army in its tracks and resisted fiercely for seven months, result-
ing in many losses on both sides, and ending with a mountain of corpses
at the door to the city and in its streets. In the heat of summer, the corpses

quickly spoiled, and infectious diseases spread rapidly. Alexander the Great tried to leave Tyre as soon as he had conquered it, but, despite his best efforts, many of his men fell ill, and they began to die. The city was plundered, all its wealth hauled away . . .

Alexander the Great always left looted cities behind, and his victorious army brought thorough extermination and inhuman suffering to Asia Minor . . . Next, it was the turn of the city of Persepolis, and the man leading the battle there was Ptolemy, Alexander's friend and loyal companion since childhood; waging war, Ptolemy was even more bloodthirsty and cruel than Alexander himself. The inhuman ferocity of the Macedonian conquerors who had buried Asia Minor in a terrible storm stirred many rumors about their lust for blood, planting an overwhelming fear in every city. Persia could no longer hold back the lion's onslaught, and many cities succumbed to Alexander's armies . . . One division, under Ptolemy's command, surrounded Persepolis, a major Persian city, and reduced the beautiful city to ruins within a week. Ptolemy had a weakness for women, and he followed the advice of his mistress, Thaïs the Athenian, and burned Persepolis, leaving nothing but rubble behind. Persepolis was not burned in the course of fierce fighting for the city. It was burned at the whim of a hetaera.

Leaving the incinerated city behind, Alexander the Great and his army advanced to the east. The scouts following Darius's trail reported to Alexander that Darius's army had fallen apart, his soldiers fleeing in all directions, and that Darius's closest advisors had forged a conspiracy and murdered him. Alexander the Great's soldiers were overjoyed to hear the news; it meant victory over their greatest foe, and they threw their swords and spears into the air with shouts of joy . . .

In the intense, burning heat of summer, Alexander the Great decided to continue marching his army forward . . . The terrible heat suffocated the soldiers, and the horses refused to move and fell to the ground, one after another. The sun burned without mercy in the sandy desert they traversed. Desperate for even a single drop of water, the soldiers could no longer move forward, and the last of their strength was lost . . . A quiet discontent spread among the troops. Whatever he knew or didn't know, whatever he heard or didn't hear, Alexander the Great remained calm . . . Nobody could have advised him to turn his army back . . . Even the news that his chief enemy, Darius, had been killed by the conspirators could not sway Alexander from his chosen path. . . . After three days and three nights marching across the enormous desert, in a low spot between dunes, they found an abandoned well. When Alexander drew near to this well, he saw an astounding sight. There, lying at the well, were the bodies of the four men with sliced-off ears and shaved heads, and the body of the blind boy with the little bell, whom he had seen in that long-ago, almost-forgotten dream. Their corpses had been so abused by desert insects and jackals that their dry bones were visible in places where chunks of flesh had been torn away . . . Nobody knew what misfortune had brought them to the middle of this endless desert. Alexander the Great immediately recognized the boy whose eyes he had personally put out, and the little bell tied to his hand gleamed in the sun . . . This boy's beautiful, clear eyes floated through Alexander's memory . . . Now, dark holes occupied their place on his face. Alongside the twisted body of the boy was his scalp, with its thin, black curls . . . A vision of the boy's eyes, clear as the blue sky, appeared before Alexander, those clear, extraordinary eyes which he had put out with his own thumbs, and these empty eye sockets, where the fire had been extinguished, these black holes seared by the sun, reminded him of those eyes, so genuinely pure, so genuinely gorgeous. Just at that moment, two tiny, silver snake heads appeared in those empty eye sockets . . . The snakes' skin glimmered as if wet in the sun, a strange gleam, like the shine of something anointed with oil . . . The snakes looked like the kind who could strike their victim with the speed of lightning. (Olympias, Alexander's mother, used to tell him that the venom of the serpents who ruled the vast desert was the strongest of all. She said these silvery, lightning-quick snakes quickly grew accustomed to human beings, and were very loyal to their master, obeying his or her every command, and if the master asked the snake to attack someone, it would not hesitate to wreak its master's vengeance. That made them different from other snakes. The Persians kept such snakes hidden in secret places, and fed them by hand, and sicced them on their personal enemies, when necessary, in order to destroy them . . .)

Not only did Alexander the Great seize Persian lands; he had also completely destroyed the greatest city in Darius's empire, the city of Ecbatana.

This was a great and holy city for the Persians, the center of their religion, and it boasted a monument to Zarathustra, god of the sun-worshipers. Alexander the Great had ordered that monument destroyed, to erect in its place the symbol of his own empire: the statue of a lion. The believers in the Sun considered the lion a personification of the devil's dark forces, and yet Alexander the Great had trampled on the sun-worshipers' sacred faith and declared: "In this world, there is only one God, and I am Him!" He ordered the execution of everyone who believed in Zarathustra and worshiped him, and he ordered the Avesta, the Holy Book, to be burned . . . The sun-worshipers cursed Alexander the Great and started looking for ways to kill him . . . The spirit of the Persian lord of dark forces, Guzasta, awoke, and the people called Alexander the Great a devil-man. The sun-worshipers conspired and agreed that they would erect a golden statue of whoever killed the devil-man, and the prophets would give him eternal life . . . (Guzasta dispatches his two lightning-quick silver snakes, with orders to kill Alexander the Great . . .) Human beings rarely even notice snakes so quick and nimble . . . The horses jerked and reared up in fright when they sensed the snakes in motion . . . Then, one snake, holding itself straight and firm as a wire, shot like an arrow toward Alexander the Great . . . Alexander remembered the seer's words about how a snake's bite would kill him. Moving its head, the size of a fingernail, the same way it moved its slender tail, the snake approached the hooves of Alexander the Great's horse . . . When the horse, frightened by the snake, skittered sideways, Alexander the Great flew from the saddle. The soldiers saw all this and directed a hail of arrows at the quick-moving snake. Barely one step from the spot where Alexander fell from his horse, an arrow pierced the snake's head. The snake coiled itself around the arrow, its jaws gaping wide but powerless, its venomous fangs shooting the poison meant for Alexander onto the ground . . . The snake whose head had been pierced by an arrow one step from Alexander still stared fixedly at him, its eyes bright as diamonds, as if trying to enchant and bewitch him . . . The snake's eyes seemed to be shooting arrows, too, and their sting was unpleasant . . . Alexander's hand felt for the handle of his sword. He gripped it feverishly, but felt a helplessness in his body, a complete apathy in his soul, preventing him from striking the snake as it writhed before him. He saw the horse's hooves and smelled the dust they raised. In the blink of an eye, turmoil sprang up all around him. When Alexander, whose legs seemed to have been taken away from him, finally did lift his weapon and strike the snake that had shot like an arrow toward him, the blade hit a rock, and a spark flew . . . The snake had darted smooth as an arrow, rushing madly toward Alexander. Bodyguards hurried to where the emperor lay on the ground, surrounding him from all sides. They supported Alexander and helped him to stand . . . Nobody noticed that this event, which passed in an instant like a flash of lightning, had set Alexander trembling, sending a cold fear through his soul. What struck him the hardest was not the appearance of that lightning-quick snake, but the connection between this event and the soothsayer's words, the perfect match between what had been said and what had transpired . . . Alexander the Great picked up the arrow that had pierced the snake's head, right between its eyes, and turned to his soldiers. "Whose arrow is this?" "Mine," answered a bodyguard. Alexander gave the guard a clap on the shoulder and high praise for his marksmanship . . . That was the first snake he had seen since the seer had predicted a snake would cause his death. No, this was no ordinary snake; it was a true silver arrow . . . The silver snake that had crawled out of the blind boy's other eye socket disappeared as if it had fallen through the earth. Since ancient times, people have said that silver snakes always hold a grudge. None of the soldiers saw where the second snake went . . .

Alexander the Great ordered his guards to bury the bodies of the four men with sliced-off ears and the blind boy . . . As soon as they had buried them, the second silver snake's small head flashed in the sun, and it sank its venomous fangs into the heel of Alexander's bodyguard, the one who had shot the first snake, and then, in the space of a split second, it twisted around and vanished from view, shooting like an arrow into the sand . . . The soldier bitten by the snake could not say a word. He fell to the ground, dead . . . At this, his first sight of a snake's vengeance, the jagged thoughts that stole Alexander's peace of mind gripped him again, like shackles . . .

Before the sun set, Alexander the Great had left the great desert behind and emerged in the Euphrates River Valley . . . Here, his soldiers, tired after their long journey, pitched tents, lay down in a row, and fell into a deep sleep . . .

Now the road before him led to Babylon . . .

Nobody knew that the second lightning-quick snake had crept onto a cart, and clung to a feed bag, and arrived here with them to complete its quest for revenge . . .

The snake meant to strike back against Alexander the Great.

The snake meant to strike back against Alexander the Great . . .

Babylon.

There, what awaited the conqueror of half the world, the Great Emperor, was not the triumph of victory but the funeral of his closest friend, Hephaestion. The terrible news of his friend's poisoning, which Alexander received several months before he arrived in Babylon, burdened him with a heavy grief and thousands of dark thoughts and suspicions. The news seemed to strip the skin from his body. Alexander the Great had extraordinary respect for the friend he was now mourning and had cherished him immensely. He had loved him beyond all measure . . . The sudden loss was a terrible burden to him. For the Emperor, to whom human life was always balanced on the edge of a sword blade, the death of his closest companion, the man with whom he had dreamed of great victories, lay like a stone in his soul, like a knife in his heart . . . Alexander the Great sent a messenger to inquire from the oracle of Amon whether Hephaestion could be declared a god, and be given all the divine honors to accompany him to the next world . . . The messenger brought good news back from Amon, and the answer was passed to Alexander: his close friend could be elevated to the rank of Hero and buried with the rites that came with that rank. Alexander the Great was extraordinarily glad to receive that news. He made plans to shower every honor on his dear friend, worthy of godhood, and see him off to the other world with immense respect and honor. Alexander, who had declared to all the peoples he conquered, large and small, that he was God, made the unthinkable decision to destroy the central Persian temple in Babylon and make it into a Temple to Worship the Emperor (Alexander), Recognized as God of the Gods. Many people frowned upon this decision by Alexander the Great. When the Persians heard of it, they debated the topic passionately, and the flames of displeasure began to smolder. This temple was sacred to them . . . With this act, Alexander the Great was transgressing the limits of the permissible, spitting at the Persians' souls, and he seemed to have no understanding that his unconscionable decisions were provoking the people's ire and making them his enemy. It was more evidence for the whole world that Alexander the Great, who considered himself God's incarnation on Earth, felt there was nobody equal to him in honor or respect in the world, nobody who might give him wise counsel or rebuff him in any way that mattered . . .

Under cover of night, a soothsayer was brought to Alexander and warned him that terrible events were imminent. Alexander heard that he must leave Babylon immediately, deserting the city. Babylon was a spoiled place, a city facing the wrath of God, with a people cursed by God . . . (And I saw an angel sent down from heaven, and its glory illuminated the Earth . . . And with a terrible voice it called out: "Fallen! Fallen is the mighty city of Babylon, the refuge of the mad, the nest of all impure spirits, the den of all sinful beasts and repulsive birds, the city drunk on the maddening wine of lust, fueling hatred in every people for all others." And I heard a voice from the heavens: "O, my people, do not descend into the sin of this city, do not take its misfortunes and calamities upon yourselves, but leave it in haste!" . . .) The seer told him in detail that there were dark forces thirsting for his death, and that he could see secret plans being forged against Alexander. These words infuriated Alexander the Great, whose stallion beat his hoof against the moon, for whom there was no one in this world who could make him stop or think. "I AM THE GOD OF GODS. IS THERE ANY WHO DARES STIR THE WRATH OF GOD?!" he shouted, and ordered the seer to be taken from the palace and executed . . . All the preparations were underway for his closest friend's funeral . . . Alexander the Great, who had taken Hephaestion's death close to heart, let his wrath fly, furiously attacking everyone responsible for aspects of the funeral, whether they were generals or his closest advisers, bodyguards or soldiers or palace servants. He vowed that after Hephaestion's funeral, he would expose everyone guilty of conspiring to kill him, all the secret plotters, and execute them on Babylon's biggest square . . .

On that day . . . the day of Hephaestion's funeral . . .

Babylon played host to Hephaestion's funeral rites, and in his honor, a great feast was held . . .

Invited to the great feast were the men who managed Alexander the Great's court, the people he most trusted, and his military commanders. The bountiful meal was to take place in Semiramis's Hanging Gardens. These Hanging Gardens were a slice of Paradise, a miraculous place built high as a vast pyramid, where flowers and astounding trees brought from every corner of the world grew, where one could hear the glorious songs of an unprecedented variety of birds and the babbling of brooks. As for running water, there were waterfalls and cascades, enough to feel like heaven. Like the Garden of Eden, it was a marvelous place of pleasure. The funeral feast began. When the mourning was over, Alexander planned to go on expanding the borders of his empire, to conquer Arabia to the south, Carthage to the west, and Italy to the north . . .

The first toast was raised in honor of the mighty Hercules and the poisoned Hephaestion. The death of his blood brother Hephaestion was a grievous loss for him, yet this pleased him, because the oracle of Amon had declared Hephaestion a divine hero . . . Alexander quickly drank the wine poured into his silver cup . . . Everyone sitting at the table watched the Emperor drink, but they were not merely watching with pride; they were waiting for his gulps of that wine to send the famed commander into the embrace of death. The oracle of Amon had guessed which of these closest companions were expecting this moment, but the oracle found it difficult to hint . . . Many people were anxious for the Emperor to die. There were his close friends, thirsty for the throne, and the military commanders competing among themselves, and his secret enemies, and those who hated him with all their hearts, and the Emperor's jealous wives Roxana, Stateira, and Barsine, and his younger half-brother Arrhidaeus, and his adviser Aristotle, and his regent Antipater . . . But nobody at the table gave themselves away, although they had all been waiting impatiently for the death of Alexander, who had conquered the world . . . Alexander never sensed or guessed their secret desire . . . He did not know that his death was there at his lips . . . When Alexander finished his wine, his whole numb body was seized by fire, a burning heat, and he tried to grab hold of something, because he could no longer stand on his weakened legs . . . Like an arrow still on the string, a soundless weapon, a saber with a blade of wool, a spear with no sharp tip, they struck the Emperor down . . .

From every direction came scattered shouting: "The Emperor! The Emperor!" and the hands of the people who came running dug into Alexander's body, light as down, to hold him . . . Everyone was wrapped up in the commotion . . . Upset, amazed, unable to believe their eyes, they lost their minds, not knowing what to do . . . The Emperor's three wives, who had been invited to the feast, let out piercing wails and embraced him from three sides, falling down next to him . . . "They wanted to consume him, and they did! They wanted to murder him, and they did!" shouted the first, and her wail pierced the universe . . . The Emperor could feel that he was not yet dead, and through a fog, he could see what was happening around him, and he heard the thumping of his own heart, just barely . . . Everyone crowded around the prone Emperor, as if hoping to pull him from the claws of death . . . The Emperor had not yet died, no, he was still breathing . . .

That was the end of the funeral feast . . .

Alexander the Great's soul was balanced on a bridge, fine as a single strand of hair, between life and death . . .

That night there was an uncommon abundance of stars in the sky over Babylon . . . Strewn across the whole sky, the stars were especially bright and beautiful as they glowed . . . Finding its way in the light of those stars liked spilled millet grains, now clinging to carts, now to empty saddlebags, the lightning-quick snake also arrived in the Hanging Gardens . . .

It slithered along the canals and past the springs of this paradise, under the sweet-smelling blossoms, beneath the cypresses and almonds and oleasters, past all the elegant fountains, and straight into the palace . . . Only the birds, who raised a cry, and the horses hitched to their carts, who snorted with alarm outside, sensed the snake's appearance there . . . Obeying the curse crafted by Guzasta, lord of the dark forces, the lightning-quick snake had slithered along many roads and crossed many gullies, and finally reached this palace . . . There was only one thought in the snake's mind: to use Guzasta's dark powers to find its way to Alexander the Great and sink its poisonous fangs into his body, and, after that, it wouldn't matter even if the end of the world came, or if the whole world collapsed into ruins . . .

Alexander the Great was half dead . . .

The narrow bridge between life and death could barely hold his weight. Like a drying piece of fruit, the body of the Great Emperor who had conquered and ruined all the world was now shriveling and shrinking. Occasionally, he let out a weak moan, and his eyes closed as he sank ever deeper into the swamp of a great darkness, traveling ever further into the embrace of that darkness . . . Once he had flown like a hurricane on his horse, but now the Great Emperor lay still; his powerful hands, which had gripped swords and spears, and pulled bows taut, now lay powerless like rags. Only a weak moan, now and then, revealed that he was still alive. None of the noblemen and hangers-on who had always sought his favors before, the ones who had always prayed over his shadow and dropped to kiss his footprints, were with him now. Only two servants stayed close by, watching over the Emperor's condition . . . He sensed that nobody would listen to his wife, and wouldn't want to, as she hurled accusations at everyone complicit in his poisoning, all her suspects, hoping to avenge him. Everyone had been thirsting for Alexander the Great to die like a dog, and the battle over the great sovereign's throne had already begun, though his body was still warm; a war to the death was underway . . . Those closest to the Emperor were ruled by suspicion now, each trying to get rid of the rest. Babylon was bursting with rumors and slander. All the talk among the people was about Alexander the Great, on the doorstep of death, and about who would take his place . . . Everyone began dividing things up, determining who would receive what portion of Alexander the Great's accumulated riches and the countries he had conquered . . . Olympias suspected a handful of Alexander's retinue and bodyguards in the attempt on his life, the ones who had always been around him . . . Her suspicions fell on Antipater, and she heard rumors that the man harbored a secret hatred and had turned his sons Iolaus and Cassander against Alexander. Olympias suspected Cassander in her son's murder, but she herself would soon be killed, stabbed in her sleeping quarters . . . When Olympias died without discovering who had poisoned her son, the situation in the palace only grew worse. The battle for the throne grew more and more desperate . . . Nobody knew what state the great Emperor was in on the sixth day he lay close to death . . . There were black clouds gathering thick over Alexander's head, and the whole palace was beset with fear . . . In Babylon, cursed of God, everyone felt balanced on the blade of a knife . . . Only the loyal Perdiccas and Alexander's two servants knew the state the Emperor was in. Death came ever closer to Alexander the Great, and on Perdicca's orders, under cover of night, they carried him across the Euphrates and hid him away from prying eyes, deep in a garden, in a secret place. Perdiccas understood that if people knew the Emperor was still alive, many would try to put him to death. They moved Alexander the Great across the river and laid him in a dark room, in a small house, in an abandoned garden . . .

Guzasta's lightning-quick snake did not find Alexander the Great in the Hanging Gardens when it arrived in Babylon, cursed of God. Guzasta's lightning-quick snake had one highly honed trait: once it smelled a scent, it never forgot it. Now it could smell that Alexander the Great was in the gardens on the other side of the river . . . That night, the snake swam across the Euphrates, and found the little house in the garden, and crept into the dark room . . .

When the snake crept into that room, it saw Alexander the Great lying in bed, unconscious, near death, with torches burning brightly on either side of him. The snake was afraid of fire, so it could not creep any closer to the Emperor, and the servants who had just left the room had smoked it well with juniper, chasing away all the dark forces, demons, and devils. The scent of that smoke kept the snake from coming further into the room . . . The smell held the snake at the threshold, but it knew that Alexander the Great could not get away now, and it was in no hurry . . . The night would pass and the morning would come, and after the morning the hot middle of the day. The heat of the sun makes snake venom stronger. Lightning-quick snakes never bite at night. In the afternoon, when the sun's fire scorches everything with its heat, the venom becomes concentrated and especially powerful. The snake decided to wait. How long it had waited for this day, how many roads it had slithered down—and now, with the help of the power Guzasta had given it, the snake was ready to bring his curse to its conclusion . . . The snake coiled itself in a corner and waited, and it decided that before it bit Alexander, it would first make itself known, and enchant and hypnotize him . . . The snake spent those minutes remembering the female snake the arrow had killed, remembering the magical time when the two of them had been together and content . . . The snake crept to Alexander the Great's body . . . Just as the soothsayers had predicted, a snake would cause his death; the cold snake crept onto his body . . . Alexander's lifeless body, hot as fire, felt its coldness, and, despite his oblivion, he trembled in fear . . . No longer coiled tight, the snake unwrapped itself and moved, its forked tongue flicking, onto the nine layers of blankets that made the royal bed, and it lifted its tiny head and hissed loudly, then stretched straight as a wire and crept slowly into the darkness, the utter darkness. The fear that pierced through Alexander the Great was like a flame running across his body, and the snake's hiss came ever closer, slow and unstoppable, to the man locked in this utter darkness. The two of them may have been the only ones left in the world, and it seemed that if a gap were to be suddenly ripped open in this utter darkness, his unfortunate soul would gladly leap through it to the outside. Both night and light froze, just as the man's heart faltered. It might have been better for the earth to absorb his soul, better for his weakly beating heart, and his body which could still sense this world, to die. Then this frigid fear would never have entered him and made him tremble. He had been given a glimpse of his death in advance and feared nothing his whole life except for snakes; now he was ready to tear his own soul from his chest. The terror clung like a snake to his whole trembling body. The snake crept slowly, drawing nearer to Alexander's eyes, closer and closer. The man let out a piercing cry, trying to penetrate this cursed darkness; he wanted to tear open his own chest, he wanted to die, he wanted to vanish, but he could not. The whole universe tensed. On this diminutive square of earth, too small to accommodate one stretched cowhide, two souls, two living creatures of this world, were deciding which one of them would survive in the darkness. Clenching his fists, Alexander thought to smash the snake's head, but he could not see its body, only its two eyes, which stared at him fixedly from a distance like two small, glowing coals. The man's whole body trembled, he shouted long and loud, but that shout was heard by nobody but himself; the cry seemed to have taken off, crashed into the darkness, and returned to him. That cry returned, along with the fear. Paying no attention to the human shout, the snake kept its burning eyes on the man, and again coiled its body and lifted its tiny head. Again, the snake hissed, making sure the man knew exactly who it had come for. The coiled snake began to feel sorry for the person there before it . . . Alexander the Great of Macedon, who had once thought of himself as an equal to the Creator, called himself God, and declared himself the God of Gods, who was guilty of spilling blood and butchering men, who had wanted to swallow the whole world in a single gulp and stamp it out, who had exterminated entire peoples, who had stolen land from so many, who had taken everything with no regard for the curses of the elderly or the tears of children, who broke the backs of his best warriors like kindling, who singled out the most ravishing beauties and raped them, who considered others to be subject to his law, who relished exercising his power, who had beat the drum of the End of Days, who had flooded the whole world with blood . . . now this man lay before him, unwanted, like a poor wretch despised by all . . . For six days, nobody knew whether he was alive or dead . . . In Babylon, Alexander the Great's closest associates, vying for the throne and his crown, had already carved the empire he built into tiny bits, and begun to murder one another . . .

Again, a great ocean of darkness covered Alexander's eyes . . . A fog veiled his sight, his arms lay motionless, and though he couldn't tell if it was real or a dream, a succession of linked thoughts paraded before his eyes, pictures of incomprehensible, interchangeable events and phenomena . . . Again, he saw before him the lame soothsayer, and the blind boy . . . Thin streams of blood ran from the boy's eye sockets . . . And the sky looked down at Alexander the Great through the eyes of the boy, and it was not the heavens gazing at him across the whole bent bow of the sky, but the boy's eyes . . . This vision cut through Alexander . . . The entire sky was the boy's eyes . . . The entire sky gazed at him with those eyes . . . Those eyes held a love for life, and the astonished Alexander the Great gazed back at those eyes, so clear, so radiant . . . How many similarly radiant eyes, glowing with fire, had he extinguished? How many similar eyes had he put out like so many burning coals, extinguishing their light forever? . . . And now thin streams of blood ran from those eyes . . . As if the whole world had been bathed in blood, the earth stank of it . . . The lame soothsayer, in the center of this vision, barely stood upright before Alexander, leaning on his stick . . . but the most astounding part was that the soothsayer's head was lying on the ground . . . and this head on the ground was saying, "I sense a warning coming from above, a warning of great calamity . . . It draws nigh . . . I saw one angel of the Sun, flying through the heavens . . . He cried out to all the birds and all the feathered beasts: 'Fly now to God's great feast! Gather and take your refreshment from the bodies of kings, the bodies of the strong, the bodies of warriors, the bodies of horses, the bodies of slaves, bodies big and small . . .' I saw the souls of those decapitated for the word of God, and they came back to life . . . but the devils who wanted to seduce them have been tossed into a burning lake of fire, and all the sinners and false prophets will be tormented forever . . ." Alexander the Great understood nothing of what the soothsayer said . . . The lame soothsayer continued to speak . . . "They were thrown into the burning lake of death and torment. This is the second death. Anyone not inscribed in the Book of Life will be thrown into the burning lake!" The blood streaming from the boy's eye sockets turned to fire, raging flames . . . "This is hell!" said the lame old soothsayer . . . "Today, the Book of Life will not open to you, for you are destined for the cauldron of torment and suffering . . . Today, as I told you, you will die of snakebite . . . But only your body will die. Your soul will go on living . . . Your soul will not die, because it must answer for the sin of the blood you spilled and deaths you caused, the sin on your shoulders, for which your soul will bear its castigation . . . Today, your line has withered and died, Alexander the Great . . . Cassander has killed your mother, your wives Stateira, Roxana, and Barsine have been cut down with swords, your half-brother Arrhidaeus has died at a traitor's hands, your children have died at the hands of your friends . . . Your line is exterminated . . . You declared yourself the son of Zeus, and brought down the wrath of Zeus when you did . . . Babylon is completely destroyed, its dust rising up to the heavens . . . And now your hour has come . . . Death stands by your head, you are not eternal, you are a Person like the people whose heads you sliced off, whose bodies you tossed in mountainous heaps . . . They

were people, just like you . . . They were people who wanted to catch the
rays of the rising sun, bathe in the rain, savor the scent of flowers, count
the stars in the night sky, take joy in the flight of a butterfly, walk barefoot
through the grass, and wet their feet in dew . . . They were people just like
you, but you wanted to make yourself a throne out of their deaths, and
put on a crown, and conquer all the world and rule them . . . You thought
you were an equal to God, you called yourself God, you sent heralds to all
corners of the world to announce that you were the God of Gods . . . Now,
thoughts of death once more remind you that you are a human being and
make you feel human again . . . Death reminds us of everything. Death
is pure . . . And eternity is a lie . . ." The voice of the lame soothsayer
injected itself inside him, and now it spoke from inside Alexander the
Great . . . "I have come for your soul, Alexander the Great . . . I will give
it to thirty-three living creatures, and the thirty-third will be a descendant
of the snake whose bite will kill you today . . . Today begins the castigation of your soul, its punishment in payment for your sins . . . Today, your
soul will move into the body of a mosquito, because, of all living creatures
on Earth, only mosquitos feed on human blood and live off that blood;
what makes you any different? . . . Your soul will reside in the bodies of
thirty-three living creatures. The first creature will be the mosquito . . .
the second, a lizard . . . the third, a fly . . . the fourth, a jackal . . . the fifth,
a cat . . . the sixth, a sparrow . . . the seventh, a monkey . . . the eighth, a
tortoise . . . the ninth, a crow . . . the tenth, an elephant . . . the eleventh,
a boar . . . the twelfth, a rat . . . the thirteenth, a bee . . . the fourteenth, a
donkey . . . the fifteenth, a scorpion . . . the sixteenth, a frog . . . the seventeenth, a mule . . . the eighteenth, a hoopoe . . . the nineteenth, a bull . . .
the twentieth, a vulture . . . the twenty-first, a magpie . . . the twenty-
second, a partridge . . . the twenty-third, a camel . . . the twenty-fourth, a
dog . . . the twenty-fifth, a badger . . . the twenty-sixth, an antelope . . . the
twenty-seventh, a buzzard . . . the twenty-eighth, a deer . . . the twenty-
ninth, a lynx . . . the thirtieth, a wolf . . . the thirty-first, a groundhog . . .
the thirty-second, a pig . . . the thirty-third, a snake . . . At the end of its
journey, your soul will enter the body of a black snake, and that snake will
bite a Man, and your soul will enter the body of that man along with the
snake's venom . . . This man will not be a normal person; after the snake's

bite, he will be insane, and the soul of Alexander the Great will find its place in the soul of this madman and bear its castigation in the madman's body." The lame old soothsayer said those words and vanished like steam before Alexander the Great's eyes . . .

A bright light flashed through the dark chamber. The scorching rays of the noon sun penetrated the room . . . The sun's heat gave the snake the heat it needed . . .

Alexander the Great felt the snake's body wrap around him like a chain . . . The soothsayer's words dug into his brain like thorns: "You will die of snakebite . . ." Once the snake wrapped its body around Alexander, it crept to his motionless head, and lifted its own tiny head quickly above his neck, its forked tongue flicking . . . Alexander's eyes could barely see, but they registered the cold, unblinking serpent's eyes before him . . . Two pairs of eyes . . . the man . . . the snake . . . stared at one another, noiseless, intent . . . In this crowded square of the vast world, two pairs of eyes regarded one another, entranced, unblinking . . . Alexander the Great's body was beaten and lifeless, and he could not even move his lips . . . The snake felt how small the world was, how tight time could be, and it felt this because between these two living creatures there was something that joined them, linked them; the man did not know this, but the snake did. To the man, it seemed that if only he could get rid of the snake, the world could turn upside down or crumble and it would be all the same to him; he had only one goal, one dream: to kill the snake. How could he kill it? . . . If only there were a stone or a stick nearby . . . That thought was what tormented Alexander . . . Alexander the Great, who had conquered the entire world, was tormented, and he suffered . . . Is there any worse suffering in the world? And all this time, viperish people fought over the Emperor's throne, swallowing one another whole . . . Only now did it occur to Alexander the Great, only now did he understand, why he had seized this world, why he wanted to rule this unfortunate world, and be a God in the universe . . . Yes, he realized, he, too, was a hapless slave of God, he, too, was an ordinary person . . . Maybe it had been that untamed desire to make himself equal to God, to rule over the world with no deference to the Creator, that had brought him to this fate? . . .

After resting for a while on Alexander the Great's cooling body, the snake decided to show the Emperor who had conquered half the world who the real victor was . . . Victory was partial to the snake . . . It lay there under its cold body . . . And hatred and revenge would have to eventually come to an end . . . The snake slithered onto the man's chest . . . and sank its venomous fangs straight into the place where the man's heart was still, just barely, beating . . . The Great Emperor Alexander the Great, whose body gave a jerk at that bite, knew that death had come . . . His body twisted . . . His vision failed . . . And his featherweight soul entered the mosquito that had been flying around the room all that time, taking occasional sips of Alexander's blood, and it flew out of the little house through a window into the fresh air . . .

The servants came into the room, and when they caught sight of the snake, they tried to catch it and kill it, but the snake immediately vanished through a crack in the floor . . .

The servants dropped to their knees before Alexander the Great, whose head lolled lifeless to one side on his high pillows . . .

The years passed . . . The centuries passed . . .

Once Alexander the Great's soul had resided in the bodies of thirty-three living creatures, it returned, at the end of its journey, to the breast of a Human Being . . . Before that, it lived in the bodies of thirty-three living beasts . . . The first was a mosquito . . . the second, a lizard . . . the third, a fly . . . the fourth, a jackal . . . the fifth, a cat . . . the sixth, a sparrow . . . the seventh, a monkey . . . the eighth, a tortoise . . . the ninth, a crow . . . the tenth, an elephant . . . the eleventh, a boar . . . the twelfth, a rat . . . the thirteenth, a bee . . . the fourteenth, a donkey . . . the fifteenth, a scorpion . . . the sixteenth, a frog . . . the seventeenth, a mule . . . the eighteenth, a hoopoe . . . the nineteenth, a bull . . . the twentieth, a vulture . . . the twenty-first, a magpie . . . the twenty-second, a partridge . . . the twenty-third, a camel . . . the twenty-fourth, a dog . . . the twenty-fifth, a badger . . . the twenty-sixth, an antelope . . . the twenty-seventh, a buzzard . . . the twenty-eighth, a deer . . . the twenty-ninth, a lynx . . . the thirtieth, a wolf . . . the thirty-first, a groundhog . . . the thirty-second, a pig . . . the thirty-third, a snake . . .

. . . Strange . . .

He used to read a lot about the real Alexander the Great, though now he couldn't remember the names of the books or who wrote them. All he remembered was that the only thing Alexander the Great feared in this world was snakes, and they were also the only thing in life that terrified him. He compared his own life with his, and it turned out he wasn't the only one afraid of them. So was Alexander the Great, who had conquered the whole world. Their names connected them, and so did this fear. Maybe that fear of snakes was the reason he announced, in the nuthouse, that his name was Alexander the Great? . . . Snakes scared him, the fear made his heart skip beats, as if it had lurched up and gotten lodged in his throat, making it impossible to breathe, like it was about to leap out of his chest. That heart, which had lurched up and gotten lodged in his throat, hopped outside and vanished into the surrounding darkness, but not a moment had passed before the heart returned and went straight back inside him, carrying with it the soul of someone who had died long ago, and it began beating. When the person's soul skipped out, he absorbed a completely different soul and started to feel very similar to Alexander the Great, who gave up his soul in ancient Babylon, and who was mortally afraid of snakes.

The Seven

On a torturously hot day, the type of day when the noontime heat boils
the brain, when the heat of the endless sandy desert scorches the skin . . .
When the Holy Land was just a little farther away, the Emperor died.

The remaining six felt dispirited. They threw up their hands in
despair, and they all stopped believing in all those lovely fairy tales about
the Holy Land, which the Emperor had once told them through his sobs,
and which had turned out to be a desert devoid of life . . . The hope they
had once had in abundance was now a chunk of stone.

The Emperor's body had been lying on the sand for one day and one
night, and a disgusting stink had begun oozing from it . . .

They decided to wash the Emperor's body before they buried it, and
they walked off in different directions to search for water . . . If they could
not find a handful of water somewhere, they would have to bury the
Emperor's body under a sand dune . . .

After searching the whole area and finding no water source, they all
returned, and Lear brought with him a very old man he had found wandering the desert . . .

Lear led the old man by the arm into the slight shadow of a sand dune,
where the Emperor's stinking body lay . . . Before burying the Emperor
and consigning his body to the earth forever, they wanted to follow tradi-
tion and bathe his body, at least a little . . . All six of them searched for
water all around, but found nothing, and returned tired and distressed.
Only Lear had met this old man in the desert and led him by the arm
back to their meeting spot at the Emperor's body . . . The old man had
seen much in his time, and now he stood unspeaking among them . . . He
looked emaciated and exhausted . . . The blind old man held his tongue

sadly and wiped the sweat from his forehead with his dirty sleeve . . . Of the six, only Cleopatra and Kozuchak sobbed, quietly, trying to keep their weeping inside, and moaned with grief . . . The Emperor had died with his eyes open . . . Alexander the Great tried to close those lifeless eyes with the palm of his hand. But the Emperor's eyes wouldn't close . . .

Now the eyes of the deceased Emperor who lay in the sand gleamed lifeless . . .

The air reeked of carrion; the body stank . . .

Genghis Khan peered intently at the vultures flying over them, the scavengers of the desert, already circling the Emperor's body . . . He had the feeling that everything was waiting for the Emperor's body . . . the beasts who lived underground, lizards, snakes, and the desert's rats, worms, and ants . . . and there were the hungry vultures flying in the sky . . . They were all waiting for that body . . . As Genghis Khan stood in a sad silence, pressing his lower lip tight between his fingers, the thought of the Emperor's soul came into his head . . . Where was that soul now?[4] Where had it flown? . . . The Emperor had talked to Genghis Khan about the human soul often and at great length, in great detail . . . He remembered his words: "It's not that a person dies, it's that their soul doesn't return to them again . . . The soul travels into a different body. There are only two limitless things in this world: the human soul and its sins . . . Truly, although the human soul is immortal, the time inevitably comes when it must pay for its sins, and if someone is not castigated for them, the castigation will be borne by the children and family they leave behind." When he heard those words, a strange feeling seized his soul, and for a moment

4. Day 1: the big toes; 2: the ankle; 3: the muscles; 4: around the elbow; 5: the elbow joint; 6: around the thigh; 7: in the groin; 8: the kidneys; 9: the ribs; 10: around the shoulder blades; 11: the forearm; 12: the palms of the hands; 13: around the neck and thoracic vertebrae; 14: in the ears; 15: throughout the flesh; 16: the inner ear; 17: around the breast; 18: the palms of the hands; 19: the forearm; 20: the shoulder blades; 21: the ribs; 22: the kidneys; 23: around the breast; 24: in the groin; 25: the elbow joint; 26: around the elbow; 27: in the muscles; 28: the ankle; 29: the calf; 30: throughout the flesh (Tibetan astrologers, writing about the relocation of the spirit within the human body on various days of the month).

he closed his eyes, and he felt as if he were flying through the days, years, and centuries to the source of all time, as if he were galloping at the head of the real Genghis Khan's enormous, dark legion of soldiers . . . Suddenly, his heart winced, and he shuddered . . . and came back to reality . . . He lumbered to his feet, like an eagle with a broken wing, then sat down again, and after that he only pretended to be listening to the Emperor, and felt an emptiness in his soul . . . Perhaps the Emperor's sly voice had merely bewitched him, somehow, or perhaps that was the moment that he first experienced the feeling of his soul relocating into a different body . . . His thoughts raced in different directions, and he understood nothing . . . The Emperor's open eyes, which Genghis Khan, too, had tried closing with the palm of his hand, seemed to be staring straight at him now . . .

(The Emperor scrambled anxiously, unable to find the road . . . He was looking for the light . . . He heard a roaring underground and saw the mountains crumble, the gullies cave in and spread thin, and black steam bursting from the cracks in the earth, and the white, boiling mirage in the air was cloaked in darkness; he heard a battle raging between two unidentified armies, as if a furious ocean were throwing itself against the rocky cliffs of the shore, and the thunder of it grew stronger and stronger; everything small and movable flew up into the air in a mad spiraling vortex, and he heard the deafening thunder of a thousand lightning strikes splitting the sky, and then . . . suddenly, this insane apocalypse paused and froze . . . A calm descended, a great silence . . . It was the era of a muted world, a world in impenetrable darkness. Time stood still . . . The vortex seized the Emperor and carried him off into the abyss . . . He was soaring, floating on a universal current . . . All the heaviness and weight of his body flew away like a molted snake skin . . . And he soared, floating, down, on the featherweight fluff of a dandelion . . . The Emperor had never felt anything so pleasant as this lightness, this weightlessness, of his body . . . The longer it lasted, the more his flight over the abyss became an infinite pleasure, and now he saw, at the bottom of the vortex, the earth coming closer . . . All feelings vanished from the Emperor's breast, both the pleasant languor he had just been experiencing, and the fear of snakes; now his heart felt nothing . . . Indifferent to it all, he soared easily downward, straight into the nest of the snake that had hunted him all his life . . . One snake wrapped itself around his leg to make its way to his neck, and coiled around it, and lifted its head to gaze intently into the Emperor's eyes . . . The Emperor felt nothing. The terror, the fear that made his whole body shake—it had all disappeared, gone away somewhere unknown . . .

The Emperor departed for the world of another life . . .)[5]

The Emperor's body lay before the six of them, covered in sand up to the neck . . .

"I couldn't find even a drop of water!" Lear complained, shaking his tousled ash-colored head, after he brought to them the blind old man with the thin beard who had been wandering the desert. "There's nothing!"

"Who is that? Where did you find this blind old man?" asked Thaïs the Athenian, staring at the newcomer. "Don't tell me he's one of them who wandered the desert barefoot following Moses for forty years," she added wryly. "Because he looks like it!"

The old man stood there frozen in silence . . . Seeing his wide-open eyes, nobody would have said he was blind. He always looked in the direction where the voice he heard was coming from, and if anyone stared hard at him, his face changed instantly . . .

"Ask him yourself! Bloody hell!" Lear winced, disgusted.

"He's a vagrant, by the looks of him . . ." said Genghis Khan. "He looks a little . . ."

"All you care about is how he looks! What do you care? Planning to take a gulp of him instead of water?" Alexander burst out. "Have him show us the way out of this desert . . . Your Holy Land doesn't exist, not even on

---

5. "The intelligent beings who commit sins and have therefore been demoted from their original stations in accordance with the severity of their sins are invested with bodies as a punishment; but when they are made clean, they rise again to their previous stations, having shed their evil and their bodies entirely. They may take on bodies in punishment, subsequently, a second or third time, or many times over. For it is fully possible that many different worlds existed and will continue to exist, some in the past, others in the future . . . As a consequence of the fall and cooling of life in the spirit, something arose which we call the soul, which nevertheless is capable of ascending to its original station" (Origen, *On First Principles*, book 2, chapter 8, paragraph 3).

the other side of this desert! Let's bury the Emperor and . . . go back to the Nation of Nutters."

"Enough of your nattering, you worthless rag!" shouted Genghis Khan, his face red with anger. "Blubbering nonsense in the presence of the dead! What's wrong with you?"

The old man listened, his head bowed, his face turned toward the shouting Alexander, and then his lips trembled as he attempted to speak: "I . . . I truly am . . ."—his voice was a low, unpleasant wheeze—". . . one of those forty who journeyed with Moses . . ."

The six of them froze, confused, not having expected such a confession from this unsightly old man. Shivering as if she'd been surprised by a splash of cold water, Thaïs the Athenian barked out rudely: "Or maybe you're the prophet Jesus, or Moses himself! . . . Look at you! You must be the traitor who sold out Moses?" Thaïs the Athenian was raving, as usual.

The old man kept his sad silence, unoffended by her words. The remaining six waited impatiently to hear what on earth he would say. The old man turned his gloomy face toward the woman talking, then suddenly, with no stutter or hesitation, in a clear voice, he said:

"It is truly so . . . I am the traitor who sold out Moses."

"The traitor?" Genghis Khan repeated mechanically. "The traitor?"

The silence was broken . . . Hearing that, they all came to life instantly, raising a ruckus.

"There you go!" shouted Thaïs the Athenian. "I can see right through them! My eyes are sharp as pins! This is the asshole who sold Moses for crumbs!"

"Why Moses? Who's the traitor? When did all this even happen? This is the twenty-first century!" said Cleopatra, her eyes big and round. "It's impossible!"

"Oh, it's impossible? Bloody hell!" Lear's crazy eyes bulged from his face, his chest puffed out, and his heart beat like mad. White froth crept onto his lips and a cold sweat soaked his whole body. A spell of madness had seized Lear. This malady, which Lear thought he had long ago left behind, grabbed him now by the scruff of the neck and sent tremors through him. "What do you mean, impossible? What do you mean, twenty-first century? What century? What hour? What time? What's time to us? What are we, servants of time, slaves of time? I have no concept of time and space. I don't care about anything! I'll show you time!" Lear punched himself in the throat. His body contorted and dropped to the ground, and he held his ear to the sand, and even seemed to hear something, and started jerking his arms and legs spasmodically. It was his illness. He was losing himself, going mad, shouting everything that came into his head. He remembered his old theater monologue, the one he started sputtering now, through his sobs:

"No," Lear began in a whisper, and then his cold eyes began glowing with fury, and his voice turned low and dull. "These late eclipses in the sun and moon portend no good to us . . ." Again, he pressed his ear to the ground, clutching fistfuls of sand. He sighed heavily and got to his knees, his whole body shaking and shivering, and he went on speaking angrily. "Though the wisdom of nature can reason it thus and thus, yet nature finds itself scourged by the sequent effects. Love cools, friendship falls off, brothers divide." Here, he started to cough, as if needing to clear his throat, and stopped reciting for a time. When he was finishing coughing, he continued his monologue in a hoarse, creaking voice. "In cities, mutinies; in countries, discord; in palaces, treason; and the bond cracked 'twixt son and father. The king falls from bias of nature: there's father against child. Machinations, hollowness, treachery, and all ruinous disorders follow us disquietly to our graves." As if he had been talking to himself all this time, Lear trailed off for a while. "The essence of human beings is that . . ." Tears came to Lear's eyes. "We make mistakes the Gods never make . . ."

He fell back to the ground, and lay motionless for some time, breathing heavily. Then he slowly began to move . . .

"Easy . . . Easy . . . I'm not upset . . . I am not upset at all . . . I am calm . . . calm and cool as snow . . . Easy . . . Easy . . ." Finally, he stood up, as if cleansed in cold water . . . he stood up a normal, healthy man . . . After an attack, Lear usually did not remember what he had said and done. That happened this time, as well.

Everyone had been so carried away with Lear's monologue that they had forgotten all about their previous conversation.

"She's right! Why are we talking about some prehistorical Moses and some traitor? Their bones rotted in the earth long ago . . . They turned to dust . . ." That was Kozuchak getting involved, standing up for Cleopatra. "He's lying!"

"I . . ." whispered the old man. "I am one of the forty who were with Moses . . . I experienced it all with him . . . his fire, his cinders, his pain, and his hell . . . I still live . . . Now I have only one wish, one hope . . ." The exhausted old man said nothing for a while and gave a deep sigh. "And that is to receive death . . . but even death won't take me . . ."

"Death?! Yes please, but here he is still alive!" spat out Lear, unhappily. "Still breathing air!"

"Damn you!" Genghis Khan burst out angrily, slapping his thigh. "What good would death do you? . . . Your bones would rot here in this goddamned desert, unburied!" Genghis Khan slapped at the air with his hand and spat heartily onto the ground.

"What were you, born immortal, Moses-betrayer? If you have some secret nobody knows, you'd better tell us, so we can wander this dry desert forever like nutters, too," said Thaïs the Athenian. "I'd much rather live in Paradise for just a day and die there happy than spend a thousand years in the desert! Everyone will say we died in Paradise! Right?"

"He said himself he's a traitor. So that's that . . . He told us who he is . . . And how would we know? Maybe he's a sly old man with the devil hidden inside him, or maybe . . . maybe he really is a traitor . . . He's got the face of a ghoul, and if he could sell out Moses, what's he going to do to us? . . . He'll take care of us in a flash . . . He'll drive us mad, and hand us straight to the Devil, and that will be that!" The furious Alexander the Great shot lightning from his eyes, and the muscles clenched in his cheeks. "Instead, why don't you tell us how to bury the Emperor? We've already been delayed enough. If this stupid old man hopes and dreams of dying, like he told us . . . Here, we can use this knife and cut him down . . . and we'll bury him, too . . . so the Emperor's body doesn't have to lie in the desert alone!" Alexander the Great pointed his knife at the old man and moved his hand like he was about to stab him.

All the rest, who never expected Alexander to do such a thing, froze, stunned . . .

"Don't be afraid of the man who says he wants to kill. Be afraid of the one who says he wants to die. How could we bury this traitor beside the Emperor?" Thaïs gave them all a disapproving glare.

The old man walked over to the raging Alexander and knelt before him and kissed the hand that held the knife. Then the old man bowed down to the ground. Alexander was black with fury, shaking all over, and could not calm down. The old man's actions stunned them all, Alexander included.

They froze, silent as the grave.

"Nothing can take me, not sharp knives, not arrows, not a dagger to the heart," the old man said quietly, barely breathing. "On the day that I betrayed Moses . . . I was made eternal . . . left to wander this desert . . ."

"What crime exactly is that a punishment for?" asked Kozuchak, staring at the old man.

"He sold out Moses! He sold out a prophet, a messenger of God! . . . And you think he's worthy of our Emperor? The earth won't even take him! He's cursed!" Lear truly regretted bringing the old man to them, and his face burned with hatred. "Let him pray for our Emperor. The Emperor wasn't a prophet, but he was like a prophet to us . . ."

"That's the truth." The old man turned his face to the source of the voice. "I am a traitor. I betrayed the man who led me through the desert for forty years . . . hoping to instill the truth in my heart . . . One of the punishments on my sinful head is this," said the old man, his voice growing stronger and higher. "I can never be reborn . . . A traitor's soul cannot be resurrected; it can never resettle in anyone's body . . . My soul bears its castigation in my body . . ." The old man seemed turned to stone. "My body is a prison and a tomb for my soul . . . It is bearing the castigation for a mortal sin . . . It is an ancient curse . . . and a punishment," he said, then sighed deeply. "God doesn't receive the rotten souls."

The Emperor promised to lead them all to the Holy Land, and then he died on the journey . . .

When he died, he took with him everything he knew about the Holy Land . . . They had followed his instructions and escaped from the Nation of Nutters, but the six of them lost their guide in the middle of the endless sandy desert, and they were left in utter confusion. Now, the Emperor who had told them secrets about the Holy Land had turned to dust, a lifeless, breathless body . . . The six did not know where they were or what to do, and the question of how to act and where to go tormented them . . . The question was driving them mad . . . In which of the seventeen thousand worlds was this cursed Holy Land hiding? Or was it just a fantasy of the Emperor? . . . And what if there wasn't a Holy Land? . . . The question gave the six no peace . . . Their road to the Holy Land had come abruptly to an end, like someone had cut it off with a pair of scissors . . .

"Let's give the Emperor's body to the earth," said Lear. "Let the earth be a cushion for him . . . How are we going to wash the body?" He looked around at them all.

Alexander took Lear's elbow, led him off to one side, and whispered in his ear:

"Maybe that old man wandering this endless desert will have an idea? . . . We should think it over . . . He's more complicated than he looks," said Alexander. He lowered his voice and twitched nervously. "He's old enough. He's seen a lot!"

As if he'd heard Alexander whispering, the old man walked toward the dead man, picked up the Emperor's hands, marked with a thick net of blue veins, and carefully crossed them over his chest. When the old man's thin hands touched the Emperor's face, his eyes, gleaming and clear as they had been in life, closed. Then, wanting to shut the Emperor's half-open mouth, the old man tore a strip of cloth from his long shirt, and wrapped it tightly around the Emperor's head.

Alexander watched every move the old man made. He saw him glance quickly over the people surrounding the dead man, and in a barely audible voice, he rasped out:

"We'll give his body to the earth clean . . . The women should step aside. We'll wash his body." Thaïs the Athenian and Cleopatra obediently walked a short distance away. Cleopatra began to cry, gasping, her whole body shaking. "I cannot wash the body clean . . . One of you will have to do it . . . But I'll tell you how," said the old man.

Genghis Khan spoke up. "I will wash him."

The mysterious old man took a deep breath and said:

"Until we consign the body to the earth, the angels will keep questioning his conscience. Let's not delay. We will bury him quickly. We will wash the body with sand . . ."

The old man moved a few steps away from the body, and turning his gaze to the sky, he quietly whispered a prayer. He recited the prayer with effort, taking pains . . . When he was finished, he spoke loudly to the others:

"Don't be afraid . . . Wash the body with sand . . . This is an Arabian custom . . . When people who live in the desert can find no water, they wash a body with sand and bury it . . . And we will do the same," said the old man, and he gave a dry cough. "And I will tell you how."

The old man turned to Genghis Khan, who had volunteered to wash the body.

"You want to wash him?"

Genghis Khan answered succinctly:

"I do."

"May it come to pass," said the old man. "You will do this work not with your own hands, but with the hands of a kind angel." The old man sighed and began to chant out what to do and when. "First remove all his clothing, and then cross his arms over his chest again."

Genghis Khan tried to do everything he said. One tug at the Emperor's shirt collar was enough for the tattered old garment to come apart at the seams. Then began the sacred ritual of washing the Emperor's body with sand. By then, his face had turned blue, and his body was beginning to reek.

The Emperor's body lay in the sand, in the crooked shadow of a dune.

"Now remove his hands from his chest and lay them, palms down, in the sand . . ." As he spoke, the old man kept his lifeless eyes trained on the sky. After every phrase, he muttered something to himself. "Pile a good quantity of sand in a heap near the corpse," he told the others. "We need clean sand to wash the body."

Hearing those instructions, the rest of them began carrying over handfuls of sand, making a pile.

"Now . . ." The old man spoke more slowly. "Take sand in your hands and rub your hands with it . . ." Genghis Khan rubbed some of the newly collected, clean sand between the palms of his hands. "Remove every particle of sand that is stuck to your palms . . . Fold his arms across his chest again," said the old man. "Rub sand into his face, brow, and head. Be careful no grain of sand remains in his hair when you are done . . . Rub his arms with sand, up to the elbows . . ." The old man continued to guide every movement.

When the washing of the body was finished, the old man unwound the turban he was wearing. "Wrap the dead man in a shroud . . . Use this cloth," he said. They had distrusted the old man before, even detested him, but they were all moved by this gesture. Only Kozuchak remained dissatisfied. "Are we really shrouding the Emperor in the turban of the traitor who betrayed Moses?" he asked.

"Hush! Shut your mouth," Lear snapped at Kozuchak. "What does the dead man care? . . . He won't feel a thing," said Lear with a sigh.

"He promised to bring us to the Holy Land!" said Kozuchak, biting his lip to keep from crying.

"That's what the Emperor wanted . . . And now he's there . . . We're next in line," said Alexander glumly. "He was unblemished . . ."

The old man, who had born many burdens and heard plenty of talk like that in his time, paid them no attention. He went on directing the rites.

"Now, dig a grave," he said.

"Where should we dig it?" asked Lear.

"Where the boy Kozuchak is standing," said the old man.

Kozuchak, who very much disliked this old man, and could barely keep himself from shouting something rude at him, kept standing where he was, pretending he didn't know what they were talking about.

"Move it!" Lear shoved Kozuchak aside, then bent over and began digging sand with his long, thin hands. Everyone immediately joined in. Soon they had dug a grave. The old man decided to get down into it to test its length. Lear helped him, holding him by the arms. The old man went down into the grave, and on the end pointing toward Mecca, he piled up some sand with his hands, making a slightly raised area.

"Give me the dead man," said the old man from the grave. The four of them lifted the body, shrouded in the fabric of the white turban. "Hand him down with his head toward Mecca," he told them.

The old man laid the Emperor's body with his head toward Mecca, on the pillow of sand he had made. When the man had finished arranging the body, following all the rules, he lifted his arms, and Lear pulled him from the grave.

The old man took a handful of sand, whispered some words over it, and tossed the sand into the grave. Then the rest of them started tossing sand, filling in the grave . . . Kozuchak, distraught, joined in.

The Emperor was given to the earth . . .

The travelers buried the Emperor in the middle of the untamed, sandy desert, strewn with countless dunes, in a quiet place protected from the winds. Deserts are constantly in motion, changing; the dunes are indistinguishable one from the other, and once they had gone a short distance away from the place and looked back, they could no longer see the burial spot . . . The blue sky seemed to have turned into a boiling cooking pot that had been overturned, and its steam scorched their faces . . . To mark the burial place somehow, the four men searched the area and found some sturdy saxaul branches, long dried out, almost petrified . . . and they stuck them in the earth around the grave . . . That was to signify that the Emperor lay there . . . Kozuchak vowed to himself that once they reached the Holy Land, he would return, dig up the Emperor's body, and carry it back to the Holy Land, God willing, and bury it there . . .

The Emperor's body was between two worlds . . .

The Emperor's soul, robed in a human body,
stood at the door to the other world,
trying to use these last moments of existence
to remember its whole slipshod life,
and straining all the neglected days of the past
through the sieve of orderly thought,

all that it had seen ten, fifty, one hundred, three hundred, five hundred,
one thousand years ago . . . It tried to catch fragments
of memories about this body's birth, its childhood and youth, its
adulthood, and to remember its births and deaths before this body
in the bodies of other living beings,
in a snowdrop, in a juniper,
all its experience moving into the bodies of animals and plants:
this soul remembered, as it said farewell to this world . . .
If it could just recall, now, the place it was born,
its birthdate, its epoch, its family, its clan,
the various days of sadness and joy, all the calamities,
the black and the white, the griefs and pains,
its happiness, its good fortune,
everything it had seen in this life, everything
for which it had lived this life,
and if it could set a goal for itself now,
one it simply had to achieve, then it would
be able to be born yet again . . .
Only then would it be resurrected, and be
able to go into one more body . . .
But the destiny assigned and the new life it was fated for—
that was how God predestined it, for each according to his fate;
and that predestiny determined whether it would be reborn
a handsome person or repulsive cretin or stupid fool
or insect, or in the hide of a wild animal,
where the soul would find its place, or bloom into this life as a
dandelion or a buckthorn on the riverbank, a barb to stick in the feet
or a saxaul to grow in the desert—nobody knows any of this,
but let that soul be reborn as it is destined,
let it revive as it is fated, and as soon as it is reborn
all its new thoughts, worries, and ideas are born along with
it, along with its whole lot in life . . . There was his soul,
shoveling through these thoughts, such a heavy load . . .
between two worlds, between life and death . . .

Kozuchak made himself a vow: he would bring the body to the Holy Land and bury it there . . .

He told nobody about his vow. He hid it deep inside his heart.

❧

That day, the desert blew its top . . . A grim darkness swept away the over-heated sun . . . From nobody knew where, thunder clouds came to carpet the sky, piling on top of each other . . . A sandstorm began . . . The quick-creeping desert wind, hissing like a snake, lifted the light sand into the air; its dancing funnels sucked up all the trash and filth from the ground and flung it into the air. The scourge gathered strength, more and more, directly over the spot where the Emperor's body lay, sweeping the sand from the dunes, jamming their noses and mouths . . . The six of them . . . and the old man . . . they all felt the storm was connected with the Emperor's soul, with the torments it was experiencing. The Emperor's departing soul was burying all their hopes . . . The harmless, playful breeze that had sprung up from nobody knew where suddenly transformed into a wild force and, scaring every living thing to death, seemed to have grabbed this arid desert by the shirt, given it a good shake, and thrown it into the sky . . . When this happens in the desert, it is hard to find shelter or any safe, calm place. The sandstorm wanted to strip their clothing away, pull-ing and yanking at their skirts and sleeves. It harassed the women most of all, tugging up their dresses, baring their thighs and smacking their rear ends. Cleopatra, embarrassed, tried hard to keep hold of her skirt, grip-ping it tightly in her hands. The storm wouldn't let them open their eyes. They set off, following the old man, until they had trudged to the foot of a tall dune, and there they collapsed, pressing their bodies to the ground. Meanwhile, trying to nip in the bud the unruliness of the wild wind, thun-der crashed in the sky, lightning flashed, and rain poured to the earth as if from buckets . . .

The heavens seemed to have collapsed, and the flood came pouring in . . .

While the crashing thunder made the earth tremble, the lightning split the storm clouds to blind the world instantly, with such a bright light that anyone could have found even a needle in the sand. After the lightning, the thunder went on crashing, sending another tremble through the ground, stripping the last courage from every heart. Once every thousand years, in the desert, this happens; all its long-tailed life, all the skittering and slithering lizards and other beasts, and even the masters of the desert, the snakes, have all gone deep under seven layers of sand, burrowing in, seeking shelter, saving themselves from the scourge. The rain began to drill holes through the enormous cloud of sand the wind had lifted into the sky, and heavy with raindrops, that cloud began to fall back to earth . . . To the seven suffering people lying at the foot of the big dune, it seemed the ground was floating under them; the rainwater, soaking the sand as it mixed itself in, seemed to swamp their hearts and stomachs with sand, and sand rained down upon them. The downpour only got stronger, and at the peak of its strength, it had complete control of the territory.

And terrible sights were revealed to our travelers in the blinding flashes of lightning, with an incomprehensible rumbling clamor from far in the distance . . . The dunes soaked up all the water they could hold, and the water washed the sand down and away . . . This debauchery of nature, set in an all-encompassing pitch black, when they could not budge from where they lay, when they could not even open their eyes because of the wind, sand, and rain, stole all the will to live from our travelers . . . The seven of them, lying on the ground where they'd fallen to save themselves from the wind, became covered in rain-soaked sand . . . Now that their bodies were under the sand, they put all their painful effort into moving their heads and lifting them free. Their heads stuck out from the sand, here and there, just like the heads of corpses rising from their graves . . .

The storm ceased around midnight . . .

The desert is fickle. In an instant, the raging desert calmed; the black thunderclouds that had covered the whole sky, and the lightning that flashed like sabers in a battle, and the deafening roar and endless rumble of the thunder and wind all disappeared, and through the breaks in the clouds, innumerable stars appeared, strewn across the sky like spilled millet, and winked merrily; a blissful serenity reigned in the nighttime desert, as if none of it had ever happened . . . The impervious night, the starry sky . . . Calm reigned all around . . . It was near midnight when the desert's madness ceased, the buckets of rain stopped pouring down, and only a gusting breeze seized up the loose sand and spread it everywhere, like grains of wheat in a current, as if covering its tracks . . . With all their strength sapped, the six people buried up to their necks in sand slept in the night's embrace . . . Only Kozuchak shook his protruding head, spat the sand from his mouth, and gazed intently at the sky over the nighttime desert . . . He looked around. His traveling companions lay covered with sand, like unburied corpses . . . He looked at Cleopatra in the starlight, lying an arm's length away . . . She was sleeping sweetly . . . None of the hardship they had borne was reflected in her lovely face, and he saw it was as pretty as ever . . . At that moment, a star tore itself from the sky and fell . . . Kozuchak thought the sky was one star poorer . . . And he was poorer, too. He imagined himself to be a man deprived of everything. His world had become so narrow, and his thoughts meager, just like his body, buried in sand . . .

Kozuchak had a dream . . . In this dream, he was sleeping with a woman for the first time . . . And, as he had sensed he might, he was sleeping with his traveling companion, Cleopatra . . . Kozuchak had never imagined anything like it, not in a dream and not in real life . . . In this dream, they were both in the Holy Land . . . Fragrant flowers bloomed all around them, and cypress trees; butterflies played, unbelievably gorgeous birds flew by, and ripe apples bright as flames hung from the trees; golden oranges and heart-shaped pomegranates dropped from the branches . . . And he, Kozuchak, was there in this wondrous place, in the Holy Land, and so was Cleopatra, both completely naked, bare as the moment they were born . . . Kozuchak noticed . . . that the real-life Cleopatra was just as lovely and sweet as the dream Cleopatra . . . and her pale body was so astonishingly alluring . . . Kozuchak carefully moved toward her and pulled off her soft blanket. Without that soft blanket, Cleopatra's whole body was revealed . . . He gazed at her hungrily, devouring her beauty, and as he tried to let his eyes, brimming with love, have their fill, he moved, carefully, so carefully, and quietly. If Cleopatra were to suddenly wake up, Kozuchak would die of shame . . . He worshipped Cleopatra . . . And now he could savor this perfect body, feast on it with his eyes . . . His gaze moved to her breasts, the protruding nipples, and then lower, stopping at the soft down between her thighs . . . This was Kozuchak's first time seeing a naked woman, and he didn't care at all whether he was awake or dreaming. While he examined her naked body, going out of his mind with lust, Cleopatra suddenly woke up . . . "Kozuchak!" said Cleopatra, surprised, in her gentle voice. A smile played on her lips . . . Kozuchak, mortified, blushed all over. But Cleopatra was not the least bit shy before Kozuchak, who had surveyed her naked body, and that made her all the more attractive and alluring . . . Kozuchak still felt shy before her, and he had covered his private parts with a leaf; when she saw that, Cleopatra giggled quietly, and Kozuchak lost the ability to hide his embarrassment, and he laughed loudly along with her . . . When Cleopatra pulled him to her and pressed herself close, Kozuchak felt his penis thrusting forward like a pointed stake . . . The woman's intoxicating aroma delighted him . . . When Cleopatra grabbed and squeezed the banana leaf that covered his most intimate part, Kozuchak felt something stunning . . . Cleopatra tore the banana leaf away . . . and pressed herself to him again . . . What happened next, Kozuchak couldn't remember, because he had lost his ability to think. His amazing dream, full of pleasure, broke off just at the moment he sprayed his seed . . . When he opened his eyes, he saw he was still in that desert, cursed of God, and his head was poking out of the sand, and more sand was stuck to his salivating mouth . . .

The heads of his traveling companions stuck out here and there around him . . . Not far from him was Cleopatra's head, lit by the moon . . . With a barely noticeable smile on her lips . . . maybe Cleopatra was dreaming of Kozuchak, too . . . Kozuchak had made love for the first time in his life, and so what if it was in a dream? . . . He felt as if he'd become a real man . . . Kozuchak had never felt such a heat before, the kind that seized him head to toe, stirring chaotic thoughts in his head and disquiet in his soul. He could not remember a single night like this in his entire life, one that had kneaded his heart like bread dough, although he had grown up quicker than others, and seen things both bitter and sweet in his short life, things rising, things falling. Could this night, which had filled his breast with new sensations, filled it with the heat of passion—could it have burned away his whole essence? How could Kozuchak have known that this miraculous night would turn his whole internal world upside down, rob him of peace, burn him with fire, and that this one inconceivable dream would shake him so powerfully that he was soaked in sweat and couldn't catch his breath?

Or maybe this was that particular, mysterious night of his life . . . the one he had waited for, with all his tangled thoughts . . . and it was that liquid from his loins that had kept him from sleeping and tortured him all night long . . . He had suspected, before, that some unknown power was hidden inside him, but what kind of power was it that it constantly bothered him and ate at his insides like a worm? A power he had only started to sense now . . . Could this have been that night of torment? . . .

Maybe it was . . .

That night, in the middle of the desert, after the wild sandstorm, there was nothing but peace and quiet . . .

There, before dawn, not a trace remained of the storm that had passed through . . .

The desert slept serenely, glowing as if rinsed in milk . . .

The dawn began to be born . . . The storm had vanished, leaving no tracks, only a deep calm . . . The desert slept peacefully, covered in a blanket woven from the wool of sandy sheep . . .

The old man's moans and groans wrecked the peace of the dawn. He was not quite weeping, not quite wailing . . . There was a loud fart, and a hoarse voice lamented:

"Oh, my unfortunate head! My damned, stupid head!" He struck himself in the head. From the crack in his skull, blood began to flow. "O Lord, will the day of my death ever come?! You've shown me torment and grief, all the torments and all the griefs! Let me die!" whined the old man, still hammering himself in the head . . . His shouting frightened Kozuchak, who was somewhere between a dream and the waking world, and not strong enough to emerge from his morning dream . . . He just managed to dig himself out of the sand, and when he stood up, he saw the venerable old man, completely naked . . . Thin, legs like sticks of kindling, shoulder blades sticking out like a camel's humps, he resembled a tree that had withered and died long ago . . . Blood trickled down his pale face, and from his neck down along his whole body . . . He had decided to kill himself . . . Nobody knew where the night's typhoon had vanished to, the one that had torn off his clothing and the rest of the turban that had been wrapped around his head . . . Between his legs, there drooped something like a wrinkled turkey's neck . . . Once Kozuchak managed to pull himself from the sand, he hurried to the venerable old man who had resolved to murder himself . . . When he got close and tried to say something, the venerable old man shouted again, and hit himself twice in the skull with a rock . . . The blood flowed faster from the old man's head wounds . . .

"Stay away from me! Stay away, I tell you! . . . Don't come any closer!" shouted the old man, and went on hitting himself, frothing at the mouth . . . Kozuchak screamed, he couldn't help it, and he grabbed the old man by the legs and forced him down into the sand . . . He felt the weight of the kindling-thin man . . . Light as dry cotton, the old man fell to the ground, shaking all over and panting, and he began to weep bitterly . . .

"Oh, the night won't take me, and the earth won't take me, and the desert won't take me, and the grave won't take me! . . . Kill me, and you'll go to paradise. Kill me, here, whack me in the head, take this rock! . . . Kill me, I tell you! Destroy me . . ." the insane old man begged Kozuchak. "Kill me!"

Kozuchak held on to the old man for a long time, pressing him against the ground, firmly, until he settled down . . . The rock fell slowly from the old man's skinny hand, onto the sand . . . While the other travelers woke up, Kozuchak spent the time looking around for some kind of rag to cover the old man's dried-out body . . . The enraged wind that had torn off the rest of his turban had hung it up on one of the saxaul branches they had stuck around the Emperor's grave . . . When he saw the cloth, waving like a white flag, Kozuchak went to it . . . At that spot, Kozuchak froze, and his eyes bugged out in terror . . . The rains of the night had completely washed out the Emperor's grave . . . The desert scavengers had eaten his body down to the bones, and all the various insects, lizards, scorpions, and black beetles, which had come running from all over and piled them-selves into the open grave, darted under the sand to hide when they saw Kozuchak. Only one black snake, long and thick as a woman's braid, lifted its head and stared out from one of the Emperor's empty eye sockets . . . That snake was the master of the desert . . . At least, that is how Kozuchak imagined it. (That snake was not the master of the desert. It was the snake the Emperor's soul had settled inside.[6])

Once, the Emperor had told Kozuchak that a snake would bring him death. Kozuchak remembered those words now . . .

(Up till this day, the snake had followed the Emperor everywhere, because the Emperor's soul was destined for that snake . . . The snake was waiting for the Emperor's soul . . . It constantly appeared in his dreams, and that is probably why the Emperor was always so desperately afraid of snakes . . . The very word "snake" was enough to drive him mad, to make his food taste like glue, and his drink taste like rot . . . This was one of the reasons he fled the nuthouse . . . The snake had appeared in the Emperor's room at the nuthouse . . . After that, he couldn't sleep in his room at night, lying there waiting for the moment the snake would bite him . . . He escaped, not just from the nuthouse but from his room there, where the vermin's hole had appeared . . . At night, the Emperor read out loud from the Holy Book that belonged to the person they called the Holy Man, who later vanished to nobody knew where (nobody ever did find out

---

6. "People are afraid to equate themselves with their bodies because they are afraid of death. Our bodies decay before our eyes . . . our bodily eyes. But the soul seems to be undying. What 'seems to be' is not necessarily true. Spiritual life begins when we understand that spiritual death also exists. The soul disintegrates, just as the body does. Worse, decaying souls are much more terrifying. A person can have a young body and a rotten soul. This is the plot of *The Portrait of Dorian Gray*: the portrait containing the protagonist's soul ages, while his body, lacking a soul, feels fantastic. The difference is that the body can decay to such an extent that it ceases to exist, becoming simply a cluster of atoms. But it would be presumptuous to assume that the soul cannot disintegrate in the same way. That state is what some call the eternal torments of hell, when the soul no longer exists as an integral entity but only as a diffuse mist. People are sometimes given to experience an alienation not only from their bodies, but from their souls. In many prayers, people address their souls—their souls, not their bodies!—as if the soul is a separate, third party. This kind of alienation is an opportunity for salvation, for restoring unity within oneself. There is one eternal life for the body and the soul. A person looks like a dead body when he is separated from his soul, but that does not mean that a soul without a body is alive. A soul does not like being without a body. Belief that the dead will be resurrected is also a belief in the resurrection of souls and bodies" (hypotheses from an unknown individual).

who he was: a person, or a prophet, or just God's toady?), and he used the words from that Holy Book to force the snake back into its hole . . . Once, a nuthouse staffer happened to find the Holy Book under the Emperor's pillow. The Emperor no longer had a Holy Book to read at night . . . The day they took the Holy Book away, the snake came back . . . And, on the day the snake reappeared, the Emperor resolved to flee the mental hospital . . . That's when he came up with the myth of the Holy Land, and started agitating other nutters to run away with him, and started looking for ways and opportunities to escape . . . He did not know himself, really, if there was a Holy Land anywhere in this world. Leading his gang of six, he escaped the nuthouse. Not a single soul had ever escaped the Nation of Nutters before, but the Emperor did, and not alone! He brought six others with him . . .)

Now the snake stuck its head out of the Emperor's right eye socket, just like it was sticking it out of its burrow, and its tail hung out where his left eye had been, and the snake stared intently at Kozuchak . . . If Kozuchak moved at all, he thought, the snake would immediately sink its poisonous fangs into him. There was no flesh left on the Emperor's body, buried just yesterday, only bones . . . The breath froze in Kozuchak's lungs . . . He froze, too, as if turned to stone . . . The snake twitched its tail, which stuck like the hard grip of a whip from the skull's left eye socket . . . and slowly crawled straight toward the venerable old man . . . The old man stood there, just barely, his arms and legs trembling like a newborn calf's, and he was still screaming like a madman . . . The snake came right to the long-bearded old man's feet . . .

"I was so happy to think I wouldn't survive the night . . . If only the lightning that struck my head had killed me! . . . I kept running to where the lightning struck, trying to catch it . . . waiting for it to strike me down. But nothing caught me, not the wind, not the pouring rain, not the storm!" the old man complained . . . When he felt something unusually cold, he went quiet . . . The snake had started slowly winding itself around the old man's right leg . . . It wrapped around his leg, in no hurry, and lifted its little head, and slowly climbed on . . . The old man was startled at first, but then he suddenly shouted in joy, waving his hands: "Yes, finally, you've heard my voice! . . . A snake . . . yesss . . . a snake! It's come to bite me! I'll die of the snake's venom!" He folded his hands in prayer and looked to the heavens, overjoyed . . . The snake crept along the thin, dried-out body, its small head up, and slithered around the man's neck, up to his head, letting its own head hang before his face, and it stared directly at him with its steely eyes . . . As Kozuchak watched, a slight tremor shot through his body. Then every part of Kozuchak's body was shaking, and he could not tear his frightened gaze away from them, as if the snake had crawled up his own body to bite him . . . He did not have the strength or the will to grab the snake and toss it far away from the old man. Kozuchak's trembling body would not obey him . . . And, meanwhile, the snake, sensing its liberty, looped its long body around the old man three times, like a garland, its forked tongue flicking playfully . . . The old man's lips spasmed, and his whole body was coated with perspiration . . . Then the snake moved differently, like it was preparing to bite the old man in the head, and it let out several short hisses . . . The snake's body tensed, and a small tremor shot through it, as if all the strength of its body was shifting from its tail to its head and its tiny brain . . . Kozuchak's knees shook as he watched it happen . . . Fear seized Kozuchak's body and deprived him of all his will. He didn't know what to do . . . Shrinking into himself, he wanted to run, but his legs would not listen to him . . . He was shaking all over, just slightly, as if it was him the snake was about to bite . . . The trembling seized Kozuchak, and a storm swirled inside him . . . His whole body was shaking . . . The snake peered into the old man's eyes, intently, for a long time . . . The old man and the snake each seemed hypnotized by the other . . . The snake slowly crept down, off the old man, onto the ground, and . . . it slithered into the sand and disappeared . . . As if he'd finally flung some unbearable load off his sweating body, Kozuchak heaved a sigh of relief . . . He rubbed his tired eyes. The night's darkness had started to yield to the coming dawn.

"Damn it, damn it all! Even the snake thinks I'm unworthy of death! . . . Couldn't even spare a drop of venom for me!" whined the old man pitifully . . .

He was lonely, bone-dry, and completely naked . . .

Kozuchak took the remnants of the venerable old man's turban off the saxaul branches stuck into the Emperor's grave and wrapped the cloth around him. As he did, the other five came limping up to them . . . The first thing they saw was the Emperor's grave, washed clean by the rain . . . Not an ounce of flesh was visible on the body, only bones, as if the body had stewed all night in a giant pot of saltwater. It was not the Emperor's body lying on the sand, only his bones . . . Now they buried the Emperor's bones for the second time . . .

They buried them in a new place . . .

Yesterday's grave had been washed away entirely by the rain that had poured down all night long . . .

"Now who will lead us to the Holy Land? Who?" asked Cleopatra.

When she asked that question, they all looked at each other, lost. None of them could say a word.

"You lead us," said Thaïs the Athenian to Lear. "You're the oldest."

"I don't know the way," Lear said, and he frowned and stepped slightly away.

"What about you?" Thaïs the Athenian asked Alexander the Great. "Show us the way, Alexander the Great . . . We're waiting!"

"Oh, come on." Alexander the Great had to clear his throat in surprise. "I don't know where the Holy Land is. I don't even know which way is east, which way is west, and which way is Mecca!"

"Numbskull! Lout! He doesn't know, he says . . . What have you got in that head of yours? Brains or straw dust, eh? Where the sun rises, that's east, and where it sets is west! . . . How do you not know that?" Thaïs the Athenian's face was splotched red in anger.

"Then you lead us, Genghis Khan," said Cleopatra, looking at Genghis Khan with hope.

"Me?"

"You, yes, you," said Thaïs the Athenian. "You and the Emperor were friends, weren't you? Inseparable! You fed on each other's stink. Poor Emperor! He must have told you everything, all about the way to the Holy Land."

"Not a word! He didn't tell me a goddamn thing," Genghis Khan swore. "Fuck me if he did!"

"Then . . . what are we going to do?" asked Cleopatra, dismayed.

"What else can we do? Spit in our hands and go whichever way the wind blows it! That's how we'll get to the Holy Land . . . Ha-ha-ha!" cackled Thaïs the Athenian.

"But maybe the old man can lead us . . . Let's ask him." Cleopatra's face lit up with a sudden hope.

"That guy? Don't you know who he is, girlie? Well, I'll tell you. He's a parasite! A traitor! . . . He sold out Moses . . . You'd do better with me in the lead than following him!" shouted Thaïs the Athenian. "Why would we follow him, anyway? He betrayed a Prophet with his tricks . . . What do you want, for him to live another billion years? . . . Moses's curse is enough for him! . . . He can fuck right out of here!" said Thaïs the Athenian.

"I will lead you," said Kozuchak.

Nobody expected such a thing of him, and they all asked in chorus: "You?!" And they all gave him a curious look.

"Me!" Kozuchak answered with confidence.

"You sound sure of yourself. That's worth something. You must know what you're talking about. Lead on!" said Thaïs the Athenian.

"But what are we going to do with the old man?" Cleopatra asked them all.

"Leave him alone . . . He's on a different road . . . Even if we all die in this desert and turn into sand, he'll go on living. That's his curse!" said Thaïs the Athenian.

"Then let's go," they all said, looking at Kozuchak. "Come on. Get up."

When they were all on their feet and ready to go, the venerable old man spoke up.

"Wait now, just a little, just a little . . ." He walked toward them on his trembling legs, and they all stopped, watching him. "I have something to say to you," said the old man. The six of them turned to him, and stood silent, waiting to hear it. "I am a traitor . . . Please listen to me, even though you call me a traitor," he said, his voice shaking, his face long and drawn. "If I don't tell you this, this sadness will always remain inside me . . . So listen . . . I am a man whose soul has died inside his body . . . And you! Do you know who you are?" the old man asked.

"Us?" Thaïs the Athenian responded, wrinkling her nose. "Allow me to introduce us," she said, her mocking glance trained on the old man. "That one, with the little beard?" She pointed to Genghis Khan. "He's a scientist, an astronomer. He studies the composition of the solar system and the Earth and other planets," she said, wry as ever. "And that's not all! He discovered the secret of the universe, its formula! He discovered the secret of this world and . . ." She stole a glance at the sky, and then, as if she didn't want anyone to hear her, she went on in a whisper: ". . . and not just the secret of this world, but the secret of the Creator, and when he went to announce this great discovery of his, he lost his job in academia! . . . All that work for nothing! . . . He meant to solve the riddle of our world, but they left him high and dry . . . Yes, yes, he lost everything. And now . . . here he is skittering across the desert, at God's mercy . . ."

Genghis Khan nodded, as if in agreement, and stared at his feet.

"And that one!" Thaïs the Athenian pointed at Alexander the Great. "That one's a scholar of religion who wanted to change the world! . . . And he would have changed it, too, but he couldn't change himself . . . And where do they send people who can't change themselves? Off to the nut-house! . . . He escaped from there, and now here he is, skittering across the untamed desert . . . The rest of us, well, we're all small fry, starting with me . . . I'll just tell you a little about us." She pointed at Lear. "That one is the Antichrist. He's ashamed of nothing! That yellow-mouthed nest-ling there, he's a botanist, and he broke himself studying too hard and got dumped in the nuthouse . . . Hmmm . . . And this lovely lady . . ." Here, Thaïs the Athenian shot a glance at Cleopatra, and spoke even more sarcastically. "She's the most innocent of creatures! Simply an angel . . . a woman in angel form . . . phenomenally bright, devilishly attractive, yes . . . divinely beautiful, blindingly honest, super-active, hypersexual . . . basically, the most fantastically modest little person you'll ever meet! . . . Isn't that so, my dear! . . . What sweet little eyes you have. The whole mys-tery of the world is in those eyes! How many men would have died just for one look from you!"

Cleopatra grinned at her funny tirade.

"No laughing!" Thaïs the Athenian glowered at her. "This mademoi-selle really stood out at the nuthouse for her excessively good looks . . . But then there's me. The daughter of a mother with brains, and a father who was off in the head. That's the truth! . . . We're all struggling to be individuals here, unlike all the rest . . . and we're all going to the Holy Land!"

The old man did not like Thaïs the Athenian's joking delivery one bit. "But do you know who you are?" he asked again.

"Yes, we do," said Lear, without even pausing to think.

"No, you don't know . . . so I'm going to tell you." The old man took a deep breath, gathering his courage and his strength. "You're insane." The other five hadn't expected that, and they burst out laughing. Thaïs the Athenian even clapped her hands.

"Don't you laugh! Stop laughing," the old man told them, scowling at them all. "It's the truth!"

"How true can anything be when a traitor says it? Shut your mouth, you," Lear said angrily. "Or . . ."

"Don't be angry! Let me speak. Don't be angry!" The old man's voice was more confident now, and louder, as if he knew something extremely important. "You're a fool and a sex fiend . . . Only you know how you've been cursed for your fiendishness, but you don't feel like telling anyone! You think I don't know about that? Well, I know, but I don't want to talk about it . . . You thought you'd have no divine castigation, and you could drag that sin along with you, bearing all its weight, didn't you? . . . Just try to deny it! . . . I know you'll answer for that . . . and you know it, too," said the venerable old man. "And this woman! She may be short, but her sins are stacked higher than any building." The old man turned to face Thaïs the Athenian. "Don't you try acting innocent . . . Don't you pray to the Creator . . . Nobody's going to hear you . . . You've got the castigation of a curse around your neck, too . . . and you know it yourself," said the old man.

"Well, well! . . . Look what we have here! Who does this blind old man think he is, an all-seeing fortune teller, or what?" Thaïs the Athenian lunged at the old man to claw him in the face, but Genghis Khan grabbed her and stopped her, even as she cursed him out. The old man paid her no attention and went on speaking as before.

"And this little Kozuchak—so young the mother's milk hasn't dried on his lips—he might have been touched by the hand of a Prophet . . ." The old man turned to face Kozuchak. "But you drank the milk of a spirit . . .

you dirtied your mouth . . . unfortunate boy . . . You're not clean, either, young one," said the venerable old man to Kozuchak. He said nothing for a while, readying himself to speak to the other three.

"Who are you?" he asked, turning sharply to Alexander the Great. "You want to tell me you're Alexander the Great? No, no . . . you're not him . . . You're a genuine nutter . . . Yes, you're a nutter! . . . Don't be offended at the word . . . Alexander the Great's soul is bearing its castigation in your body . . . It's inside your body." The old man slowly turned his head toward Genghis Khan. "And Genghis Khan's soul is in your body." He turned to Cleopatra. "And Cleopatra's soul has found its refuge inside of you . . . Accountability! Accountability for everything in this world. You all have to answer for people who have long dropped into oblivion, and their souls are now in your bodies . . . The human soul is eternal, and so are the demands upon it! . . . Human sin pursues a person's descendants . . . Not a single soul has ever escaped a sin, not easily," said the old man. "When I betrayed the Prophet, I was doomed to the castigation of immortality . . . It's not your own sins, but the sins of the people whose souls you carry in your bodies, that you're trying to take to the Holy Land to be cleansed . . . But does that Holy Land exist? . . . If it does, then where is it? What is it? Some place? Or this whole ever-changing world? . . . What is it, eh? . . . Nobody knows! . . . It's all a riddle, a mystery! The world, mankind, every-thing! . . . My body is a tomb, and my soul will always bear its castigation in my body . . . but you're carrying souls in your bodies that will never pay off their sins, and will bear their castigation for all eternity . . . That's where you and I resemble one another," said the venerable old man.

They all listened to him without uttering a word. After what the old man said, absolute silence reigned among them . . . Though the old man had been speaking earnestly, as if trying to impress upon them a bitter truth, the passionate, searing words of a man who had betrayed a Prophet, who was roaming the desert all alone, constantly praying for God to give him death, had no effect on them whatsoever.

"Each person is all alone in this world," the old man went on sadly. "We know we'll die eventually, and death is our only close friend . . . Know-ing that death exists, it's only through death that we can understand the true meaning of life . . . To understand life's value, we have to experience all its difficulties and torments, because only those things can awaken a genuine love for life in our breasts, a love for the joys of existence . . ." The old man looked at the sky, reverentially, thoughtfully. "This is a love both for life and for death . . . This is happiness, and this love is inside you, but all I have is the most extreme curse of eternal immortality."

The old man whom the earth wouldn't take, exiled from many lands, privy to many secrets, sighed deeply . . .

"Oh, to hell with you! Enough of your nonsense!" Thaïs the Athenian walked up to the old man, grabbed him by the shoulders, spun him around roughly to face the east, and spoke, meanly. "You need to go *this* way, and we'll go *that* way," she said, pointing west. "You're not on our way . . . not even close! . . . What a weirdo! All this time, and he doesn't admit his guilt! What an asshole!" Thaïs the Athenian got even angrier. "Millions of years he's lived, and he still doesn't get it . . . May your turban catch fire!" She shouted at him, furious.

Then she turned to Kozuchak. "All right, kid. Go on and lead us. Forget all that claptrap! Show us the way!"

🍂

Dangerous omens:
The Alatyr stone
Narcissism
Water
A wave
A mountain
Mount Agung
Lightning
Rain
The Earth
Stone
Fire
The sea
The ocean
A bridle
A planet

A rainbow
A river
Dew
Great Mount Semeru
The Sun
Salt
A meteorite
The philosopher's stone

The venerable old man set off for the east, while the other six headed west . . .

Again, the six set out on their long journey, having decided to go west, and finally cross the broad, sandy breast of this hot, never-ending desert . . .

In the lead walked the yellow-mouthed boy Kozuchak, the rest in a clump behind him . . . Starving and exhausted, they fell to sleep instantly whenever they could, and then walked some more, a little at a time, slowly covering the endless distance . . .

Sometimes the world is vast, and sometimes it is so small that there is no place to set your foot. The edge of this desert, cursed of God, turned out to be infinitely far away . . .

Kozuchak walked in the lead. Next came Thaïs the Athenian, strong and sturdy, who never felt tired and who was always brewing up plans along the way, chatting on without pause; now, though, she walked with her head down and her teeth clenched . . . this was another sign of their long journey . . . She was explosive by nature, and vivacious, but also vexing, when she squawked on nonstop like a magpie, or when she heard some unlucky word and burst into another conversation. But she was leagues ahead of many men in terms of courage and resilience . . . Thaïs the Athenian's long-unwashed hair carried a thick crust of dandruff . . . The desert pulled the strength even out of her, and she, too, was exhausted and downcast, barely hanging on . . .

The cruel law of this untamed desert tied them all together, and there was only one thought driving them forward: to get out of the desert while they still could. Now they were scared to even mention the Holy Land . . . And nobody knew what was happening inside the unspeaking Genghis Khan and Alexander the Great, what they were thinking, what fire was burning in their hearts. Both seemed to be stuck in bottomless wells, each quieter than the other, only rarely moving their lips to mutter something, in a general conversation, or when someone asked them a question; otherwise, nobody could get a word out of them. They both were tired of the endless journey, completely worn out . . . How else could they be? There was no escape from the exhaustion. They wished they could break from the group, somehow, and walk off into that mad, wild desert. "Your Holy Land can go to hell!" That was the fire burning inside them . . . But the two of them cannot just walk away from the rest, or say to hell with it all . . . They have to stick together. Their common goal binds them. Where would they go if they left the rest of them? What did east, west, north, and south mean in this endless, untamed desert? That question drove Genghis Khan completely insane . . . And for that reason, he walked behind everyone else, like a dog on a lead . . .

In that desert, scorched by the heat of the Great Fire, mirages wavered all around, seeding temptation everywhere . . . Nothing but sand was visible, as if a snake had swept the place clean with its tail. Unless you counted the desert wildlife, who flashed into view timidly, once in a while, here and there, their eyes could see only three things: the endless sands, the sun, and the sky . . .

In the desert, time stood still, and a wild kind of calm reigned all around . . .

Alexander the Great had taken to hunching over as he walked, lacking the strength to even speak about the pain, hiding his long, thin neck between his protruding shoulders, seemingly afraid to lift his head in case it got torn off . . . The burned skin on his neck was swollen and putrefying . . . and all because of this God-damned journey . . . It had brought them so much disaster . . . And, for that reason, disillusioned with everything and feeling cold toward them all, he wants to walk away; but he can feel how weak he is, so he has to stay . . . and his soul burns in that scorching flame . . . The clothing on Lear's thin frame has long since burned through and lost its color in the baking heat of the desert . . . Sometimes, madness seizes him, the wild force of madness suddenly overcomes him, and he succumbs to the power of that madness . . . When insanity takes him, he is strong as a wild boar, ready to knock over anyone who stands in his way, and raise a genuine storm . . . Just try to calm him down when he's in a state like that. He'll knock the whole world to pieces. He has to collapse on his own somewhere, exhausted, like a pricked balloon; there is no forcing him to calm down, no pacifying his rage . . . His insanity swoops in on an unexpected breeze, a sudden storm . . . At times like that, he does not know what he is saying or doing, and he cannot control his own body, and has no mastery over himself, like a doll in someone else's hands; his insanity controls him completely . . . But no matter how far out of his mind he goes, frothing at the lips, spraying saliva in all directions, he remembers the monologue imprinted on his brain like it was carved in stone, and he enters into that theatrical role and delivers the speech, giving it his whole soul and—most intriguing of all—never forgetting, never skipping, a single word from that monologue, never deviating from his role in any way . . . But, in his normal state, he can't remember a line of that long monologue . . . Lear truly had been a very interesting person . . . Women had always loved him, adored him for his long, slender fingers, the look in his eye, his height, the way his hair swept back on his head . . . The man who had betrayed the holy Moses had first given him a good, long look, and then, without hesitation, let the words drop: "You're insane." And he had said he knew everything about Lear, things even Lear didn't know, and that hit Lear where it hurt. Lear truly had been a womanizer . . . In his old notebook, he'd even written down which women he slept with, and when. According to his calculations, according to the notebook, there were 1001 of them. He'd written everything in that notebook: each woman's name, age, habits, the things they did in bed, even the loving words they spoke. Then he read those notes for pleasure . . . Once they had done a search in the nuthouse, and they found his notebook and took it away. He even had his own philosophy: "A woman is made for a man's pleasure." Once, he had read that sex fiends would be the first ones dumped in the boiling cauldron of Hell and interrogated in the other world, and he had laughed for a long time over that. He often waged war with the words, "It's my life, mine! I live the way I want!" That last night still hounded him . . . The girl who had been in Lear's arms . . . that little prostitute was his daughter, he'd slept with his own daughter, a punishment for recognizing no gods, for spitting at the heavens; yes, finally, the day of reckoning had come . . . Whatever the case, that night he had not had the strength or the will or the courage to push away the girl who was sharing his bed, and tell her: "I am your father." . . . Now he remembered that girl, his daughter, to be precise, and he frequently thought about her . . . He did more than that; he had gone back two or three times, after that night, to the brothel, but he never saw the girl there again . . . The women at the brothel hadn't been able to give him her address . . . He just couldn't forget that girl . . . that girl . . . his own daughter . . . The morning after that utterly dark night, he fell into a serious depression, and lost his mind . . . He had gone against his God, he had disavowed the Creator, he had shrunk from the very word "God" and had burned quite a few holy books in his arrogance . . . The castigation arrived together with his daughter, straight into his embrace . . . There had been a time, recently, when he had held a conversation with the Creator in every dream he had . . . Was it a conversation, or an insane fantasy? If only he knew for sure . . . Was he insane? Had those dreams blown in on the winds of imbecility? . . . What could it signify? What could it mean? . . . He simply had no idea . . . Every night, somebody calling himself God told him about the mysteries of the universe, the ones he could not penetrate with his rational mind, the ones he could not understand in the slightest . . . He did not know where those cursed visions came from, or what they were for, and once, before dawn, he prayed to God in fear, yes, he started praying to God . . . And, just as he asked, that night, the Creator stopped appearing in his dreams. He saw plenty of things in his dreams after that . . . everything but God . . .

Like a gemstone lying in the mud, none of the torments and troubles that Cleopatra bore along with the rest of them had chased the beauty from her face. It was as perfectly radiant as before. The difficulties of the long journey in this desert could not extinguish the light of her clear eyes, or her gentleness, or her femininity, or her world, full of her dreams and imagination . . . The old man's words had made Cleopatra think. She was the kind who, once she heard something, tended to keep it inside, suffering silently, ashamed to reveal her feelings, not to anyone, no matter what went on in her soul. The old man's words got through to the young woman, like worms eating into her soul. Usually, Cleopatra kept everything she heard inside herself, and worried and suffered in private, not letting on to anyone. She . . . and also the real Cleopatra, her soul . . . (and what completely discordant, stupid words! How could they have anything to do with this young woman?) In the nuthouse, it was only after they shoved the sharp needle into her, by force, torturing her, that she lost her mind, carried away in visions, experiencing such strange feelings . . . That was the only way . . . How could the words of that unpleasant old man apply to her . . . She just couldn't understand it . . . From what she remembered, it was the chief physician at the nuthouse who had named her Cleopatra . . . She did not know for sure. Maybe her real name was Cleopatra, given to her with all the proper ceremony when she was born? . . . it would be difficult to find out . . . The nuthouse seemed to have wiped her memory clean, and every time she tried to remember something, there was the nuthouse before her . . . that man in black who came to see her once a month . . . the oatmeal they served . . . a voice on the radio . . . the hospital's hubbub . . . people shouting . . . it all seemed like a genuine hell . . . She didn't regret joining this group and fleeing the nuthouse, not at all. The hardships of the journey seemed much easier to bear than all that torment and suffering . . .

The night before, Cleopatra had a dream. In the dream, she was using an axe to chop down a cherry tree dotted with ripe, red fruit . . . She didn't understand why she had picked up the axe and was hacking at that cherry tree, and when she sank the blade into the trunk, thick red blood flowed from the tree, like it was a human body. After two or three swings of her axe, the cherries dropped from the tree . . . Red as burning coals, the cherries fell to the ground like tears. Plop! Plop! . . . Cleopatra woke up, terrified . . . She told Kozuchak about it. Kozuchak listened, and then he told Cleopatra about a strange dream of his own. In the dream, Kozuchak decided to hang himself from a tall tree growing in the middle of a hilly wasteland. He took off his belt and tried two times to toss it over a branch. Finally, he did it, but the branch broke under Kozuchak's weight, and he fell, and his hand touched something cold. He felt the thing to find out what it was, and it turned out to be an axe. Kozuchak picked up the axe and chopped off some twigs, then swung the axe against the trunk of the tree a few times and chopped it down . . . They decided to go to Thaïs the Athenian to have her interpret their dreams, but she had had a dream, too, in which she was chopping down a fig tree hung with fruit. At first, the three of them thought that their dreams just happened to have been similar, but it turned out that the rest of them had also been dreaming of chopping down trees all night. Alexander the Great had felled a pine tree, Genghis Khan's was a poplar, and Lear thought his was some kind of tree that grew in Yemen . . . They gave each other puzzled looks and asked what those visions were and what they meant, but none of them could offer any clear explanation. If just one person had had that dream, then fine; but they were all chopping down trees in their dreams, and that was incomprehensible, inexplicable. There were no trees in the desert. They all could have used one, and they needed the shade of a tree in this solar-powered oven . . . How strange that they had cut them down.

Those mysterious dreams gave rise to doubts and suspicions. Did they herald some disaster? . . . The question gave them no peace . . .

"Get up!" When Lear kicked Kozuchak, Kozuchak did not even move. The boy was too worn out from the long, difficult journey, and his body felt beaten. Now seven days and seven nights had passed since Kozuchak began leading this small band of people . . . For seven days, the six had trudged stubbornly straight ahead, unblinking, with only one desire: to finally cross through this rotten desert . . . He walked forward, despite their moaning and complaining . . . even the boisterous Thaïs the Athenian found it difficult to move her feet, feeling helpless, her spirits down. They were all exhausted by their journey, and they all collapsed on heaps of sand wanting just to sleep for a while . . .

Dawn was gathering, and the life of desert had begun to awaken . . .

They always set out early, before the desert's heat was in full force, hoping to reach the Holy Land . . .

The kick from Lear surprised Kozuchak . . .

Dawn had begun in the desert . . .

Kozuchak stretched his neck and peered through his narrow eyes into the distance . . . Genghis Khan, on his knees, was pissing toward the west . . . Lear, his towering body blocking the sunlight from Kozuchak, kicked him until he woke up . . . When Lear took a step away, the rays of the rising sun pierced Kozuchak's eyes like needles . . . Alexander the Great had risen before them all and was pacing back and forth, thinking . . . Kozuchak remembered the nighttime whispering between Alexander and Genghis Khan . . . Kozuchak had been drowsy, and he'd only barely listened, and he'd soon fallen asleep. But he had overheard part of their conversation. "I don't like what that traitor said . . . Did you hear him? . . . He pointed at me and said: 'You are carrying the soul of the genuine Alexander!' I want to believe him, but I can't. Where would I have picked up Alexander's soul? When I'm barely alive myself . . . He told the truth about me. Maybe he lied about you. When I heard what he said, it was like some mystery force wrapped around my chest, honest to God . . . I didn't know what it was . . . Or was I just scared? Maybe the old man's a dervish wandering the desert? . . . Why Moses? . . . Why this traitor? . . . say what you want, but there's power in his words, you feel like believing him . . . Did you see it? That flame that popped out of his chest? For some reason, I believe him . . . What do you think?" Alexander the Great asked Genghis Khan. "That old man said I've got Genghis Khan's soul inside me. Why Genghis Khan? Why me? . . . Or do I look like him? They say he had narrow eyes and crooked legs, and wasn't very tall, and had two strands of hair for a beard! What do he and I have in common?" They talked, the two of them, for a long time, discussing what the old man had said . . . Kozuchak remembered their conversation . . . The old man had said he had drunk a spirit's milk when he was a baby . . . When Kozuchak remembered those words, his whole body jerked, as if he'd been shocked . . .

Dawn was emerging at the horizon of the desert . . . The sun was coming up . . .

Kozuchak saw Thaïs the Athenian and Cleopatra walking around a dune to answer the call of nature away from the men.

Not far from Kozuchak, Genghis Khan said to Alexander the Great: "This place looks familiar to me. We've been here before . . ."

"When? Don't be ridiculous," Alexander the Great said to Genghis Khan. "All this way we've already come, everything looks like everything else . . . The mountains are mountains, the steppe is the steppe, the desert is the desert . . . You're imagining things . . . See that bird in the sky? There's a reason it's there . . . That bird has a tuft of floodplain grass in its beak . . . We must be getting close to the Holy Land . . . We just need to walk a little farther, and we'll be done with this wild desert . . . Hang in there . . ." Alexander the Great had barely finished speaking those words when a piercing shriek came from the other side of the dune, where Thaïs the Athenian and Cleopatra were. Astonished, they immediately rushed toward the scream.

Kozuchak was the last to run up.

When he arrived, he saw the other five standing in the place where the Emperor was buried . . . Kozuchak could not believe his eyes, and cold sweat squeezed out of him . . . Had they made a circle and returned here? That was impossible! Kozuchak had been walking toward Mecca, but he seemed to have led them in the completely opposite direction . . . Kozuchak was still panting from running to the spot, and now his whole body began to quiver . . . he whispered to himself: "Impossible!" The Emperor had often told him that the Holy Land was in the same direction as Mecca, and that they had to keep walking west . . . Kozuchak had done that, walking always toward Mecca, in the direction where the sun sank into its nest . . . What devil had tricked them and led them back here? . . . Everyone was shocked . . . Everyone was distraught . . . The thoughts scrambled together in their heads . . . a messy slop of thoughts . . . Terror took root in their bewildered souls, because now it seemed they would never get out of this cursed desert; they had put all their last strength into walking, full of hope, trying to overcome the endless expanses of this desert, and now here they were, back where they had started, as if traveling the mill wheel of some crazed miller . . . Nobody had made Kozuchak speak up, the day they buried the Emperor, nobody had made him volunteer to lead them all . . . and that embarrassed him worst of all, the knowledge of his guilt draining his last strength . . . Everyone standing at the Emperor's grave shared one thought: that now they would never be able to escape this untamed desert, and that thought birthed another terrible thought: about how impossible a peaceful death would be here, about how they would all rot alive in this desert and become food for the insects and other creeping beasts . . . That idea was like a dagger in everyone's heart . . . There was a red rag tied to one of the saxaul branches they had stuck around the Emperor's grave . . . And a little off in the distance, the edge of a rock poked out of the sand like a tooth . . . all of this . . . all of it, they were seeing again, like looking at a painting . . . The usually boisterous, sharp-tongued Thaïs the Athenian looked completely broken down, drained of all strength, like a nomad after three straight seasonal migrations . . . They said nothing for a long time . . . Who would speak first? Who would explode first? Who would blame whom? . . . Now it seemed that Time itself was standing still . . . Thaïs the Athenian finally lost all patience and broke the dead silence with a piercing, plaintive wail.

"I've had it!" she screamed. "We're gonna die and rot here just like him! You said there was no such thing as the end of the world, but here it is! Is it a worldwide flood? An ice age? An earthquake? Planets colliding? Total destruction? What do we care!" Thaïs the Athenian's face convulsed into a strange shape. "We've got the end of the world right here! It's this desert, this endless sand! . . . And the one we pray to, the one we're devoted to, the one we beg for help, isn't worth a damn!" Her eyes grew big and round, her hands shook, and as her body trembled, she shouted loud enough for the whole desert to hear: "Everything has a beginning and an end! The universe is choking on our poison! I've had it!" Thaïs the Athenian's words stunned them all, and they shivered as if a storm had swept in. "We told that creep to lead us to the campfire, but he led us to total shit! . . . We should have seen it! Now we do!"

"Seen what?" asked Genghis Khan, apparently hypnotized by Thaïs the Athenian's crazed screaming.

"What do you think?" Tears flew from Thaïs the Athenian's eyes. "You and your thick head! . . . We're gonna rot and die in this God-forsaken desert!" she yelled, her face twisted by another spasm. "We're all gonna die!"

"Die?" The word was a thorn in the soul for them all.

Genghis Khan went pale when he heard it, and his lips trembled; his arms jerked like he'd grabbed a live wire, and terror shot through him, making him want to pray to God, though his idiotic tongue wouldn't obey. The sensation of fear crept through Genghis Khan's whole body, through his veins, and it made his throat clench. He sank to the ground and stared angrily at those around him, he fell to the ground, weak, and he scooped

up two handfuls of hot sand and flung it at the people standing around
him . . .

"Here's death for you!" he yelled.

The sand Genghis Khan had grabbed and thrown into the air soon
sprinkled down on them all. His narrow eyes flashed, mean as a rabid
dog's, and he started to shout hoarsely. Thaïs the Athenian and Genghis
Khan shouted insanely together, and their shrieks split the sky . . .

"Everything has a beginning and an end!" shouted Thaïs the Athenian.

"Here's death for you!" shouted Genghis Khan, throwing sand.

"The universe is choking on our poison!"

"We're not dying of poison, we're dying of our own stench!"

They both shouted like people possessed, now Thaïs the Athenian,
now Genghis Khan . . .

Their mutual madness grew stronger and stronger . . .

Alexander the Great, unable to believe his eyes, froze where he stood,
feeling lost. He stood there glum and mute . . . Robbed of the strength to
say a word, make a noise, or even scream; he felt someone had stuffed his
mouth with sand, and he couldn't move so much as a hand . . . Thaïs the
Athenian's high, piercing shriek started to take them in, it started to heat
their blood, making it run faster through their veins, slowly drawing them
all into a frenzied, all-encompassing riot . . . Only Cleopatra and Kozuchak
stood still, like gravestones pounded into the ground . . . The rest started
screaming like wounded beasts, flinging handfuls of sand at them, and
they stopped understanding what they were doing and what they were yell-
ing . . . Filthy words shot from their mouths like streams of fire, their red
eyes glowed like coals, and just as if the great storm at the End of the World
had begun, the storm that would turn the whole Earth upside down, and
knead their bodies like dough, and lift them up to the sky and fling them
into an enormous bonfire, they raised a maddened hue and cry . . .

"What is a lie?" In the midst of this noise, shaking all over, Genghis
Khan grit his teeth and tried reciting the lines of some poet[7] he'd suddenly
remembered:

7. Şayloobek Düyşeev.

In a flash it twists into being,
Thin and lovely as a liar! . . .
Sorely tempting all of us,
Passion driven,
Stealing the water
Sanding the well
Paying no heed
to conscience or soul,
We have trespassed
against shame and honor,
Trespassed: do not trespass the Koran!
We have trespassed
against holiness
against God in Heaven!

After every line, Genghis Khan flung a handful of sand into the air . . . As he recited, the veins on his neck swelled, his face twisted, and spit flew from his mouth. Genghis Khan reached his boiling point. He was deranged, as if a dragon had awoken inside him . . .

"This is the path you led us along?"

"Where's the Holy Land?"

"Where is it?"

"You bastard!"

"Crazy asshole!"

"Fuck you!"

"Asking some snot-nosed brat to lead us!"

"You've led us to Hell!"

The shouts, the scorn, the oaths rained down on Kozuchak from all sides.

"This Devil tempted us!" Thaïs the Athenian said coldly. "It was the Devil, following the Emperor's orders! Stone him! Stone him! Do you still believe that traitor to Moses? He's a debaucher who drank a spirit's milk! A devil debaucher! Stone him! Stone him!" Thaïs the Athenian quickly bent over to look for rocks, and she found one the size of a walnut and threw it, and it hit the boy Kozuchak square in the forehead. A thin trickle of blood flowed from the wound . . .

"Stone him!"

"Stone him!"

"Stone him!"

All the others started throwing everything they could get their hands on, too . . .

Kozuchak didn't know what to do. He didn't understand what was happening, who was doing what, or why, and he couldn't see the people throwing sand at him, just stood there, empty of all will and thought . . . His head was spinning, and the sounds outside weren't getting through to him . . . He stood there, insensate to the rocks that hit his body and the sand they threw in his face . . . Next to him, Cleopatra sobbed, almost deafened from all the shouting . . . The earth seemed to be swimming underfoot . . .

"The Holy Land! The Holy Land! I'll show you!" The furious Genghis Khan started digging up the Emperor's grave, clawing at the sand with his fingers . . . "This is all his fault!" he said as he clawed through the sand of the burial mound. "You're the one who brought us here! I'll disturb your slumber! I won't leave your soul at peace! We're all idiots for listening to you! We're worse than dogs! The Holy Land, the Holy Land . . . I piss on your Holy Land! You damned trickster, you didn't want to lie here all alone, did you? You wanted us to die and rot in this desert along with you!" Genghis Khan kept growling, seething with madness, as he used his hands like shovels to dig the sand from the Emperor's grave and toss it behind him, like sowing wheat . . .

Alexander the Great began digging out the grave along with him . . . Very soon, the two of them had dug it up entirely, and they each grabbed a leg and pulled out the Emperor's corpse . . . The Emperor's corpse did not have an ounce of flesh left on it, because that had all been eaten long ago by insects and scavengers, so that the bones gleamed white . . . The eye sockets, the nose bones, the ridge of the brow—those all looked a little like the Emperor's face, just a resemblance . . . Both crazed madmen grabbed the corpse and tossed it roughly from the hill of sand . . . The hard landing took off the Emperor's head . . .

"And you believed him, too! . . . You're the one who talked me into listening to him, you cretin!" The raging Alexander the Great was shouting at Genghis Khan now, pointing at him and glaring. "If you hadn't tempted me, I never would have experienced any of this! Go to hell!"

"Me?" Genghis Khan demanded.

"Yes, you!" said Alexander the Great in his fury.

"Me? *I* tempted *you*?" Genghis Khan was beside himself with anger. "You're the one who kept harping on . . . 'The Holy Land! The Holy Land!' . . . And now you want to punish *me* for all this because you can't punish the Emperor. Isn't that right, you infidel? But he's the one who tricked you!" Genghis Khan pointed at the corpse of the Emperor, lying on the ground. "If you're so tough, go ahead and take your revenge! Teach his soul a lesson!"

"Oh, I will, I will!" said Alexander the Great.

"Good! If you're so tough, piss on his skull! Get your revenge!" Genghis Khan was still shouting, spit spraying from his mouth.

Alexander the Great wasn't shy. He pulled his penis out of his pants.

"I'm going to piss on him! You think I won't do it?" He started to pee on the Emperor's corpse . . . "What about you? Are you a man or aren't you? . . . Don't be a sissy! Go ahead and piss!" Alexander the Great told Genghis Khan threateningly. "Piss!"

Genghis Khan hadn't expected that and paused.

"Me, too?"

"Yes! You, too! Take your revenge!" Alexander the Great stared at Genghis Khan. "Come on, do it!"

"Oh. Yeah! Why would I deny myself the pleasure! I'll piss on him!" And Genghis Khan started to piss on the Emperor's corpse, freshly dug from the grave.

"Me too! We have to piss on him so the dog gets the death he deserves!" Thaïs the Athenian called out, and she squatted like a hen over the Emperor's skull and peed, spraying urine everywhere. Then she hopped over to his body, picked up her skirt, and started to shit on it like an animal:

When the last star falls from the sky,
When the sun moves behind the hill,

A page is torn from the calendar,
An end to the year . . . redder than red.
Satan dances on the face of the moon,
The moonlight brings shame to our eyes,
And everything has the bitterest taste,
everything emerges, by and by,
Doom and destruction will swallow this world!
When doomsday comes, Satan laughs out loud,
phantoms emerge from the fires of hell,
and pursue all living beings . . .
Doomsday will come, heaven's face hidden
by the darkest, deadliest night,
our lungs will fill with poisonous gas,
The earth will be ruined, a great collapse . . .
And the great horned Satan dances!
In the most fearful minds!

Thaïs the Athenian was jumping up and down on the bones. Crack! Crack!

These six unfortunates had helped each other across the merciless desert in hopes of finding the Holy Land, losing themselves to sleep wherever they could, for a very long time . . . and, gradually, they came to hate each other and transformed into truly savage animals. Now, nobody could have said what demon had cursed them . . . Their veins are distended, their eyes burn with disdain, and their hatred boils. The sight of each other is too much for them, to say nothing of loving one another . . . Or have they now reached the last waypoint on their way to the Holy Land the Emperor had told them about? Or were they simply outraged to have enslaved themselves to those words about the Holy Land, to have sacrificed themselves in this bare, wild desert? Or were they simply out of patience? Those questions hung in the air, unanswered . . . Nothing could sway them anymore: they were sure their lives were ending, and at that moment, they had no choice but to suck out all the sweetness it could offer, and everywhere you looked there was a dark murk, not even one slender ray of light . . . They thought that moment was their last minute before the End of the World, that this was a sign of Judgment Day . . . And the thought that they would not die with dignity but simply drop dead, get snuffed out, no funeral rites, no graves, obsessed them . . .

The chosen day was short, and it burned in flame . . .

"Take that!" Alexander the Great sprayed his stream of urine right in Genghis Khan's face. "Can you do that?!"

"Take that!" And both of them forgot all shame and started hopping around, cackling savagely, spraying each other with urine . . .

When he saw what those two were doing, Lear rushed up and whacked Genghis Khan in the forehead, so hard that his knees buckled, and he tumbled onto the sand . . . And when he swooped down like a black bird on Alexander the Great and punched him in the head, Alexander the Great flew backwards, collided with a sharp rock sticking out of the sand, and fell next to it . . . The morals of a wild boar were at work inside Lear, and he shoved Genghis Khan into the sand and hit him in the stomach. Coughing blood, Alexander the Great curled into the fetal position there on the sand . . .

A scream ascended to the heavens . . .

They had once been as close as the fingers of a single hand, they had seen things on their journey that even wild dogs never see, and Fate had tied them together, but suddenly they were in a mad frenzy, boiling hot, renouncing God, rushing each other with teeth bared like predatory beasts, in a deranged and bloody bacchanalia . . .

Cleopatra watched it all happening, whispering prayers, but all she could do was weep, sitting by herself off to one side, helpless and powerless . . . Rabid and raving, Lear tore out of the ground one of the decaying saxaul trunks from around the Emperor's grave and shouted at Kozuchak:

"What the hell use was that route you led us down?! Was that your route?" And he struck him twice on the back with the saxaul.

"Don't hit him! Stop!" Cleopatra shouted.

When she rushed into the melee to defend Kozuchak, who had become close to her, her other half, somebody burst out of the crowd and shoved her violently out of the fight. Cleopatra limped away, out of strength, her legs like rubber, and fell onto the sand. Alexander the Great and Genghis Khan could barely stand, but now they turned to beating each other bloody . . . For no reason at all, they were now mortal enemies. A mad force that recognized no God had taken root inside them . . .

And what had possessed Thaïs the Athenian? . . . Like some sort of hash fiend, she was oblivious to everything going on around her, and to her own actions, and she'd lost every shred of judgment . . . She sat astride the bloodied, helpless, bewildered Kozuchak like a witch on a broom, shouting any incomprehensible words that came into her head, now howling, now muttering as if cowed or insulted, now shouting ardently, excited . . . Thaïs the Athenian lowered her reeking mouth to Kozuchak's lips and started to kiss him . . . Kozuchak took a deep breath, tensed his body, and bent double, abruptly tossing off the woman sitting on him . . . When she toppled onto the sand, Thaïs the Athenian laughed loud enough to rock the desert, and her laughter sounded nothing like laughter, only like the plaintive howl of a jackal . . .

The beating midday sun scorched everything with its heat . . .

A bird in the heavens, looking down on this human beastliness, soared lazily, slowly, indifferent to who among them would die and who would live . . .

But the people on the ground were pitching a bloody slaughter . . . Like sworn enemies, they saw nothing, too busy beating and kicking one another till the blood flowed, as if the Devil, snoozing until then, had now woken up inside of them . . . Too weak even to wave a hand or stand on their feet, Genghis Khan and Alexander the Great collapsed within reach of each other on the sand . . . They were sure they were at the doorstep of the End of Days . . .

Sobbing and gasping for breath, trembling like a blade of grass in the breeze, Cleopatra held Kozuchak's head in her hands where he lay until Lear stumbled up to her, swaying on his feet, and swooped down on her like an eagle. He grabbed hold of her and hit her on the back of the head, then dragged her away. Cleopatra kicked and fought as hard as she could, pulling Lear's hair . . . Lust was at a boil inside him, and he paid no attention to anything she did . . .

Lear lugged Cleopatra to a sloping dune out of sight of the others and tossed her onto the ground . . . Cleopatra's head was on a rise in the ground, like a pillow, and then Lear's strong legs were between hers. When he got hold of the collar of Cleopatra's dress and ripped it open, one pale white breast, round as an apple, spilled through the tear . . . Lear clamped his lips to her breast, her nipple, and sucked it red, relishing all the feminine flavors it still contained . . . Cleopatra screamed at top volume and fought him desperately . . . but Lear was strong and ignored her screams . . . Lear's long body was between her legs . . . Drunk on her breath, on the aroma of this young woman, he worked to free the upright stake from his pants . . . Still, she fought as hard as she could, and she never stopped shouting: "Kozuchak! Kozuchak!" . . . Flattened by Lear's heavy body, her face beneath his broad chest so that he cut off her air, she was starting to suffocate . . . Cleopatra groped for some sand and threw it in Lear's eyes . . . The sand hit him in the eyes, and he tried to rub it out with his hands . . . but his eyes were too full of sand, and he couldn't see . . . She grabbed more sand, hot from the sun, and pressed it hard against his penis, making Lear recoil with a shout . . . Kozuchak regained his wits and looked around for Cleopatra . . . When he saw Lear's tracks heading to the other side of a dune, he picked up a saxaul branch that had marked the Emperor's grave and rushed off in pursuit . . . Kozuchak caught sight of Lear rubbing the sand from his eyes, and Kozuchak swung the saxaul with all his strength straight into Lear's head . . . He hit him so hard that Lear's eyes practically popped out, and his skull cracked . . . He hit him so unbelievably hard, with such fury . . .

The same snake as before emerged from the Emperor's eye socket . . . When the snake saw Thaïs the Athenian cavorting on a pile of bones, shouting everything she could think of, naked from the waist up, it set off slowly crawling in her direction . . . The dead man's ribs began to crack and break under Thaïs the Athenian's dancing feet, the bones that had lain under the sand and under the beating sun . . . but the woman paid that no attention, enraptured by her sense of total liberty and freedom, as usual—now cackling, now sobbing, now screaming, now laughing, as if the cracking sounds of the bones breaking under her feet gave her more and more power, and she spun in a circle, waving the hand that held her long skirt, shaking her stout thighs, as if her dance was giving her unthinkable pleasure, and she lost her mind entirely, luxuriating in it, weeping, arousing herself more all the time, dancing without a care in the world . . . She could feel nothing, as if heaven and earth had merged into one . . .

The snake that crept from the Emperor's skull had a head full of venom . . . When it had been lying inside that skull, the scent of urine had filled it with disgust . . . Its whole body went tense with the desire to sink its poisonous fangs into that woman . . . Nobody . . . not the woman dancing and laughing on the loudly breaking bones, not Genghis Khan or Alexander the Great, who had dug the body out of the earth to at least take revenge on the corpse . . . nobody knew that the snake's gleaming body held the soul of the Emperor . . . Only Kozuchak might have known, because the Emperor had told him, when he was alive, that his soul would be given to a snake . . .

Evening started to descend on the desert, and it started to grow dark . . .

The immense cruelty of the fight between the people who had used to be so close and caring had shown, again, how little removed people are from their animal essence, and here it had suddenly awoken . . . That sad day was a disastrous one, a day that burned away everything human inside those people, when each one turned on the others like a predatory beast, and on this last day before the End of Days, nothing human remained in them . . . their souls grew a coat of rough fur . . .

After Kozuchak struck him in the head with the saxaul branch, Lear lay where he fell, still as stone, unmoving, not a hand or foot twitching.

Lear lay helpless and still, and the snake bit him . . . His heart stopped instantly.

That evening, the dusk was red with the scarlet setting sun . . .

The disk of the sun seemed to melt over the horizon, and soon it would vanish completely . . .

Thaïs the Athenian did not see the setting sun, as scarlet as the coals of a fire. This woman, who had frolicked topless on a pile of bones, who had held her head high through this whole arid desert . . . the snake from the Emperor's skull shot at her like lightning and bit her . . . The snake's venom spread quickly through her body, and she fell to the ground and died in terrible torment. Thaïs the Athenian's old hat lay next to her half-naked body . . . Thaïs the Athenian was no longer so sharp of tongue. Bitten by the snake, she fell down dead, into an eternal sleep . . . Not far from Thaïs the Athenian, Genghis Khan and Alexander the Great had also been lying for a long while, bleeding; they had beaten each other nearly to death, mercilessly, and in the last moments of that twilight, they also gave up their souls to God . . .

The snake sank its venomous fangs into their bodies, too . . .

When they caught the scent of human blood, all the creatures of the desert began to creep their way.

By late in the evening, only two people remained alive in that endless desert: Kozuchak and Cleopatra.

When darkness falls in the desert, all the creatures of the desert creep from their holes . . .

Epilogue

By late in the evening, only two people remained alive in that endless desert: Kozuchak and Cleopatra.

When darkness falls in the desert, all the creatures of the desert creep from their holes . . .

When the twilight thickens and the night's darkness lays its claims, the real life of the wild denizens of the desert begins . . .

They sleep all day under the sand, then creep to the surface in search of food and begin to prowl the night. An uncountable army, they amass throughout the deserts of God's earth, they peer at the stars twinkling in the sky, and then they begin to search for a good meal, leaving their lace-like tracks in the sand . . . Here is one rule of the desert. Whenever the desert marmots sense something dangerous or unusual close by, they whistle, soft and thin, like the sound of the wind. That is how they tell everyone that there is something in the vicinity they don't encounter every day, something that could cause trouble or danger. And that whistle from the desert marmots serves as a special signal not just to others of their own kind, but also for all the other inhabitants of the desert, both the kind who run and the kind who slither . . .

That night required such a warning . . .

The beasts of the desert had never met two-legged creatures before and didn't know where they had come from . . . The smell carried on the breeze made it clear who they were, and how many. Four of the creatures who had arrived from who knows where had stopped breathing. They were lying in the sand, showing no signs of life . . . A little farther away, there were two more, also lying on the ground, holding each other tightly, their heads tilted toward one another, frozen in absolute silence . . . But from those two, there came the almost imperceptible sound of breathing. The desert beasts have a perfect sense of hearing. What's more, the snake, the lord of the desert, was lying there, its whole long body wrapped around them. And if the lord of the desert was encircling something, the other, smaller beasts had no right to it.

That night was an unusual one for the inhabitants of the desert . . .

Because these four two-legged creatures, who didn't respond even if you tickled the souls of their feet, were dead, feeling nothing . . . These four . . . one of them, tall, strong, handsome, lay there with his head bashed in and bloody. That was Lear. The half-naked woman face-down in the sand, whose plump rear end was glowing in the moonlight, was Thaïs the Athenian, and the other pair of them, who had collapsed side by side in their fight—one face-down, one on his side—that was Genghis Khan and Alexander the Great.

As darkness fell, a new day began for the local animals . . .

Although they knew that the blood had long stopped running through the veins of these prone creatures and their breath had halted long ago, they still approached them with caution. Most of them decided to wait a while to see what would happen. But the little desert mice weren't afraid of anything. They ran straight to the corpses, climbed up, and scurried under their clothing . . .

The desert marmots, as usual, had been sending out their long whistles, summoning all the desert's inhabitants . . . When they heard that whistle, the tiny creatures of the desert set off running for the place, pausing sometimes to cock their ears and lift their tiny snouts before they continued hurrying toward the sound. By now, five or six of those small creatures were poking around on Thaïs the Athenian's half-naked body . . . Once the rest of them, a larger group, realized there was no danger, they began scampering bravely over the corpses of the other three, leaving no crack or crevice unexplored . . . The desert marmots' whistling grew louder and stronger, and more desert-dwellers gathered all the time . . . The furry desert jerboas with their long tails came leaping, baring their sharp incisors, and the desert lizards scurried in, close to the ground, tongues out, and the spiders, and the scorpions and black widows, and the fast-moving snakes . . . The jackals came, too, tails pressed under them, running toward the scent of human blood . . . Such a generous feast, apparently fallen from the heavens, was especially pleasing to the jackals, their eyes glowing like lanterns, who attacked the lifeless bodies in throngs and were the first to tear off chunks of flesh. They hurried first to the half-naked body of Thaïs the Athenian, who looked like the juiciest, and they started gnawing at her fatty buttocks . . . Then the marmots, the heralds of the desert, stopped whistling and rushed at the bodies lying there, right after the jackals, and surrounded them to gnaw and chew . . .

When would anything like this ever happen again? That small corner of land is suddenly too small for all the desert creatures gathered inside it . . . The only sound is the gnashing and clacking of teeth. The animals fall on the four bodies like a flock of black jackdaws and tug at them from every direction, sinking their teeth into the places with the most meat, tearing it away and swallowing it down . . . Sometimes the jackals, their snouts smeared with human blood, growl and lunge at one another, their greed not yet sated . . . The desert mice, who ordinarily hide from the jackals, are only thinking about food today, and they have also attacked the bodies, paying no attention to the jackals . . . All the smaller creatures of the desert have come to the feast, as well . . . the scorpions and lizards, the desert snakes, the desert rats . . . and not only them, but also the venomous and nonvenomous spiders, and the beetles and other insects, who hide from dawn to dusk deep under the sand where some moisture resides, and creep out into the air only late in the evening—they feast alongside everyone else . . .

Countless numbers of desert dwellers had gathered in that dark night, and very likely, none of them missed the chance to sample a piece of Genghis Khan and Alexander the Great. They ate all the flesh from the bones, and then, as if taking revenge on them for something, they swallowed the bones, too, growling, snapping and gobbling them down . . .

Some mysterious sense had awoken inside these wild animals, a sense that had been stored inside them for century upon century. After all, in times long, long ago, in some era of the distant past, in some year vanished from memory, these untamed beasts who had streamed here like a furious flood had lived in this world as human beings . . . They sensed this inside themselves, like life itself, and they had come running, crawling, and hopping here to satisfy their ancient craving for vengeance, some against Genghis Khan, who had wrung the blood from the lands he conquered, and some against Alexander the Great, who had vanquished half the world and chopped off thousands of heads . . . These wild animals sensed this, and as animals who carried inside them the souls of long-dead people, they bore it as an incurable, traumatic illness . . . In those long-ago times, they had died at the hands of these two men, and for a millennium or more, their souls had moved from one animal's body to another . . . The souls of the human beings who had been unable to take their revenge on those two men who had shaken the universe had settled in these animals, now . . . and now they devoured and sucked dry all the bones and tendons in their bodies, the bodies where Genghis Khan and Alexander the Great's souls had settled . . .

To an ordinary person thinking stereotypically, this scene indicates how a day will come to this perverted, inconstant world when we will answer for our past sins . . . These living creatures remind the blinded, mortal man that sins must be repaid, in this world, not only on Judgment Day: there is also a Judgment of the Soul to which we each must respond and bear the castigation we deserve . . . There is only one responsible party in this world, and that is the Son of Man . . . These tiny wild creatures, crawling and darting across the earth, were born of the will of God, just like human beings, and carrying in their bodies all the souls born of the Great Creator, they have lived to see this day . . . The Earth is circular, and so is the fate of every living being, and one day, if not today, then tomorrow, it will return to its proper place . . . Everything in the world is connected . . . That idea is at the very foundation! . . . O God, are these the inviolable laws of your perfectly clever world? . . . The truth is not in the animals' wild morality, or the vengeance of living creatures, which they carry through century after century, because the law of life is wound around this circular world, one narrow ribbon, and each person is an impenetrable mystery of the universe, and all this is tied into such a tight knot of creation that nobody can unravel it—the destiny and the hope of this egg-like Earth, and the people, and the animals, and its mountains and waters, steppes and deserts, oceans and sky—everything . . . everything . . . It is all glued to the thin shell of the Earth . . . Only the soul fails to dissolve into the ether of this world: it is life in motion, and by an immortal, eternal law, it gives motion to the entire world . . . This motion is the Soul. The Soul is the Creator's great gift . . .

By midnight, nothing remained of the four of them except their bare bones. The residents of the desert who had run to the place had devoured, chewed, sucked dry, and licked clean everything else . . . When the jackals, their bellies round and full, had sated their initial hunger, they headed for the two people lying a short distance away. When they drew near, their eyes gleaming, the snake who ruled the desert, who was guarding them, its whole long body in a ring around them, lifted its head abruptly and gazed all around, making sure the jackals understood that these people were under its protection . . . At the first sight and scent of the regal snake, the jackals immediately turned around and retreated, less bold than before . . . In this desert, where the regal snake ruled, beasts far stronger than jackals feared it . . .

The night sky was sprinkled with countless masses of stars, as if someone had strewn seeds everywhere, and the full moon shined brightly among them . . .

The world went on living according to its laws . . .

Gradually, the eastern side of the sky over the desert began to grow lighter, and the milky light of the coming sun crept farther and farther across the dark sky . . .

Over the horizon, a first sliver of the sun appeared, splashing its rays in every direction . . .

When Cleopatra's bare foot nudged the snake's cold body, she gave a start . . .

"A snake!" Cleopatra whimpered, and tucked her foot up under her body.

"Don't move. Don't kick!" said Kozuchak, almost whispering, when he saw the snake lying so close. It was an extremely long snake, which had wrapped its body completely around the spot of ground on which they lay. It lay there with its head, the size of a fist, turned just slightly, and it seemed to have taken them prisoner. When Cleopatra's bare foot nudged the snake's body, it startled both of them, the woman and the snake . . .

Dawn came, and peace and quiet reigned in the desert . . .

Kozuchak and Cleopatra had slept through the night in a deep slumber, pressed close to one another . . . That cursed day which had made their bodies tremble seemed to have cut them down, and they'd collapsed where they stood and slept until dawn without moving. Neither of them knew what had happened during that night, cursed of God. Kozuchak's whole body was battered, and Cleopatra had barely stopped the blood flowing from his wounds; in the darkness, they had walked a lariat's throw away from the other four, and now they didn't know what had happened to the others or how they were . . . Everything had flashed by like a flying arrow . . . The only thing Kozuchak remembered was how he had bashed the saxaul branch into Lear's head with all his might. And he remembered Cleopatra dragging him, half dead, to this place. She had used her bare hands to wipe the blood from Kozuchak's face and body, and she had torn a strip of fabric off her skirt and bandaged his head. Yesterday, when he had hit Lear with the branch, he put his last drop of strength into the blow and struck him as hard as he could. That much he knew . . . Yes, he hit him, then collapsed to the ground, himself, right there . . . He didn't remember anything after that . . . But now Cleopatra's frightened gasp woke him up. Kozuchak had been sleeping sweetly, but now he opened his eyes wide and saw the snake that lay in a circle around them.

Both of them were very frightened of snakes . . . and the snake seemed frightened of their screaming and tightened the ring it was forming. This snake was not like other snakes. It was enormous . . . Its body contracted, it began to turn . . . As if it understood them when they shouted "A snake!" and "Don't move!" the snake froze for a moment or two, to avoid frightening them, only flicking out its narrow tongue every now and then. Then it carefully brought its slender tail to its head . . . It lay motionless for a while, giving them time to calm down and think clearly, watching them, and then, slowly, carefully, it started to move, rippling like something made of silk. Kozuchak winked imperceptibly and whispered to Cleopatra: "Easy . . ." Lifting its head, the snake slowly crawled first over Cleopatra's legs, then over Kozuchak's, caressing them gently with its body . . . They both froze still as stone. They were afraid that if they so much as twitched, the snake would bite them . . .

By then, dawn had broken, and a light morning breeze was blowing . . .

The snake slithered away, nobody knew where, and vanished, leaving a curving trail behind it. They felt the biggest relief of their lives, as if they'd shed an enormous burden . . . The snake had stirred panic and fear inside them, making their hearts pound like mad . . . It was probably that fear that sent a piercing pain through Cleopatra's heart . . . (It was on that very day, one thousand years ago, that Cleopatra the queen died of snakebite. That very day.) A snake's ferocity can drown a person in fear. When the snake had looked them in the eye so intently, they read plenty in its gaze. But then it seemed the snake erased everything they had read, and they couldn't have remembered a thing, even if someone had asked . . . When Kozuchak got to his feet and stood up tall, his head began to spin, and his vision went dark . . . His head hurt badly. Cleopatra, who had sat there holding his head most of the night, never letting her eyes shut, had only dozed off very late at night . . . Now Kozuchak could feel all the pain from the rock that had hit him the day before. Kozuchak looked around, but he saw no sign of Thaïs the Athenian, Genghis Khan, King Lear, or Alexander the Great . . . The only thing he remembered was how he'd hit Lear on the head with the saxaul branch. Nothing else.

"Where is everyone?" Kozuchak asked Cleopatra. Cleopatra looked at Kozuchak without answering. She was surprised that he remembered nothing of the day before.

"What do you mean? Don't you remember?" she asked, giving him a helpless look.

"I can't remember . . . I think I remember hitting Lear . . . Why? . . . Did I . . . kill him?" Kozuchak's voice trembled. "Or is he OK?" He looked hopefully at Cleopatra.

She only shrugged, not making a sound, to tell him she didn't know . . . Kozuchak sensed that her eyes could not lie . . .

"If he's alive, then that's it . . . He'll crush me . . . That's what he's like," Kozuchak said. That comment told Cleopatra he truly did not remember. She took the dizzy Kozuchak by the hand.

"They stayed on the other side of that sand dune . . . I barely managed to drag you over here . . . To tell you the truth . . . I'm not sure what happened to them, or how they're doing now," she said quietly, avoiding his question. "Lear . . ." Cleopatra's lips trembled, and she put her hands to her chest, where her collar was torn. "He . . ."

"I know. I remember that," Kozuchak said flatly. "Let's go . . . Let's go check on them . . . We'll see how they're doing . . . Come on," said Kozuchak.

"You go. I'll wait for you here," Cleopatra said, unhappy. "My feet hurt."

"Let's go. Don't be afraid. I'll be with you." There was a new, commanding tone to Kozuchak's voice.

With Cleopatra to support him, Kozuchak began trudging toward the sand dune.

When they were almost at the flat top of the dune, there was a raucous flapping of wings on the other side, and all the desert's feathered scavengers took off in flight. There were thousands and thousands more like them on the other side of the dune. When they saw the people approaching, they beat their wings and rose like a black thundercloud into the air . . . At the place they took off from, human bones still lay on the ground. When Cleopatra saw those bones, she let out a loud scream and cowered closer to Kozuchak . . . Those bones . . . they belonged to Thaïs the Athenian, Genghis Khan, King Lear, and Alexander the Great, who had become food for the desert animals . . . With all those bones scattered across the sand, it was difficult to tell which belonged to whom . . . Near some bones on one side there was a pair of corduroy pants, torn in a thousand places, and Lear's leather belt . . . And that was where Kozuchak had hit Lear in the head with that branch, yes, he could remember it clearly now . . . Those bones, lying near a woman's hat, were much smaller than the other bones; they were female bones, Thaïs the Athenian's bones . . . The bones tossed helter-skelter, legs here, arms there, heads somewhere else entirely, those were Genghis Khan and Alexander the Great's bones . . . their leather shoes were there, too . . . And farther off still, there were the bones Genghis Khan and Alexander the Great had dug out of the grave. Those were the Emperor's bones. His metal teeth still glinted in his skull . . . Kozuchak took note of all these things as he wandered among the bones, examining them . . . He was shaking all over, and tears gleamed in his eyes . . .

Cleopatra was wracked with sobs, her teeth chattering as she cried and shook, as if her heart were about to burst . . . The sight was too much for

Kozuchak, and he gave a piercing cry and fell to his knees. "Oh, God!"
The boy's shout carried across the entire desert. Sitting behind him,
Cleopatra did not know what to do, or what to say, and she felt as shriveled
as an autumn leaf. She repeated:

"Oh, God!"

And she wept silently . . .

The earth seemed to tremble with her weeping, the sky seemed to
break, and lightning struck . . .

When they were both sitting still, not knowing what to do, the snake
appeared again from one of the eye sockets in the Emperor's skull . . . The
snake terrified them . . . As soon as they saw it, they froze. Not a movement!
Not a sound! . . . This snake, long as two paces by an adult man, slithered
from the Emperor's skull and slowly crawled, curving this way and that,
across the hot sand toward them . . . The snake came close and wrapped
its cold body around Kozuchak's legs, all the way around, twice, and then
it reached like ivy to Cleopatra's legs and wrapped around them . . . They
were afraid to move, afraid that the instant they budged, the snake would
sink its fangs into them . . . Its eyes gleamed as it wrapped around them, as
if binding their legs, hot from the burning sand, with its cool body . . . And
the snake did more than bind them: it pulled them both as hard as it could,
tugging their legs close together . . . Kozuchak and Cleopatra felt how strong
the snake was, and they looked each other in the eye, too weak to move,
shivering with fear . . . Quietly, they closed their eyes and lifted their faces to
the clear sky and hot, brilliant sun . . . At that instant, they both thought the
snake was about to kill them . . . They thought it would be better to die than
to be left alone in the desert . . . They prepared themselves for Death . . .
They were expecting it . . . The thought of death made them fonder of each
other . . . It was a warm feeling, that came to them along with the idea of
death . . . that feeling was a secret, intimate feeling, the kind born in the
hearts of a young man and young woman . . . At that instant, that warm feeling somehow far outweighed their terrifying thoughts about death, for both
of them . . . Kozuchak remembered the dream in which he had relished the
joy of Love with Cleopatra . . . They forgot about the snake wrapped around
their legs and began to kiss . . . Warmth spread through their bodies . . .
They stopped feeling the cold body of the snake, and it seemed to them the

way they felt could melt any ice . . . That feeling completed washed away
their fear of death, conquering that fear completely . . .

(O, God! . . .)
The great Word came into the hearts of the two of them . . .
it came and . . . it conquered their thoughts of death . . .
and more, it sowed the light of hope in their hearts . . .
That light . . . it warmed their bodies, and from their chests . . . from
    their beating hearts . . . the ice-cold thought picked up and left . . .
    vanished somewhere very far away . . . and that thought, like a leaf
    fallen from a branch, flew away on their breath . . . the fear . . .
    vanished completely . . .
and feeling, that moment, endlessly happy . . .
on the wings of wondrous thoughts
 they felt just like cranes soaring
    straight through the sky,
        and they both bowed
            to the light of the Creator,
                and spoke pure words
                    (great words, sacred words,
                            radiant words,
                                exquisite words,
                                    heartfelt words):
                                        (O, God!)
            "God!" they said,
            (a word in the soul of every human being,
             on the tongue of every human being,
            on the mind of every human being . . .
        in everyone's heart,
        as the heart beats,
    so it is spoken . . .)
        that sacred word
            burst from the depths of their hearts
                like a volcano . . .
                    (O, God! . . .)

At that moment, they heard the gentle ringing of a bell, coming from they didn't know where. Ding! Ding! . . .

The bell was ringing and dinging . . .

At the sound of the bell, the snake that had wrapped like a vine around their legs slowly dropped to the ground . . . The snake could feel, through its skin, all the passions boiling inside them . . . How could these young people have known that the Emperor's soul had settled inside that snake? . . . The Emperor's soul was in the snake's body, and that soul approved of the warm feeling, the feeling of love, that had sprung up between them . . . only that feeling could give them the strength to win . . . The snake was pleased by that feeling . . . Hearing the sound of the bell, carried from some unknown place, the snake decided to slip away . . . Released from its grip, Cleopatra and Kozuchak held each other tight, and peered in the direction the sound came from . . .

The bell went on ringing, gently, monotonously, and that ringing came closer and closer: Ding . . . Ding . . . Ding . . . Ding . . .

The sound kept coming closer . . .

It was the sound of a small bell . . . From the place the sound came from, over the dunes, a camel's head came into view, and then an old man on the camel's back, with a beard down to his waist . . . The old man whipped the camel on, coming closer and closer . . . The bell was tied to the camel's long neck, and with every step the camel took, it dipped its head, and the bell rang . . . The two of them ran to meet these visitors . . . and stopped three paces from them . . . The ringing of the bell paused, and they stood there staring at the old man, confused . . .

The old man stood up in his stirrups, and said:

"Greetings! A good journey to you! Which way are you headed?"

"Greetings to you!" they answered in unison.

"We're going to the Holy Land," said Cleopatra.

"The Holy Land," Kozuchak hurried to add.

"Can you show us the way to the Holy Land?" Cleopatra asked, with a hopeful look.

Hearing this, the old man peered at them thoughtfully.

"I can," he announced.

"Which way should we go?" she asked.

The old man gave them one more thoughtful look, and then uttered, slowly:

"You have already come to the Holy Land."

"We've already come?" they asked together, turning to look at each other.

"You are standing inside it. The Holy Land you seek is under your feet," said the old man.

"Under our feet?" Neither of them understood.

"Whenever a person sets foot on the land, it is always Holy," said the old man.

Kozuchak and Cleopatra felt the warm earth under their feet . . .

"Are you saying the Holy Land we were searching so hard for, and suffered so terribly for, is under our feet?" asked Kozuchak.

"Yes, under your feet!" said the old man with certainty, as if sharing a treasured secret. "A person can only find the truth after surviving quite a lot . . . The truth you were seeking is that the Holy Land is everywhere," he said.

The old man arranged himself more comfortably between the camel's humps.

"I know," he said, nodding his head. "There were seven of you . . . The Emperor was the first to give up his soul to God, and he was leading you to the Holy Land to cleanse yourselves of sin." The old man nodded to where the Emperor's bones lay, as if he knew all about it. Then he went on. "He gave his life to explain to you the truth of this world . . . His gift lit the lantern of human feeling in your hearts." The old man squinted his eyes, knit his brow, and sighed deeply. "But the other four!" He gripped his whip more tightly. "They became food for the wild beasts of the desert, the insects, worms, and scavengers . . ." The old man paused meaningfully and sighed again. "The demands on the soul last forever. Genghis Khan's soul and Alexander the Great's soul got what they deserved . . . a final repayment," said the old man, nodding toward the bones lying in the distance. "And the other two answered for their consciences."

The old man looked thoughtfully at the sky. For a while, he did not speak.

"Their souls will face the same fate, sooner or later," he continued. "People like that can never understand the value of the Holy Land . . . The Creator gave a soul to the Son of Man, and the conscience looks out for the purity of that soul, born of the love of God . . . The power of the Creator is not far from each person," said the old man, and he sighed again.

Strung across the camel's back, hanging down on each side, were two sacks of saplings . . .

"Are you bringing saplings across this arid desert?" Kozuchak asked the old man. "Are you sure saplings can thrive in the desert?"

"I will give these saplings to you," the old man replied.

"What are we supposed to do with them, in this desert?" asked Cleopatra, surprised.

"Plant them," the old man answered, quite seriously. "Plant them today."

"You want us to plant them here, when we don't even know which way to go?" Kozuchak did not understand.

"You must plant them . . . Plant them today, no later," the old man ordered them.

"But why today?" asked Kozuchak.

"Because tomorrow the End of the World will come. Plant them today," said the old man, and he handed a sapling to each of them . . .

The old man turned his camel, and the bell rang as he slowly rode away . . .

The bell rang for a long time . . .

Ding . . . Ding . . . Ding . . . Ding . . . Ding . . . Ding . . . Ding . . .

Translator's Note

Acknowledgments

Translator's Note

You have just read a novel that opens with seven travelers wandering the desert, a beginning that may have led you to make certain assumptions. By now, you will have realized that *Castigation* is not, in fact, a biblical tale or a morality play, and it is not an adventure story or a love story, though it is partly all of those things. Nor is it pure historical fantasy, despite all the historical characters (or fictional characters named for them). And even though the interplay between various deities and human souls plays an extremely significant role here, the book is not exactly a religious tract, either.

As someone who has taken this book apart and put it together again in the process of translation, my advice is to give up all attempts to fit this tale into any frame you've previously encountered. Unless, of course, you've encountered other post-Soviet apocalyptic romantic religious allegories positing a postmodern critique of politics and mental health and righteous condemnation of the excesses of Genghis Khan and Alexander the Great, because this book is one of those.

Author Sultan Raev began his career in the Soviet Union, where creative writing was as centrally regulated as any other public endeavor. This book, however, reaches into Central Asia's distant past (including the eras of warring Mongolians and Macedonians) for many of its religious, cultural, and historical references. And it was written and originally read in independent Kyrgyzstan, a state we can justifiably say was created and then abandoned by the Soviet Union. *Castigation* can be read as the author's response to being suddenly set adrift, newly untethered from all certainty, and left to wander with other former inmates, all as a result of processes none of them can fully comprehend. What sort of leaders emerge in such a situation? Who can be trusted? Where are any of them going? How many snakes will there be, and what does God think of it all? This is one of the rare novels from the region to try grappling with these questions.

A few Soviet relics that figure in the plot require a brief explanation. King Lear's lines are from the most famous Russian translation of Shakespeare's play during the Soviet era, the version by Boris Pasternak. I have translated those lines back into English in a way that is not quite Shakespeare, to respect the differences that came with Pasternak's version. A more despicable aspect of the Soviet legacy in *Castigation* is punitive psychiatric treatment, notably with sulfosin, a painful concoction of sulfur and oil that remained common in Soviet psychiatry long after its use was banned elsewhere. A thorough history of the drug can be found in M. Marco Igual, "Sulfosin: A Centennial Drug between Therapy and Punishment," *Neurosciences and History* 9, no. 2 (2021): 55–68. To stress the drug's Soviet associations, I chose to use a transliteration of its Russian name: sulfozin.

This translation is the result of some textual triangulation. Raev provided me with an anonymous, unpublished Russian translation of his novel, as well as his own Kyrgyz original. Because Russian is the non-English language I know the best, and I have rarely worked with Kyrgyz, my first instinct was to use the Russian translation as my primary source. But obeying that instinct would have been lazy and also counterproductive. Kyrgyz strongly resembles two languages I can read well (Kazakh and Uzbek), so I found I was able to navigate through the original without problems. That was fortunate, because I quickly discovered that the Russian text was not entirely reliable. For one thing, it tended to either smooth over or ignore many specifically Kyrgyz images and cultural references, applying a domesticating approach. Translating the Russian versions of those passages would have been tantamount to Russifying this book for English-language readers. It also contained some objective errors I would not have liked to replicate in English. To avoid those pitfalls, I realized I would need to pay equal attention to both versions as I translated. I have done my best.

Acknowledgments

I am immensely grateful to author Sultan Raev for entrusting me with his novel and patiently explaining what it means to him, as we worked together to help readers discover it in English. He was patient and gracious in answering my questions. I would not have encountered *Castigation* in any language without the advice of Duisenali Alimakhyn, who has high hopes and bright ideas for Central Asian literature. I was encouraged at the enthusiastic response my readings from this translation received from my colleagues at conferences of the American Translators Association (ATA) and American Literary Translators Association (ALTA) in the fall of 2023. Also that year, the online journal *Turkoslavia* did us the honor of publishing a lengthy excerpt of this translation and my essay about translating it in their second issue. Finally, I offer my thanks and respect to that anonymous translator into Russian, whose work made it possible for me to begin mine.

Shelley Fairweather-Vega
Seattle, Washington

Sultan Raev was born in Soviet Kyrgyzstan in 1958. Trained as a journalist, he was the first editor of an independent newspaper in Kyrgyzstan. His short stories, novels, and stage plays have won multiple awards. After the collapse of the Soviet Union, Raev served in various government advisory posts, notably as minister of culture. In 2022, he was elected head of TÜRKSOY, a multinational cultural organization. He is considered one of the brightest stars of the new literature of Central Asia.

Shelley Fairweather-Vega is a professional translator in Seattle, Washington. She specializes in new poetry and prose by writers across Central Asia.

www.ingramcontent.com/pod-product-compliance
Lightning Source LLC
Chambersburg PA
CBHW062029070825
30733CB00005B/12